# THE DESERT PRINCESS

# THE FOUR KINGDOMS AND BEYOND

# THE DESERT PRINCESS

## A RETELLING OF ALADDIN

### MELANIE CELLIER

LUMINANT PUBLICATIONS

Luminant Publications
PO Box 201
Burnside, South Australia 5066

melaniecellier@internode.on.net
http://www.melaniecellier.com

Cover Design by Karri Klawiter
Editing by Mary Novak
Proofreading by Deborah Grace White

*For Intisar and Hannah,*
*thanks for cheering me along and sharing the writing journey with me*

ROYAL FAMILY TREES


THE FOUR KINGDOMS

**KINGDOM OF ARCADIA**

King Henry—Queen Eleanor

*Parents of*

Prince Maximilian (Max)—Alyssa of Arcadia
    *Parents of*
    Prince Henry (Harry)
    Princess Rose

Princess Lily—Prince Jon of Marin
    *Parents of*
    Prince Owen
    Princess Hope

Princess Sophie—King Dominic of Palinar
    *Parents of*
    Prince Arthur
    Princess Grace

(Deceased: Princess Mina, younger sister of King Henry, married to Prince Friedrich of Rangmere, *parents of* Prince Damon)

**KINGDOM OF RANGMERE**

King Josef (deceased)—Queen Charlotte (deceased)

*Parents of*

Prince Konrad (deceased)—Princess Clarisse of Lanover

Queen Ava—King Hans
  *Parents of*
  Princess Ellery

(Missing: Prince Friedrich, older brother of King Josef, married to Princess Mina of Arcadia, *parents of* Prince Damon)

## KINGDOM OF NORTHHELM

King Richard—Queen Louise

*Parents of*

Prince William—Princess Celeste of Lanover
  *Parents of*
  Princess Danielle

Princess Marie—Prince Raphael of Lanover
  *Parents of*
  Prince Benjamin
  Prince Emmett

## KINGDOM OF LANOVER

King Leonardo—Queen Viktoria

*Parents of*

Prince Frederic—Evangeline (Evie) of Lanover
  *Parents of*

Prince Leo
Princess Beatrice

Princess Clarisse—Charles of Rangmere
*Parents of*
Princess Isabella
Prince Danton

Prince Cassian—Tillara (Tillie) of the Nomadic Desert Traders
*Parents of*
Prince Luca
Princess Iris
Princess Violet

Prince Raphael—Princess Marie of Northhelm
*Parents of*
Prince Benjamin
Prince Emmett

Princess Celeste—Prince William of Northhelm
*Parents of*
Princess Danielle

Princess Cordelia—Ferdinand of Northhelm
*Parents of*
Princess Arabella
Prince Andrew

Princess Celine—Prince Oliver of Eldon


BEYOND THE FOUR KINGDOMS

**DUCHY OF MARIN**

Duke Philip—Duchess Aurelia

*Parents of*

Prince Jonathan—Princess Lily of Arcadia
    *Parents of*
    Prince Owen
    Princess Hope

Princess Lilac

Princess Hazel

Princess Marigold

## KINGDOM OF TRIONE

King Edward—Queen Juliette

*Parents of*

Prince Theodore (Teddy)—Princess Isla of Merrita

Princess Millicent (Millie)—Nereus of Merrita

Princess Margaret (Daisy)

## KINGDOM OF PALINAR

King Dominic—Queen Sophie
    *Parents of*
    Prince Arthur
    Princess Grace

## KINGDOM OF TALINOS

King Clarence—Queen Sapphira

*Parents of*

Prince Gabriel (Gabe)—Princess Adelaide of Palinar

Prince Percival (Percy)

Princess Pearl

Princess Opal

## KINGDOM OF ELDON

King Leopold—Queen Camille

*Parents of*

Prince Oliver—Princess Celine

Princess Emmeline

Princess Giselle

## KINGDOM OF ELIAM

King George (deceased)—Queen Alida (deceased)

*Father of*

Queen Blanche (Snow)—King Alexander

# KINGDOM OF MERRITA

King Morgan—Queen Nerida (deceased)

*Parents of*

Princess Oceana—Lyon of Merrita
  *Parents of*
  Prince Edmund
  Princess Eloise

Princess Coral

Princess Marine

Princess Avalon

Princess Waverly

Princess Isla—Prince Teddy of Trione

(General Nerissa and Captain Nereus—brother and sister of Queen Nerida)

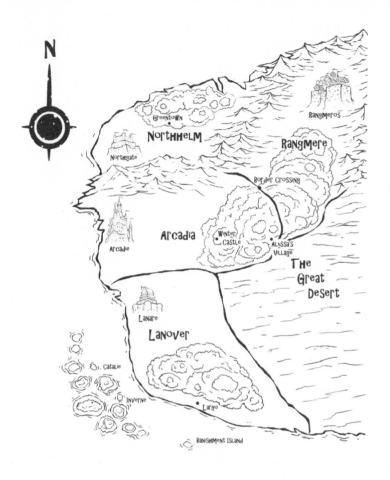

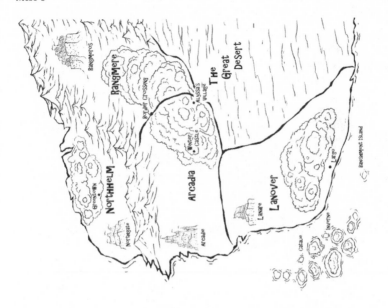

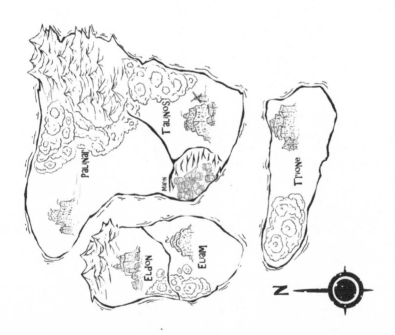

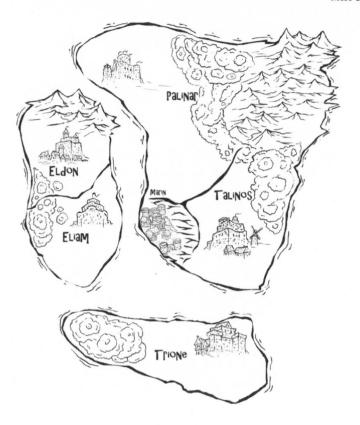

# PART I
# THE DESERT

$\mathscr{I}$ sat alone in the small, dark space, my legs curled beneath me. I didn't bother pressing my eye to the single pinprick of light provided by the hole in one wall. I could follow the conversation of the two men in my uncle's study without the view it provided.

"Your visit is an unexpected honor," my uncle said, his measured tone hiding the surprise I knew he felt at the king's appearance at our remote castle in the southern forests.

"The crown is grateful for the service your family has rendered our kingdom," King Leopold replied.

I smiled at the stiff note in his voice, even as I straightened in excitement at his words. My uncle had flatly refused to include me in the meeting, using the well-worn excuses that I was only fourteen years old and not even his heir. But the king had said *your family*, and these days it was only my uncle and me.

"I know my son and his new bride recently passed through here on their wedding tour," the king continued, and my excitement mounted. Princess Celine had become a friend of sorts and knew all about my dreams for a life beyond this small estate—she had even promised to help me achieve them.

Surely the next words out of the king's mouth would include my own name—Cassandra.

"It was a pleasure to host Their Highnesses," my uncle said, hitting just the right note of respect.

"They enjoyed their stay, and Oliver mentioned that your nephew and heir is soon to return from Eliam," King Leopold said. "I would like to invite him to spend a season or two at the palace, getting to know my son and learning valuable skills for his future. I'm sure the court will have something of value to offer to a young man who will one day take your place among the nobility."

"I will gladly accept your generous offer on behalf of my nephew." Real warmth entered my uncle's voice, drifting through the walls to burn my ears.

I deflated, all hope that it was me the king meant to invite to the palace draining away. I should have known he was here about Olvin, my uncle's nephew by blood, despite Olvin's absence from Eldon for the better part of two years. He had played no role in our rescue of the kingdom—but as heir, of course he was to reap the rewards.

I balled my hands into fists, trying to will away my feelings of resentment that such a prize went to someone who wouldn't properly value it. But it wasn't Olvin's fault he was staid, responsible, cautious, and old enough to be more uncle than cousin—he wasn't one to dream of adventure. And it certainly wasn't his fault he was Lord Treestone's direct nephew—and, therefore, heir—rather than a relative by marriage from his wife's side like me. Most days I could even acknowledge that he would one day fill my uncle's role well—they were similar in both temperament and ability.

But the king's words were still a crushing blow after allowing myself a moment of hope. For once my usual thirst to know everything happening around me disappeared, and I crawled silently out of my hidey-hole into the narrow, hidden passage

4

behind it. I didn't want to hear any more of their conversation as they planned the logistics of Olvin's good fortune. After the excitement of the last six months, I had nothing to look forward to but a return to boredom.

I stopped to rest my forehead against the cool stone of the wall. I still hadn't bothered to light a lantern, every step of the hidden passages which honeycombed the castle familiar to me after all these years. I welcomed the darkness as I let my frustration well up, a single tear escaping to run down my cheek.

My uncle might not understand me, but I knew he cared for me, and for years that had been enough as I spent my time learning about his estate and exploring these long-forgotten passages and nooks of the castle. Uncle was aware I knew more than I should about everything that went on here, but he seemed determined not to ask too many questions or make any serious attempt to discover how I came by my knowledge.

Sometimes I wondered if he didn't want to know because he doubted the outcome of the battle of wills that would follow any significant attempt to curtail me—and so he chose willful ignorance. Instead he channeled all his determination into a single issue. I was to remain here, at the estate, where I would be raised to be just like my mother. An illusion he could only maintain if he didn't look too closely at my daily activities.

I groaned and pushed off the wall, hurrying down the dark passage. I didn't remember much of my mother, but she and my aunt had been twins, and from all accounts they had both been gentle, nurturing women who cared for the people of the estate while my uncle took care of the practicalities of running it. While he admired strong, opinionated women like Princess Celine, he couldn't let go of the idea that he owed it to his dead wife and her sister to raise his niece to be just like them.

Never mind that I had clearly inherited my personality from the father who had died shortly after my birth. I was nothing like my few treasured memories of my mother, and no one had yet been guilty of describing me as sweet, gentle, or biddable. Maybe if my uncle had dealt with his grief over the loss of his wife by actually getting to know the real me, instead of attempting to mold me in her legacy, he might have mentioned me to the king and sent me to the capital along with Olvin.

I blew out a breath. There was no point in hoping for the impossible.

I stepped from cool stone onto a threadbare rug, plopping down onto one of the worn cushions I had used to make the small space into a hideout. This was where I came when I wanted time to think without being disturbed, like now. Brushing away the lingering moisture on my cheek, my hands found the lantern I always left here, lighting it in an efficient manner.

The time for self-pity had passed. Only a few short months ago, we had felt helpless in the face of the curse consuming our kingdom, and yet we had prevailed against it. And I would also prevail against my uncle's determination to keep me sequestered at his remote estate. Princess Celine might not have sent King Leopold to rescue me, but she was still on my side. She knew the part I had played in the events of the previous months, and she would help me find somewhere where I could make true use of my abilities and interests.

If a princess, like her sister, could be an intelligencer, then the niece of a minor noble could be as well.

My heart seized at the thought of Celeste, the famed beauty who had become crown princess of the distant kingdom of Northhelm. During her visit, Celine had confided that her sister was also Aurora, infamous spymaster of a network that spanned the entirety of the Four Kingdoms.

I had never visited any of that group of kingdoms, but even out here, I had heard whispers of her name. She hadn't been present at Celine's wedding to our own crown prince, but she was supposed to be planning a visit to Eldon soon. If I could find a way to impress her, maybe she would take me on as one of her agents. Surely my uncle could not prevent my accepting a place as lady-in-waiting to a crown princess, even one who lived an ocean away. And once I was free, he couldn't prevent me undertaking other, more secretive and interesting duties.

Hope filled me, my returned heartbeat speeding up. At thirteen years old, I had helped free an entire kingdom—surely I could prove myself worthy of Aurora's time and attention. And then I could finally escape this one small corner of the world and explore not only the rest of our lands, but also the faraway kingdoms across the sea. I had been dreaming of seeing them ever since our group of kingdoms had rediscovered their existence after generations apart.

Surely Aurora would be like Celine—unlike my uncle, she would see my true capabilities and allow me to use them to free others as I had done in Eldon. Visions of rising to be one of Aurora's trusted lieutenants filled my mind. I would save another kingdom and prove myself to everyone once and for all. Then my uncle would finally see me and value me for who I truly was, instead of looking at me and seeing only the ghost of those he had lost.

I smiled giddily at the blank wall before sobering. Other than my contribution to saving Eldon, my efforts until now had been mere child's play—discovering every secret of my uncle's domain merely to prove I could. If I wanted a future as one of Aurora's intelligencers, I would have to prove I wasn't a child.

An intelligencer needed determination, intelligence, patience, and meticulous skill. They had to see everything and remember what they saw. If I was to be accepted among their ranks, I could expect no less of myself. The apothecary who had workrooms at our castle had to remember every herb, medication, and concoction he prepared, and he had started teaching me the memory palace method he used to keep the information straight. I would work harder to learn the technique—which involved remembering large amounts of information by associating it with familiar physical places. By walking the rooms of my palace in my mind, I could remember the pieces of information attached to each location—honing my brain to needle sharpness in the process. I would prove my worth and find my place—no matter how long it took.

# CHAPTER 1

NEARLY FOUR YEARS LATER

*I* watched Celine sail away in our damaged ship with a furrowed brow. When I had promised myself I would meet Aurora and earn a place in her network, I hadn't pictured it taking nearly four years.

Aurora had visited Eldon to meet her sister's new husband, as expected, but it had unfortunately coincided with Olvin's return from his stay at the capital. My uncle had insisted it would be an insult to his heir for me to leave immediately, even though Olvin and I didn't know each other well after all his absences. Since revealing the true reason I was desperate to meet Celine's sister wasn't an option—it would only ensure I was never allowed to leave home again—I had been forced to accept the disappointment, however bitter.

When I wrote to her, Celine had promised to include me when she took a delegation back to her home kingdom of Lanover—the richest among the Four Kingdoms. But the trip had been delayed several times, and I had started to think I would never make it.

And now that I was here, my feet firmly buried in the sand of a new kingdom, something had already gone wrong.

For years I had been pinning my hopes on this trip, with the expectation my friend would be with me to introduce me to her sister. I hadn't expected us to be parted before we even set foot in Arcadia—the first kingdom of our tour.

Without Celine, I would have to rely entirely on my own abilities to make an impression on Aurora, and I hadn't made a good start. Something wasn't right, and whatever it was, I should have discovered it during our voyage across the ocean.

A well-built and maintained royal ship didn't just spring a leak. And I wasn't the only one to think it. The captain's eyes held concern as he oversaw our disembarkation, even if he hadn't voiced it. I had spent some time with him during the voyage, curious to learn about the many aspects of a sea-faring life, and he usually took problems comfortably in stride. But this leak had overset his usual calm.

After four years actively preparing myself to be an intelligencer, I had failed at the first test—noticing neither clues nor warning signs. I still had no idea what had gone wrong or who might be responsible. If the leak was the result of foul play, I had missed the perfect opportunity to prove my worth to Aurora.

I sighed and turned away from the ocean. The ship was out of my reach now, and there was nothing I could do about the leak, natural or otherwise. The only thing I could do was look to the future and find a different means of impressing Aurora and convincing her to let me stay in the Four Kingdoms. After all, if it had been foul play, there might be more to come.

I tipped my head up to the sun and let a lighter mood wash over me. The weather, at least, was cooperating, the day perfect for an extended walk. A smile even stretched across my face as I considered how unnatural my uncle and cousin would find my delight at the prospect of further calamity.

Suppressing a chuckle, I turned the smile on Princess Giselle, entering into the talk of the other three girls.

"Cassie, Cassie, Cassie." Princess Daisy pulled on my arm, her mood teasing. The thirteen-year-old was caught up in the excitement, and not even the steadying presence of Daria was enough to keep her from bouncing on her toes as she chattered away about the excitement of our hurried departure from the ship.

But even as we joked and talked, a part of me remained alert, determined not to fail again. A strange look between one of the guards and Giselle's personal maid made my muscles tighten, my body responding to the unease of my mind. The maid had struck me as odd from the moment I met her, but when I failed to observe any suspicious behavior on her part during the voyage, I had dismissed it as the sort of foolish fancy my mother might have indulged in—exactly the kind of emotional whimsy my uncle would have liked me to display in place of what he called my hard-headed insistence on sticking my nose where it didn't belong.

Giselle spoke with the guard, her relaxed attitude confirming I had no reason to suspect him, and the group began to form up. We had agreed to leave this remote beach and begin walking to the Arcadian capital, rather than waiting for the carriages that were supposedly being sent to meet us after our unexpected and hurried departure from the ship. Hopefully we would meet up with them before those of us with less than appropriate footwear began to feel the pinch of our shoes.

Daria didn't notice the movement of the group, her attention on the departing ship as it grew smaller and smaller. I called to her, gesturing for her to fall in beside Daisy and me. I liked Daisy, but I didn't want to be the object of her undivided attention for the entire walk. I had too much occupying my mind.

Thankfully, Daisy didn't appear to notice my abstraction, chattering to me at full speed as we walked under the shade of a line of trees, following a road between fields being readied for spring planting. Everything about the scene spoke of order and harmony, and a sliver of doubt crept in. Was I willing there to be intrigue where in fact there was none? Maybe the ship really had just sprung a leak and the concerns of the captain were about safely delivering the rest of his royal charges to Lanover.

Daisy continued to talk at me about her plans for making the most of the unexpected adventure. As a princess, she was usually watched over far more closely than she liked, and she had already told me how she envied my childhood. From her perspective, it sounded idyllic to be left free to explore our ancient castle's secret passages or map the nearby forest. From what I had seen of her, I suspected she would have found it lonely in reality, however.

After a while she must have noticed my minimal answers because as we entered a copse of trees, she fell silent, drifting a few steps away from me. I paid her little heed since an unspoken tension had gripped some of the guards, catching my attention. Many of them looked toward the front of our small procession, their gaze lingering on the guard who had earlier spoken to Princess Giselle.

My eyes narrowed as I watched him, my earlier doubts resurfacing as I tried to catch some sign of the source of their unease. A sound in the trees to our left distracted me. The noise had been quiet, but I wasn't the only one to catch it. Daisy, even closer to the source than me, stepped off the path, as if she meant to investigate.

Neither Daria nor Giselle had responded to the initial sound, but both reacted to Daisy's departure. Giselle hurried after her, but movement at the front of our group pulled my attention away from the other girls. My eyes narrowed as the guard looked back in our direction.

Sudden apprehension gripped me, and I opened my mouth to call to Giselle. But before I could do so, several things happened at once.

A flicker of movement in the corner of my eye was followed immediately by Giselle screaming Daisy's name. Giselle's unusual horse, Arvin, already in motion, knocked her to the ground. And the guard I had been watching shouted something I couldn't catch, causing many of those around us to draw their swords and attack.

The attacking portion of guards focused first on the other guards, no doubt perceiving them as the greater threat. But with the element of surprise on their side, I was still frozen when the closest one dispatched the guard beside him—leaving him bleeding on the ground—and turned toward Daria.

Daria was caught completely off guard. She stumbled backward, her arms rising in front of her in an ineffectual attempt at defense. I ran the few steps between us, thankful for the mobility allowed by my full skirts as I kicked high, my foot firmly connecting with the guard's stomach.

Winded, he dropped his weapon and doubled over.

My uncle's captain of the guard had taught me that move, claiming it would give me time to run away. And that was exactly what I intended to do now. It was the only strategy that had any hope of success given we were outnumbered and unarmed.

I hesitated, however, unwilling to abandon the other girls. Daria, the only one in reach, was staring at the battle being waged around us, apparently still in shock. I didn't have time to talk her out of it, and I couldn't trust she'd respond to a verbal command.

Grabbing her arm, I dragged her off the road behind me and into the shelter of the trees. As soon as we were under cover, I paused, and she pulled herself free. I could hear her drawing deep, shuddering breaths, but my focus was on the other side of the road. I had reacted instinctively, heading for the closest shelter, but the road now separated us from Giselle, while Daisy had disappeared from sight completely.

I hesitated again, but the sight of Arvin beside Giselle gave me pause. He had known something was wrong and acted before I did. I didn't know his history, but he clearly wasn't an ordinary animal. If Giselle and Daisy escaped on horseback, none of the traitors would have a hope of catching them—especially since they didn't have mounts themselves.

Giselle caught my eye and gestured wildly at the woods behind us, clearly telling me to keep running. Daria caught the message as well, but she didn't move, seeming torn.

I threw a quick glance at the road, drawing in a hissing breath as I saw the fight was over. It hadn't gone our way. If we were going to have any chance of escape, we needed to leave now.

"We need to run!" I said, and Daria nodded, her eyes sick, but her face determined.

Afraid she was still in shock, I reached for her arm again, ready to tow her all the way through the woods if necessary, but she shook her head.

"We'll move faster separately."

Relief at the return of her good sense filled me, and I didn't wait for any further conversation, running at full speed into the trees behind us. Daria followed at my heels, keeping pace.

"Where can we go?" She gasped out the words, her breathing already ragged.

"Away." I shot out the single word, fear keeping me focused. I knew nothing about the area, or even about our attackers. All I knew was that they were killers, and our only hope lay in putting as much distance between us and them as possible. I wasted a moment of thought hoping Giselle and Daisy were already far away on Arvin's back before a loud shout behind us made me find a new level of speed.

It required all my focus to avoid the trees and not trip over any of the undergrowth. A large bush appeared in front of me, and I veered right, only to realize Daria had gone left. But the guards were almost on our heels, and I couldn't slow or change direction.

To my disappointment, they split up to follow us. I had briefly hoped they might abandon Daria to follow me, clearing the way for her escape. But at least by splitting, they had reduced the number either of us had on our tail. Hopefully we could find each other again on the other side of the trees. If we survived that long.

A new scent caught my nose, making me jerk my head further right. Smoke.

I hesitated for a brief second before changing course. The smell wasn't coming from anywhere near the battle I had left behind on the road, so it must belong to someone other than my attackers. My instincts told me introducing more elements to the situation would increase my likelihood of finding a way to escape. I needed the guards distracted—I just hoped I didn't get any innocents hurt in the process.

The bright flicker of a flame was the first thing to appear between the trees. I ran toward it, giving a great shout as I did so. I didn't want the guards catching the people at the camp by surprise.

My shout elicited curses and angry yells from behind me. My ears strained to hear the corresponding sound of voices and confusion ahead of me, but it didn't eventuate. Instead, I caught only the ring of drawn steel.

I let out a soft breath of relief. Clearly I wasn't leading the guards toward unarmed, unprepared victims. And hopefully the sight of armed strangers would give my pursuers pause.

I swerved at the last minute so as not to burst out of the trees directly into the campsite. Instead I skirted around the small clearing. My curving movement took me temporarily out of view of the guards behind me, a thick clump of trees and bushes shielding me momentarily. I turned my eyes to the trees ahead of me, looking for the right one.

There!

Barely breaking stride, I jumped, grasping the branch and swinging myself into the tree. Trying to quiet my breathing, I scrabbled against the bark as I desperately scrambled higher into the foliage. As soon as I was confident I was out of sight, hidden by the thick green leaves, I froze.

The two guards pursuing me came into view, their headlong pace slowing as they caught sight of the campfire between the trees. They glanced at each other, peering around as if trying to determine which way I had fled.

After a minute, one of them grunted, jerking his head toward the clearing ahead of them. They approached, moving at a more cautious pace now, clearly wanting to see if I had sought refuge with the unknown group.

I looked down into the small clearing and got my first proper view of the camp. It was empty.

Two horses, clearly interrupted in their grazing, stood at alert, their heads up and ears pricked. A small cart sat a short distance from them, various lumpy packages covered by a stretch of canvas. A couple of bedrolls lay beside the small fire, and a cooking pot sat to one side, its contents steaming. But I could see no sign of any cook.

A strangled gasp from the direction of the guards made me whip my eyes back toward my pursuers. They hadn't made it to the edge of the clearing.

Both of their bodies lay sprawled in unnatural positions, struck down before they could investigate more closely. I gulped at the sight of their killers.

The two men looked far too large to have concealed themselves in the forest, and yet they had clearly taken the guards by surprise. Even I had seen no sign of them from my hidden perch. Their size and clothing marked them as a pair, although in every other respect they looked like opposites.

One had the palest skin I had ever seen, other than a small patch around his eyes that looked closer to my own olive tone. His long hair only completed the colorless effect, bleached so white blond he could have passed for a grandfather if not for his menacing air.

The other had ebony skin and a bald head that shone in the reflected light of the flames. He looked contemplatively down at the two dead guards while his companion scanned the nearby forest. I held my breath, irrationally afraid he might see me despite my screen of dense leaves. He didn't even look up into the treetops, though, shrugging instead and turning back to his fire.

"Whoever they were pursuing will have run far by now. If they're wise, that is."

The other gave a rough laugh before frowning back into the trees. "There might be others. They have the look of royal guards."

His companion shrugged. "Let them come."

His grin showed too many teeth and elicited a similarly unsettling smile from the other man who followed him back into the campsite without further dispute. They both took the time to carefully clean their blades before returning them to the scabbards strapped to their waists and sitting once again beside their fire.

I drew quiet, even breaths, the way I had taught myself to do when watching people unobserved. In some ways, the role felt familiar, and yet I had never spied on anyone as clearly dangerous as these two. Aside from their easy dispatch of the two trained guards, something in their manner made them far more intimidating than my pursuers had been, even in the midst of my flight. I knew, with utter certainty, that I could not let these men catch sight of me. They hadn't hesitated to strike down my pursuers, and I was utterly confident they would treat me the same way without a second thought.

Which meant I couldn't climb down from the tree. I was stuck.

# CHAPTER 2

*C*aptive on my perch, I listened to the conversation around the campfire. The position of the two men made it hard for me to see them clearly or to distinguish who was speaking. Their voices blended together, both speaking with the same accent—one I didn't recognize. Even in my position of peril, this small ignorance cost me a pang. If I was a local, I would no doubt understand the significance of the accent. Such lapses in knowledge might disadvantage me with Aurora.

Clearly these men had nothing to do with the attack on the road, but I still followed their words with interest. Whoever they were, they didn't strike me as normal travelers, and their uncon-cern over killing two men they believed to be royal guards intrigued and terrified me in equal measures. Who were they that they considered themselves outside the reach of any conse-quences?

At one point I caught the name Malik, although they seemed to be referring to a third person—one who wasn't traveling with them. Most of their conversation was unintelligible, their refer-ences to their home, their business, and their lives too unfamiliar for me to parse. But the longer I listened, the more intrigued and unsettled I became.

I had questioned whether I was imagining nefarious happenings on the ship, but I had clearly been right. This time I had clear evidence the men below me were without normal conscience or check. And the certainty these weren't ordinary criminals grew the more time passed. Although clearly warriors of some sort, they struck me as having something of the alert watchfulness I strove to achieve myself. Was it possible they were intelligencers?

I rejected the thought after a moment's consideration. Unlike me, with my small stature and unusually young looks, these men could hardly pass through a crowd unnoticed. Their sheer bulk, let alone the air of menace they wore, drew instant attention, and their pairing only increased the effect. No one would choose them for a mission that required discreet observance.

They were something else then. Something more than a mere guard or brigand. A sense of excitement thrummed through my bones, making it hard to retain the necessary stillness. Could this be the opportunity I needed?

Now that the initial shock of the attack on the road had subsided, shame had taken its place. I had left home certain of my ability—confident that my uncle's desire to shape me for a quiet life at home was an underestimation of my true potential and gifting. And yet I had traveled all that time on the ship and not seen the sinister plot underway.

For all my nerves, at heart I had been sure the training I had given myself in the past four years, as well as my previous success, were enough to win acceptance from Aurora. But if she could see me right now, she would dismiss me as worse than a fool. I had wasted my time on the ship, and people had died in consequence.

But with these two, I had stumbled upon an entirely separate conspiracy. If I could find out some concrete information about their plans and purposes, she might overlook my failure with the traitorous guards. At the very least, the prospect gave me something to think about other than my uncomfortable position in the tree or my concerns for my companions' safety.

The smell of the men's meal wafted up to me, and I pressed my hand against my stomach, willing it not to gurgle. The ship's leak had disrupted our day, and I couldn't remember when I had last eaten. At least I had my water skin strapped across my back, although I didn't dare retrieve it while balanced motionless in the tree.

When they had finished eating, the bald one stood and looked in the direction of the fallen guards.

"Someone will come searching for them eventually." He spoke without inflection, but a question lurked in his words. His companion also stood.

"Malik told us not to draw official attention." He sounded regretful. "I suppose we should find another campsite for the night."

Without further conversation, the bald one threw dirt on their fire while the bloodthirsty one went to the horses. I frowned. They couldn't leave. I hadn't discovered anything of use about them yet. I hadn't redeemed myself.

Working together, they harnessed the two horses to the wagon, shoving their bedrolls and cooking pot in the back without unclipping the canvas. It was unusual for a cart that size to have a double harness, but given the size of the men themselves, I could understand why they needed two animals to pull it.

Before they climbed up to the seat at the front of the wagon, however, a distant sound made them pause. The bald one cocked his head, his eyes focused on the trees before they both took off. They moved impossibly silently, melting into the trees on the far side of the clearing, back in the direction of the road and the battle. More of the guards must have made it this far.

Suddenly alone on the edge of the clearing, I found myself sliding down the tree before I realized my own intent. Seeing my opportunity to redeem myself slipping away, I didn't stop to second guess my actions. Dashing across the short open space, I pulled myself into the back of the wagon. Lying on my tummy, I wiggled under the canvas, winding around the various haphazardly placed packages until I reached the very back. It was stifling all the way back here, and I didn't even have enough room to sit up. Doubt gripped me, and I nearly backtracked. But before I could move, the wagon dipped and creaked as someone climbed onto the seat above me.

I stifled a gasp. The men had returned as silently as they had left. If I had moved a few seconds earlier, they would have caught me leaving the wagon. I dropped down and lay still.

The rumble of voices sounded.

"We could have eliminated them easily."

"No doubt," the other replied. "But our mission is better served by our departure." He gave a low laugh. "There will be victims enough to satisfy even your blade when Malik returns with his army. Patience."

The other grunted, as if dissatisfied with the idea of patience, but my mind had caught on the previous words. Army? He spoke as if an invasion was imminent.

The self-centered interest that had driven me onto the wagon dissolved before a far more important concern. If these were scouts for an invading army, then far more futures than mine might hang in the balance. I needed to find out where they came from and then get back to Giselle as quickly as possible. She and Arvin must have made it to the palace in Arcadie by now. Once I had the information, I would find my way there.

I just hoped Daria would be able to do the same. I refused to consider the idea that she might have been caught.

We bumped along the rough ground of the forest, weaving between trees. I could tell from our direction that we continued to move away from the road that had seen the battle, but there must have been one on the other side as well because we soon hit level ground.

Our pace increased, and I strained to hear any conversation above the sound of the wheels. The two men rarely spoke, and when they did, their voices remained at an indistinguishable murmur.

From their earlier words, I had been expecting them to find a new camp within the trees, but clearly something had set them on a different course of action. Instead, the wagon rolled further and further away from where I had crawled aboard.

The terrifying exhilaration of hearing about a planned invasion faded, replaced with a gnawing anxiety. My stomach roiled more now than when the path beneath us had been bumpy. Where were the men unwittingly taking me? If we went too far, it might become difficult to get back given I had neither resources nor provisions.

But it was too late to worry about that now. I had no choice but to wait for them to eventually stop and make camp. At least it would be easier to make my escape under the cover of dark.

I bit my lip as I considered creeping away in the night. Despite the one shocking revelation, I hadn't heard any significant details. If I slipped away immediately, I wouldn't have any information about their origins or plans to report to Princess Giselle.

But despite my desire to impress Aurora, I didn't fancy getting myself killed in the process. The longer I spent near these men, the more chance I would be discovered.

For the moment, there was nothing I could do about it, however. The wagon rolled on, and I remained stuck in the back. Hours passed, and even the dim sliver of light that filtered in from the back of the wagon had long since died before our movement finally slowed and stopped. I spared a thought for the poor horses as I carefully stretched, trying to limber sore muscles in preparation for a desperate dash for freedom.

The wagon rocked again as the pair climbed down, and I froze as one of them approached the back and began to pull out the items they had hastily stowed before leaving the last camp. If they intended to unclip the canvas and access all their cargo, I would be discovered before I had even attempted escape.

I held my breath, not daring to make the smallest movement, while they retrieved the bedrolls and cooking supplies. A long moment passed and then another. The canvas remained untouched.

I breathed a silent sigh of relief as I listened to them strike a fire and set up camp. The distant rumble of their voices sounded only occasionally, and one of my feet jiggled as I waited for them to settle into sleep.

Now that I was faced with the reality of the moment, I realized the task I had set myself wasn't going to be simple. Stuck in the dark, I had no way to identify the right moment for escape. They moved so silently that one of them could be pacing up and down beside the wagon keeping watch for the night, and I wouldn't hear a thing. If I was fortunate, they would both snore.

Sure enough, eventually a rasping rhythm reached my ears. One of them, at least, was asleep.

I waited, but no other sound joined the first.

I had reached an impasse. It was possible the other didn't snore, but it struck me as more likely that they slept in shifts, leaving one on guard at all times. Which meant sneaking away might be impossible.

My breathing hitched and tried to speed up, but I steadied it with an act of will. Fear and rash action wouldn't serve me now. I needed to move carefully and slowly and to think my way out of the situation, just as I had been training myself to do.

But no amount of thinking produced any solution other than creeping to the lip of the wagon as silently as possible and hoping I could get a sight of their bedrolls. Eventually I gave up on any hope of a brilliant alternative and wormed my way to the edge of the canvas. At least I was wearing a deep blue gown and the dark brown of my hair also worked in my favor in the dimness of night.

Ever so slowly, I poked the top of my head out of the back of the wagon. Shafts of moonlight lit up the new campsite. Open fields stretched around the small area of churned up dirt that had clearly been used by many travelers before now. In the distance I caught a glimpse of the road before my eyes fastened on a dark figure, striding away from me.

The man stopped, starting to pivot back in my direction. With a stifled gasp, I scuttled backward into the depths of the wagon. As soon as I was well out of sight, I froze, my heart pounding. Had he turned because he heard me, or had he merely reached the edge of his appointed sentry area?

Long seconds passed as I waited, but no shout of alarm sounded, and no one approached the rear of the wagon. Whatever his reason for turning, he didn't appear to have seen me. This time.

I lay for a long time, considering and rejecting again all the ideas that had previously run through my mind. I needed to get out of this wagon, but I couldn't do it with a sentry on duty. In the woods it could have been achieved with careful timing, but here the ground was far too flat.

Reluctantly I concluded I had no choice but to wait until the wagon reached different terrain—perhaps even a town. And I would have to hope the men didn't need anything from further back in their wagon before that happened.

Moving as silently as possible, I retrieved my water skin and took a drink while I considered my situation. I would have to sleep. It had been a long and difficult day, and despite the fear and uncertainty, my body was reaching its limits. Lying here motionless in the dark, I would soon sleep regardless of my intentions. Would I wake at the first sound, or would my exhaustion propel me into a deep slumber?

My elbow bumped against a sharp corner of wood, and I suppressed a grumble. That particular crate had already delivered several blows during the journey. I pushed at it, trying to clear myself some more room, and it moved surprisingly easily. No wonder it had bounced against me on the drive, despite its size.

My hand ran along the edge. Just how big was the crate?

The side stretched on further than I could reach, and I scooted awkwardly around so I could find the far corner. My surprise at the crate's light weight grew. It was more than half my length, and wider than my shoulders. Big enough, in fact, to fit my whole body if I pulled up my legs.

Carefully, I pushed the lid ajar and reached inside to feel the contents. My fingers plunged into loose curls of sawdust. No wonder it was so light. I hoisted myself up and plunged my whole arm in, seeking the contents protected by the sawdust. I found nothing.

Further exploration still revealed nothing. I frowned. Why would anyone have a crate of sawdust in the back of their wagon? There must be something in there. But if there was, it was too small for me to find from my hampered position.

I hesitated for one final moment before shrugging. I needed to sleep, and it would be easier to relax in the security of the crate than lying exposed among the boxes and packages in the bed of the wagon. Even if the men came looking for something in the morning, they wouldn't see me concealed among the sawdust.

# CHAPTER 3

*I*t took me some time to maneuver the lid off, given my limitations and the need for silence. I eventually managed it, however, scrambling inelegantly inside. When I pulled the lid back over the top of me, some of the tension inside loosened. Even if it was largely an illusion, I felt more secure now I was hidden from casual view.

My muscles relaxed, my mind slowing as I tried to squirm into the most comfortable position. As I pushed through the now-flattened sawdust, my leg bumped against something. Twisting, I managed to get it in my hand. At first, with no light, I couldn't tell what it was. Then my fingers found a clasp, and I realized it was a small leather case. Wiggling it open, I pulled back the lid, exposing two slim glass vials nestled inside.

Now that I knew what to look for, I managed to find two more such cases hidden among the protective packaging. It was a lot of sawdust to protect so few cases. Had there been something bigger stored in here previously that had recently been removed? Or had there been many more cases and vials and these were the only ones left? In that case the size of the crate suggested they had originally transported a significant number.

I chewed on my lip. Whatever the reason, these cases must

hold something valuable. I considered climbing back out of the crate and wriggling closer to the front of the wagon so I could get a look at one of the vials. But fear of being spotted kept me immobile. And in my exhausted state, I couldn't be too sorry for an excuse not to try.

Sight wasn't the only sense of use, though. The apothecary's workroom had always been filled with different scents, and I had learned to recognize many of them. If I could identify the main ingredients, I might be able to guess at the purpose of the contents.

I slowly rolled onto my stomach, raising my head as far as the lid of the crate would allow so I could keep the vial upright. Working off the stopper, I held the vial in front of my nose, using my other hand to waft the fumes inside toward my nose.

Disappointment registered at the totally unfamiliar scent before my mind grew fuzzy. For a moment I tried to hold on to my thoughts, a sense of imminent danger pushing against the rising dark. But without conscious volition, my hand went slack, releasing the vial, and a moment later my head sank to the bottom of the crate. A last rush of fear fought to keep me alert, but the darkness overwhelmed me, and I slept.

A jostling movement made me groan and stir. Why did all my muscles ache? A deep, groaning roar made me bolt upright, only to hit my head against something hard and flat above me. I fell back, moaning and rubbing at my forehead.

My elbows hit two walls on either side of me, and memory returned in a flood. I bit back a gasp. What had happened to me? How long had I been unconscious?

I felt around frantically, scrabbling through the sawdust, but the vial must have rolled away. Did that mean we'd been traveling while I lay insensible in the crate? If the vial had leaked liquid, it had since dried because I couldn't even find any moisture.

I almost groaned again at the thought of moisture, desperate for some water to soothe my parched mouth. How long had I been lying curled in this box? No wonder everything hurt.

Memory of my uncertain situation momentarily drove away the thirst. Whatever gas was trapped in those vials, it was strong enough to knock someone out. Had I missed my chance to escape from the two men who drove the cart while I was unconscious? Why had I opened the vial then and there instead of taking it with me to investigate later? I had finally done what my uncle had always warned and stuck my nose where it didn't belong—in this case in the most literal sense.

And even if I could escape, how far might I have to travel to get back to Arcadie and my friends?

I shook my head. I could worry about that once I was safely away.

Before I could even consider pushing up the lid to get a peek at my current situation, the crate moved again. This time it went beyond a rough sliding motion. Someone actually picked the crate up and swung it through the air.

I stifled a squeak as I lurched upward and then dropped part way toward the ground before being steadied.

A grunt sounded above me followed by a curse. Someone was unloading the crate, and that someone seemed taken off guard by its weight.

"What did you put in here?" an annoyed voice asked, the accent familiar from the conversations I had previously overheard.

"Nothing," the other man called back.

He sounded suspicious, and my mind flashed to the tiny dagger concealed in my boot. But even if I could reach it, what good would it do? It certainly wouldn't intimidate either of the men who had so easily dispatched the traitorous guards. And the lock picks concealed in my hair would be even less use.

Before I had time to come up with a course of action, my crate was roughly dropped on the ground. I suppressed a groan at the jostling of my bruised muscles, but a cry burst out of me when the lid was removed and dazzling sunlight pierced my burning eyes.

Instinctively I threw one arm across my face while with the other, I pushed myself upright. I lurched wildly, completely unsteady, but I refused to lie helpless before whatever was coming for me.

"What in the—" The man cut himself off, letting out a string of curses.

His companion gave a wordless cry of outrage from somewhere to my right as I scrambled to my feet. I had barely found my balance when the sound of drawn steel made me force my arm away from my eyes despite the pain of the bright light.

I stepped backward, but my foot didn't quite clear the lip of the crate, and I stumbled. By the time I managed to right myself, both feet firmly planted on the ground beside the crate, a dark, solid shape stood between me and the approaching sword.

"Get out of my way, Aron."

I squinted, my eyes slowly adjusting. Two blurry shapes resolved into the men from the clearing, facing off against each other. The bald one—apparently Aron—didn't move out of the way, and the other grunted in frustration. He didn't, however, attack his companion.

I slowly edged backward, but I hadn't made it more than a couple of steps when Aron's hand shot backward and grabbed my arm. He turned a dangerous look on me before glancing back at the other man.

"Don't be so hasty, Samar. I have questions, and I'm sure Malik will as well."

Samar, his hair now tied back into braids, spat on the ground. "I have no questions for a filthy stowaway."

"No." Aron sounded bored. "But then you've always been rash. Why do you think Malik always sends us out together?"

Samar muttered something I didn't catch because my heart was now beating so hard I thought my legs might collapse from under me. Although now that I got a good look at our surroundings, I realized the weakened state of my body might be attributable to more than just fear.

Patches of tough grass grew out of the dirt beneath us, but only steps away, the dirt was overtaken by sand. It stretched out, rising up and down in vast dunes that extended further than the eye could see. I had studied maps of the Four Kingdoms before embarking on our trip, and there was only one place this could be. The Great Desert.

If we had reached the edge of the Great Desert, then we had traveled even further than I had feared. I must have been unconscious for an extended period of time.

Dizziness washed over me, and I no longer knew if it was fear, shock, or dehydration.

"Please don't hurt me. I didn't mean any harm." I tried to sound as weak and pitiful as possible, but both men just stared at me in disgust.

I flinched, cowering away. If I was to have any hope of getting out of this situation alive, then I needed them to underestimate me. Thankfully adults had always had a tendency to do that due to my small size.

"What were you doing in our wagon?" Aron asked.

I let tears leak out of my eyes. "I was just seeking shelter. Some men were chasing me."

"The girl from the woods." Samar narrowed his eyes. "Let me get rid of her so we can be on our way."

But Aron raised an eyebrow. "The woods? That was a long time past." He gave me a thorough inspection. "She looks weak enough to have been in there that long." He let out a short bark of laughter. "She won't be putting up much of a fight." He rubbed his hand along his chin, still examining me.

Samar shrugged. "Weak or strong, you can't imagine she would cause me any difficulty either way."

Aron gave him a disgusted look. "I'm not questioning your ability to kill, Samar. It's a different purpose I have in mind. Back there," he jerked a thumb away from the desert, "she would have been a liability. If she escaped, or if anyone saw her...But out here." He gazed across the barren dunes, and I swallowed, new fear rising inside me.

"Please, just let me go," I whispered. "I won't say anything to anyone—"

"Silence!" Aron cut me off, his voice managing to convey a threat despite his obvious abstraction.

I went quiet, not wanting to goad them into hasty action. But the wind blew sand around my legs, and I shivered despite the heat. I had been hoping to lure them into thinking me weak and helpless, opening up the opportunity for a later escape. But if they intended to head into the vast, lifeless desert...

"She clearly found one of the vials," Aron said after a moment's thought. "I can smell it on her." His eyes snapped to me. "Which means you know we can easily get you across the desert with or without your cooperation. But I can't guarantee what another extended period without food or water would do to you. So if you want to stay conscious, don't cause any trouble."

"You can't be serious!" Samar frowned at him. "You want to drag her across the desert with us?"

"She's not much to look at, but need I remind you she managed to hide herself in our wagon and make it this far without being discovered? I'd wager she's wilier than she looks. Who knows what useful information she might possess?" He grinned suddenly, the expression almost as frightening as his glare. "You have enemies here, girl, clearly. So perhaps you'll find you can come to an arrangement of mutual understanding with Malik."

Samar scoffed. "We don't need assistance from the likes of her. You saw for yourself that these lands are ripe for the picking."

Aron shook his head. "I saw a number of interesting things. The Four Kingdoms are not so weak that we can ignore a potential advantage." He shrugged. "And if she doesn't prove to have useful information, Malik will find another use for her. She looks young enough to be bound to the ring."

At that Samar finally gave up on further argument. Instead he squinted at me before shrugging. "Malik does like his games, and I suppose she might be pretty enough with some food and a bath." He wrinkled his nose. "If you have use for ornamentation." His tone made it clear that Malik had such a use but that Samar considered it a weakness.

Their words made little sense to me, but I took hope from their decision not to kill me immediately. Of course, if their superior hoped to get information about the Four Kingdoms out of me, he would be disappointed. Even if I had been inclined to help him, I had so far spent the vast majority of my time in these kingdoms unconscious. His own men must know more about these lands than I did. But I was willing to take any reprieve and trust in my ability to escape before we reached this mysterious Malik.

"I won't cause any trouble," I said quickly. If I could convince them I was willing to work with them, they might keep less of a close watch.

"No." Samar balanced his sword on one finger before sliding it cleanly back into the scabbard at his waist. "You won't."

He turned away from me, indicating with his unprotected back that he considered me no threat. I carefully kept my face locked in a mask of timid fear, but inside I cheered. The buoyant emotion faded as I caught a glimpse of Aron's expression, however. He watched me with an alert air that didn't bode well. Samar might be the rash, bloodthirsty one, but Aron was the one I would need to watch.

I turned slightly away from him, surveying the scene around me now that I had a moment of leisure to do so. My fumbling fingers, weak from the long period of confinement and deprivation, opened my water skin. My throat ached and scratched from the sawdust, desperate for a drink. As I took a slow swallow, wincing at the discomfort, I examined the creatures whose cries had startled me awake. Camels.

We appeared to be alone, so I didn't know where they had come from. But Aron and Samar were clearly half way through transferring their load from the wagon to the backs of two camels. Another two camels wore saddles for riding.

Now that my fate had been so casually decided, the two men returned to their task with brisk efficiency. Without changing the direction of my gaze, I tried taking a couple of steps backward. Aron instantly stilled, his eyes on me with a silent threat. I froze and didn't try it again.

If I had been at full strength, I might have attempted to run despite his watchful eye. I was usually quick despite my small stature. But the extended period of time in the crate had weakened me to the point where the effort would be futile. Which left me with no choice but to remain as their captive for now.

But for all my desire to gather intelligence and prove myself, I had no desire to be taken deep into the desert. Or as far away as southern Lanover, which was their only possible destination. Given I hadn't expired from lack of water, we must be at the northwestern tip of the Great Desert, the closest point to Arcadie and our original location.

The desert stretched along the whole eastern edge of Lanover as well as along the southern border of Rangmere and part of Arcadia. The endless sand dunes were impassable, but a series of oases allowed traders to travel up and down the western portion, carrying goods back and forth to southern Lanover. While Aron and Samar didn't travel with a traditional desert trader caravan, they must have some connection to them since the traders carefully guarded knowledge of the location of the hidden water sources.

Cautiously, not wanting to draw Aron's attention, I tried to shake off the sawdust that coated me, stretching out my weak, aching muscles in the process. They spasmed, making me gasp with pain as my eyes stung. If I had any excess moisture left in me, they would no doubt have watered. But I pushed through, desperate to have my body returned to working order. I needed to be ready as soon as a possibility of escape presented itself. It might even be possible to escape in the desert, after all, if I could memorize the route we took to the closest oasis. The sooner I could get away, the less distance I would have to backtrack.

I needed more water first, though. And some food as well.

As if reading my mind, Aron threw something in my direction. I reacted on instinct, my hands flying out to snatch it from the air.

He raised an eyebrow. "Quick reflexes."

I remained silent, upbraiding myself for the unintended display. The smell of the small chunk of bread, heavy with dried fruit, quickly drove all other thought from my mind, however, and I had to exert all my self-control to eat it slowly. The last thing I wanted was for my stomach to reject the food after going so long without eating.

When everything was loaded onto the camels, Aron directed me to refill my water skin at a small stream a short way behind us. I took the opportunity to drink again before filling my skin to bursting. I didn't know when I would have the chance to get more, and I was starting at a disadvantage compared to the two men.

Aron stood threateningly over me while I crouched beside the water, and the moment I was finished, he lifted me into the air and deposited me on the back of a camel. He climbed on in front of me, and the creature lumbered to its feet. Samar watched us contemptuously from the back of his already standing camel. The two pack camels had been secured behind him in a mini string while our beast moved freely. Of course, with Aron in front of me, there was no possibility of goading my mount into making a break for freedom— even if I could have worked out how to do it.

We began to move, and I clutched convulsively at the saddle in front of me, suddenly aware of how high up we were. But we moved at a steady—if bumpy—pace, and the growing heat of the sun soon drove all other thoughts out of my mind. By the time we had left all sight of greenery behind us, it was impossible to remember it was only spring.

Both men had wrapped themselves in voluminous robes that exposed only a small portion of skin around their eyes, explaining the odd patch of tanned skin on Samar's face. At first I had been horrified at the idea of wearing so much material in the heat, but after an hour in the direct sun, I changed my mind.

"I need a robe as well," I said to Aron's back.

I braced myself for a swift denial, but he said nothing. Picking up a length of rough material draped across the saddle in front of him, he handed it back to me without even turning to look in my direction.

Astonished, I nearly dropped it, seizing it at the last minute and gathering the material in my lap. For a moment I just stared at his back. Once again Aron had surprised me, anticipating my need from the beginning. Although he hadn't had the compassion to act before I made the request.

It took me several attempts, but I managed to cocoon myself in something approaching the style of my captors, who now closely resembled traders. Slightly heartened by the success of my request, I spoke again.

"Are you desert traders?"

"Silence, captive," Aron replied quickly, but not fast enough to override Samar's response.

Turning, Samar spat valuable moisture onto the sand beneath us. "Desert traders? We're not filthy traitors like those—" He broke off as if suddenly remembering whom he addressed. Giving me a disgusted look, he turned back to face forward.

After that, we rode in silence.

I tucked the piece of information away in my mind, further questions tugging at me. The desert traders operated separately to the Lanoverian crown, but they gave them loyalty. And their ties had been recently strengthened by a marriage of alliance. So who did Samar consider the traders to be traitors against?

The buzz of curiosity slowly faded with no possible way to assuage it as we traveled on and on.

I took careful, slow sips of water as we traveled. I wanted to conserve my supplies, but I was conscious of my desperate need to rehydrate. Hours passed in uncomfortable monotony as we traveled deeper and deeper into the desert. When the sun finally began to set, I welcomed the break from movement.

I expected the men to put me to work, but instead they continued to ignore me. Working in what was clearly a practiced routine, they set up a small camp, producing an evening meal and even a large container from which they filled their individual water skins. Samar hesitated for a moment after filling his own before glancing at Aron and imperiously holding out his hand for mine.

I risked his displeasure by taking a few valuable seconds to gulp down my remaining water, letting it spill out across my face when he made a noise of impatience. Sighing in satisfaction, I handed my skin to him to be refilled. Now that I knew we would have refreshed supplies at night, I would ration better during the day.

Neither man spoke to me, other than to bark sharp orders, but Aron threw me a blanket as they settled into their own bedrolls. I shook it out and laid it over the sand which I had done my best to sculpt into a makeshift bed. I certainly couldn't imagine putting it over me given the heat that still lingered in both the air and the sand beneath my feet.

An hour later I had changed my mind, however. As the chill night air leached the remaining heat from the sand, I rolled myself up in it, wishing for a second one. Only hours ago I would have considered this kind of cold in the desert to be an impossibility. Clearly this was going to be an uncomfortable journey.

$\mathcal{N}$othing on the second day belied my expectation of discomfort. And Aron and Samar barely spoke, even to each other, so I had few chances to glean even the smallest bits of information about either my captors or our destination. My curiosity chafed at the lack of information, fueled by the fear that I wouldn't find a way to escape when the time came.

But on the third day, a niggling certainty that I was missing something important distracted me from the unrelenting boredom and discomfort. It took me hours to put my finger on the source of my unease, however.

When I did, I couldn't help exclaiming aloud.

"East! We're still traveling east! Shouldn't we have turned south by now?"

"No," Aron said without inflection. "We're crossing the desert."

"We're what?" I stared at his back, trying to make sense of his words.

I had just assumed his earlier statement about taking me across the desert had been a reference to traveling through it on their way to southern Lanover. There was no other possible interpretation. It was a well-known fact that no one in the Four Kingdoms had ever found a way across the Great Desert.

"It will take us many more days to traverse the Sea of Sand and reach Ardasira."

"Ardasira? I don't understand. What's Ardasira?" I'd studied the map of the Four Kingdoms enough to know there was no city with that name.

"The kingdom of Ardasira is our home," Aron said. "And now it will be yours. Whether it will be a welcoming home is entirely up to you."

"And Malik," Samar called across with nasty mirth in his voice.

"And Malik," Aron agreed. "So I suggest you resolve now to be cooperative and tell him whatever he wants to know."

Their threats failed to reach me, my mind entirely occupied with this stunning revelation.

"There's a kingdom called Ardasira across the Great Desert? And you know how to reach it?"

"Of course we know. We came from there." Samar's impatience was clear, and I reluctantly stemmed the questions bubbling to my lips. Everything about the man warned me not to push him too far.

We continued on in silence, like before, but now my mind buzzed, spinning in circles. Excitement filled me at the idea of an entire unknown kingdom. Aurora couldn't possibly reject me when I came bearing information like this. It was the most important discovery since the impassable storms cleared, allowing travel between the Four Kingdoms and my own lands.

What connection did this Ardasira have with the Four Kingdoms? Aron had called the Great Desert the Sea of Sand, and from what I'd read, only the desert traders used that name. And yet my captors had denied association with them.

But as the camel plodded on, my excitement faded, lost in a growing list of concerns. Aron and Samar had spoken of Malik returning with an army. Was Ardasira planning to invade the Four Kingdoms?

Staring out at the endless sand dunes around us, it was hard to think we could be at risk from anyone on the other side of all this. And yet Aron and Samar clearly knew a route through. I couldn't discount the possibility of a threat.

A heavy weight settled over me as the foolhardy nature of my actions hit me afresh. Despite all my efforts to sharpen my mind, I had let my emotions rule me. Driven by my desire to redeem my previous mistake, I had made another even greater one when I dove into the wagon and then opened that vial.

As far as I knew, I was the only person in either the Four Kingdoms or my own lands to know anything of the existence of this Ardasira. And I had lost the opportunity to report Aron and Samar's presence with enough time for the authorities in the Four Kingdoms to follow them or question them as to their origins. The hope of everyone I had left behind now rested on my shoulders, and the burden felt suffocatingly heavy. Southern Lanover had seemed a world away, but the other side of the desert was another prospect entirely. From Ardasira, there would only be one way back.

I twisted in my seat to look behind us. Sand stretched away as far as the eye could see, occasionally undulating into dunes, big and small. I looked forward again to an identical view. My hope of escaping before we reached our destination and retracing my steps in the desert already looked foolish. I knew nothing about tracking in this vast wasteland and even less about camels. And when we finally reached Ardasira, I would face an entirely unknown kingdom and people. Escape had never been so important nor so impossible.

I straightened, pushing back against the creeping feeling of despair. I had made mistakes, certainly. But I had also wanted a chance to prove myself to Aurora. Before me now was an opportunity greater than I could have imagined. I would just have to make sure that I didn't let my emotions get in the way of my good decision making again.

I would let Aron and Samar take me to this Ardasira, I would escape, I would learn as much about the kingdom and its plans as I could, and then I would find a way back across the Great Desert. These two couldn't be the only ones who knew the location of the oases. I would have to find a way to earn some money and then pay someone to guide me back.

I just needed to stay strong.

The days blurred into each other in our seemingly endless journey, until I almost lost count. The further we rode, the clearer my own foolishness became. I had been certain I was cut from a different cloth from my mother, and yet clearly I was subject to the whim of my emotions after all. And now I might live out the rest of my days alone—a prisoner, or at best a street urchin in a place where I knew no one.

Despite my return to physical strength, several times I had to rouse myself from an increasing torpor, using only force of will. Eventually, alarmed by my own condition, I gave myself a stern lecture. I couldn't change the past, but I could hold on to hope that I would find a way back across the desert. And I could resolve to think like an intelligencer going forward. I couldn't do anything to escape immediately, but I could at least occupy myself by building a memory palace.

After a lifetime of exploring my uncle's castle, it was easy to use it as the base to store the information I was learning about Aron, Samar, Malik, Ardasira, and the plot against the Four Kingdoms. Unfortunately I knew almost nothing about the final point, and I could gather only little about the others. But I hoarded every scrap of information I could, hoping it would be of help later.

As long as I asked no questions, they conducted their own conversations in front of me, clearly not considering me a threat of any kind. Unfortunately they seemed to feel no need to discuss the mission which had taken them to the Four Kingdoms or the invasion they had referenced previously. I did, however, learn that Ardasira was a wealthy kingdom, ruled over by Sultan Kalmir. I gathered we were heading for the city of Sirrala, which I took to be the capital, although occasional mentions of a place called Qalerim cast that into doubt.

I gradually created a picture of Sirrala as a city built around a giant oasis—a green jewel on the cusp of the desert. Further in, the kingdom became more temperate—or at least I assumed so from the occasional mention of crops and all four seasons.

The intriguing question of the men's connection to the desert traders who plied the western portion of the desert, moving north-south along the length of Lanover, remained. Perhaps goaded on by my earlier question, Samar made frequent disparaging references to the traders, which Aron never disputed. But I had done some reading about them during my preparation for Celine's delegation, and much of the daily reality of our trip across the desert brought back memories of their practices. I wished I had met some traders in order to make a more direct comparison.

If the traders had some connection to Ardasira—perhaps had even broken away from them generations ago and found their way to the Four Kingdoms—did they still remember the existence of the distant kingdom? Were they clinging to an enormous secret, or did any direct contact lie so far in the past that they no longer remembered or believed their true origins?

One night, Aron and Samar discussed a neighboring kingdom —Kuralan. But any momentary hope they might exercise a restraining influence over Ardasiran dreams of conquest quickly died. A strong kingdom, Kuralan apparently didn't have the wealth or luxury goods of Ardasira, but they made up for it with the size of their army. Samar spoke of them admiringly, as if they were allies in whatever venture Malik was considering.

Malik himself remained shadowy, however. Although his name cropped up more frequently than most other topics, they never mentioned his role in Ardasira. I could only guess at his importance based on the idea he had an army at his disposal.

I walked my memory palace often in my mind, examining each clue stored away in it, desperate to keep my mind active despite the monotony of the journey. Even my fear had long since faded. As long as I drew no attention to myself, both men largely ignored me, providing me necessary food and water but otherwise avoiding all interaction.

Eventually they relaxed their vigilance enough to let me fetch my own food and water from the camels. Surrounded by desolate sand, with no immediate threat, it was impossible for anyone to remain in a state of alert indefinitely.

I encouraged the relaxed attitude between us by speaking rarely and showing no hint of defiance. Despite the change in our situation, I still hoped to lull them into a sense of complacency toward me.

I did conduct the occasional, subtle examination of the luggage attached to the two pack camels, however. And when I discovered the leather cases that had once been stored in the wooden crate, I hesitated for only a moment before pocketing the one that held only a single vial—its partner having already gotten me into this mess. With so many unknowns in front of me, I needed every advantage I could get.

The stolen treasure seemed unnaturally heavy in my pocket, and briefly the old tension returned. But neither man ever opened any bags except the ones holding the necessities for our journey, and my small theft wasn't discovered. Soon I ceased to even think of it.

My favorite days were when we camped at an oasis, the lush patches of green providing welcome relief and shade from the unrelenting sun and sand. I eagerly followed the example of the men, submerging myself in the water fully clothed and drinking to gorging throughout the time we camped there.

The oasis stops were few and far between, although by far the longest gap had been between the edge of the desert and the first one. I could see how impossible exploration of the desert would be. Finding an oasis by chance would be like finding a particular grain of sand in a dune—and at such distances, any mistake could be deadly.

Aron and Samar seemed to enjoy the occasional stops as much as I did, and I learned to anticipate them by a certain change in the air of the two men on days that ended at an oasis. So when I noticed the suppressed energy around both of them only a day after leaving the last oasis, I came to full alert myself. No oases had been so close together before. Were we reaching our destination at last?

All the fear and energy that had been missing for so long came flooding back, as if it had been breeding unseen for all those days. I did my best to hide my awareness, pretending to be oblivious to the change in the others. I suspected my best chance of escape would be if I acted quickly, disappearing in the initial distraction of reaching the city—which meant I needed to be ready.

When we stopped for a short break, I made sure to wrap my robe securely around me, arranging it so my legs would be as unhampered as possible. If everyone in the city wore such robes all the time, it would make it a lot easier to disappear into a crowd, but I didn't want to count on that being the case. Aron had made several mentions of the beautiful gardens of Sirrala, so there must be shade enough not to require such garments.

My body thrummed with energy as we topped yet another dune, my eyes straining against the glare, trying to make out something ahead of us other than endless sand. For a moment I thought I was imagining the distant shapes blocking the horizon, but they solidified as we started down the other side. After so many days of nothing but sand, we were finally approaching a distant spur of rocky mountains. I couldn't make out any green, but it must surely lie somewhere along the base of the cliffs that faced toward us.

We had reached the other side of the desert at last.

The camels continued on, uninterested in anything but the next step, and I had to suppress my rising impatience. We had crossed an entire desert, but now that the end was in sight, this last stretch dragged almost beyond endurance. My gaze swept back and forth, looking for something that resembled the Sirrala of my imagination. But all I could see was dusty cliffs, their yellow-brown almost indistinguishable from the sand they rose from.

As we approached closer, I caught sight of the occasional hardy scrub, clinging to the stark rock. But none of it resembled a lush oasis city. I cast surreptitious glances at Aron and Samar, but neither of them gave anything away. Perhaps I had been wrong about our destination? Or maybe I had been mistaken about the city's proximity to the desert.

Just as disappointment swirled in my belly, we reached the closest spur of rock. The sand still stretched everywhere, but it now blew loosely over a firmer surface beneath as we rounded the closest tall outcropping, entering a protected stretch of ground with mountains on three sides.

I gasped as a new angle of the sheer cliff face came into view. Set into it, carved directly from the mountain itself, was an enormous building with columns and windows and elaborate decorative embellishments. Behind the impressive facade, it promised multiple levels and a vast number of rooms. And yet, if they existed, they must be inside the mountain itself.

I shook my head. I had completely mistaken the nature of the city. Aron and Samar's talk of gardens had given me an entirely different picture, but a deep desire to see the beautiful gardens that grew inside a mountain now seized me. Pushing away the thought, I readied myself.

The camel, which was a much gentler creature than I had pictured from the little I had read about them, must have picked up on my tense state. His even pace faltered, and he lifted his head, tossing it to and fro.

Aron responded with a calm murmur that would likely have soothed our mount if not for the timing of a loud bleat that sounded from the mountainside ahead of us. Our camel balked, spitting in the direction of the hardy mountain goat that stood on the trunk of a small tree that grew almost horizontally from the steep layers of rock. The wild creature turned tail and fled up the mountain, although we were still some distance away, its bleat ringing out in the semi-circle of mountains that now enclosed us.

My eyes, trained from a lifetime of seeking out hidden passages and secret openings in my home, caught on a shadow where the goat had previously been standing. If I hadn't been looking closely, I wouldn't have seen it, but now that I had, certainty swept through me. The magnificent carved facade wasn't the only opening into the tunnels that must riddle the mountain.

Murmuring a quiet apology to the poor camel, I let out a wild shout and kicked both of my heels against his side with as much force as I could muster. The unexpected sound ricocheted around us, echoing off the stone surfaces and growing far more fearsome than I could have hoped. The camel, already on edge, took off at a run.

Clutching at the saddle in front of me, I gave a real scream at our bumpy pace. I had read camels could run fast, but it hadn't prepared me for the reality of swaying wildly so far above the ground. Aron, caught by surprise in a twisted position as he turned to look back at me, took several moments to steady himself.

He kept his voice and hands calm, however, steering us slowly left, away from the cliff face that held the city. I couldn't have that.

I kicked as hard as I could with my left heel. The camel gave a loud bellow and turned its head right. Aron didn't try to fight him, instead changing his own momentum to guide the animal right instead. Apparently he didn't mind which direction we circled in.

I needed to seize what might be my only chance of escape, but the camel's flashing legs discouraged any attempt to slide down from his back. I couldn't afford to lose the opportunity, however. While Aron was calm with the animal, he would be furious with me once he had the situation back under control.

I pulled up my legs, bracing my feet against the camel's hump in an awkward crouching position that made keeping my seat at speed difficult. We had already raced past the carved entrance to the city, but since we had curved back toward the right, we would soon pass it again, much closer this time. I fixed my eyes on the opening I had seen in the rock face just this side of the building, preparing to leap.

As soon as I was into the tunnel, I would have to run faster than I'd ever run before. Without my unsettling influence, Aron would soon have the camel calmed and be after me.

Already the animal had slowed considerably, making my difficult task a fraction easier. I hoisted up my robes, hooking the folds over my shoulders so there was no chance they would catch in my legs. As we passed beside the opening, I pushed off with my feet, propelling myself into the air and away from the camel.

I ignored its bellow and the shout of Aron behind me, my leap already carrying me clear. My reaching hands found the gnarled tree trunk that had held the goat and clamped around the wood. My momentum continued to carry my legs forward, and my feet hit the side of the cliff. I scrabbled for purchase but could find none.

I squeezed tighter with my hands as my feet fell, leaving me dangling in the air, part way up the cliff. Shouts and the clomp of feet sounded behind me, distracting me from my task. Samar was attempting to goad his string of camels to a faster pace, his angry gaze fixed on me, but Aron was closer. Already he had our camel under control and was turning it back in my direction. His intense, furious gaze promised retribution, and my hands began to move while my mind was still fixed on the approaching threat.

Slowly—too slowly—I inched along the trunk, one hand after another. The cliff face grew closer. Finally I could reach out with one hanging boot and touch rock. My toes found a small lip. It cost precious seconds for my other foot to find purchase, and I still didn't dare let go with both hands.

Reaching with one arm, I gripped the base of a small bush growing on the edge of the small, cave-like hole I had spotted from afar. But as soon as I pulled, it came loose, its shallow roots giving up without a fight. I dropped it, my racing heart increasing its pace.

A sound from behind made me flinch and glance backward. Aron was maneuvering his camel up as close beside the cliff as it would go, and he would soon have me in reach. With renewed desperation, my fingers ran along the ground just inside the hole, grasping on to a small overhang of rock.

Letting go of the tree completely, I gripped the rock with the tips of my fingers. Using every ounce of my strength, I strained, my boots slipping and sliding against the side of the mountain as I hauled myself up toward the shadowy entrance.

I got one knee over the lip, trembling and gasping now with the effort. But just as I tried to pull the other foot up, fingers grasped my ankle.

I flew backward out of the hole, yanked by my loose foot. I screamed, my hands grasping at everything flashing past them, finally wrapping around the base of the tree trunk.

My sudden resistance pulled back against his momentum, jarring my shoulders but also upsetting the camel. It stirred, pulling away and nearly unseating Aron. His grip on my ankle loosened as he seized back control of his mount. As the animal responded to his direction, stepping back toward the edge of the cliff, the tension on my leg eased.

I tightened my grip, putting everything I had into a single, desperate movement. As my free leg swung upward, I lashed out, driving my boot toward Aron's head.

I missed, hitting his shoulder instead. But he let out a shout of surprise at the blow, making the camel jerk into motion once more. My other foot slipped from his hold completely as he slid down the far side of the camel.

A crunch sounded as he hit the ground, and despite everything, I winced. That had sounded like breaking bone. His strangled yell certainly sounded pained, and the camel took off, running back toward its brethren. I didn't stop to see how the swearing Samar intended to handle the situation. Neither did I have time for self-pity that I once again had to pull myself up.

Reaching upward with determination, I found the same overhang of rock and pulled. Grunting and groaning, the sweat running down my face now, I scrambled my way completely over the edge. As I had expected, a dark opening stretched ahead of me, nearly black to my sun-bright eyes.

I hesitated only a moment, glancing back over my shoulder. Aron still lay on the ground, clutching at one leg. The small pang I felt at his injury disappeared when I remembered his cold unconcern over taking lives. He wouldn't be chasing me into the mountain, and I allowed myself satisfaction at that fact.

Samar had dismounted but was attempting to keep control of the agitated camels, calling something angrily toward Aron as he looked between his downed companion and me.

I didn't wait to see whom he would choose. Ducking slightly, I plunged into the mountain.

## CHAPTER 5

or some time, I was able to run in a straight line, unimpeded despite the dim light. And the further I got, the more my eyes adjusted. It wasn't as black as it had appeared from outside, small openings here and there letting in bursts of sunlight and fresh air. And occasionally a stream of light seemed to appear from nowhere, further illuminating my surroundings.

Whoever had created this place had been a genius—their placement of small shafts through the rock ensured no patch of tunnel was completely dark. For a moment I wondered if they utilized a system of mirrors to reach the more remote corners, but I didn't slow my forward progress to investigate.

The shouting of my captors soon faded, however, lost in the maze of stone. While I had appreciated the lack of turns while my eyes took time to adjust, I needed to move away from this straight tunnel. Once Samar made it up here, it would be too easy for him to pursue me.

I watched carefully for side openings, my ears straining for some hint of the bustling sounds of a city. I heard only my own footfalls and echoes of my labored breathing.

When a branch appeared, I took it without hesitation, locking the right turn away in my memory as I had long ago trained myself to do. Out there in the shifting sands of the desert, I was lost, but in this twisting maze of tunnels and hidden openings, I was at home.

I turned and turned again, bearing back toward the main, carved entrance whenever I had the chance to do so. Surely the heart of the city lay behind that incredible facade.

It was easy to hold my direction in my mind, a mental map unfolding behind my eyes. I was good at this.

I passed a number of openings which led not to more tunnels but to large, rough caves, but I kept moving. And the further I went, the more uneasy I became. The silence continued, stretching out unnaturally. Where were the people of the city?

I seemed to be moving in the right direction since the tunnels smoothed out, turning into something more like a normal passage or hallway, regular sconces appearing on the walls. I passed an opening that actually had a door, although it was ajar. I stopped to peer inside.

I had yet to hear any sound of pursuit, and a new fear was fast overtaking my previous anxiety about recapture. The room behind the door was as empty as the caves I had seen, although its walls were smoothed and several empty niches had been carved, as if to hold vases or other decorations.

I stepped back into the hallway, fear now clawing at my throat. Dust covered everything, and sand piled up in hidden corners, while the occasional bleat of a goat echoed back from the far distance. Every instinct screamed at me that these tunnels were deserted.

The front facade hadn't lied—a whole network of tunnels and chambers lay behind it. But it wasn't a thriving city. This place was long abandoned.

No wonder Aron and Samar hadn't been prepared for my escape attempt. This wasn't Sirrala. Nothing waited here but a lonely death.

I shivered, rejecting the dark thought. Just because this city-within-a-mountain had been abandoned didn't mean it was entirely devoid of those elements required for life. People had clearly lived here once. There must be water somewhere. And the goats suggested there was at least limited vegetation. Surely I would find something I could eat.

I didn't resume running. Deep in the mountain it was hard to remember the tension that had driven me earlier. The outside world felt a long way away.

I walked through the corridors, moving deeper into the more polished part of the city. Instinct told me any remaining resources would be in this section.

It was beautiful, in a sad, neglected sort of way. What had it looked like in its glory days when it bustled with life and echoed with the noises of untold people? The expansion into rough tunnels and natural caves suggested it must once have housed as many people as it could hold.

Elaborate carvings along the corridors attempted to make up for the absence of windows, and I stopped to admire several of the intricate designs. Twice I even came across small sections where the usual thin shaft had been widened, allowing not only an influx of extra light but a view of blue sky and bright sun far above. Both spots appeared to have once been used as gardens, although only a few hardy mountain shrubs remained.

In one, the goat whose bleats I had previously heard contentedly munched on his find. He immediately bounded away at my approach, and the rejection brought a fresh surge of hope. Did he know that humans were a source of danger? If so, then perhaps this place wasn't completely abandoned after all.

I continued on with renewed purpose, searching for any sign of habitation. As I walked, I thought ruefully of the fantastic gardens I had imagined might grow here. Whatever had once existed, I would find no such living wonders here now.

The mental map I was building grew as I walked deeper into

the city. I locked each twist and turn into my mind, seeing it unfold behind my eyes. After the thousands of hours I had spent building the memory palace of my home, it was surprisingly easy to construct a new map.

I had taken enough turns now to feel confident Samar would have little hope of finding me. And Aron wouldn't be climbing into the city at all—not with a broken leg. My two ex-captors were no longer my primary concern.

Some of the rooms I discovered led to other rooms, whole apartments big enough to house a large family. I even began to find instances of stone furniture left behind—tables or chairs or even beds, their mattresses long gone. But despite the beauty of their design, none of the furniture excited my interest like the discovery of a fireplace that still held ashes.

Dipping in a finger, I gave a small whoop at the feeling of residual warmth. Someone had been here. Hours had passed, certainly, but not days or weeks or years or centuries. Someone could still be found here among these empty rooms.

My speed increased again, new hope lending me fresh energy. Before long, my straining ears picked up a new sound, although it wasn't one made by any human. If anything, it was even more welcome. Water.

I wanted to run after the alluring rush of moving water, but I forced myself to be cautious. Sound moved strangely in this stone maze, and I couldn't afford to lose my way.

After two false turns, I finally came out into a cavern—the largest I had yet seen. Cutting through the middle of the space, a fast river flowed, gushing and tumbling and full of beautiful, wondrous, life-giving water. Although the size of the cavern suggested the space had occurred naturally—exposing this stretch of the subterranean river by happy chance—the previous inhabitants of the mountain had clearly made use of it. An elegant bridge had once arched across it, giving access to the other side of the chamber, but it had lost the middle section at some point.

I knelt beside the river, carefully filling my water skin before drinking deeply and refilling it. I was just wedging in the stopper when the sound of a clearing throat startled me so badly, I nearly toppled into the fast-moving water.

A steadying hand gripped my arm, holding firm until I had regained my balance and then immediately letting go. I spun around, leaping up to a standing position, and stared in shock at the young man in front of me.

Any fear that Samar had found me disappeared instantly at my first sight of my rescuer. Despite his height, I estimated he had only a couple of years on my own seventeen. His skin was several shades darker than mine, but his hair was a similar deep brown. However, unlike the hint of green in my brown eyes, his were enlivened by flecks of gold.

Awareness of my dusty, tangled robe and my many sweat streaks swept over me. And I didn't even want to think about the state of my hair. I flushed.

When I had imagined someone lingering in this desolate city, I had been picturing an old and grizzled shepherd, left behind while the rest of life moved on. But no one could accuse the man in front of me of such a thing. I had never met someone so vital and alive in my life. Purpose and certainty radiated from him, and he took in my appearance without comment or hint of surprise.

"Who is it?" a female voice asked from behind him, startling us both and breaking the unexpected intensity of the moment.

A girl appeared—my age, or perhaps a little younger—her features regular except for enormous dark eyes which lifted her pretty face into true beauty. They widened at the sight of me, her mouth dropping open.

"A newcomer? But we never get newcomers—unless we bring them here ourselves."

"And yet, here she is."

"But how?" the girl demanded, still staring at me.

"How would I know, Kayla? Perhaps you should ask her." The boy turned to me, his manner courteous. "What is your name?"

"I'm Cassie," I said, almost as astonished by the girl's arrival as I had been by the presence of the boy.

I could only imagine that my confused expression at the simple question must have marked me as a complete fool, as if I didn't look bad enough already. But the man responded as if it had been the most ordinary of introductions, giving a shallow bow even while his laughing eyes made a mockery of such formality in the circumstances.

"I'm...Zaid." I couldn't interpret the swift sideways glance he gave Kayla as he hesitated.

Determined not to be outdone, I dropped into the deep curtsy I had learned in preparation for our tour of the Four Kingdoms. "Pleased to meet you, Zaid and Kayla."

Kayla shook her head. "I'm delighted to meet you, of course. But how did you get here? And *why*?"

"I..." I hesitated, unsure how much to say. "It was an accident. I'm not from around here, and I thought this was Sirrala."

"Sirrala?" Kayla went off into gales of laughter. "You thought this was Sirrala?"

"Kayla." Zaid sounded disapproving.

"Sorry." She mopped at her eyes with her sleeve. "But can you imagine? I suppose that would make me sultana—ruler of all I survey." She gestured around the vast empty chamber.

I grinned back, sensing no malice in her amusement. "It seems like great riches to me. I don't think I've ever been so glad to see anything as I was this river. And I'm almost as pleased to see the two of you. I was starting to fear this place was entirely deserted, and I was going to starve or die of dehydration before I found a way out."

"Qalerim isn't a place you want to find yourself lost and

alone." Zaid's eyes conveyed a sympathy that went beyond his words. As if he sensed there was more to my story.

"Qalerim?" I repeated, remembering hearing Aron and Samar use the name. "This is Qalerim?"

"It is indeed." Zaid swept his arm out with a dramatic flourish. "Welcome to the ancient city of Qalerim, once the pride of the desert."

"And now abandoned to the goats," Kayla added.

"And you," I said. "For which I'm extremely grateful."

"But where are you from?" Kayla asked, "to not know of Qalerim?"

"I'm not from Ardasira," I said, thinking fast as I decided how much to say. I had no idea what these people thought of the Four Kingdoms, but if war between our peoples was coming, it might not be a good idea to announce my origins. "I came here with a camel train but became separated from the group."

"Oh, I'm sorry." Her ready compassion endeared her to me after so many days with only Aron and Samar for company. It was hard to believe she could be complicit in an invasion. "Where were they going? We can help you find them again."

I shook my head. "No, there's no need. We were traveling companions, that's all. They will have continued on to Sirrala without me, and I will need to make my own way from here." I bit my lip. "While your assistance to find Sirrala would be welcome, I must admit I have no coin to offer you in exchange. I was hoping to find work in the city."

Kayla shrugged. "Do you think any of us would live in Qalerim if we had any coin? Qalerim is a refuge for those of us who have no other home." She grinned at Zaid. "And for Zaid, who takes pity on us sometimes and graces us with his sunny disposition."

Zaid grinned for the first time, the expression transforming his face. I could feel the warmth creeping back up my cheeks and ruthlessly suppressed it.

"Who can be depressed by life with you around, Kayla?"

She flipped her long, dark braid over her shoulder. "No one, of course." She pushed past him and linked her arm in mine. "Which is why you should stick close to me, Cassie. Never mind Sirrala, you can stay here."

"Here?" Despite my surprise at the suggestion, I had to admit Qalerim seemed an excellent place to stay if you wanted to keep hidden and out of sight.

"Of course! Come on, I'll show you where we live. There's plenty of room. In fact, you can have your own room. Or ten." She chuckled at her own joke.

I followed along, feeling as if I had been swept into a dream. In some ways Kayla reminded me of a child, but I caught the occasional flash in her eyes that belied such youth. Something had driven her out here to this refuge, and the awareness of it lurked out of sight.

As for Zaid, he seemed utterly out of place in this dusty, forgotten city—and yet as comfortable as anyone could be. I couldn't make sense of him at all.

Kayla led us both out of the river cavern and back into the corridors, making several turns that seemed to lead us closer to the impressive front facade. Eventually we emerged into a corridor wider than any of the others, illuminated by bright sunlight at the far end, beyond which I could see the bright gold of sand. But instead of turning toward the exit, she led me in the other direction, stopping at the first door we encountered and ushering me into a large apartment.

One glance was enough to determine this had once been the elegant home of someone rich and important. Intricate carvings decorated the doors and walls, and a profusion of niches waited to house beautiful items.

One such alcove held a slingshot and a small pyramid of dirty stones. Another displayed a single shoe with a worn-through sole alongside half a coconut husk. Most of the remaining stone furniture had been covered haphazardly with drapes made of ripped blankets or desert robes, as if the occupants had entered the room and thrown them on the first available surface.

"Let me fetch the others," Kayla said brightly, dropping my arm and disappearing through a door on the far side of the room.

I remained still, taking in the extraordinary scene.

"They did leave for Sirrala," Zaid's soft voice said from just behind me. "In case you were wondering."

I stiffened. "Who?"

"Your traveling companions."

I spun around to face him, a question in my eyes.

He met my gaze, his own expression inscrutable. "After a short and heated debate, they left in search of medical aid for the injured man."

"Oh. I see." I examined his face, waiting for some kind of accusation. None came.

"I just thought you'd like to know," he added.

"Did they..." I trailed off, not sure how I wanted to word my question.

"They didn't see me," he said. "Most people don't know anyone still lives here. From their conversation, I believe they expect you to perish, wandering lost among the maze of tunnels."

I let out a deep breath, a weight falling off my shoulders. While I still had a myriad of problems before me, one at least had been lifted.

"Thank you," I said.

He shrugged before smiling, the expression once again robbing me of breath.

"If you stick with us, Kayla won't let you end up lost, Cassie of foreign lands. It's an odd life here, but there are worse ones."

I sucked in a slight breath at his reference to my origins, again waiting for an accusation. But again none came. And whatever lurked behind his words, I couldn't read it in his face.

I stood up straighter. "Actually, I'm not prone to getting lost. And I don't mind tunnels."

A new warmth lit his eyes. "All the better. Maybe you'll even like it here, then."

I glanced around the odd room. "I think I might."

The answer slipped out, surprising even me. I still had much I needed to accomplish, but I could have started my time in Ardasira in a far worse situation than this. And when I pictured leaving, something in me rebelled. There were secrets here, I could sense them. I couldn't leave without making the smallest attempt to uncover them.

Kayla bounced back into the room, a lanky youth slouching behind her. "They've all gone off searching." She shot a look at Zaid that I couldn't interpret. "There's only Elias still here. Cassie, this is Elias. Elias, Cassie."

Elias gave me a startled look as if he hadn't believed Kayla's claims of a newcomer.

"We have a new recruit," Zaid said, increasing the astonishment on Elias's face. "Sort of."

Kayla, however, bounced up and down. "You mean she's going to stay?" She ran up to me. "You won't regret this, Cassie. We're going to be best friends. I can sense it."

Despite myself, I grinned back. There might be secrets between us—on both sides—but I couldn't help responding to her warmth. I had arrived here alone and afraid, but already I didn't feel alone anymore.

# CHAPTER 6

"*W*hat's this about a new qaleri?" A tall, pale youth burst into the apartment, his eyes raking over the ten or so young people in the room before resting on me.

I met his gaze steadily. "Qaleri?"

Kayla, who had been busy in the kitchen creating something that smelled incredible, rushed back into the central living area. Zaid had long gone—apparently he didn't live in the abandoned city, although he had offered no information about his home—so only she remained to champion my presence.

"That's what we call ourselves," Kayla explained. Her bearing seemed tense, but she still threw me a grin. "That's the name used by the people who once lived in Qalerim, so why are we any different? Sultana of all I survey, remember?"

The new boy snorted. "Does that make me sultan, then? I like the sound of that."

Kayla rolled her eyes before fastening them on the boy. "Josef, this is Cassie. She doesn't have anywhere to go, so I told her she could stay with us. Qalerim always has room for outcasts."

I looked back and forth between the two, unable to miss the warning in Kayla's tone. What was she concerned about? The new arrival clearly considered himself to have some sort of authority among the self-styled qaleri—a ragtag group of youth from what I had seen so far. Was she afraid he would refuse to let me stay? I didn't want to cause trouble for my new friend.

"She came on her own?" Josef asked slowly, and Kayla nodded.

My eyebrows creased at the relief evident in the lines of her body. If she could detect a change in the boy's antagonism, then she was more discerning than me.

But apparently Kayla's reading was accurate because a moment later he shrugged.

"Very well, then. I don't care who chooses to spend their days in this drafty mausoleum." He let the bag he was carrying drop to the ground before casting a rough spun robe over the closest chair and sprawling himself across several cushions on the far side of the room.

I tried to refrain from wrinkling my nose, although I knew I shouldn't be surprised. I guessed Josef's age at fifteen, and he was hardly the first of his age to possess a loose relationship with tidiness.

"Zaid found her at the river and brought her here." Elias deposited a large, newly filled water jug in the kitchen and crossed toward Josef.

The rest of the youths in the room brightened at this news, as if my standing had just increased significantly in their eyes. Only Josef gave no such reaction. Instead, he leaped to his feet and slung an arm around Elias's shoulders.

"Zaid, hey, Cousin?"

"Yes." Kayla stuck her head back out of the kitchen, giving Josef another intense look. "Zaid was the one who found her, and he suggested she stay. So she's staying. And that's all there is to the story."

Josef ruffled Elias's hair as if he were a small child, although the lanky boy had already told me he was fourteen. Elias looked pained, shrugging away from his cousin.

A small smile crossed Josef's face, as if his intention had been to ruffle his young relative in more ways than one.

"Very well, then," he said. "I've no desire to interfere with anyone's fun. Anybody who's willing to help with the chores can live here with my goodwill."

"I'm ready to do my part," I said quickly, hoping to restore things to their previous amicable status.

As the apartment had slowly filled over the course of the late afternoon, I had been introduced to a group of nearly ten youths whose young ages made the sixteen-year-old Kayla into a mother hen. All had greeted me with some degree of curiosity, but no one had challenged my arrival until Josef.

"Food's served," Kayla announced, bringing out a large pot and plonking it in the middle of the table.

Glad shouts greeted this news, and flying arms and legs filled the room as everyone except me scrambled to retrieve a bowl and utensil and serve themselves some of the stew.

My eyes widened at the unexpected melee, and Kayla collapsed down beside me, a bowl in each hand. She cast me a sidelong glance, a tinge of shame coloring her face before she straightened her spine.

"There's no need for civilization out here in the ruins." Her mouth twisted in a wry smile.

"No, indeed," I said quickly, mortified she had thought I was judging her.

Her grin reappeared as she handed me one of the bowls. "You'll learn fast, I'm sure—for instance, never announce the meal until you've served yourself."

"And always make friends with the cook," I quipped back, accepting the food.

She chuckled. "Words to live by."

For a moment there was silence as we each scooped up spoonfuls of the delicious spiced dish. I could pick out familiar individual flavors, but the combination was new, and I could tell it would have been tasty even if I hadn't been starving.

The front door of the apartment banged open, and another boy rushed in. He dropped everything he held on the floor, as Josef had done, and dove straight for a bowl.

No one took any particular note of his arrival, the others having settled into various positions around the room. Conversation was sporadic as everyone focused on the important business of eating. I was similarly occupied, but I watched them all from the corner of my eyes while I scraped my bowl clean.

They lived together in one large apartment, but they didn't act like a family. I revised my mother hen analogy. Kayla and Josef might be the oldest of the group—viewing themselves in some sort of leadership role—but I could see no sign of a parental interest in the others. No one had even asked about the missing boy when the food was served, let alone considered delaying the meal. And his late return had evoked no especial reaction from anyone.

Elias and Josef were cousins, but none of the others had claimed kinship or connection beyond their shared housing. So if it wasn't bonds of friendship or family that held them together, what was it?

Selina, a tall girl with warm brown skin who was the youngest of the group at barely thirteen, stopped on her way to refill her bowl. "Kayla said you're going to share our room."

I nodded. "But only for now. She's going to help me make up my own bed pallet tomorrow, and then I'll find a spot of my own."

"That's a good idea. I can help, too." Selina's myriad of tight black braids bounced as she gave an enthusiastic head nod before shooting me a look. "Not that I mind you joining the qaleri, of course. It's just the room is a little small for three."

"I can find somewhere else to stay for tonight," I suggested. "I don't want to impose on anyone—"

She shook her head emphatically. "No, of course not. I don't mind for a night or two." She smiled. "It's actually nice to have something new and unexpected happen. It gets monotonous around here."

"There are worse things than monotony," Kayla said in an under voice, and the warmth disappeared from Selina's eyes.

I glanced between them, but neither said anything more, the younger girl hurrying away toward the pot of stew. I watched her go with interest. She hadn't sounded as if she liked her life out here in Qalerim. So what kept her here? Was she like me with nowhere else to go?

"Don't mind her," Kayla said with bright cheer, as if trying to cover the awkward moment. "You'll be at home here soon enough."

"So you all live in this one apartment except Zaid?" I asked.

Kayla tensed slightly at his name before relaxing. "Yes, that's right. It's simpler since we share cooking duties and supplies."

She suddenly bounced upright, her whole face lighting up. "Unless you want to move next door with me?"

"Next door?" I tried not to sound as confused as I felt.

She nodded vigorously. "Josef and I were the first to come here, so of course we wanted to stay together." She grimaced. "You may have noticed he has something of an abrasive personality, but I figured he was better than no one. At least he would stop me being nibbled to death by goats in my sleep." She shuddered dramatically.

"Nibbled to death by goats?" I couldn't keep the laugh out of my voice.

"Don't laugh, goats will eat anything!"

This time I gave a full chuckle, unable to help myself. Underneath, however, I sympathized. For a short time I had thought myself alone in this vast place, so I knew exactly how unnerving it could be. I would have wanted to stick close to my one companion as well.

"Every time someone new came, they just moved in." She shrugged. "It was easy, I suppose. But now it's starting to smell." She wrinkled her nose, and I grimaced.

"That might be me. Sorry. It's been a long day, and I started it on a camel."

She laughed. "Believe me, I've been living with Josef in the next room for years—you couldn't smell that bad if you tried."

I bit my lip, trying not to laugh aloud as I watched the tall youth attempt to impress several of the younger qaleri with some tale of his day's adventures that was almost certainly exaggerated. A couple of them were listening with attention, but several others had already disappeared—presumably retreating to their rooms.

Kayla watched one of the only other girls, a fifteen-year-old named Sari, slip out of the room. "None of the newcomers wanted to share a room until Selina arrived. She's a good room-mate, but she's been reluctant to make a full break from the group with just the two of us. But maybe three will be enough to convince her. It's not like I want to go to the other side of the city. And we'd still share supplies with the group, obviously, since—"

She cut herself off and then tried to cover the lapse with a cough. Before I could think of a subtle enough question to get her talking again, Elias joined us. From the resentful look he cast over his shoulder and the way those around Josef were chuckling, I suspected he was fleeing his cousin more than seeking us out.

"What's on the other side of the city?" he asked.

"Nothing, that's the point," Kayla said. "Selina, Cassie, and I are planning to move to the next apartment along."

I smiled, appreciating her confident way of approaching the undecided issue.

"Moving?" Elias straightened, once again casting a look back at his cousin. "Can I come with you?"

"Of course! That's perfect." Kayla grinned. "Selina can't

possibly say no if there are four of us. And you two are the only ones here who don't leave trip hazards everywhere you go." She frowned at the various items littering the floor.

"I'll be able to have my own room instead of having to share with Patrin. He snores." Elias seemed increasingly pleased at the idea. "I don't know why you didn't think of this earlier, Kayla."

"Think of it earlier..." Kayla spluttered, but Elias had already stridden away, presumably to start packing from the sound of his mutters.

"Yeah, Kayla, why didn't you think of it earlier?" I said with a straight face.

"Oof!" She pulled the threadbare cushion from behind her and threw it at my head. I dodged and grinned at her, relieved at the way the situation had worked out.

I didn't want Selina to agree to move just because of my presence when I didn't know how long I'd be able to stay around. Despite my initial relief at keeping well out of the way of Aron and Samar, I would eventually have to track them and their mysterious superior, Malik, down. I hadn't forgotten the threat that hung over the Four Kingdoms, and even possibly my own lands. I was just grateful I would be able to get a good sleep before I had to tackle it.

# CHAPTER 7

"**K**icked out already? Who did you offend?" an amused voice asked from behind me, startling me into dropping the sleeping pallet I was attempting to haul out the door single handed.

I spun around, clutching my chest as my heart rate soared, only steadying when I saw who stood there.

Zaid raised an eyebrow. "You're twitchy, Cassie."

I shrugged. If he had seen my escape, he knew I had a reason to be jumpy, but I didn't intend to be drawn into a conversation about it. Pushing down the feeling of relief that I had managed to wash and find fresh clothes since our last encounter, I eyed him suspiciously.

"Are you here to search for treasure?"

"I make a hard rule never to search for treasure," he said with a straight face. "So you can rest easy."

I rolled my eyes. "Resting is precisely what I can't do. Kayla was very insistent we move apartment today—and yet no sooner had the day started, than they all disappeared one by one. Apparently they've gone off searching for some sort of riches they're convinced are hiding somewhere in the mountain. Selina informs me that's what they do every day." I shook my head in disbelief before gesturing at the now abandoned pallet. "And so you see me trying to move on my own."

"That's industrious of you," Zaid said, as if surprised I would do anything so helpful.

"Well I can't just sit around all day." I gave him a pointed look. "Are you going to help me?"

"Certainly," he said promptly, sliding through the door to pick up the other end. "Direct away."

I gave him a hard look, but he seemed perfectly serious, so I lifted my end and shuffled backward into the corridor. It took a little maneuvering, but we soon had the pallet inside one of the bedrooms of the new apartment.

"So is there really treasure hidden somewhere in Qalerim?" I asked skeptically as I led the way back to the main apartment.

Zaid sighed. "It seems highly unlikely. After all, an entire city of people used to live here. Surely they would have discovered it if so."

I stopped in the doorway to Kayla's room to frown back at him. "That's what I thought. But I can see from your expression it's not an argument that finds favor with the others."

Zaid hesitated. "The qaleri certainly seem...obstinate on the issue."

I snorted. "Hardly shocking given their age, I suppose."

Zaid raised an eyebrow. "You say with the benefit of your vastly superior years."

"I'm older than I look. I'll be eighteen in a couple of months."

He looked surprised at that news, like most people were when they first met me.

"Don't worry, you'll adjust to it soon enough," I said. "Everyone thinks I'm younger when they first meet me, but no one ever thinks it for long."

"That sounds ominous," Zaid said with a chuckle.

I grinned back. "My uncle has also been known to inform me that I was never a youth. While he seemed to view that as a negative, I feel it gives me full rein to comment on the obstinacy of youth."

"I may have only met you yesterday, but you're not going to convince me you know nothing about obstinacy," Zaid said, the smile still lingering around his mouth.

"Are you going to help me with this or not?" I asked, pointing at Selina's pallet. "If not, I'll just have to go back to *obstinately* dragging it on my own."

Zaid promptly picked up one end of the pallet. "What exactly are we doing?" he asked as we edged it out the door of the room.

"Kayla, Selina, Elias, and I are moving to the next apartment over," I said. "We've taken a solemn pact to keep our new home tidy and as sweet smelling as is possible with a boy of fourteen in residence."

"Goodness, you've been here one day, and already you're shaking things up."

"I can't take any credit. It was all Kayla's idea. I'm just being dragged along."

Zaid gave me a quizzical look that struck me as more serious than his earlier teasing. "Are you? You don't strike me as the sort of person to allow yourself to just be swept along by life."

I looked away, uncomfortable with his accurate analysis. I had spent my life influencing events from the shadows, wishing to be taken seriously by my uncle and the adults around him. But now there were no shadows—just golden-brown eyes that looked straight at me—and I found myself longing for anonymity again. Could Zaid see how shaken my confidence was? How conscious I was of the many mistakes that had led me here?

"What about you?" I asked, deflecting the question. "If you don't have a mania for treasure like all the others, what are you doing here?"

"I came to check up on the newest qaleri, of course," he said with an easy smile.

I sternly told my heart not to even consider speeding up its rhythm. I had an important job to do, and sighing over an attractive face wouldn't help me do it.

"You seem to be settling in excellently," he said. "I needn't have worried."

We exited the apartment, heading down the wide corridor to the next door along. I surreptitiously watched Zaid as we adjusted our angle to fit through the doorway. When he had left Qalerim the night before, I hadn't expected to see him again so soon.

"Do you prefer to camp in the open air?" I asked, keeping my voice light and my face open.

"Camp?" He gave me a strange look. "No, of course not."

I frowned. "Where do you live, then? Kayla said you don't stay here, in the city."

His expression lightened. "I keep forgetting you're not familiar with the area. I live in the capital, Sirrala."

"Sirrala?" I stopped my progress through the living area of my new apartment to stare at him. "But how are you back here already, then?"

"Sirrala isn't far away. This section of the mountains isn't very wide, and it's just on the other side."

I slowly resumed my progress as I digested this information. If the city was in such easy reach, maybe I could stay here longer than I had thought.

"I want to see it," I announced as we deposited the second pallet with the first one in the largest of the three bedrooms. "Will you take me there?"

"Take you to Sirrala?" Zaid seemed disproportionately thrown off by my request.

"You said you only came here to check on me, so I assume you'll be going back soon. Let me come with you. Selina said they'll all be out searching all day, so no one will miss me."

Still he hesitated.

"Please?" I gave him my most winsome look.

He sighed. "I can't take you into the city, but I can take you to a spot with a good view."

I grinned triumphantly, willing to take what I could get. I wasn't used to being so reliant on other people, and I wanted to get to know my new surroundings as quickly as possible. A small voice in the back of my head told me I was just focusing on what felt achievable in order to avoid thinking about the insurmountable challenges ahead of me, but I squashed it down.

It took us almost no time to get Elias's pallet into one of the other bedrooms, but I decided Kayla could tackle the job of deciding what else was transferring across. Whatever reluctance Zaid had felt seemed to have been cast aside, and he didn't hesitate to lead me out into the main corridor.

Rather than heading for the main exit, however, he ducked into a side tunnel that led to a steep set of stairs hewn from the rock.

"This isn't the way you went yesterday," I said suspiciously.

"There are lots of ways out of the city. I'm taking you to the one with the best view." He glanced over his shoulder at me. "I promise it will be worth it."

Intrigued, I picked up the pace. "What's it like?" I asked. "Sirrala?"

"It's the largest city, and the most prosperous," he said, pride in his voice. "And in my opinion, also the most beautiful. Travelers come from all over to see it."

"From all over?" I asked tentatively. I hadn't heard any mention of the Four Kingdoms since my arrival, but it was possible the topic just hadn't come up. None of the qaleri had so far asked me questions about my origins—possibly because they all seemed equally reticent to discuss their own histories.

"Oh yes," he said. "Even the Kuralanis acknowledge the wonders of Sirrala and come to admire it."

"But no one else?" I asked, still hesitant.

"What do you mean?" He shot me a surprised look. "The

desert nomad clans? There are precious few of those families left, and even those that did remain seem to have disappeared in the last decade or so. Have you met some of them? I'm sure the royal officials would be eager to hear of it if so."

"No." I shook my head. "I just wondered…"

"It would be nice to think they had found new places to visit and would soon return," Zaid said. "But unfortunately it seems more likely they met a darker fate out there in the desert." He glanced in the direction of the dunes, although the solid rock of the mountain blocked his view.

I silently considered his words as we continued along another tunnel, this one rising at a steady pace, the light growing constantly brighter. It almost sounded as if the locals were as unaware of the Four Kingdoms as the Four Kingdoms were of Ardasira and Kuralan. But if that was the case, how could Ardasira be planning an invasion?

"Through here." Zaid interrupted my thoughts to usher me ahead of him out of a rough tunnel entrance.

I stepped out onto the mountainside well above ground level, with a view in several directions. Behind me, rough mountains cut across the unbroken blue sky. Sand blew around their base, drifting from the desert at their feet.

But in front of me, a city sat, like a jewel in the midst of the yellow sand and dusty rock. Sirrala—just as I had imagined it on my journey across the desert. It stole my breath, and I had the feeling it always would, no matter how many times I came out through this tunnel.

High walls encircled the city, keeping out both raiders and the desert sands—although its location, tucked behind the mountains that housed Qalerim, protected it from the worst of the sand storms. Lush green softened the pale stone, gardens filling every inch of unoccupied city.

And rising from the center, atop a raised mound, stood the

palace of Sultan Kalmir. Its many towers drew the eye, surmounted as they were by domes of either gold or silver.

I could easily believe that people traveled from all over the kingdom and from neighboring Kuralan to view the oasis city of Sirrala and the wonder of the sultan's palace.

There could be no doubt Qalerim was a marvel of its own, and I was almost starting to grow fond of the ancient city. It was certainly a feat of construction to turn rough caves into a beautiful honeycomb big enough to house an entire people. But I couldn't blame the inhabitants of this region for abandoning it in favor of Sirrala.

"It's beautiful," I whispered, and Zaid made a satisfied noise of approval.

"Why did the people ever live in the mountain?" I asked. "For all its marvels, they must have longed to see the sky. Was it for protection?"

Zaid stepped up beside me, also gazing out at the view. From the corner of my eye, I saw him shrug.

"It happened long enough ago that it can be hard to distinguish true history from poetry and story. But apparently the people fled the destruction of their previous home to Qalerim. Eventually they grew too large for the mountain, but when they did, a new string of oases appeared where the city now stands. So they ventured forth and built themselves a new home."

"The High King provides," I said softly. It certainly sounded like the sort of thing a godmother would do.

I shook my head. "I can't believe it's so close!" It certainly made more sense now as to how the qaleri had ended up in their unusual home. I could see how it might seem an obvious solution to those with nowhere else to go.

"Where's the army?" I blurted out, unthinkingly, when I registered the peaceful feel of the scene.

Zaid gave me a concerned look. "Where they always are, of

course. The royal guards patrol the city and the palace, and the armed forces are spread out around the kingdom, ready to defend and assist as needed. I understand Kuralan employs a similar arrangement, even if they do have superior troop numbers to us."

"Oh. Yes, I'm sure…" I bit my tongue, annoyed with myself.

When would I start using my head? I couldn't just blurt such things out—not until I'd worked out who was involved in the plot and what their feelings might be toward someone like me. I had just been taken by surprise. When I pictured Sirrala, I had been imagining a tent city alongside it, housing the gathering troops preparing to march across the desert.

But Zaid wasn't a qaleri. He lived in the city and walked its streets every day. The people of Ardasira might not know of the Four Kingdoms, but they would surely know if a force of any significant size was gathering.

A tight band across my chest eased. The invasion Aron and Samar had referenced must not be an imminent occurrence. I had time to find out their plan and warn the people on the other side of the desert. Suddenly my overwhelming task felt a fraction more manageable.

I gazed out at the rooftops. Somewhere in there, Aron and Samar were lurking. I had memorized the route from the apartment to the exit, and I would need to make the full journey down into the city some day soon. But I was still hoping to gather more information so I knew where to start looking.

The persistent voice in my head scolded me for hesitating and delaying. I still didn't know how much time I actually had. But acting rashly was what had gotten me into this mess. I hesitated, glancing sideways at Zaid. He lived in Sirrala—maybe he could give me some information.

But his attention had been caught by something below us. I followed his gaze to where an undulating road ran along the base of the mountains, guiding travelers from what must be southern Ardasira to an enormous gate in the city's western wall.

I couldn't immediately see what had captured his gaze until a large man driving an overladen wagon lifted his whip to lash the exhausted looking donkey harnessed to it. I frowned. That cart was far too heavy for the size of the donkey. He lifted it again, and I flinched, despite the distance between us.

The blow didn't fall, however. A small lad sprang up from the back of the wagon, jabbering something to the man that we were too far away to hear. Whether the boy cared for the animal, or was merely concerned they were going to cripple their only means of transport, I didn't know. And the man apparently didn't care. Lifting his whip, he used the base of it to whack at the child, sending him sprawling back into the base of the wagon with a sharp cry we heard all the way on our high perch.

Beside me, Zaid growled. "We do not permit the abuse of either children or animals in Sirrala," he snapped. "I must go. Can you find your way back without me?" He stepped forward onto the rough trail that led down the mountainside, waiting for my answer but clearly anxious to be gone.

I gaped at him. "I can get back fine, but you'll never reach them before they disappear inside the city." Already the wagon was nearing the gate.

"Even if they're inside, I'll find them," he called back over his shoulder, already leaping down the slope with the surety of a mountain goat. "Royal guards patrol the city. I can enlist them to assist me."

I almost started down after him but hesitated. As much as the man's behavior made my blood boil, I had no experience on the track or in the city. I would be more hindrance than help. Instead, I held my position, watching Zaid's progress.

He reached flat ground faster than seemed possible, merging with the light traffic on the road. The wagon had now stopped at the gate, talking to the guards there. My eyes flashed back along the road, looking for Zaid's moving head, but I could no longer see him.

I frowned and leaned forward, scanning up and down the flow of people, horses, and carriages. When I looked back at the gate, the wagon had disappeared through. Zaid must have somehow moved with even more speed to catch up with them.

I bit my lip. The man had been large, and clearly prone to violence. I didn't like to just leave, not knowing how his altercation with Zaid would progress. But if they were already inside the city, standing here would do no good. With a last piercing look at the city gate, I stepped back into the mountain.

# CHAPTER 8

*W*hen Kayla returned that afternoon, she helped me collect sand to fill a basic mattress. I took the opportunity to relate the story to her, but she seemed to share none of my concerns.

"That's just like Zaid," she said. "And if you try to bring it up later, he'll just change the subject. He doesn't like you to point out his good deeds."

"That's a glowing testimony." I glanced at her sideways. "Is there something between the two of you?"

She put down her bucket of sand and stared at me. "Between me and Zaid?" Before I could confirm, she threw back her head and burst into a full-throated laugh. Her amusement lasted for a good minute, eventually subsiding into gurgles.

"Oh, that's too much. No, there's nothing between us." She mopped at her now streaming eyes.

I waited for her to go on and explain why it was so amusing to think of being interested in someone who was good-looking, kind, charming, and considerate, but she offered no explanation for her amusement. I almost asked the question but pulled myself up before I could start listing Zaid's virtues aloud. I didn't want Kayla getting the idea I was interested in him. For all the good qualities I had already witnessed in Zaid, there were far more mysteries. I had to keep my emotions firmly in hand and lead with my mind. Leaping without thinking had already cost me too much.

We resumed filling our containers, the occasional chuckle still burbling out of Kayla. Unable to entirely put the matter out of my mind, I asked a related question instead.

"Why does Zaid come here to Qalerim?"

I had a suspicion as to the answer, but I wanted to hear her response. And I couldn't dismiss the possibility he felt quite differently about a connection between them.

"He's a good person," Kayla said with conviction. "He wants to help us. We should probably tell him to leave us alone, but he's too easy to like. And Selina was right. It gets monotonous out here."

"Why don't you leave, then?" I purposely didn't look directly at her as I asked, trying to keep the question from sounding too confronting.

My strategy didn't work, however. She merely shrugged, bustling to her feet and starting back toward the entrance to Qalerim. I followed her more slowly, taking a moment to admire the incredible façade. It was still hard to believe this was my home, however temporary.

And it was a home full of mysteries. I watched Kayla's retreating back. It wasn't the first shrug I had received—from her or the other qaleri—in response to a direct question.

And the answers I did receive were often like her response about Zaid's visits—they told me almost nothing. From the protective instinct I had witnessed in him, I had already guessed he wanted to help the qaleri. But visiting them in their isolated home seemed a strange way to do it.

The desire to unravel their secrets itched at me, but there were no hidden nooks here or formal meetings to be observed. Once I would have thrilled at the challenge, but now uncertainty tugged at me. Maybe the limited world of my uncle's estate had given me an overblown sense of my own capability?

I stepped into the apartment behind Kayla to find Selina waiting for us. "Goodness, you look positively fierce," she said when she caught sight of me.

"Do I?" I shook my head, clearing my expression. "I didn't mean to."

I tried to push away the feelings of self-doubt and focus on what needed to be accomplished. I was separated from everyone I had ever known by an enormous desert, and I had a potential invasion to stop. I didn't have time to fall in a heap.

"I was actually wanting to ask you both something. Have either of you heard of someone by the name of Malik?"

"Malik?" Selina looked to Kayla instead of me, her face a question.

Kayla didn't respond, however. Nor did she look at me. Was her studied distraction out of embarrassment for me at my ignorance? Or was she suspicious?

I groaned silently. For all my resolutions to behave with more intelligence, I had clearly just misstepped. Was Malik someone everyone in these kingdoms knew? Would they guess I came from elsewhere? What would they do with that information if so?

"Why do you ask?" Kayla asked slowly, still not looking at me.

"Curiosity." I forced a grin. "It's a besetting sin, I'm afraid. I've heard his name mentioned."

"Here in Qalerim?" Selina sounded shocked, and my interest in his identity increased.

"No, before I arrived."

Kayla gave Selina an odd look. "Of course she didn't hear him talked of here. What use do we have sitting around chatting about the sultan's Grand Vizier? What would we have to do with the most highly ranked official in the kingdom?"

Selina flushed, but I was too busy being shocked at the revelation of Malik's position to give much attention to her unusual sternness toward the younger girl. My earlier relief at finding no signs of an imminent invasion weakened.

I tried to cover my confusion. "I was actually wondering where he lives, mostly," I said. "Could either of you show me his house sometime?" When both girls gave me equally blank looks, I hurried on. "I'm sure it must be a fine one—second only to the palace itself, surely."

Kayla shrugged. "Yes, I suppose you're right. But you don't need us to show you. Anyone you see in Sirrala could do that."

I filed that information away since clearly neither of my new housemates were eager to get too close to someone like the Grand Vizier. And since I had my doubts about the way they acquired their supplies, I couldn't exactly blame them.

I went through the rest of the process of making myself a bed in a distracted daze. So Malik was the Grand Vizier. Any hope that he was some small-time bandit with delusions beyond his means was gone now. If Malik was Ardasira's Grand Vizier—a position that sounded equivalent to the king's Chief Advisor back home—The Four Kingdoms were in trouble. And no one even knew it but me.

If I was going to avert war, I would have to be craftier, cleverer, and more observant than I had ever been before. Starting now.

## CHAPTER 9

"Cassie! Oh, thank goodness someone's here!" Selina slumped, panting, in the doorway of our apartment. "I already tried next door, but no one was there."

I leaped to my feet and hurried over. In the week I had been here, the qaleri had gone out treasure hunting every day, but none of them had ever returned like this.

"What's wrong?" I asked as she accepted my assistance into the closest chair, visibly limping as she did so.

"I twisted my ankle." She grimaced. "But never mind me. It's not a serious injury—it just meant it took me forever to get back here."

She let out the smallest whimper as I crouched down to examine the ankle in question.

I chewed on my lip. "I'm no doctor. I can't tell how bad it is. But it can't have helped to hobble all the way back here alone. Didn't you go out with Elias? Where is he?"

"That's just it!" she cried in despairing tones. "A section of the floor collapsed, and he fell. I was running back for help when I rolled my ankle."

I shot back to my feet. "He fell! He's not…"

She shook her head. "He was alive when I left. I could hear him shouting at me to hurry. But I don't know..."

I whirled around, my eyes flying over the neat piles of items Kayla stored in the various display niches of the room. Earlier I could have sworn I saw...

"There!" I pounced on the tight coil of rope in the furthest one.

Selina watched me with concern. "I was hoping some of the others would be here. How are you going to pull him out by yourself?"

I hoisted the rope over my shoulder. "I'll just have to find a way."

"A way to do what?" asked a new voice.

I spun, a smile of relief filling my face.

"Zaid! Excellent timing! I'm about to mount a rescue expedition."

His smile disappeared, replaced with a look of concern as he dumped the sack of flour he carried on the floor. "Rescue?" His eyes flashed around the empty room. "On your own? Who needs rescuing?"

"Elias fell through the floor," Selina said. "I told him the room didn't look safe, but..." Her eyes flashed first to Zaid and then to me as she fell silent.

"There's no time to lose," I said, ignoring whatever she was leaving unspoken. "We don't know how badly he's injured. Where did it happen, Selina?"

She frowned. "We went into the new section that Kayla found last week." The lines of her forehead deepened as she strained her memory. "I came back right, left, third fork, right. I think." She threw us an apologetic look. "It was next to a section where the hallway had collapsed—that's what made me wary about the room."

"Oh! I know that spot. Kayla showed it to me yesterday." I turned for the door. "Let's go. I can lead us there." I glanced over my shoulder. "We'll be back soon, Selina. Don't try to move while we're gone. You could make your ankle worse."

She murmured agreement, shooing us both out the door with her hands. As soon as we were on our way down the main corridor, I turned to Zaid.

"I don't know enough about ankles to know how badly she's injured—let alone whatever damage Elias has managed to do to himself. We don't have any doctors in Qalerim."

"Don't worry," he said, calm and assured as always as he strode quickly beside me, his long legs allowing him to easily keep up with my jog. "I can take them both into Sirrala and get them treatment if needed. You just get us to Elias. I don't know this place as well as everyone else. I didn't have any idea what Selina was talking about."

"No one could expect you to know the city as well as the others," I said, maintaining my hurried pace since we had a fair way to go. "I certainly don't. They seem to spend morning, noon, and night exploring it."

I watched Zaid out of the corner of my eye as I led us down a branching corridor, wondering again what he thought of the qaleri and their obsession with treasure. He certainly didn't seem to share it, although he showed no discomfort at spending time in the abandoned city. Had he been more successful than I had in getting answers from them? I certainly felt the pull to confide in him, despite how little I still knew of his own story.

I stopped abruptly, so distracted by Zaid's presence I had nearly missed the door we needed. I shook myself. Here was yet more evidence of the danger of getting swept up in my emotions.

"In here." I led the way through the door—a plain wooden one, otherwise identical to all the others in the long corridor.

Zaid followed with a confused look. "Selina mentioned a number of turns..." His voice dropped away as he stepped through and saw we had entered a large room with a number of corridors exiting from it in multiple directions.

"This is what Kayla discovered last week," I explained, making for the hall on the left. "She was excited enough to even drag me out to see it. We have no idea why they made it look like a regular apartment door from the outside. Josef is convinced it must have been because there was something back here they wanted to hide."

I shrugged as I led us into another turning. "But given the number of corridors and apartments back here, a lot of people must have known about it back when a whole city lived here. Maybe it started as an apartment and then they found further caves behind it when they needed to expand and used the original apartment as the beginning of the tunnels?"

"That makes sense." Zaid sighed. "But the others wouldn't have been able to resist."

I nodded. "They certainly seem focused on finding this treasure they're all convinced is hidden here somewhere."

Zaid grimaced. "The Treasure of Qalerim. Did you really not grow up with stories of it?"

I shrugged, pretending I didn't see the curious look he threw me. Zaid, more than the others, knew there was more to my past than I was sharing.

An impulse to open my mouth and blurt out the truth nearly overwhelmed me. Zaid radiated dependability, and he had a lurking hint of sympathy in his eyes when he looked at me that made me want to tell him everything and ask for his help.

But I reminded myself about the stakes and the costs so far of following my emotions, and I kept my mouth tightly closed. Besides, secrets swirled through the air of Qalerim. No one here was telling me their secrets, and I couldn't afford to tell them mine. Not when there might be four entire kingdoms at risk.

And besides, I liked Zaid and the qaleri—all of whom seemed to be orphans who had once lived on the streets. I had to assume Malik was dangerous. Given the brutal Aron and Samar were mere lieutenants, obeying his orders, I'd be wise to consider him very dangerous. If the others believed me—rather than writing me off as a liar—and if they didn't hold my origins against me, they might want to help. And while I might need that help eventually, for now I didn't want to catapult them into a potential danger I didn't understand.

I glanced again at Zaid. Despite my firm convictions that butterflies in my stomach shouldn't control my actions, I cared far more than was logical that I not push Zaid into danger. I couldn't allow my emotions to overcome my judgment. My heart might want to tell Zaid the truth, but my mind was in control. And I would just have to make sure it stayed that way. I would keep my background safe until it made sense not to.

I led us around a left turning, slowing down as I did so. "We should be cautious from here. See, there's the collapsed section of hall." I pointed further down the corridor where the open passage ended in a short slope of tumbled rock.

Zaid glanced back the way we came. "I thought Selina said the last turn was right. But we just went left."

I looked at him in surprise. "Have they never explained their system to you?"

"I never go with them on their treasure hunts. I..." He stopped abruptly and remained silent, despite my questioning look.

I gave a soft sigh. Zaid might be separate from the qaleri, but in some ways they were far too alike.

"They don't have a proper system of marking routes. Instead Kayla taught them all to memorize their turns as they go—but opposite and in reverse order. So if you take a left turn, you start chanting in your mind *right*, then if you make a right turn, you make it *left, right*. Whenever you want to turn back, you just follow the instructions in your mind. So in that case, you'd make a left and then a right, and you'd be back where you started. It's more complicated, of course, but that's the basic idea. So I had to reverse the directions she remembered."

Zaid stared at me, appalled. "If you hadn't been here, I could never have found my way."

I sighed. "It's not ideal. But this is the first time anyone's gotten into trouble. I'm guessing it doesn't happen often." I stepped through the only open doorway accessible in the corridor. "We need to be quiet now so we can listen for Elias. And watch your step. Test the ground before you put your weight on it."

I inched carefully forward toward the gaping hole in the middle of the apartment floor. My pulse began to race at the unnerving silence.

"Elias?" I called, keeping my voice calm and steady despite my rising panic.

A loud groan echoed from the hole, and I drew a breath of relief. Elias had been growing in confidence since the first day I met him—perhaps the effect of moving out from his older cousin's shadow—and I was starting to like him almost as much as Selina. It had been too horrible to think that someone so young and full of potential might be dead because of a futile search for treasure.

"Zaid and I are here to rescue you," I said. "Don't try to move."

I tried to take another step forward, but Zaid put a hand on my arm, holding me back.

"We don't know how stable the floor is near the edge of the hole," he said in a low voice. "The last thing we need is for the rest of it to collapse and send both of us plummeting down to join him."

"What do you suggest?" I asked. "We can't leave him there."

"Just give me a moment." He took the coil of rope and looped the end of it around his waist, securing it with a quick knot. The other end he attached to a decorative pillar beside the door.

"Take hold of me like this." He demonstrated, gripping my lower arm while I gripped his. "Now go slowly."

I tried to ignore the way my heart raced at his touch, shuffling back toward the hole, with Zaid following behind as my anchor. When my feet reached the edge, I let our joined hands take my weight, leaning out over the jagged opening.

Elias stared up at me from below, his eyes wide in a face streaked with dirt and blood.

"Cassie?" he called weakly. "Is that you?"

"It's me." I tried to make my voice as cheerful as I could. "And we'll be down to get you in just a moment."

Zaid pulled back against my arm, helping me to right myself. I traced the loop around his waist with my eyes.

"How secure is that rope?" I asked.

He raised an eyebrow. "Secure enough. What did you have in mind?"

"Do you think you could lower us both down to him?"

Zaid frowned. "I could. But how would we get back up? I could probably climb the rope, but there's no way Elias could while injured."

I noticed he diplomatically refrained from voicing doubts about my ability to achieve such a feat.

"We wouldn't need to climb back up. I got a good look at his surroundings, and he's a level down in one of the public bathhouses. Given I know the route we took on this level, I'm confident I can lead us all back from down there."

"How confident?" Zaid regarded me with some doubt. "I don't much like the idea of spending my last remaining hours wandering lost through the tunnels of Qalerim."

I chuckled. "Thanks for the vote of confidence. I can do it. Remember, I told you on my first day that I'm familiar with tunnels, and I'm not prone to getting lost."

"Very well, then." Without losing further time to debate, he untied the rope from around his own waist, and looped it around mine.

Warmth filled me at his trust, but I said nothing, pretending to be unaffected by our close proximity as he tugged the rope tight and secured the knot.

"I'll lower you down first," he said. "As soon as you reach the ground, untie the knot, and I'll pull the rope back up and come down myself."

I considered asking how he would manage without someone to lower him but decided to give him the same trust he'd shown me. Instead I just nodded, beating back the rush of nerves as I contemplated stepping over the edge of the hole.

# CHAPTER 10

Zaid directed me to make a small loop in the free length of rope and slip my foot inside the hole to help me stay upright as I was lowered down. Not wanting to spend more time on the insecure floor than necessary, I sat down on the edge of the hole and eased myself straight over the side.

For a dizzying moment, I swung, nothing holding me up but the rope and Zaid somewhere out of sight at the end of it. I gripped it tightly, pressing down on the foot inside the loop as I began to move toward the ground. Only a grunt of effort from above gave any indication of Zaid's part in the process. Just as I thought to wonder if the jagged edge of the hole could fray the rope, my feet touched down on the scattered rock beneath me.

I stumbled for a moment before managing to right myself. As my fingers fumbled at the knot around my waist, my eyes sought out Elias. He lay at the center of the shattered pieces of rock, several steps away from where Zaid had deposited me. The end of the rope finally slipped free, and I let it drop.

"Pull it up!" I called but didn't wait to see if Zaid obeyed.

Picking my way over the uneven lumps of ceiling, I reached Elias. Dropping to a knee beside him, I spoke softly, trying to sound confident and knowledgeable.

"Where does it hurt? Can you move? Did you hit your head?"

My fingers cradled his skull, feeling gently for the source of the blood. I breathed a sigh of relief when I found nothing but a shallow scrape near his hairline that had already stopped bleeding.

"Not my head." He sounded hoarse. "I landed on my left leg. And I braced with my arms." A small whimper escaped. "I think I've broken my right arm as well as my ankle."

I sucked in a breath. An arm and a leg was going to make moving him difficult. I tried to keep my concern from my face, however, straining to remember the basic medical information I had picked up from listening to my uncle's doctor when he visited the apothecary's workrooms to discuss cases and medicines.

"What about your chest? Are you having any difficulty breathing? Any severe pain?"

Elias shook his head. "It's my arm and my leg that hurt the worst. By a lot." His last words sounded strained.

"That's a good thing." Zaid landed amid the rubble with a small thump. "If you'd broken a rib, you'd feel it. And a broken rib might threaten your lungs. Whereas broken limbs may hurt, but they're about the safest injuries you could have in this situation." He walked over to join us. "A doctor can also set a limb, while there's not a whole lot we can do to fix broken ribs other than live through the pain until they heal."

"Thankfully we're not dealing with that." I said the words briskly, but I shot a look of intense relief at Zaid. I had been fearing finding Elias in worse shape.

"I hope," Zaid said to the boy in a mock stern voice, "that you've learned your lesson about exploring rooms right next to collapsed sections of corridor."

Elias managed a weak grin in response. "You know me, Zaid. I never learn my lessons. I'm famous for it."

I groaned. "Why did I agree to live with you lot, again?"

Elias chuckled, the sound cutting off and turning into a groan half way through. "It's Kayla. She has that effect on people. Before you know it, you can't escape."

"That sounds about right." Zaid laughed, but there was an emotion in the sound I couldn't identify.

I shot him a single, searching look, before sternly reminding myself to stay focused on Elias's situation.

"We're not going to try to get you back up through that hole," I said. "I think we'll find the stairs challenging enough."

"I have a basic knowledge of splinting broken bones," Zaid said, taking his pack off his back and dropping it on the ground. "And I have something we can use in here."

"You do?" I stared at him.

He shrugged, not looking up from his examination of the inside of his bag. "I have a very basic knowledge only. He'll definitely need a doctor to look at both his arm and leg as soon as possible, but hopefully I can at least work out a makeshift solution to get him into Sirrala without further injuring the limbs."

"I'm glad you turned up when you did! I don't know the first thing about splints or setting bones."

He grinned up at me. "Just like I'm glad you're here to lead us out of these tunnels. We make a good team."

I smiled back, trying to ignore the sparks attempting to ignite a fire in my belly. Elias groaned, extinguishing the warmth.

I grimaced down at him sympathetically. "I wish I had something to give you for the pain. Sari found some of that numbing plant two days ago, but it needs to be brewed into a tea, so we couldn't bring it with us."

"We can stop for a rest at the apartment and give him some before we start the journey to Sirrala," Zaid said. "In the meantime, he'll just have to cope." He raised an eyebrow at Elias. "You can cope, can't you?"

The challenge had a bracing effect on the younger boy who stiffened and nodded.

"Of course I can. I'm tough."

"A very good thing, since this whole process is going to hurt." Without any more preamble, Zaid produced two solid batons about the length of my arm from his pack.

I raised both eyebrows at the sight of the unfamiliar weapons. Zaid caught my confused look, a flicker of surprise or interest flashing through his eyes.

"These are haryat sticks," he said. "The local guards are trained in a fighting style that makes use of them."

"You're a guard?" I asked, leaping on the morsel of information.

"Zaid? Hardly!" Elias said, but Zaid shushed him, telling him to keep still while he used strips of his own robe to cushion and secure the injured limbs.

I tucked away the information that Zaid wasn't a guard but was a trained fighter as I followed his orders, helping to immobilize Elias's arm against his chest, and to wrap his ankle from calf to toes. As Zaid tied the final knot, a deep groaning sound made us both freeze and look up.

"Is that—?"

I broke off, as Zaid shouted, "Go!"

Scooping up his pack, I took two long strides to where Elias's bag still lay where it had fallen. Snatching that up as well, I darted for the door, taking care where I placed my feet.

With a single swift apology, Zaid scooped Elias up and slung him over his shoulder. He moved as if the lanky boy's weight was feather light, not slowing at Elias's quickly suppressed shout of pain.

I reached the door a stride before him, bursting through and jumping sideways out of the way. Zaid followed behind me just as a screeching sound preceded an earsplitting crash. A cloud of dust enveloped us.

I coughed violently, dropping the bags and waving my arms in front of my face to try to clear the air. My efforts were ineffectual, but with no further disruption, the dust slowly settled, and I had a clear view of Zaid.

For a breathless moment, our wide eyes met in silence. Both of us were now as covered in dirt as Elias.

"That was close," I said, the words making the dust in my throat scratch and setting me coughing again.

"I guess the floor couldn't handle all our activity. We can just be thankful it didn't give way sooner."

I gulped. "Let's not think about that. Are you all right, Elias?"

He nodded, the strain on his face suggesting he was in too much pain to talk. I transferred my gaze to Zaid.

"How are we going to get him back? He can't walk."

"Give him a minute," Zaid said. "The pain should settle. He's got one good leg, so I'm hoping he can manage to hobble along with help now that he's splinted."

"Yes," Elias gasped. "It is getting better. It was the sudden, unexpected jarring. Not that I mind," he added hastily, with a glance back at the room we had just exited.

Moving slowly this time, with me for support, Zaid lowered Elias onto his good leg.

"Here, throw your good arm over my shoulders. Thankfully the good arm is on the side of the broken ankle."

I pushed him lightly out of the way. "No, you're too tall. Put your arm around my shoulders, Elias."

Zaid tried to protest, but I gave him a stern look. "It will be much easier for Elias this way since we're closer in height. And it will allow you to keep your strength so you can carry him when needed. I'm sure he'll appreciate the occasional break, and you'll need to carry him up the stairs at the very least."

Zaid reluctantly agreed, and we had soon arranged ourselves and begun hobbling slowly down the corridor.

"I wonder if any of the others have returned and found Selina yet?" I asked brightly, conscious it was going to be a long and painful journey for Elias.

"How is she?" he asked. "I heard her call she was going for help, but then she was gone for so long, I feared…"

"She rolled her ankle, I'm afraid. Nothing serious, but it slowed her pace considerably."

Elias grimaced. "I suppose I'll have to apologize since she was hurrying for my sake." He threw a guilty glance at Zaid. "She did warn me not to go into the apartment."

"I suspect she'll consider you punished enough," he said with a grin, and Elias's face lightened slightly.

It had been obvious since my arrival in Qalerim that Elias looked up to Zaid even more than the others did. I just hoped his determination to appear to good advantage in front of his hero would help him through the continuing ordeal.

"It's hard to believe," Zaid said in a conversational tone, "but Cassie here isn't familiar with the tale of the Treasure of Qalerim. Apparently her childhood was greatly lacking. Perhaps you could tell it to her so she knows why you're risking life and limb in these back tunnels."

I opened my mouth to tell him that while I hadn't heard the story as a child, I had certainly heard enough chatter about the qaleri's search for the treasure to understand the basics, but one look at his face made me swallow the words. I should have realized immediately his intention was to distract Elias, not inform me.

"You've never heard it before? I thought everyone knew the story." Elias stared at me, suggesting Zaid's strategy was a masterly one.

"You all mention the treasure constantly," I said with a chuckle. "But I don't think anyone's told me the whole legend."

"It's a good one," he said with the tiniest hint of enthusiasm. He glanced at Zaid. "You don't want to tell it?"

"No, indeed. You're the expert," he said, bringing a small glow to Elias's eyes.

The boy cleared his throat and began, dropping into a cadence and tone he must have learned at his mother's knee.

"Once, long ago, the eastern half of the Great Desert bloomed with life."

"What?" I stared at Zaid. "Is that possible?"

"Shhh," he said. "He's started the story. You can't interrupt."

The mischievous twinkle in his eyes made me throw him an exasperated look, but I apologized gravely to Elias and resumed my attentive silence.

"As I was saying, the eastern half of the Great Desert bloomed with life. It supported a mighty empire, ruled over by three brothers."

"All three of them? That sounds problematic."

"Cassie!" Elias gave me an irritated look, and I grinned.

"Sorry! I'll be quiet this time, I promise."

He shook his head and continued. "The first two brothers were good rulers, loyal to their people and to the other brothers. But the youngest brother had a greedy heart."

"Uh oh," I whispered, too quietly to earn a reprimand. Although I did get a warning look from Elias and an amused one from Zaid, who seemed to have cottoned on to my efforts to keep Elias as distracted from his pain as possible.

"At first the younger brother contented himself with stealing from his brothers and people, amassing vast riches. Since he could not keep them in the palace, he secreted them in two caves on opposite ends of the empire. But his greatest treasure he wore on his finger."

"Oooh, was it a giant jewel?"

"Not just a jewel," Elias said, seeming to take this comment as being more in spirit with the tale. "It was an enchanted object. A wise woman had gifted each of the brothers a ring that would ensure unswerving loyalty from anyone who swore their fealty to the bearer and kissed the hand that wore the ring."

"A godmother, you mean?" I asked, startled. Was it a true story, then, and not just a children's tale?

"A godmother?"

I nearly replied it was the name such women were known by in my own lands before suddenly remembering what the statement would reveal. I bit my lip.

"Sorry, continue!" I said quickly, forestalling further questions.

Elias hesitated briefly before plunging on.

"After a while, the younger brother was no longer content with his hidden riches. He grew more and more unhappy at having to share the rule and wished to be emperor over his brothers."

He paused, grunting as his bad foot hit a loose rock in our path. For a moment there was silence as his breathing turned labored, but after a moment he shook his head and returned to his recitation.

"To this end, he went to them and proposed that they each swear loyalty to the others and kiss their rings. He claimed that it would ensure they could never be made to work against each other by either cunning or threat."

"And the brothers fell for that?" I asked, incredulous.

"Unlike the youngest brother, their hearts were pure," Elias said with a reproving look. "They knew nothing of the perfidy hiding in their younger brother's soul. They agreed to his plan and, in age order, they pledged their loyalty to their two brothers, starting with the oldest. But when the middle brother had finished pledging his loyalty, the youngest revealed his true nature, refusing to take his turn."

"Predictable," I muttered under my breath.

This was why the kingdoms needed people like Aurora. If the older brothers had possessed an advisor like her, they would have been safe. She would have seen through the plan in a moment.

"The younger brother ordered his two older brothers to relinquish their rings to him. Bound by the oath they had made, they were forced to hand over their greatest treasure. Using another enchanted object, the younger brother combined the gold of the two rings with other metals that strengthened the initial enchantment, tying it to the power of his own ring. Using this new material, he crafted a lamp. The lamp could compel not only loyalty but absolute obedience."

"A lamp? Why a lamp?"

Elias stumbled over a loose rock in our path, jolting his limbs. "I don't know!" he snapped before drawing several deep breaths. "Sorry. That hurt."

"The steps are just up there." I pointed ahead of us. "Maybe you could carry him for a little, Zaid?"

"No, I'm fine, I don't need—"

Zaid ignored Elias's words, crouching to lift him over his shoulder much more gently than he had done in the collapsing rooms.

"I would like to emerge from these tunnels some time today," he said, a humorous note in his voice. "So you will not be hobbling up those stairs."

"Oh, very well," Elias muttered, but I could hear the smile in his voice, his momentary bad humor vanished.

I trailed behind them, admiring the ease with which Zaid managed the injured youth. Even if I had possessed his physical strength and skill, I would never have managed so well on my own.

"But seriously," I said, when we reached the top of the stairs, and Elias was placed back on his feet. "Why a lamp?"

He shrugged. "It's a bedtime story. I've honestly never thought about it."

"But it's not *just* a bedtime story. At least, you must believe it's based on truth, or you wouldn't be searching the city for the treasure."

"Yes, but we—" He cut off abruptly, his eyes flying to Zaid as he fell silent.

I frowned but didn't bother asking any further questions. Whatever mystery hung over the final inhabitants of Qalerim, I already knew I was going to have to discover it for myself.

"So what about you?" I asked Zaid as I directed him to make a left turn. "Do you know why a lamp?"

He considered the question. "I've always assumed it to be symbolic. A lamp guides our way in the darkness. The younger brother was stating that he alone would lead and choose the way forward."

I shrugged. "I suppose that's as good an explanation as any. So what did he do with this lamp?"

"He placed it in one of his treasure caves, of course," Elias said. "He still had his ring, and as long as he possessed the lamp, he could use its power through the ring. He knew that after his betrayal of his brothers, everyone in the empire who was not already bound to him would attempt to steal the lamp."

"And what of his brothers?"

"He had them executed. And so great was the crime of the younger brother's betrayal, the earth itself turned against him, and his once beautiful empire transformed into desert. The people rebelled, and he was forced to flee. He ran to the mountains, thinking to hide in his cave and retrieve his lamp. But the people overwhelmed his loyal guards and overtook him before he could reach it. He was slain, and the people discovered the network of caves of which his cavern was one. They did not know how to access the treasure he had hidden, but they recognized the greater treasure he had overlooked—the mountain itself and the river within. They built on the natural cave system that already existed, carving Qalerim out of the rock and building for themselves a new empire."

"But the treasure was never found," I finished for him. "And it is hidden still somewhere deep within the mountain." That was the part of the story I had heard several times since joining the qaleri.

"Exactly. The lost Treasure of Qalerim. Many have sought it, but none have found it—yet."

## CHAPTER 11

For a moment there was only the sound of Elias's labored breathing as I considered the activities of the qaleri in light of the tale.

"If no one found it when a whole city's worth of people lived here, what hope do you think you have?" I couldn't help asking.

He shrugged, looking uncomfortable. "What else should we do all the way out here?"

"You could return to Sirrala," I suggested.

Elias kept his gaze awkwardly on the far wall. "Actually we couldn't do that." He paused. "There's no place for us there."

I wanted to tell him he should carve a place for himself if that's what it took, but I couldn't bring myself to criticize someone who was in so much pain. But Elias seemed to sense my thoughts, his eyes swinging to me, heat in his voice and a faint flush to his pale skin.

"And what of you, Cassie? Why have you stayed with us instead of continuing on into Sirrala if starting a life there is so easy?"

Now it was my turn to flush. In my interminable trip across the desert, I'd had ample time to consider my own inadequacies in a number of areas—including my ability to earn my way. My only training was what I had given myself in spycraft, and I could hardly earn a living in Sirrala using that. The brutal truth was that as a destitute stranger, untrained in any trade, and far too old to be an apprentice, I had no chance of providing for myself.

"You're right," I said, owning to my error. "I'm not versed in a trade, so I would have little to no hope of finding a job in the city."

"There are some jobs you can come to without skills," Zaid said, his voice carefully free of judgment, which only made his words sting all the more. "But it is true you generally need connections to be chosen for them. And most start such roles younger than you." He looked sideways at me. "Are you sure you have no relevant skills or training?"

My flush deepened. I had never felt so utterly useless in my life.

"I'm afraid not."

Elias, apparently taking pity on me, grinned in my direction. "Then it's a good thing you found us. It doesn't require any prior training to join the qaleri."

"I can't tell you how grateful I am for all of your generosity." I shook my head ruefully. "But unless I stumble across this lost treasure, I don't see how I'm going to contribute. I can't keep taking your supplies without giving back."

I bit my lip. I was skirting perilously close to a dangerous topic, but part of me wanted to push harder and see what Elias might say. Kayla was too good at dodging my questions, and I'd been wondering all week where their food and other essentials came from since Kayla had admitted on the first day that they had no coin.

"Yes, your supplies," Zaid said, his voice a little too light. "Where do you source them again?"

My eyes jumped to him, instantly suspicious of his overly casual demeanor. Perhaps I wasn't the only one who wanted to know how the qaleri supported themselves.

Elias swallowed, his Adam's apple bobbing.

I had been asking Kayla in the days since my arrival to take me into Sirrala and show me around. I wanted to see the city and observe how the gate guards operated before I attempted going in on my own. But every day she and the others were too busy with their treasure hunting to make the trip.

Yet the evening meal two nights before had included fresh dates and even a cake no one in Qalerim had baked. When I questioned Sari about it, she had casually mentioned Josef and Patrin's supply run into the city earlier in the day. After that, I hounded Kayla until she admitted it was her and Selina's turn to go next. My anticipation about the upcoming trip was mounting, but my questions about the source of their provisions had only grown.

The silence grew too long until Elias eventually spoke. "We don't take them from the sultan, if that's what you're suggesting." His belligerent tone was a shock, directed as it was toward Zaid, and I received the instant impression it was a desperate mask, assumed to hide his lack of reasonable response.

"From the sultan?" I asked, astonished. Surely he didn't think Zaid was accusing him of stealing from the sultan himself?

"He means the sultan's provision," Zaid said to me, calm in the face of Elias's sudden about face. "The sultan supplies necessities for those who truly need them—those unable to work from injury or illness, as well as the very old and very young."

"None of which applies to us," Elias said. "Any of us would be ashamed to claim the provision in place of someone who might truly need it."

Zaid met my eyes, neither of us willing to challenge the assertion that the qaleri were not children in need of support. At least Elias's impassioned declaration of civic duty undermined my previous fear that they were stealing on their trips into Sirrala. But it was hard to think of another way they could so quickly amass provisions at will.

I added it to the growing list of mysteries that surrounded them. I still hoped to one day understand what was going on with the qaleri, but in the meantime, I needed to think of a way to contribute. The lingering fear we might be living on stolen goods only amplified my desire not to rely on the other qaleri to supply all my needs.

"Elias! They're back!" The shout echoed down the large main tunnel, followed by the sound of many running feet.

The other qaleri soon swarmed around us, Josef stepping in to take my place under Elias's shoulder. As cousin, he declared that it fell to him to provide support for the rest of the way into our apartment.

When we arrived inside, I dropped into a chair, trying to hide my exhaustion. It had been a long trip back.

"Are you all right?" Zaid asked quietly.

I mustered a smile. "I'm fine. Just tired."

I should have known Zaid would notice. He observed most of the subtleties going on around him—too many sometimes as far as I was concerned. He would make a good intelligencer.

Selina declared her ankle was already feeling better and refused a visit to a doctor. But Zaid wanted to get Elias down the mountain as soon as possible. After an extended conversation, it was decided a stretcher would be fashioned, and Josef and Zaid would carry him down using the widest path.

After that, everyone scurried around, discussing ways to construct the stretcher while I continued to rest and recover under Kayla's orders.

"You managed to have all the adventure without me," she declared, looking honestly put out. "The very least you can do is let me earn some gratitude now by my ingenious solution."

"I'm all curiosity. What will it be?" I asked.

She pushed up her sleeves. "I don't know yet. But I'm sure I'll think of something."

And in the end, she did. It was still bright daylight when Zaid and Josef set off, each carrying the end of a makeshift stretcher made from several blankets and the frame of an ancient and threadbare tapestry that one of them had discovered at some point deep in the mountain.

Those of us left behind waited anxiously until Josef returned part way through the night to report that Zaid had placed Elias in one of the public healing halls.

"Surely that must cost coin?" I asked, concerned, but he assured me Zaid had taken care of everything and would visit Elias daily.

This blithe assurance only increased my curiosity about the mysteries surrounding Zaid. He dressed without ostentation, but his clothes lacked the patches and tears of those of the qaleri. He clearly visited often, dropping in unannounced and always to a warm welcome. And I could understand why the qaleri looked forward to his presence. When he remained absent over the following days—presumably busy overseeing Elias's recovery—I felt the lack of his company far more than I was willing to admit.

His friendly manner, quick intelligence, and the hidden laughter in his eyes had made him impossible to dislike from the beginning. But the more I saw of him, and his strength and compassion, the stronger my liking became—and the harder it grew to ignore it, as I remained determined to do.

I started joining Kayla and Selina in their daily searches, curious to see more of Qalerim as well as hoping to glean valuable information from my friends in the course of the day's conversation. But my true focus was on our upcoming trip to Sirrala. Once I had access to the city, I could begin my true work.

Zaid still had not returned when the morning of our visit finally arrived, and I couldn't help wondering if we might run into him in the city. I wanted to ask the girls about the possibility, but I held my tongue, reminding myself of the far more important information I needed to seek in Sirrala. Such thoughts only proved why I needed to stop thinking with my heart.

As we came out of the tunnels and I once again drank in the view of the oasis city behind the mountain, I marveled that I had been living in Qalerim for less than two weeks. Already the mountain felt comfortable and familiar.

I followed Kayla and Selina down the track, picking my way carefully. They moved slowly in consideration for my inexperience, reminding me again of my good fortune in finding them. I could almost believe I had a godmother who had guided me to them, despite my lack of royal parents.

When we reached level ground, we slipped onto the road between two large groups of travelers. Kayla took the lead, increasing her speed until we were hanging on the fringes of the group ahead of us.

She had explained the qaleri strategy over breakfast. While access to the city was unrestricted in daylight hours, they didn't like to draw the attention of the guard. "They'll stop anyone they think looks threatening," she had said, "or just out of place in any way. And you look younger than me, so you'll draw their eye if you appear to be traveling alone—or even just with the two of us. The best way to avoid catching their attention is to walk close enough to a large group that you slip into the city as one of them."

The plan turned out to be simple to execute. We all paused briefly while someone at the head of the group exchanged a few jovial words with one of the guards, and then we strolled through without question.

"Josef, and even Elias, are getting tall enough that they're starting to get noticed," Kayla whispered once we were past the gates. "But us girls can still slip by without attracting attention."

I barely heard her. The noise and smell of Sirrala hit me with almost physical force after the vast emptiness of Qalerim and the fresh air of the mountains. It wasn't unpleasant, exactly, but the mix of people, animals, spices, and flowers produced a scent and volume of noise that momentarily overwhelmed me.

I had thought I was prepared to enter the city after so many days of waiting, but now that I was here, apprehension seized me. What if Aron and Samar caught sight of me on the streets? I had dismissed the danger earlier, telling myself I had spent our entire journey across the desert wrapped head to toe in my robe. But now that I was here, surrounded by a crowd of strangers, I couldn't help the spike of anxiety.

Selina pulled me out of the way of a passing carriage, tugging me along behind Kayla who sidestepped a camel before weaving her way between a number of carts. I shook myself, throwing off the momentary paralysis to focus properly on my immediate surroundings. I couldn't hide in Qalerim forever. I simply had to keep my eyes open and my senses alert—which was exactly what I'd spent years training myself to do.

I stepped up beside Kayla, examining the passing crowd with interest. I had already marveled from afar at the differences in the physical environment between Sirrala and my own kingdom —the desert, the sand, the gardens, the golden domes, and the way the heat hung in the air like a physical presence whenever the breeze disappeared. But this was my first chance to walk among the people of this kingdom.

In appearance they looked much like those who inhabited the kingdoms on the other side of the desert—their skin tones reflecting the full range between Aron and Samar. But their clothing fascinated me—beautifully embroidered robes and jackets caught my eye everywhere I looked, and the sashes and turbans were a far cry from the tall fur-lined boots favored by the inhabitants of my own capital. I wished I had made it as far as Lanover in the Four Kingdoms so I could have a comparison with the fashions of that hot, sticky kingdom.

The voices that swirled around me spoke with the cadence I had grown used to on my desert journey with my two captors and then during my days in Qalerim. I had even practiced while exploring with Kayla so I could speak the same way myself. But it sounded different in the loud cries and murmured hum of a large crowd.

I grinned as my eyes darted in all directions. Now that I had gotten past the initial shock, the hustle and bustle was invigorating. In Qalerim mysteries hung in the air, but the thriving activity of Sirrala seemed to promise a wealth of answers.

Kayla led the way past a group of children playing games in the street. She was heading toward the closest patch of greenery, and I followed eagerly. She stopped, however, in front of the carefully manicured entrance which invited passersby into a large formal garden. The group of children we had passed earlier raced by, spilling onto the grass before disappearing from sight.

I gave my friend an inquiring look. "Is it a public park? Can we go in?"

She shook her head. "It's the home of one of the nobles."

"Look there." Selina pointed toward the heart of the garden. "You can see part of the house between the trees."

"A private home?" I glanced at a mother and child who gave us looks of mild curiosity as they strolled past on their way through the entrance. "It looks more like a park."

"It's both, really," Kayla said. "All the nobles in Sirrala maintain large gardens around their homes and allow the people of the city to access them freely. They even forgo fences, using small ditches to delineate their properties."

"So it's more like one big garden," Selina explained, "since it's easy enough to jump the ditches. Which means if you keep going that way—" she pointed north, "you'll reach Malik's house. His is the last one in this particular row. And it's the largest in the city as well. You can't miss it."

"Since you said you wanted to see his house," Kayla added with a bright smile.

I opened my mouth only to close it again. The two of them had clearly planned this in advance as a way to get rid of me while they fetched their supplies. But while part of me longed to call them out on their obvious stratagem and demand to accompany them, I couldn't do it. I couldn't put my curiosity, however strong, above the much more important task of finding out about Malik's intended invasion. I had already delayed too long.

"Thank you," I said instead, before hesitating for a moment. "You're sure I can't miss it?"

"One of his ancestors—no doubt a previous Grand Vizier—had an excessive love of gilt," Kayla said dryly. "You won't miss it."

"Lots of people think it's beautiful," Selina added. "Visitors often stop to see it on their way to or from the palace."

"We'll meet you back here just after noon," Kayla said, tugging on Selina's arm. "You can't get too lost if you stick to the gardens."

I nodded, watching as they plunged back into the crowd. I had to crush every instinct to follow behind them, but I managed to keep my feet firmly planted until the temptation was gone. I couldn't let this opportunity to investigate Malik pass me by.

I hurried into the garden, passing the mother and child I had seen earlier. Surrounded by greenery and unhampered by traffic, my pace increased. My earlier anxiety attempted to return, now that I walked alone, and I had no desire to linger despite the beauty around me. Firmly seizing control of myself, I forced my head to take the lead over my emotions, focusing on every detail around me in an effort to drown out the unhelpful feelings.

As Kayla had predicted, I had no issue jumping the small ditch that lined the northern border of the first garden and the southern border of the next one. Moving from home to home, I admired the different styles and layouts without stopping to examine any of them. I did enjoy the shade of the many trees, however. With the sun already beating down on the city, I could see why so many flocked to these spaces.

Despite my sharp lookout, which only increased as I moved further along the row of houses, I saw no sign of the hulking figures of my previous captors. I took solace in my original observation that they weren't the type to disappear in a crowd, although I couldn't forget the silent way they had moved through the trees.

When I stepped across yet another ditch, I immediately noticed the difference in the next garden. The soft splash of fountains came from multiple directions, while there was no sign of the house itself among the increased number of bushes and trees. I strode deeper into the large, verdant space, fighting to keep my breathing steady. Was this it? The final house?

As soon as the building came into view, I knew I had found the abode of the Grand Vizier. Gilt edged the doors and windows, as well as the peaks and domes of the elaborate roof, just as Selina had promised. Complex patterns decorated the screens on the windows while engravings bordered all the doors.

Two men stood in front of it, gazing at the details admiringly while they conversed in low tones—visitors to Sirrala, perhaps. I gave them a wide berth, circling the west facing front of the building to approach the long northern side. An ornamental bush ran all the way along it, and while the gap between the vegetation and the wall wouldn't have allowed a full grown man to fit, my small stature should allow it. I glanced around, strolling on when a group of women came into sight. By the time I reached the back of the house, they had disappeared again into a small clump of trees.

Dropping to my knees, I crawled between the bush and the wall of the enormous mansion, heading back toward the front of the building. As I shuffled along, prickles caught at my clothing. I ignored them, focusing on the windows on my other side. Almost half way along, I found what I was searching for—not only one, but an entire row of windows with their screens thrust wide to let in the breeze.

I stopped under the first one, holding my breath while I listened for sounds. I could hear nothing.

Rising ever so slowly, I inched my head above the windowsill until I could peek into the room beyond. I managed one sweeping glance of the large hall before whisking my head back down again. No outraged cry sounded to suggest the occupants at the far end had seen me, but I stayed motionless and silent for some time anyway.

My mistake had been in assuming each window opened onto a different room. Instead, all of the open ones looked into a cavernous hall, meaning I hadn't heard the quiet sounds of people all the way at the other end. Thankfully it sounded like none of them had been glancing my way.

From the look and size of the space, I guessed it to be a servants' hall—the kind of place where people would be congregating or working throughout the day. And an excellent place for gathering gossip.

When enough time had passed, I continued crawling. I stopped at the furthest open window, guessing the current occupants of the room to be just inside it. Sure enough, down here I could hear their quiet murmurs.

I leaned my back against the wall, getting as comfortable as I could, and settled in to listen. Three hours later, I crawled carefully back out of the bush, frustrated and sore.

In all that time I had heard nothing but the usual chatter of a large household. Not even the faintest allusion or significant pause had suggested activities beyond the normal daily routine of the Grand Vizier's household. And while I had kept my mind busy beginning to learn the rhythms of this place, I hadn't received any actual confirmation this was the Malik I sought.

I completed a full circle of the building, taking note of the entrances, before conducting a lightning-quick tour of the garden. By the time I circled back to the front, I had to hurry to avoid being late to meet Kayla and Selina.

Moving back from garden to garden, I no longer fixated on the possibility of meeting Aron or Samar. Instead I couldn't shake the worry they might have been referring to a different Malik.

I arrived back at the meeting place only a minute or two before Kayla and Selina appeared. Each of them carried a heavy sack, and Kayla also had a large pack strung across one shoulder. They greeted me cheerfully enough, neither of them asking about my activities in their absence. After a moment's hesitation, I followed their lead, taking the pack Kayla thrust at me without asking as to its origin.

We made the trek back out of the city, chatting about inconsequential things like the gardens I had passed through and the fashions we had spied among the crowd. They reported a visit to Elias in the healing house and relayed the news that he would soon be well enough to return home. I was disappointed to have been excluded from the visit until a casual question on my part revealed Zaid had not been there. I was somewhat ashamed of myself when my disappointment at missing the visit all but vanished after that—but I took comfort in the knowledge that a fourteen-year-old convalescent would have found two fussing females quite enough at one time.

The return trip passed quickly, and back inside Qalerim, we distributed the contents of the sacks onto the shelves of the apartments. As I worked it occurred to me that there was a benefit to the reticence of my housemates. They might not answer questions, but they didn't ask them either.

For the first time in my life, I considered the possibility of not trying to discover every secret in my vicinity.

With the heavy weight of my seemingly impossible task on my shoulders, the prospect didn't seem as appalling as I had expected. Maybe I could do it. Maybe I could live here, and be friends with Kayla and Selina, despite their silence. Maybe I could pursue my own efforts without involving them at all.

It was a surprisingly attractive proposition since I still

dreaded the possibility they might not believe me. To them, my story would surely sound impossible.

The realization that I had—contrary to all expectation—already found friends here, gave me the lift I needed after my dispiriting day. I would return to Sirrala on my own, and I would listen at the Grand Vizier's windows until I heard something to prove whether or not he was the Malik I sought. Only once I had built a full picture of the situation would I consider enlisting aid.

I purposely didn't think about what I would do if he was the wrong Malik. Because how could I possibly go about finding Aron and Samar at this point?

# CHAPTER 12

*W*hen Zaid came by with a sack of corn three days later, he found me alone in the apartment, dusting and sweeping Elias's room. It was a constant chore thanks to the sand that found its way into the front few layers of the city.

"Have you brought Elias?" I asked, trying to peer over his tall shoulder. "I've been keeping his room ready for him."

"That's kind of you," he said, and I pretended his smile didn't warm me from the inside out. "He's not back yet, though, I'm afraid. His bones are healing nicely, but after a discussion with the doctor, we decided it would be best to let them heal completely before he returns. So it will be some weeks longer, after all."

"Selina will be disappointed." I propped the broom against the wall and led the way back to the living room. "She says that despite Elias's lack of caution, Kayla is a less satisfactory search partner."

Zaid shook his head, the corners of his lips curling up. "I think our Selina might harbor a certain love of adventure herself. She probably thinks Kayla babies her. I suppose they're all out searching currently?"

He deposited his sack of corn in the kitchen, beside the cleverly contrived stove and chimney left from the previous long-ago inhabitants.

"Kayla invited me to come, but I wanted to sweep out the sand. Again." I smiled at my own fussiness. "My uncle is a careful, particular sort of person, and he expected order in our home."

"Your uncle? Did he raise you, then? Where is he now?"

I bit my lip, irritated with myself for letting the comment slip without thinking.

This was the problem with Zaid. He made me forget myself and confide things in him that I shouldn't. Here he was, waltzing in after days away doing who knew what, and I was talking as if we were old friends.

And yet, I couldn't resist telling him more about myself. It might not be safe or wise to mention imaginary kingdoms across the desert, but that didn't mean I couldn't talk about my family.

"Yes, it was just him and me growing up," I said. "My parents were both killed in the same accident that killed my aunt. My uncle raised me as a daughter, but..." I hesitated, trying to think what to say. "He lives a very long way away, and he can't help me now."

"I'm sorry," Zaid said quietly, and I wasn't sure which part of my history he was referring to.

"Don't be," I said as brightly as I could manage. "I never knew my parents, and my uncle was loving enough—even if he didn't know what to do with a child who wanted to spend her time exploring secret passageways and listening in on his meetings."

Zaid chuckled. "I would love a child like that one day. As long as they let me explore with them."

I grinned. "I would have said the same thing before I came here. But I'm starting to suspect that if I ever manage to leave Qalerim, I won't want to see another tunnel ever again."

Zaid winced. "It's that bad, is it?"

I shook my head. "Not yet. But there are a lot of tunnels here.

And apparently the others are determined to search every single one." I rolled my eyes.

"I hope none of them have gone near the damaged section since Elias's accident," Zaid said.

I shook my head. "They've headed off in a new direction entirely. Selina found a whole level they hadn't accessed yet."

"In just a few weeks you've gotten to know this place far better than I ever managed," he said. "A fact for which I'm very grateful considering you led Elias and me out the other day."

I shrugged. "I'm good at remembering things, and I've been working on developing the skill for a long time now."

"So you don't use the reverse turn chant to find your way out?" His voice held a tinge of amusement.

"No, I don't." I gave him a wry look. "It's better than nothing, but it has its limitations, as you know. Personally, I build a map in my head. As I discover new sections or passages, the map expands."

"A map?" He sounded startled. "So you can bring it to mind right now? Of the whole city?"

"Not the whole city." I busied myself with emptying the corn out of the sack. "This place is enormous, so I haven't been everywhere—but wherever I have been is set in my memory."

"But...that's remarkable!"

I shrugged. "Like I said, I've been practicing the skill since I was a young child." I didn't mention I had been attempting to hone it for a future as an intelligencer. Since I hoped to one day confess I didn't come from either Ardasira or Kuralan, that seemed like a foolhardy piece of information to impart.

Kayla burst into the apartment, filling it with her irrepressible energy.

"Zaid! Welcome!" She peered over my shoulder. "You brought corn! That's my favorite. Thank you!"

"Cassie has just been telling me about how she finds her way around in here," he said. "It's incredible."

"Isn't it?" Kayla collapsed into the closest chair, propping her feet up and letting out an exhausted sigh. "I've tried to tell her the same thing, but she's always downplaying it. But maybe you could teach some of the others how to do it, Cassie?"

"Maybe you could learn," Zaid suggested, his lips twitching.

"Oh no." She waved her hand through the air dismissively. "My mind doesn't work like that. I couldn't possibly hold so much in there at once. I was the one who came up with the current system, and it's all my poor scattered thoughts can manage."

"Maybe there's another way." Zaid looked thoughtfully between us. "If I brought enough parchment, could you make a book of maps, Cassie? If you mapped the whole of the city, then everyone could report ahead of time where they mean to search for the day. That way if there's another accident, we'll know where to look."

"Ooh!" Kayla sat up. "Would you do that, Cassie? That would be amazing! We could mark off the areas we've searched, so we don't double up that way, too. We've been putting marks on the walls of the corridors as we go, but a map book would be much more systematic."

She glanced around the room and sighed. "If this place weren't so old, we might have found some old maps left behind. Surely they must have existed once. But we haven't found any surviving parchment."

"It probably wouldn't still be here anyway," I said. "The whole place looks picked clean of anything light enough to carry. I guess with it being so close to the new city, no one wanted to leave anything of even the remotest value."

Kayla nodded. "And a good thing, or we'd have Sirralans up here constantly, rifling through the apartments. But everyone knows there's nothing here." She frowned. "Perhaps in the royal library, though…"

Zaid shook his head. "If such ancient documents exist, you can be sure the librarians won't let them out of their sight."

I laughed. "Certainly not for a bunch of penniless orphans. If we want a map book, we'll certainly have to make it ourselves." I hesitated. "But are you sure it's worth the effort, Kayla?" We'd had this conversation before, but I couldn't help making a final plea before committing to the cause. "You just said yourself that if anyone truly believed there was anything of value in this city, they'd be here in droves."

Kayla's mouth set into frustrated lines. "It doesn't matter what other people think. I'm glad we don't have treasure hunters here bothering us."

I bit my lip. Their singular obsession might not make sense to me, but it was clearly important to them. And I still hadn't found a way to contribute in any meaningful way. If this would truly be of value to them—and assist in keeping them safe in the process —then I would happily make a map.

"Of course I'll draw a map for you, if you want one," I said.

"Thank you!" Kayla sprang to her feet, her eyes alight.

"It's the least I can do, given the way you've all taken me in."

Selina popped her head in. "Are you coming across? Patrin made the stew today, and it's surprisingly good despite his last— Zaid!" She broke off as soon as she spotted our visitor. "You'll join us?"

"Never mind food, Cassie's going to make us a map," Kayla cried.

"A map?"

Kayla led the way over to the door, explaining the whole scheme to Selina as we trailed across to the other apartment behind her. The others greeted Zaid with as much enthusiasm as Selina had done, and to my surprise, despite their usual lack of cohesion, they all greeted the proposal about keeping a master map with almost equal levels of excitement.

By the time Zaid stood to leave, his belly was full, and he had promised to return the next day with stacks of parchment.

"I'll even get it bound for you when you're done," he promised with a smile that seemed just for me. "Although given the size of this place, that might take you a few years."

I laughed and brushed his comment aside, but inside my curiosity sparked. Zaid could set Elias up for weeks in a healing clinic and have a book bound as a simple favor. He clearly had access to significant resources. So what was he doing spending his time visiting Qalerim?

He never mentioned an occupation or other source of wealth —and he never mentioned family for that matter, either. The one piece of information about him I'd managed to prize out of the qaleri was that he wasn't related to any of them, so it couldn't be a matter of family obligation.

A sudden determination to take action filled me. I had claimed I had no skills, but it wasn't entirely true. I had trained myself for years in the skills of an intelligencer which meant I didn't have to meekly accept the mysteries surrounding Zaid. I might have made peace with the secrets of the qaleri, but from the moment I had met him, Zaid had always stood apart from them.

When he stood to leave, I jumped up as well. "I feel like a walk. I'll keep you company for a while."

"Company is always welcome." His smile seemed to hold extra warmth, and I turned away quickly to grab my robe so he wouldn't see the flush that rose to my cheeks in response to the light in his eyes.

Once he had said his goodbyes and we had left the apartment behind, he gave a rueful chuckle.

"Some types of company are welcome, at any rate."

I turned to him with a raised eyebrow, and he smiled quickly.

"You fall on the welcome side. Obviously."

"Obviously," I said dryly.

He shook his head, a wry smile on his face. "Ordinarily I'm

much better at not blurting out whatever I'm thinking. But there's something about you, Cassie…"

"I'm not sure whether to take that as a compliment," I said, to stop myself from blurting out that I had been thinking the same thing about him.

"I think it's how open you are," he said so blandly, and with such an innocent face, that I wanted to throw something at him.

"Yes," I said instead, equally straight-faced. "That must definitely be it. Just like you. It's like we're two peas in a pod."

He laughed, shaking his head. "Careful, Cassie. I might think you're accompanying me just to spy on me."

I pushed aside the branches that had grown over the tunnel exit we were using, holding them aside for Zaid as an excuse to cover my flush. But this time it was discomfort that brought the color to my cheeks.

I hurried to turn the direction of the conversation. "Whose company do you prefer to avoid, then?"

He grimaced. "Don't tell Josef, but I was thinking that I preferred a walk back to the city with you for company than him."

"The lack of a stretcher and severely injured companion might have something to do with that," I pointed out in fairness.

He shook his head. "You're forgetting. I walked across Qalerim with a severely injured companion—and no stretcher— with you just the other day. So I have a direct comparison."

I sighed. "It is hard to believe Elias and Josef are cousins sometimes, it's true. In some ways, Elias is a typical surly youth, but underneath he has a soft heart. Whereas Josef is too focused on himself to even notice if he hurts someone else."

"It's sad, really," Zaid said. "I suspect he deals out jibes and verbal cuts because it's his only chance to feel in control of his life. And I can hardly blame him, in truth…" He threw a glance back toward Qalerim, as if to indicate that the circumstances of Josef's life could be blamed for his irritating manner and attitude.

"No, but then life doesn't seem to have been kind to any of them. And look at Kayla. She's not a burden to live with—quite the opposite."

"I think your coming to Qalerim will be a good thing for Kayla," he said. "She needs a friend closer to her age than Selina."

"I'm glad to think I can be of some help—for as long as I'm here."

He shot me a quick look. "And how long might that be?"

I hesitated. Thinking of Kayla and Selina brought Daria and Daisy to mind. I had friends back home who also needed me. I trusted they had evaded the guards like I had, but they were still in danger.

"I don't know," I said at last. "But not forever, I hope."

His posture relaxed slightly. "No, certainly not forever. Hopefully none of you will be stuck in that ruin forever."

I frowned, trying to puzzle out the meaning behind his emotions. But when the silence drew out uncomfortably, I spoke, keeping my voice light.

"Maybe someone will come along who's the same age as Selina, too."

He immediately stiffened. "Let's hope not."

"Not?" I gave him a look of open surprise, hoping for once to get an answer.

He glanced quickly at me and then away.

"She's so young," he said. "I wouldn't wish for anyone else her age to find themselves at Qalerim."

I frowned, turning my focus back to the path ahead of us. "No, of course. I wasn't thinking."

I threw a final, darting glance sideways. His words made sense, but I couldn't shake the feeling that something else lay behind the heat of his response.

I spotted the end of the trail, not far below us at this point and, with a start, remembered my purpose in accompanying him. It was far too easy to lose track of my plans in his presence.

"I'll stop here," I said with a forced smile.

He looked for a moment as if he might protest, but with a quick look at the city in front of us, he nodded, wishing me farewell and thanking me again for my company. Freshly reminded of my duplicitous intentions, I could barely return his friendly salutations.

He left, an expression of mild concern on his face, and I shook myself. I couldn't lose focus.

Turning back, as if I meant to return the way we had come, I rounded a bend that hid me from sight. Darting down a side path, I clambered down a steep slope. Kayla had pointed out the thin track to me, explaining it was a more direct route to the city but that none of them ever took it unless they were alone and in a hurry. It was too steep and rough for comfort.

Moving faster than was safe, I slid the rest of the way and dashed between two enormous boulders. Peering around one of them, I spotted Zaid stepping onto the road. He was striding quickly now, his eyes on the level of the sun where it hung low in the sky.

Did he have something to get back to? That might help my purpose, if so. I wanted to see where Zaid lived and what he did with his days when he wasn't with us, and it wouldn't help me if he wandered around the shopping districts instead of returning home.

He joined the road ahead of a caravan of travelers. They had a mix of camels, donkeys, and carts, so they hadn't come from the desert. Perhaps a local could have identified their origin more easily, but I could only guess as to whether they had come from one of the internal regions of Ardasira or from neighboring Kuralan.

As they passed me, I seized the opportunity they provided and slipped out onto the road. With them as a screen between us, I could keep closer to Zaid.

When we stopped at the end of the short line waiting to pass through the gate, I began to worm my way through, utilizing my small size and doing my best to look young and harmless. A few of the travelers called lazy reprimands, but none of them gave me a second look.

I had soon worked my way close enough to the front to see two farmers with a hand cart who were in conversation with the guards at the gate. I frowned.

The farmers had been arriving at the gate as Zaid joined the road. He had definitely been between them and the large group of travelers. But I could see no sign of him now. Peering around the closest camel, I scanned the empty ground surrounding the road. There was no sign of him.

He had to be on this road. I had seen him join it, and it only led to the one gate. The trek to another gate involved circling much of the city.

I darted among the travelers, my eyes slipping over the milling crowd, waiting for their turn. Perhaps Zaid had merged with them, just as I had done. I could see no sign of him, however.

Confusion and concern whirled through my mind. A person couldn't just vanish. Not from the middle of the road.

But that was exactly what Zaid had done. He was gone.

I let the travelers sweep me into the city with their group, searching the streets near the gate. But I could find no sign of my friend. As the sun sank lower in the sky, I had to concede defeat. I couldn't risk returning home in the dark until I was far more familiar with the trails and the mountain itself.

And there seemed little point to the search, anyway. As long as I kept close to Zaid, I had retained some hope of tailing him in an unfamiliar city. Now that I had lost him, it would have required an enormous stroke of luck to find him again.

My initial unreasoning fear for his safety had faded by the time I trudged back up the mountain path. If an accident had befallen him, it could not have gone unnoticed so near the gate guards. Instead I had to concede that I had overestimated my own skill. Once again.

Previously that thought had stung on a personal level, but now it terrified me. I was all the Four Kingdoms had, and I was apparently much less prepared than I had thought.

As I pulled back the branches and stepped into the semi-darkness of Qalerim, I balled up my fists. I would just have to confront Zaid when he returned and demand answers. But as I walked toward my apartment, my hands gradually relaxed.

Did I intend to tell Zaid I had attempted to spy on him? He had shown me nothing but kindness despite my strange arrival and my own reticence. He had seen Aron and Samar and knew I was being less than forthcoming, and yet he had never pressed me for answers.

The earlier shame I had felt in his presence rushed back. Now that I had paused for reflection, I knew why I had decided Zaid was different from the others. For all I liked Kayla and Selina, he was the one I most desired to confide my story to.

But the safety of too many people hung on my every action. And with each passing day, I only proved the foolishness of my own heart. I couldn't risk confiding in someone whom I knew nothing about. Without knowing his circumstances, I couldn't know how he would react. His loyalty and integrity might be the very traits that would require him to report my presence to some unknown official whom he knew and valued far better than he did me. I sensed that Zaid was the type who would always do what was best for his kingdom, regardless of his personal feelings.

And so I wanted to determine his place in Sirrala and untangle his loyalties. I wanted to know I could confide in him without risking all the people I had left behind—or losing his respect. In short, I was once again thinking with my heart not my head.

I groaned. Why was it that the older I got, the more confusing everything became? Wasn't it supposed to grow clearer? And yet the certainty that had once gripped me when I prowled the hidden corridors of my uncle's castle seemed beyond elusive now.

Then it had seemed only natural that I should be privy to all my uncle's strategies. But now I found myself wondering why I thought I deserved answers from Zaid when I wasn't willing to give him any of my own. I could argue that I had good reason for keeping my secrets—reasons involving more people than just myself—but for all I knew, the same could apply to him. If I couldn't be friends with him without knowing his background, then he couldn't be friends with me, either.

The thought of losing our growing connection stung, making my steps falter. I considered the matter from another perspective. Could Zaid—a single person, and one not trained in spycraft or owing loyalty to the Four Kingdoms—really provide any significant assistance in my mission? Or was it just the comfort of a shoulder to lean on and a friend to confide in that I sought?

I was immediately forced to concede that it was the latter. My obsession with knowing more about him was personally motivated, and the wasted efforts of the day only demonstrated that the issue was distracting me from the more important purpose of finding out about Malik.

I shook myself. I wouldn't demand anything from Zaid, and neither would I attempt to follow him again. Clearly my spycraft needed more work than I had thought, but I would practice on Malik and his servants. The sooner I could find out the breadth and details of the plot against the Four Kingdoms, the sooner I could return home.

And I would be returning home. Which meant my personal reasons for wanting to know more about Zaid were irrelevant. I had already decided I was not going to allow myself to fall for him, and my heart would simply have to keep in line.

# PART II
# THE ANCIENT CITY

# CHAPTER 13

*Z*aid delivered the parchments as promised, and I began work on the book. Every day I made the trek into Sirrala, taking my position beneath the windows of Malik's servants' hall. I had long ago learned that boredom was the most difficult part of an intelligencer's role, so I made use of the time to sketch those parts of Qalerim I already knew.

My arrival and departure times differed each day in an effort to prevent being noticed by any of the household. The small adjustments also gave me the chance to observe different parts of the day—I even spied Malik himself on one occasion when he was leaving home after the midday meal.

But with each day that passed, I grew more frustrated. Malik's servants didn't even respect him, let alone fear him. They gave no sign they served a master bent on domination and destruction. And when I heard his name mentioned in the streets and markets of the city, he was talked of as a benevolent—if ineffectual—force in the kingdom.

I began to actually hope I did have the wrong Malik. If Aron and Samar truly answered to the Grand Vizier, then the man was both cunning and expert at concealing his activities. Alone in a strange land, with my erratic emotions betraying me, I no longer trusted my ability to get past his defenses.

Not that my capability—or lack of it—changed anything, of course. I had to try anyway.

As the daylight faded on my eighth day of surveillance, I packed my parchment away in my pack, having just mapped out the last of the tunnels I already knew. I had never stayed so late before, but I finally felt confident enough in the path back into Qalerim to risk staying out after dark. I needed to try watching at night because I couldn't keep coming here day after day and making no progress.

The servants ate their evening meal while I dined on a dry cake and a handful of dates which Sari had brought back to Qalerim the day before. Kayla had given me her share of the dates, claiming she didn't like them, which seemed impossible to me. Of the new foods I had tried since coming to Ardasira, they were easily my favorite.

Some of the servants lingered to talk in the hall, but eventually they all filtered out, heading to their beds. Still I waited.

But when my head jerked, returning me to consciousness after a moment of unintended sleep, I gave up. No one had come into the hall or garden since the last of the servants had gone to bed, so there was nothing to be gained by remaining here under the window.

Crawling to the end of the bush, I paused as I always did to check for passersby. The instinct saved me since a second later I heard the front door open followed by the murmur of low voices. I froze, goosebumps breaking out all over my skin as my subconscious recognized one of them before my scrambling thoughts caught up.

Samar.

My hands trembled, but I forced myself to carefully peer around the corner of the building. A lantern burned beside the elaborate front door illuminating Aron and Samar standing a few paces away from Malik. Samar looked the same as ever, but Aron leaned on a stout wooden cane, a binding of some sort still wrapped around one leg.

He neither spoke nor looked directly at Malik, instead staring out into the garden with an inscrutable expression. The rumble of wheels grew louder, and a carriage appeared up the long carriageway that led from the street to Malik's front door.

As soon as it arrived, Aron struggled into it, neither asking nor receiving help despite his injury. Samar, however, lingered, turning a disgusted expression on the vehicle.

"Get inside and be gone," Malik said in an icy voice. "I have more important matters to attend to."

Even in the semi-darkness I could see the deadly light in Samar's eyes, but Malik didn't flinch despite Samar looming over him in size.

"You're neither of you any good to me damaged, and I clearly can't trust you to manage people," the Vizier said, his voice almost as deadly as Samar's expression. "Don't expect to be called back to the capital any time soon. You can work with the army until I find a use for two such useless servants."

Samar growled, but when he snapped into motion, it was only to follow Aron into the carriage. Malik looked up at the driver.

"Take them south to our camp. And don't waste time on the way."

"Aye, Your Eminence."

The driver tipped his head before calling to the horses and guiding them back toward the road. Malik, clearly both demanding and expecting total obedience, didn't wait to see the carriage disappear.

As soon as the front door had closed behind him, I slumped against the side of the building. I had found my answer. The Malik I sought was indeed the Grand Vizier.

When I finally got myself moving again, I jumped at shadows all the way up the track to Qalerim, not feeling secure until the tunnel walls closed around me. Malik was clearly displeased with his two lieutenants—although whether they had committed some fresh transgression or whether Aron had only just recovered enough to travel, I had no way of knowing. But their absence from the city was certainly a weight off my mind, at least.

"Cassie!" Kayla bounced out of one of the chairs in the living room as soon as I stepped through the apartment door.

"What are you still doing awake?" I slung my pack onto the floor and collapsed onto a cushion. "I'm only half awake myself."

"I may have nodded off in the chair," Kayla acknowledged with a grin. "But I couldn't go to bed until I knew you'd made it back. It was your first time coming up the trail in the dark."

She announced the fact proudly, as if I were a favored pupil finally finding independence.

"And as you can see, I survived." I followed the words with a long yawn. "So next time you won't need to wait up."

"Are you intending to jaunt around at night frequently?" Kayla asked, sounding half curious, half surprised.

"Are you going to keep spending your time searching for a treasure that probably doesn't exist?"

She shrugged, and we both let the topic drop as we always did.

Sitting up, I pulled the parchments out of my bag. "I have the latest pages for the map." I thrust them at her. "They're now updated with everything I've so far explored in here."

"Sounds like tomorrow I need to take you deeper into the mountain," she said, a concerning sparkle in her eyes.

I groaned. "Please don't tell me you have something disgusting hidden away in some nook. I'm too tired."

Kayla laughed. "You're getting me confused with Josef. He showed poor Elias a rotting goat carcass on his first foray into the tunnels." She shook her head while I squeaked in disgust. "I'll take you to some of the best views. And there's even a spiral staircase."

I stood up and stumbled toward the door to the bedrooms, waving a hand back in her direction. "It all sounds lovely. Absolutely delightful. For tomorrow."

Her chuckles chased me to bed. But I had ample opportunity to regret my acquiescence when I was woken by an enthusiastic Selina at the crack of dawn. When she told me it wasn't the crack of dawn but rather a quite advanced hour of the morning, I pulled my pillow over my head and tried to go back to sleep anyway. The girl had persistence, however, and all too soon I was sitting in the kitchen, sipping a hot drink.

Usually it took little effort to commit the tunnels I visited to memory, but I struggled to focus on this occasion. I wrestled my mind into submission, however. I had promised the qaleri a book of maps, and I didn't mean to let them down.

I had intended to head back into the city in the late afternoon, ready to watch into the night again. But after very little sleep followed by a day clambering around inside the mountain, I had to skip the trip. Although I didn't like to wait now that I had the first hint of evidence, I couldn't afford to make a mistake due to fatigue.

After that, I settled into a routine. In the morning, I went exploring inside Qalerim, building my mental map as I went. I often went on my own since I moved at a much faster pace than the others, who were conducting a more thorough search. But my favorite days were when Zaid turned up at Qalerim in time to accompany me. He claimed it was safer to visit such remote corners in pairs, but I suspected he had developed something of a love for rediscovering ancient and forgotten places.

He told insightful and entertaining stories about Sirrala and its people, although he still avoided speaking of his background or current circumstances. And since I now spent a part of each day in the city, I was able to avoid looking completely ignorant as he spoke of the more prominent inhabitants.

It didn't take long to realize the lessons I had learned listening to my uncle's strategy meetings applied to much of the politics and trade of Sirrala as well. People were, at heart, much the same everywhere, although the trappings looked different.

After my explorations, I always snatched a quick nap before walking into Sirrala well before it got dark. The daylight hours I spent wandering the streets and markets, but the night was spent keeping vigil at Malik's house—or at least the first half of the night. I needed some sleep, and thankfully Malik did as well.

He seemed most active in the hours around midnight, and by lurking in the garden, I could usually follow him when he did emerge. He was always alone, apparently conducting his active nocturnal life in secret, even from his own household.

The cover of night and the reduced traffic on the roads made it much easier to follow him. On the first night, I expected Malik to go to the palace, but it was the one place he never went. Instead, each night he visited other houses or shops, conducting quiet meetings with rich merchants and tradesmen—even, on one occasion, a captain of the guard.

When I could listen to the conversations, I did. But more often I had no way to follow him into a building and instead had to resort to investigating the premise or asking about its occupant in the market the next afternoon. In this manner I soon built a picture of Malik's activities.

By day he might be the loyal Grand Vizier, but at night he masterminded a network of influential players. From the rumors in the market, he dealt exclusively with those who were known for being underhanded, duplicitous, and dishonest—by reputation if not proven fact. Some nights he took packages with him, or returned with a small cart, laden with supplies that remained hidden beneath a canvas covering.

How many of the dishonest dealings discussed in low voices in the market were carried out by these merchants on behalf of Malik? He must have amassed a fortune based on the breadth and frequency of his dealings.

The conversation with the captain of the guard was one of the few that took place outside, allowing me to edge close enough to hear their murmured words. As I listened, one apprehension grew while another lessened. The man's surreptitious words and darting eyes clearly confirmed Malik's preparation for an invasion was being done without the knowledge and approval of the sultan. I had been hoping as much, but the confirmation still provided relief. The danger to the Four Kingdoms remained, but stopping it felt more achievable when the crown wasn't involved.

The bulk of their conversation was less reassuring, however. From what I could follow, Malik had tasked the captain with recruiting soldiers to his cause. While he had found few takers in Ardasira, Kuralan had fallen on harder times recently, and a large number of men were willing to turn mercenary with the promise of good pay and new opportunities.

Not even the captain seemed to know what Malik intended to do with the army he was gathering at the mysterious southern camp, and my disgust for the man grew. He had joined the effort purely for his own enrichment, and he didn't care who these men might be enlisted to hurt.

As they prepared to part ways, he asked a final question. "You still want me to keep gathering soldiers up until the weather starts to cool?"

"If my orders change, you will certainly know about it."

Malik somehow turned the words into a threat, and the captain visibly swallowed before hurrying off into the night. I remained frozen in place in the deepest shadow I had been able to find, not moving until long after Malik disappeared. Despite the tinge of fear, I felt lighter than I had in weeks, though.

I had time. Summer hadn't even begun yet, so I still had months before Malik intended to make a move. It certainly made sense that he wouldn't want to attempt marching an army across the desert during the warmer months.

As I hurried back up the mountain trail, my feet seeming to

fly, I realized the night was more than half over—meaning it was officially my birthday.

"Happy birthday to me," I whispered, and was hit with a painful pang of home sickness at the thought of my uncle. He had always made a big deal of my birthday, apparently following the tradition begun by my mother and aunt. And this was my eighteenth, so he would have insisted on all kinds of celebrations.

What was he doing now? What was everyone back home doing? Would he have sent Olvin to Arcadia to search for me when news reached them I was missing? Olvin would certainly have done his duty and gone, but the effort would do him no good. If I was to ever see them again—or my other missing friends—I would have to find a way back myself.

# CHAPTER 14

The next morning when I rolled out of bed, it took me a moment to place the light, happy feeling that filled me. Then I remembered I had two reasons to feel glad: there was still time before the invasion, and today was my birthday.

Another pang hit me at the thought of my uncle. Hopefully he and Olvin were together, comforting each other in their reserved sort of way.

My bedroom door crashed open, and Selina catapulted inside, driving the melancholy thoughts from my mind.

"Hurry up!" She took me by the arm and started to tow me out of the room.

"Selina!" Kayla stood inside the living area, hands on her hips and flour lightly dusted across her clothes. "I told you to let her sleep."

"I did! Half the morning's gone."

Kayla threw an apologetic look at me. "Sorry, Cassie. I did tell her to let you be."

I laughed. "I don't mind. What's that amazing smell?"

"I made fresh fruit bread." Kayla looked inordinately pleased with herself.

"Bread?" I hurried over to peek inside the kitchen.

135

We never had fresh bread. It took too long to make, so the qaleri contented themselves with longer lasting supplies they could lug up from Sirrala.

"Happy Birthday!" Selina cried, the words bursting out of her, and Kayla repeated them with almost as large a grin.

"How did you know?" I asked, sure I hadn't mentioned the date to Kayla.

"I told them," said a deeper voice from the doorway, reminding me there was one person I had told.

I spun around to give Zaid a mock glare that turned into a glad cry when I saw Elias grinning over his shoulder.

"Happy Birthday," Elias said. "I thought I would bring you the best possible present—me."

Kayla groaned, but Selina greeted him with unabated good cheer. She insisted he take a seat in case the journey back had strained the injured muscles which were still regaining their strength. But she didn't wait for him to sit down before launching into a litany of complaints about Kayla as a search partner.

Elias seemed content to listen to her grumbles, lapping up the implied praise for his own companionship, so I turned to Zaid, unable to help smiling at him.

"Don't be angry," he said before I could speak again. "Kayla forced it out of me."

I shook my head as I watched the other girl triumphantly bear her baked creation out of the kitchen on a wooden board.

"She's certainly a force to be reckoned with. I'll forgive you because I can't remember the last time I smelled something so utterly delightful." I turned a suspicious look on him. "It's awfully early in the day to be bringing Elias back, though. You knew Kayla was going to be baking, didn't you?"

"I admit nothing," Zaid said, but the twinkle in his eyes betrayed him. He held out a package wrapped in plain cotton. "Does it help my case that I brought you a gift?"

I hesitated, unsure if I should accept when I had no way to reciprocate. But when our eyes met, my hands reached out on their own accord to accept it. I couldn't insult him by refusing when I knew he expected nothing in return except my thanks and friendship.

Letting the cotton covering fall, I held up a desert wrap. Unlike the one I had worn across the desert—which had chafed my skin and which Kayla had immediately repurposed into a sturdy rug for our new apartment—the material was light and airy and soft. The tan color wouldn't draw attention—something for which I was grateful—but there was no doubt it was a quality piece of clothing.

"Thank you," I said, trying to put my emotion into the simple words. "It's beautiful."

Zaid looked as if he wanted to say something back, but several people crowded through the door behind him, breaking the moment.

"What's that smell?" Patrin asked before Josef let out a triumphant crow at sight of the loaves.

"It's Cassie's birthday, which means we all get a holiday," Selina cried, and a general cheer went up.

"In Qalerim, every birthday is a holiday," Sari explained when she saw my bewildered look. "And any day there's a royal procession, too. On those days we go down to the city to wave at the sultan and sultana with everyone else."

She hurried toward the table before I had a chance to reply. I watched her go with a shake of my head.

"Given their excitement, you'd think they had a harsh overseer here forcing them to go searching the city every day," I whispered to Zaid.

I expected him to laugh, but instead he looked concerned.

"I've never seen anyone in Qalerim other than us," I quickly reassured him. "But I'm pleased to learn they do take breaks."

An odd shadow still lurked in his eyes, but Elias called to him, and he strolled over to join the boy, leaving me free to receive another round of birthday wishes.

Only half my mind was on the conversations, however, as I clutched my new robe against my chest, feeling again its softness. Even after all these weeks, much about Zaid was still in doubt. But I couldn't doubt his thoughtfulness.

I made a sudden decision. Once I had the full picture of Malik's plans—and hopefully some evidence to back my story up—Zaid would be the first person I would tell. I would ask him to believe me, and to help me save the Four Kingdoms. Now that I knew the invasion wasn't sanctioned by the crown, I had to believe he would be willing to aid such a desperate cause, even if it wasn't his own people in danger.

For a few days, the possibility of sharing the truth with Zaid filled me with equal parts nerves and excitement. But as the weeks continued to pass, panic slowly took their place.

The timeline that had once seemed so generous shrunk, contracting with each passing day. Weeks passed, and still I had no evidence of Malik's plans or even any substantial details of what they might be.

An inescapable conclusion grew. I needed to take my spying to the next level. I needed to break into Malik's house and search it, top to bottom, until I found the evidence I needed.

The certainty of it grew in my belly first, my thoughts taking longer to catch up, and it made me hesitate. Was my impatience—my desire to make progress, and to tell Zaid the truth—influencing my good sense? If I misstepped inside Malik's house, the consequences would be dire—and not just for me personally.

But although I waited, thinking it through from every angle, I could see no other option. I had to go in.

For a whole week I resumed my old position below the windows, once again sinking into the rhythm and routine of Malik's household. Eventually I could put it off no longer, however. Despite my fear of making a wrong move, I had to do something. The confidence that had led me to throw myself into Aron and Samar's wagon seemed like the naivety of youth now— a folly belonging to a far distant person. But somehow I had to muster the courage to act.

I lingered over my last meal with my housemates before the incursion. Zaid was with us, so it was a jovial occasion, out of step with my mood. As I ate, I debated giving them a hint of where I was going in case something went wrong. But I couldn't think of a way to give them the necessary information without the whole complicated, unbelievable story coming tumbling out with it. And besides, what could a bunch of orphans do if the Grand Vizier of Sirrala arrested an intruder in his home?

I caught Kayla watching me, however, as if she could sense something was wrong. I silently resolved that she would be the second person to learn the truth after Zaid. I owed it to her after all her generosity.

When I stood up to clear away the dishes, Zaid instantly joined me. I pretended I didn't see the looks he gave me in the semi-privacy of the kitchen, as if inviting me to tell him what was on my mind. Clearly Kayla hadn't been the only one to notice my abstraction.

My resolution to wait and tell him about Malik's plans only when I had some solid evidence to back my claims wavered. Zaid wasn't an indigent orphan. Maybe if something went wrong, he really could help me in some way.

But just as my good sense was buckling under the weight of my emotions, Kayla called through from the main room.

"Zaid! Cassie is about to walk into Sirrala, despite the late hour. You can keep her company."

I smiled at the evidence of her concern, but the expression dropped when I saw Zaid's face. Far from looking pleased at the prospect, his features had frozen, as if he had locked them in place while he thought of an adequate excuse.

"Actually," he said after a moment that stretched on just a

fraction too long, "I need to go next door to talk to Josef after this." He turned to me with something close to his normal smile. "Sorry, Cassie."

I murmured the right response while my insides soured. I had never once seen Zaid inside Sirrala. It was almost as if he didn't actually live in the city at all. I shook off the ridiculous thought. This was why I needed to remain focused instead of letting myself get bogged down by emotion. Today of all days, I couldn't lose my head.

The walk down to the city passed impossibly quickly despite the lack of company, and I slipped inside the gate shortly before it was closed for the night. I glanced once at the small door that lay beside it—the one that could be opened only from the inside and gave citizens access out of the city at night. For once I didn't expect to be using it again in only a few hours. I would almost certainly be in Malik's house all night—if not longer. I had enough experience of such ventures to know it was a real possibility I could get stuck in some cupboard or nook for the entire next day.

I patted the water skin and small pouch I wore slung over my back. The pouch contained some basic snacks that would be welcome in such a scenario, although I hoped I didn't have cause to use them.

I didn't waste time in the markets or streets, heading straight to Malik's house. Once there, I concealed myself in the garden and waited. I wouldn't attempt entry into the house unless Malik was absent. If he didn't leave, I would come back the next night. But I hoped it wouldn't come to that. Having keyed myself up, I wanted to make my move now.

As the hours dragged on, I walked my memory palace in my mind. I had filled it with a myriad of small details, but major connections still eluded me. Malik's dishonest business dealings had amassed enough gold to fund a small army, but it wasn't enough men to safely invade four entire kingdoms—even if they were unsuspecting. Clearly he had some other trick up his sleeve.

I massaged the sides of my head. At the moment, my entire story sounded implausible. Without the missing element, it would be too easy to dismiss. But if I could discover the nature of that key strategy, perhaps I could find some way to sabotage it?

The sound of the front door brought me to full attention. Malik slipped out and strode off toward the road, and for the first time I didn't follow him. Instead, I crawled behind the now familiar bushes, popping up beneath the second window along— the one with a faulty latch. One of the maids had been complaining about it days ago, and I had filed the information away for later use.

Working the screen open took little time, and I had soon hoisted myself over the windowsill and dropped silently into the room. For a moment I took the chance to look around me. The room felt even larger from the inside, a testament to the size of Malik's household.

I didn't linger too long, however. Malik wouldn't conceal any secrets in a room belonging to the servants.

Hurrying into the dark hall, I searched for the stairs down to the basement, intending to start my search there. But unlike the great houses from my cold, snowy home, this house didn't have any below ground level. Changing strategy on the spot, I decided instead to start with the top of the house, thinking I might find some sort of attic there.

The main staircase curved gracefully up two flights, and I crept up it, with every muscle tightly on edge. I felt exposed tiptoeing up stairs clearly designed to attract attention. But Malik had no family beyond his spoiled daughter, Jamila, so with Malik himself out of the house, I was far less likely to run into anyone on the main stairs than on the ones used by the servants.

No lanterns or candles had been left burning, confirming the idea that Jamila had retired for the night and the household didn't know of Malik's nighttime wanderings. The darkness surrounded me like a comforting cocoon, my eyes swiftly adjusting to the faint glow from the moonlight that made it through the window screens.

When I reached the top level, I crept quietly along the hall. The whisper of murmured voices sent me flying back to the stairs, however, my heart almost pounding out of my chest. The servants might all be in their rooms, but they weren't all asleep.

I abandoned any plans of searching the top floor. It appeared to house only the rooms of the servants, so it was unlikely to bear fruit anyway. The middle level looked more promising, but although I crept through a ballroom, a library, and a number of guest suites, I saw nothing out of the ordinary for the home of a royal advisor.

Twice when I pressed my ear to a closed door, I heard the quiet sounds of a sleeper and was forced to bypass that suite. Since none of the empty rooms looked as if they were in use, I was forced to conclude that one of the occupied rooms belonged to Malik. He must have a manservant who slept on hand, ready to wait on him whenever he needed assistance. Was the man in his confidence, maintaining the illusion of his presence should there be some disturbance in the household during the night?

I didn't dare confirm my theory by checking the occupied rooms, and my spirits dropped. If Malik kept the evidence I sought in his bedchamber, my efforts would prove futile.

Returning to the ground floor, I came upon an enormous kitchen. I had barely stepped inside, however, before a soft footfall sounded in the hall behind me. My eyes latched on a small door in one wall, and I flew to it, snatching it open and then easing it silently closed. Feeling around the small cupboard, I breathed a sigh of relief that I had sought shelter among a collection of brooms and not in the pantry. If the interloper had come in search of a late-night snack, the pantry was the last place I wanted to be.

As if to confirm the thought, someone began to mutter quietly over the sounds of rummaging. It took me a moment to place the voice, but I eventually recognized it as belonging to one of the grooms. A moment later his words confirmed it. From his grumbles, he had been up late helping to birth a foal.

Retrospective fear flooded me. He must have entered the house carrying a lantern, and the side door to the stables opened onto the wide entranceway in easy view of the main staircase. For all my attempts to take care, if I had come down them even moments later, I could easily have been spotted.

The minutes ticked by, each one seeming to last an hour, but eventually the man finished whatever leftovers he had managed to pilfer and ambled back out the way he had come. I waited several long breaths before easing out of the cupboard.

I had hoped to be finished before Malik returned from his night's activities, but too much time was passing. I took a moment to consider. Peeking through the windows had given me some idea of the rooms to be found on the ground floor. Many of them—like the sitting rooms and family dining room—were as unlikely to hold Malik's secrets as the kitchen or the servants' hall. If I wanted to make best use of my remaining time, I should head straight for Malik's study.

My spirits lifted as soon as I tried the handle and found it locked. It was the first room I had found barred to me which seemed more than promising.

Extracting the lock picks from my hair, I set to work on the lock. When the door swung open mere moments later, I tutted quietly to myself. There wasn't much point in such a weak protection.

Once inside, I relocked the door from the inside. I didn't want to risk Malik returning in the night and surprising me, or even an overly conscientious servant coming past to check the door remained secure.

The room contained a number of bookshelves, their handsome, leather-bound contents looking untouched. I shook my head as I headed straight for the enormous desk in the middle of the room. Clearly built to impress, the legs curved in elegant lines, and the dark mahogany of the wood shone.

My only interest lay in the drawers, however. The lock on each one required a little more effort than the one on the door, but they weren't complex enough to foil me.

The treasure trove of papers inside took longer to sift through. As I flipped from page to page, the pressure inside grew stronger and stronger—the roiling in my stomach transforming into a band around my chest that clenched tighter with the passing minutes. The servants would rise early, and I had to be gone well before then. I couldn't risk being caught in the house or being seen climbing back out the window by an early stroller in the garden outside.

But at the same time, I didn't want to leave. As I finished examining the contents of each drawer, I told myself the next one would contain what I sought. So far, everything had related to the daytime activities of the Vizier. I hadn't seen so much as the name of any of his nighttime associates listed on any of the papers.

When I reached the bottom of the final drawer, my stomach dropped, and the twisting anxiety inside doubled its efforts. There was nothing here. But surely Malik must keep a record of his dealings somewhere. He conducted far too much business to do it all from memory, and he didn't strike me as a man who would accept being cheated because he failed to remember a crucial detail.

My mind fixated on the occupied room upstairs. Did he keep all the records in his suite of personal rooms, then? My eyes flew around the study, desperately seeking something that might hold answers. But the shining marble of the enormous fireplace stared back at me, as blank and empty as my mind.

Reluctantly I turned back to the door before halting suddenly and swinging back to stare at the fireplace. It did indeed gleam, the white pristine and bright. While I didn't doubt the diligence of the maids, that shining expanse of white didn't look as if it had ever seen a speck of soot.

With summer drawing to a close, there was no need for fires in every hearth. But I had experienced night in the desert, and I didn't doubt some sort of heating would be needed in the colder months. So why did this fireplace look as if it had never been used?

I hurried over, fresh hope surging within. How had I nearly missed such an important clue? Secret rooms and passageways were as familiar to me as the tunnels of Qalerim.

I didn't have long, but I made myself move slowly, taking a step back to run my eye over the lines of the fireplace. The elaborate carvings decorating the mantle made my lips curl upward. The perfect hiding place.

Stepping close, I ran my hands over the design, feeling each knot and whorl and flower. I moved with painstaking care, and my patience was rewarded. As I neared the middle of the mantel, a small carving of a rose gave slightly under my questing fingertips. I pushed harder, and the entire shape of the flower depressed by at least an inch.

Without a sound, the back of the fireplace slid aside.

Lantern light shone out from the space on the other side, and I blinked several times, my satisfaction replaced by fear. Was someone already inside the hidden cavity?

But no one spoke or moved, and I mustered the courage to step inside.

Experience told me there would be a mechanism for closing the door somewhere, but I didn't waste time searching for it. Dawn was approaching too quickly, and I couldn't risk ending up stuck in here where there might not be anywhere to hide if Malik came in.

Instead I stepped into the middle of the room and looked

around. Shelves lined every wall except where they left a small gap for another door. I barely noticed the other exit, however, my eyes instantly drawn to what filled the shelves.

In neat rows, hundreds of vials stood upright in wooden stands. Familiar vials.

With a trembling hand, I drew the single vial I had stolen from the camel out of my pouch. I never went anywhere without it.

Cold washed over me as I looked between the vial in my hand and the ones stored in this hidden room. It wasn't my imagination—they were identical, down to the slight mist of the gas, trapped behind the glass.

After a long, frozen moment, my gaze fixed on the only other item on the shelves. Along the bottommost shelf of each set, a line of large, stoppered jugs stood.

Hesitant after my experience with the vial in the wagon, I picked one of them up and gave it a gentle shake. Liquid sloshed inside, reassuring me it wasn't just filled with more gas. I gently eased out the stopper.

Gingerly leaning forward, I sniffed at the liquid inside. Immediately I pulled my head back, inhaling gulping gasps of fresh air.

But when no darkness assailed my senses, I calmed. The smell was familiar but far less concentrated than the gas inside the vials. Had Malik turned the gas into this liquid, or had he turned the liquid into the gas?

As I put the jug back on the shelf, I shook my head. It didn't matter which had come first. Hidden in this room, Malik had the tools to incapacitate hundreds, if not thousands, of people. I had found the missing element of his plan.

# CHAPTER 15

*a* rattle from the study on the other side of the fireplace snapped me out of my shock. Someone was unlocking the door.

I didn't stop to think. In two strides I was back out of the hidden room. In the intensity of the moment, I didn't tremble or shake, my movements sharp and fast. Slamming my hand on the marble rose, I triggered the hidden door to close.

It was still slipping the rest of the way back into its place as I threw myself behind the large desk, just in time to hear the study door open. Squeezing my eyes shut, I held my breath as footsteps crossed the room. If Malik was coming to his desk, I had gambled wrong and would be discovered. But dark still lingered outside. If he was coming into his study now, surely it was the hidden room he sought.

Sure enough, the footsteps continued past the desk, stopping for a moment in front of the fireplace. I strained to hear the sound of the secret door opening and thought I heard the softest sigh as it slid away.

The footsteps resumed, only to cut off suddenly, as if a barrier had dropped between us. I waited another heartbeat and another. When I had counted to a hundred, I eased silently out from behind the desk. Sure enough, the fireplace had returned to its ordinary state with no sign anyone else had ever been in the room.

I glanced toward the screens that covered the windows—the ones that always stayed closed. Was that the first hints of dawn turning the black to deepest blue? Malik had been out late.

My nerves, shredded by the close call, told me to leave by the window at hand, but I suppressed the urge. I would have no way to re-latch the shutter from the other side to conceal my passage. I needed to stick to the plan and return the way I had come. I unlocked the study door easily from the inside but had to use my lock picks to secure it again from the outside. As soon as I was finished, I gave up all pretense of stealth and ran for the servants' hall. An early riser could be starting their day at any moment.

Throwing myself out the unlatched shutter, I fell into the bush beneath and had to fight my way free from the prickles. As soon as I could stand unhindered, I pulled the shutter back closed behind me and dropped down to make the now familiar crawl along the building.

At the corner, I hesitated as always, peeking out into the garden. A rustle made me pause while a youth, making use of the tunnel of gardens for some early morning errand, ran past. As soon as he was out of sight, I leaped out of the bushes and sprinted after him.

Long before I could catch him, however, I veered off and emerged onto the street. As the sky lightened, more and more traffic appeared around me, and by the time I reached the city gate, it had been opened for the day.

I passed through with only a curious look from one of the guards and headed straight for the nearest trail. It was only when I was half way up that I realized I had failed in my primary mission. I had left the hidden room empty handed, with no proof to show for my efforts.

∼

Even without concrete proof, I had to tell Zaid what I had discovered. I couldn't keep the information to myself. I would need to further explore that hidden room—and any that lay beyond it—and I needed someone to know the truth in case I never came back.

I prepared and ate breakfast the next morning in constant tension. Zaid didn't come every day, and I rarely knew in advance when to expect him. Everything in me wanted to take action, but I had no way to find him. I had to wait for him to come to Qalerim.

Kayla made several teasing comments about my distraction and the constant glances I threw at the door. Selina and Elias chuckled along, but I sensed an element of sympathy from them. They loved Zaid's visits as well.

All of the qaleri had accepted me by now, but I didn't generate the sort of enthusiasm he did. In me they recognized someone as alone as themselves, but it was something else that drew them to Zaid. Some indefinable quality that set him apart.

Perhaps it was his confidence and instinctive authority that called to a fractured group of youths without clear leadership. For all Kayla and Josef's seniority, neither of them were true leaders. While some of the qaleri responded to them, at least two rarely spoke to anyone, preferring to keep almost entirely to themselves. Yet even the reclusive ones liked Zaid.

I shook my head. It was more than that, though. Perhaps it was the kindness that lingered beneath the surface. The sort of kindness that motivated him to not only bring supplies to a group of orphans living outside the city but to take the time to befriend them.

Or maybe it was the light in his eyes. The way they pierced through you and convinced you that he fully saw you. Sitting at the breakfast table, I felt the heat rise to my cheeks. It was possible that last one was just me. As someone who had spent my life in the background, slipping through the shadows, there was something heady about being seen—about knowing that someone who commanded a room just by his presence had his full attention on me.

I balled my fists until my nails bit into my palms, interrupting my thoughts. With an exercise of will, I suppressed the flush, shutting down my daydreams about Zaid. It didn't matter that it felt like the desert sun had taken nest in my belly every time we happened to touch. I was supposed to be rehearsing the reasons it was safe to trust him despite his own secrets—convincing my mind I wasn't thinking with foolish emotions. Instead I was doing the opposite.

I shook my head. Head or heart, it didn't matter. I had to tell Zaid. Logical or not, he was the person I trusted most in Ardasira. Even if a small, hurt part of me wished he felt the same way about me.

I leaped from my chair the moment the door began to move, relief swelling inside me when it was Zaid who appeared and not one of the other qaleri. He gave me an odd look, making me wonder what he could read on my face. But there was no time for such irrelevancies.

"You're late," I announced, although I had no idea what the time was. "We need to go."

He blinked. "We do?"

He looked to the others for explanation of my strange behavior, and I caught Kayla shrugging out of the corner of my eye. I ignored their silent communication, calling a breezy farewell to the group and pulling Zaid straight back out the door.

"What's going on?" he asked as soon as it had closed behind us.

I shook my head. "Not here."

Concern replaced his confusion, and he looked as if he wanted to press me for more information. But after another piercing glance, he stayed quiet, instead taking the lead as we moved deeper into Qalerim, driving us to a faster pace.

As soon as we were safely ensconced in layers of deep rock, he stopped, turning to me with a look that was half curiosity, half determination.

"Tell me."

After my rush to get here, I suddenly found myself reluctant to speak. It was hard to know where to begin.

Reaching into my pack, I pulled out the small leather pouch that I had taken from the camel. Removing the vial, I held it up into a shaft of sunlight.

"Do you know what this is?" I asked.

He frowned, stepping forward to look more closely. Clearly whatever he had been expecting, it wasn't this.

"Can I open it?" he asked.

I pulled my arm back, shaking my head. "If you inhale the gas inside, you'll be unconscious for hours."

"Oh, it's nayera." He frowned. "Why do you have that? *How* do you have it?"

"I…" I hesitated. "I took it from someone."

Concern and displeasure warred on his face. "Why would you do that? Putting aside the issue of stealing, that's a dangerous item to carry around with you."

I winced at his obvious disappointment. But any attempt to defend myself against the accusation of theft required a long and involved story. I needed to know whatever he knew about nayera first.

"It's a strong vial," I said instead. "And the pouch keeps it safe."

He shook his head. "I don't mean the gas is dangerous—although it is. I mean you would be in serious trouble if anyone saw you with it. The sultan's decree prohibits anyone possessing nayera other than registered surgeons."

"Surgeons?" I stared at him, realization dawning. "Oh, they use it for patients during surgery!"

"Yes, of course." He examined me, his brows knit. "Did you really not know?"

"I've never heard of it." I bit my lip, thinking. "So no one else is allowed it? What about palace officials?"

"No, of course not. When the royal apothecary developed it several decades ago, the sultan at the time was concerned about its use as a weapon. But it's too valuable for use in medicine to ban it completely, so he permitted its development under the strictest conditions. The recipe is closely guarded and known only to the royal apothecary and his assistants. They manufacture it in small quantities and distribute it to the surgeons of the kingdom as needed."

"What about in liquid form?" I asked.

"Liquid?" Zaid took a step back, anger clouding his face. "Why would you even ask that?"

"I'm sorry. I'm just trying to understand. I saw—"

"You saw this—" He pointed at the vial I still clutched in my hand, "in liquid form?"

I nodded, fear taking hold in response to his unaccustomed anger.

"Why? What's so terrible about liquid nayera?" The vision of all those jugs lined up in the secret room filled my mind.

"In gas form, it renders someone unconscious. If you drink it, though, it's deadly. Even when diluted. That's why the sultan guards the composition so closely."

"Fatal?" My own voice sounded far away. "Even if diluted?"

The jugs seemed to parade before my eyes in endless procession. How many people could Malik kill if he poured those jugs into water sources across the Four Kingdoms? How much chaos could he sow?

Firm hands gripped my shoulders, giving me the tiniest of shakes.

"Cassie, why are you asking me about liquid nayera? Where have you seen it?"

I drew a deep breath. "In a secret room in Malik's house. He has hundreds and hundreds of these vials as well as dozens of jugs full of a liquid that smells like nayera gas. I found it last night."

Zaid's hands dropped, and he fell back two steps. "I…" He ran a hand through his hair. "I don't even know where to start. Malik, as in the Grand Vizier?"

"Yes, that Malik. But you said royal officials aren't permitted to have nayera."

"No one is permitted to have it in the quantities you're talking about! Not even the royal apothecary stores more than a few vials at a time. But…"

He swallowed, clearly struggling to process the news. How would he have reacted if I had started with the long list of other unbelievable things I was hiding? A surge of relief filled me that I hadn't let the whole story come pouring out in all its complicated confusion.

"*You* were inside a hidden room in Malik's house?" he eventually asked, settling on the least important element of the story.

"Never mind that," I said. "What are we going to do about it? We need to report it to someone."

His face turned grim. "We certainly do. If what you say is true…"

"Of course it's true! I've seen it with my own eyes!"

"Sorry." He frowned, although I didn't think the expression was for me. "I didn't mean I doubt you. It's just so incredible. Malik is…"

I waited for him to continue, but he didn't.

"He's the Grand Vizier, and therefore above reproach?" I filled in for him, unable to keep a note of impatience out of my voice.

Zaid shook his head. "No, of course not. Holding a position doesn't make you above reproach. You have to earn trust."

"And you think Malik has earned the sultan's trust?"

My unease must have sounded in my voice because Zaid

looked at me, some of the shock and concern in his face replaced with intense feeling.

"Whatever this is about, if Malik is involved in some sort of plot, it isn't with the knowledge of the sultan. Sultan Kalmir cares about his people—he wouldn't do anything to harm large numbers of them."

I bit my lip. "I certainly hope you're right," I said softly.

And I hoped the sultan cared about the people of other kingdoms as well—even kingdoms he'd never heard of before.

But maybe it wouldn't be necessary to bring the Four Kingdoms into the issue at all. My discovery of Malik's stores of nayera could solve all my problems. Letting the Ardasirans take care of Malik before he launched any of his plans would be a far preferable option to somehow beating the royal army across the desert in order to warn the Four Kingdoms they had unknown and bloodthirsty neighbors about to come calling.

"But you said it's a hidden room," Zaid said, sounding less certain.

My eyes flew to his face as I realized his concern.

"Yes. I don't think even his servants know about its existence."

"Obviously he'll deny having a secret room, let alone one full of illegal stores of nayera."

The excitement and hope drained out of me. "And I'm an unknown orphan. No one is going to believe my word over the Grand Vizier. They won't even search his house, let alone find the secret room."

"I could tell them I was the one to see the room," Zaid said, clearly thinking aloud.

My heart warmed at the expression of trust in that statement. Maybe he did trust me, after all, despite his lack of openness.

But he didn't notice my reaction, still chasing down the thread of his thoughts.

"That won't work, though. What possible reason could I give for having been in Malik's house investigating hidden rooms?

They'll guess I got the information from someone else, and they'll want to know who. But there's no way I'm involving you. When I can't give a good answer, Malik will argue I've been tricked by a lie planted by one of his rivals. And by the time anyone gets as far as investigating his house—if it comes to that at all—he'll have had a chance to move the nayera."

"I have this vial," I said, patting the pouch where it was once again tucked away. I didn't mention this particular one hadn't come from Malik's secret room.

Zaid sighed. "It's only one vial. It could have come from a surgeon or the royal apothecary. Now if we had a jug of the liquid…"

I shook my head vigorously. "Given your reaction just now, even if I had one, there is no way I would hand over a jug so that you could march into one of the sultan's public assemblies and present him with it. You'd be arrested on the spot."

For a moment Zaid looked as if he wanted to argue, but then he just shook his head. "It doesn't matter. We don't have a jug."

As soon as he capitulated, I relented. Perhaps he had some way to use it as evidence without endangering himself.

"I could go back tonight and get one," I suggested. A jug would be harder to conceal on my person than a vial, but if I timed my visit right it could be done. "Of course, after that, the sultan would need to move quickly because its disappearance would alert Malik that his secret has been discovered."

"No!" Zaid reached me in one stride, taking my shoulders again and looking down into my eyes. "On no account are you to sneak into the Grand Vizier's home a second time in order to smuggle out a jug of poison. Promise me you won't try."

I bit my lip. "But what if it's the only way?"

"No." He shook his head. "It can't be the only way. I know people of influence. I'll talk to them. I'll find a way to present the information to the sultan so that he believes it."

I hesitated, and he leaned in.

"Promise me you won't put yourself in danger, Cassie. Promise me you'll give me a chance. Do you trust me?"

When he put it like that, what choice did I have? Remembering his earlier statement of his own trust, I relented. "Fine, I won't go back to Malik's house until I hear from you."

He nodded. "Don't even go into Sirrala. Wait here until I return."

I agreed again, an invisible pressure lifting from my shoulders. After so many months, it was a relief not to carry the weight on my own.

We made our way straight back to the apartment, and Zaid left for Sirrala without even saying goodbye to the other qaleri. I didn't venture back out into the tunnels, instead pacing the room until I feared my endless circling thoughts would drive all reason from my mind. After that, to occupy my hands and keep the fears at bay, I sketched my most recent explorations.

Zaid did not return that evening, but I reminded myself it would take him time to devise a plan and talk to the necessary people. I reminded myself of that all the next day as well while I waited in the apartment for him to come. On the third day, I returned to the tunnels, unable to bear another day of idle waiting. I left a note on the table with a sketch of the section where I could be found. When I returned in the late afternoon, it still sat there, untouched.

Another day passed in the same way, and then another. By the end of the first week, I was locked in a constant internal battle about whether I should break my promise to Zaid and go into Sirrala. But what would I do when I got there? Despite all that had passed between us, I still had no idea where Zaid lived or worked.

By the end of the second week, I was finding it hard to eat, my stomach in constant knots. I told myself Zaid's plan might take time, but if it was taking longer than he'd expected, why hadn't he returned to give me an update on his progress? He'd never been away from Qalerim for so long.

He had asked me to trust him, and I told myself trust was enough. But no amount of reliving our conversation changed its outcome. Zaid had taken me seriously and had left to accuse Malik. And Zaid had not returned.

# CHAPTER 16

$\mathcal{I}$ slipped out the tunnel entrance and around the rock formation that kept it hidden from casual view. For once I didn't pause to take in the view. The anxiety that had been gnawing inside me for days drove me forward.

Hurrying down the goat track that gave quickest access to the western gate, my mind was too busy to pay more than cursory attention to my surroundings. I slipped into the city as I always did, not slowing until I reached the Grand Vizier's garden.

Malik wouldn't be there—I had chosen a public audience day on purpose to ensure it since he always stood at the sultan's side during public audiences. But even after their long absence, I still kept a wary eye out for Aron and Samar. If something had gone wrong with Zaid, Malik might have recalled his henchmen to the capital.

I saw only the usual servants moving about their business, however, along with a small but steady flow of visitors, come to admire the Vizier's carefully groomed garden. The regulars among them stood or sat in the calm beauty, soaking it in, while others passed through in small clumps, murmuring quiet praises or giving sudden exclamations as they came upon some new aspect. Some among them might even be those already on their way back from the palace, having been fortunate enough to secure one of the earliest audiences with the sultan.

Sudden determination seized me. If I could discover no sign of Zaid today, I would brave the court itself. Anyone was permitted to approach the sultan on a public audience day if they had need of justice. He would be unlikely to believe my tale, but if Zaid's life was on the line, I had to try.

I strolled behind a large clump of trees, struggling to keep the necessary air of calm unconcern. I'd learned long ago that when wanting to pass unnoticed, it was essential to look unconcerned about being seen. But it was harder than usual to maintain the posture with my pulse beating out the pace of my worries.

Where was Zaid?

Kayla and the others seemed entirely unconcerned about our friend, despite his long absence. When I pressed Kayla, she had replied vaguely, as if it was normal for him to stay away, although it was not. At least not during my time at Qalerim.

And while I tried to take comfort from her attitude, it did little to ease my tension. My friend didn't know that Zaid had gone into Sirrala to face off against Malik on my behalf.

I had questioned every qaleri who had been into Sirrala since Zaid left, and none of them had reported seeing him. Neither had they heard any talk of him on the street. I had even gone as far as to ask if there had been any disruptions at the palace or accusations made against the Grand Vizier. They had all declaimed any knowledge about unusual happenings in the city, hurrying to get away from my inquisitive conversation as quickly as possible.

If Zaid had not confronted Malik at the palace, my fear was that he had been caught in a more private confrontation—the sort that Malik might have been able to keep quiet. I had been over our conversation a hundred times in my head and concluded that Zaid's greatest concern had been the believability of his story. Was it possible he had decided to investigate Malik's house himself so as to lend his tale credibility?

I knew it was a desperate theory, based as much on my capacity to investigate it as anything else. I had no idea where to find Zaid, but Malik's household was a familiar target. If one of the servants had discovered him snooping around the house, there would surely be talk of it still.

Deeper fears ran beneath the surface, fears I constantly sought to suppress. I had watched Malik from the shadows for long enough to know that he was someone without compassion or compunction. If he had come upon Zaid alone...

I shivered at the thought. I couldn't believe Zaid—someone so full of life—could possibly be dead. I refused to consider it. Zaid had haryat sticks and knew how to use them. Surely he wouldn't have gone into Malik's home unarmed.

Alone now in a thick patch of greenery, I pulled Zaid's gift tighter around me. I had told myself I should wear the desert robe to conceal my identity in case Aron and Samar had indeed returned, but in truth it just made me feel closer to Zaid.

Dropping to my knees, I crawled behind the familiar row of prickle bushes, taking up my post beneath one of the large windows, open as usual to allow the morning breezes to flow through the servants' hall. I squirmed around until I found a comfortable position with my back against the wall and settled in to listen.

An hour passed and then another. My anxiety had been making sleep difficult at night, but the buzz of bees and the softly splashing water from a nearby fountain nearly lulled me into slumber. Still I heard nothing of interest. But I refused to give up and leave. I would stay here for as long as it took.

As another hour passed, I tried to break my mind from its endless circling. When I was younger, I never would have second-guessed myself so constantly. And I wouldn't have taken so long to follow after Zaid, despite my promise. Wasn't I supposed to gain more wisdom and certainty with age, not less?

I pushed that thought away, too. Allowing myself to dwell on self-doubt wouldn't help Zaid. Instead, I focused on the movements I could hear in the room behind me, walking my memory palace in my mind, as I often did when bored.

As I completed the mental exercises, I carefully stretched out one limb at a time to prevent myself from losing mobility after my long period of stillness. Servants moved in and out of the room, talking about the day's tasks or the movements of the Grand Vizier. I had spent enough time investigating this household to be able to identify many of them.

The maid who always worked longer and harder than all the others because she had dreams of rising to housekeeper one day. The cook who preferred making desserts, and the one who excelled at soups. The footman who was stealing silver, and the one who was hopelessly in love with Malik's beautiful but entitled daughter, Jamila. The groom who had forgotten to have Malik's favorite mount re-shod and only kept his position because the stable master covered for him.

If Zaid had been discovered, surely it had been by one of these people. They would probably have thought him a regular thief, but it would still have created a wave of excitement in the otherwise orderly household.

Two young women whose voices I didn't recognize took up positions by the window. From the sounds floating through the open frame, they were both engaged in needlework, and they chatted eagerly as they sewed. One of them had seen Sultan Kalmir's son on procession through the city the day before, and the two of them gushed about his handsome appearance and brave reputation.

I listened, my impatience rising. I didn't want to hear about the prince, I wanted to hear about Malik's activities and any hint of Zaid.

"I'm just glad Prince Zain didn't return from his trip with an announcement of his betrothal to Princess Adara."

I sighed. The maids were still talking about the prince.

"Yes," the other agreed. "He's far too handsome to waste on a Kuralani—even if she is a princess."

They both giggled as if they thought there was some chance they themselves might catch the eye of the prince. There must have been a delegation to Ardasira's neighbor which had just returned. It was strange none of the qaleri had mentioned it. There was a great deal of pomp and a number of processions every time the royals went anywhere, and my friends were usually eager to declare it a holiday and all troop into the city to join the watching crowds.

"Haven't you heard?" A new voice joined them, the breathless quality of the words suggesting this third maid had a juicy piece of gossip to share. "Jamila's personal maids haven't been able to talk of anything else."

She paused expectantly, and the others obediently filled the gap.

"Well? What is it?"

"Heard what?"

"Jamila told her maids this morning that with the prince returned, the sultan is going to announce their betrothal."

"What?!" one of them almost screamed before audibly slapping her hand over her mouth.

"Jamila to marry the prince?" the other cried, and I couldn't tell if she was horrified or giddy with excitement.

"I suppose she's the sultan's second option since he didn't come back from his trip with a marriage alliance," the first said with a hint of spite.

My earlier irritation with their topic had completely fallen away at this startling news. Jamila to marry the prince? That would make Malik and the sultan family. Any hope of convincing the sultan of Malik's perfidy started to vanish before my eyes.

A sharp gasp above my head made me flinch. All three maids surged to their feet, their embroidery clattering against the windowsill as it fell from their hands.

"It must be true!" one of them whispered. "He's here!"

I stiffened just as a familiar voice sounded from further inside the hall. Malik himself. He never visited the servants' hall. I had rarely seen him in daylight at all, although I occasionally caught sight of him from afar as he conducted his own small processions through the streets.

"As you can see, Your Highness," Malik said, "even in the servants' halls there are excellent examples of the sort of fine workmanship you have so admired elsewhere in the house. My grandfather, who commissioned the building and laid out the gardens, had an exquisite eye for detail."

"The prince!" breathed one of the maids.

They clearly considered his presence as confirmation of the coming alliance, and from the sounds above me, they had all completely abandoned their work and were avidly watching the tour.

Moving carefully, I turned around, still in a crouch, and raised my head as slowly as possible. As soon as my eyes cleared the windowsill, I froze, my gaze darting around the large hall.

As I had hoped, the three maids blocked anyone else in the room from getting a clear view of the top of my head, their backs turned to me while they kept their attention firmly fixed on the unexpected visitors to their domain. But with any luck, I would still manage a glimpse beyond them.

My curiosity roused at the news of the upcoming betrothal, I couldn't resist trying for a glimpse of the prince who was to marry Malik's daughter. While I had seen both Sultan Kalmir and Sultana Nadira go past in procession on more than one occasion, I had never caught a glimpse of their only child.

But the closest maid completely blocked both men, leaving me with no view but the embroidery abandoned on the windowsill in front of me. From the fine material and flash of gems, I guessed the outfit was intended for Malik himself.

A fresh round of giggles made me look up again, hoping the

men had moved. Instead it was the maid in front of me who had shifted, leaning to whisper to her companion, and clearing my view in the process.

My whole head and part of my body now showed in the window, and I could clearly see Malik and his exalted guest. At that moment, Prince Zain, taller than I had imagined from my view of his parents, glanced toward the giggling maids. For one shocking moment, our eyes locked. I froze, everything around me going silent for a moment and then springing back into focus with shocking volume and speed.

Zaid. It was Zaid.

# CHAPTER 17

"Thief!" Malik shouted the alarm, having followed the direction of his guest's stare and seen me, standing behind the costly garment.

All three maids whirled around, shrieking. One of them snatched up the embroidery, while another grabbed for me, seizing a fistful of my robe.

Instinct broke through my shock. I dropped to my knees and scrambled through the bushes, my flight slowed by the maid's hold on my wrap. I let the material unwind, leaving it lying on the ground behind me as I scrambled out beyond the end of the building.

Piercing shrieks still sounded from the servants' hall, so I had no time to stop or think. Tucking my head down and gripping my satchel securely across my body, I ran. Thankful for the knowledge I had gained from countless explorations of Malik's gardens, I dodged quickly out of sight, sprinting around a fountain and into a stand of trees.

I emerged out the other side and plunged through a carefully arranged flower garden, the heady scent out of place with the frantic emotions driving me. As I took the ditch on the far side of

Malik's garden in one flying leap, I risked a glance back over my shoulder.

For a brief moment, I had a clear view of the front door. Guards poured out, an angry sergeant bellowing orders behind them—as if I really had made off with some valuable possession. Perhaps Malik hadn't even stopped to check if I had actually taken anything. Or else his disproportionate reaction was a show of strength for his royal audience.

The prince. Zaid's face flashed in front of my eyes again, and I nearly stumbled, only just catching myself in time.

How could he have done it? Passing himself off as the prince to gain access to Malik's home was beyond foolhardy. If Malik was angry at my supposed theft, how much more enraged would he be when he discovered Zaid's deception?

But the thought only lasted a moment. Malik was the sultan's Grand Vizier. He must be more than familiar with the prince and couldn't be fooled as to his appearance. Which left only one conclusion.

Zaid hadn't been masquerading as the prince. This was his secret. He was Prince Zain.

It didn't make sense. None of it made any sense. But I couldn't process the thoughts while fleeing for my life. I was nearing the end of this string of gardens, and I could still hear distant sounds of pursuit. I needed all my focus for getting out of the city without being caught.

I leaped over the final ditch, launching myself into the public park that anchored this row of houses. Nearly colliding with a small cluster of people, I dodged at the last minute and landed in a bush instead.

Several people rushed to help me extricate myself, full of apologies, and it took all my self-control to avoid compulsively looking over my shoulder. These people would be less helpful if they suspected I was a thief, fleeing pursuit.

I rushed my way through a breathless apology of my own

before breaking away and disappearing into the unexpected crowd filling the park. As I threaded my way between them, I forced myself to move at the same pace as the rest of the crush of people, doing nothing to draw attention to myself.

By the time I reached the small stand of trees at the center of the park, I had discovered the reason for the crowd. A marriage ceremony was underway, and I recognized the two families clustered together at the center. Before my absence, Sirrala had been full of news of the marriage alliance brokered between two prominent merchant families. And it appeared that many residents had come to observe the happy festivities, milling behind the tight clump of invited guests.

Servants gathered to one side, preparing food and drink to be served to the guests as soon as the ceremony was complete. As I passed, one of them told the others that more food was on its way to the park. Apparently a last minute decision had been made to serve the whole crowd. The two fathers had declared that they wished the whole city to celebrate with them, so I could only assume they were both more than happy with the alliance.

Word of the planned generosity must have spread quickly because the crowd grew thicker. I continued to push my way through, trying to reach the far side of the park.

As I skirted around the denser throng of invited guests, the two fathers clasped hands and spoke what sounded like traditional words of family binding and loyalty. Their broad smiles confirmed my earlier guess at their satisfaction over the alliance, but I was glad to see the young couple looked equally pleased with the occasion.

I finally wormed my way through to the road, my satchel still clasped firmly against my middle. The crowd was already spilling out of the park and beginning to impede traffic. I darted across the road, ready to disappear into the city. But the sight of a familiar guard made me pull up and circle back into the wedding crowd.

I recognized the man from Malik's household. His captain must have sent the guards to encircle the event, keeping watch in all directions for me to emerge. I kept my head down and my feet moving, glad yet again for my small size.

With all of Malik's guards congregated here, I needed a way to get far from this park with speed—something I couldn't do on foot. Directing my progress without appearing to do so, I let the crowd carry me back to the edge of the throng.

Waiting to one side of the road stood an elaborate carriage—one I recognized. The driver watched the festivities from his vantage above the crowd, paying no attention to the people who pressed close against his vehicle.

A single glance at the well-known jeweler on the opposite side of the road told me the reason for his wait. Jamila must be inside the shop. But he couldn't stay forever. He would need to get the horses moving soon.

I slunk up beside the vehicle and peered quickly through the lattice screens on the windows. Empty, as I had expected.

A great cheer sounded from the direction of the wedding, and I used the noise and distraction to inch the door of the carriage open. Slipping inside, I shut it again. The one place the guards wouldn't be looking for me was the place I had just run from.

I had examined this carriage carefully one night while it stood unattended in Malik's carriage house. Nothing of interest had been concealed inside it, but I had discovered the two bench seats lifted up to reveal storage boxes.

I pulled the nearest one open, poised to flee back out the door if it was crammed full, offering no place to hide. But while the bags inside took up too much space to allow me to climb in, it was packed loosely enough to make me pause. Spinning, I ripped open the other one. It was the same.

My heart beat feverishly as I stuffed the bags from the front-facing seat on top of those already stored in the rear-facing one.

Combined, the various items filled the space, but I could still lower the top—just.

I scrambled into the now empty box, pulling the lid down over me just as loud voices approached the carriage. The whole vehicle rocked as the door was opened and three people climbed in.

A familiar voice issued a stream of complaints. If Jamila, Malik's daughter, had indeed been jubilant earlier in the day at her coming betrothal, she had lost her good humor in the course of the morning. Instead, she was subjecting two of her personal servant girls to the full force of her irritation. Apparently she didn't share the city's jubilation at the wedding celebration, instead resenting the interruption to her shopping.

Lying still in the dark, my heart stuttered as I realized it was Zaid Jamila claimed to be marrying. And although I had long ago decided we could be nothing but friends, I still didn't want to see him married to Jamila—a person who never showed an interest in anyone outside herself.

Surely Zaid would never agree to marry her. Surely he would not. I held the thought tightly while I listened to her complaints through the wood of the seat.

"This is outrageous." She shifted on the bench. "How are we supposed to get home when people are crowding into the street and blocking it completely? It's a hazard and should not be permitted."

One of the maids gave a soothing murmur too quiet for me to distinguish the words.

"I have half a mind to order the coachman to drive straight over them," Jamila snapped in response.

Her other attendant replied in a louder voice. "If we can't return to your noble father's home, perhaps you should visit the palace instead." She gave a loud giggle. "After all, it will soon be your new home, and the road looks clearer in that direction."

I expected Jamila to reprimand her for the suggestion, but instead her voice brightened.

"Of course! An excellent idea. The sultana has often invited me to visit whenever I like. And I'm sure my soon-to-be-betrothed will be delighted to see me."

"He's very handsome," the bold maid said with a loud sigh. "You're so fortunate."

My heart seized again as an image of Zaid filled my mind. He was handsome. Too handsome. I had already thought so before I knew he was a prince.

"Fortune has nothing to do with it," Jamila said, an edge to her voice. "I had to work for this betrothal. Without my efforts, my useless father would have dithered and dithered and achieved nothing."

One of the maids made a soft sound of concern at her disrespectful comments about her father while I marveled that even his own daughter didn't know Malik at all. Jamila was undeterred by the mild censure, however.

"And do not forget our marriage will make me a princess. His looks are not my primary concern. I would marry him regardless of his appearance."

*Or his personality*, I thought, an unfamiliar vicious tone to my thoughts.

"Then we can be thankful he is not ugly," the confident maid replied.

"Yes," Jamila conceded, the satisfied grin audible in her voice, "I am certainly most pleased with his person. It is satisfying not to bestow my own beauty on an unworthy recipient."

I almost gagged. Jamila was beautiful enough—but not that beautiful. If the sultan had agreed to a betrothal it was because of her position as the daughter of the Grand Vizier. She was probably the next most eligible choice after Princess Adara of Kuralan, who I had heard mentioned several times as having just come of age. The relevance of that point now made sense if the Ardasirans had been hoping for an alliance.

I frowned, considering the neighboring kingdom. The maids had spoken of Prince Zain returning from a trip to Kuralan. Suddenly Zaid's long absence made sense. Had he gone to Kuralan to explore a potential marriage alliance?

Anger at his abandoning me without warning stirred. And another thought hard on its heels deepened the emotion. None of the other qaleri had been at all concerned about his disappearance. And none of them had mentioned a royal delegation to Ardasira's neighbor or suggested we go into Sirrala to watch the inevitable procession. Had they been trying to conceal from me the fact that Prince Zain's trip lined up with Zaid's absence?

Did the others know he was Prince Zain?

The more I thought about it, the more certain it seemed. They had all grown up here in Ardasira and must be familiar with the appearance of their kingdom's only prince. Why had they all kept it secret from me? Was his identity somehow linked to the rest of their web of secrets?

My spinning brain could come up with nothing. Their deception seemed as bizarre as a crown prince who spent his days bringing sacks of flour to a small group of orphans living in an abandoned city. Why did his family allow him to roam around alone, with not even a single guard to accompany him?

A memory of the haryat sticks he had once used as splints came back to me. I now knew why he had been trained to fight like the local guards. He was probably equally skilled with a sword, but a long blade was more difficult to conceal.

As the carriage rumbled through the streets, finally picking up speed, I berated myself. I claimed to be an intelligencer, and yet I had been friends with the prince for months and never worked out his true identity. My earlier determination not to intrude on his privacy now seemed foolish.

And I felt equally foolish as I thought of our conversation

about Malik and how much I hadn't understood. I poured over my memories of it, straining to remember Zaid's words and expressions. He had been passionately sure the sultan could not be involved in any plot that would put his people at risk—as an invasion of the Four Kingdoms would surely do. Of course he had been. The sultan was his father.

I groaned silently. Of course he had never spoken of his family, other than in a general way. It all made sense now. The only things I still couldn't explain were his disappearance the one time I tried to follow him and the purpose behind his continued visits to Qalerim.

The carriage slowed, and I caught the distant sounds of the driver exchanging words with someone.

"Ah, here we are," Jamila said in a satisfied voice. "Naturally we shall drive through to the second gate."

I almost bit through my tongue when I remembered where she had directed the carriage to drive. I was about to be driven into the heart of the palace.

I had learned in my wanderings through the city that the general populace dismounted at the gate of the first courtyard, met by doorkeepers who directed them to the public audience room while their mounts and carriages departed again. But the Grand Vizier was one of a small honored few permitted to drive through and dismount at the second gate. And apparently that honor was extended to his daughter—or perhaps she had earned it in her own right as the future betrothed of the prince.

Either way, I wouldn't have the opportunity to slip out of the empty carriage after its driver delivered his passengers to the palace. Already inside the outer wall, he would no doubt wait at the royal stables for Jamila's return.

In my efforts to surveil Malik and his associates, I had explored much of Sirrala. But I had never been inside the palace. I knew almost nothing about it, and I had no idea how easy it would be to get out once I was inside.

The driver called to his horses, and the carriage began to move again, the surface beneath the wheels changing as we rolled into the palace courtyard. For the first time I had entered the famous royal palace of Ardasira. Now I just had to find a way to get back out without being seen.

$\mathcal{W}$e reached the second gate quickly, the carriage stopping again, and Jamila and her two maids climbing out. Jamila maintained a discreet silence, but the bolder of the two maids let a couple of giggles slip out. She must be new to the Vizier's employ. I imagined she wouldn't be given another chance to visit the palace now that she had compromised Jamila's sense of dignity. Or maybe her betrothal would put Jamila in a positive enough frame of mind that she would forgive the small offense.

My stomach turned once again at the thought of the betrothal. I couldn't fathom the idea of Zaid shackled to a partner like Jamila. And that was without considering what a terrible ruler she would make.

Sternly, I told my mind to stop wandering. I needed to focus on getting out of the carriage without being seen.

As it turned out, the task proved easier than I had feared. The carriage began to move again, going only a short way before stopping. For a few moments, I could hear a flurry of activity as the two horses were removed from the traces. Then a male voice invited the driver to join him for a drink, and everything went quiet.

I stayed in place for several minutes, straining to hear any further activity. When only silence reached my ears, I eased the seat up and climbed carefully out. Lowering the lid back down, I took special care not to let it make any noise.

But when I peered out of the carriage, the effort seemed unnecessary. The vehicle had been left in an enormous carriage house beside a number of other such conveyances. Further back in the building, even more stood, these ones with royal crests. But no people were in sight. From all appearances, I was alone.

I let myself out of the carriage, hurrying to the nearest door. In the carriage house, I looked obviously out of place, but I hoped I could pass as a member of the public once I stepped out into the courtyard. Many people flocked to the palace on a public audience day, and I could blend into their number.

I slipped through the door and took off with a purposeful stride, hoping I appeared confident. I needed anyone who saw me to assume I was where I was supposed to be. But my steps faltered, shock momentarily taking over before I drove myself forward again.

I hadn't emerged into the outer courtyard between the first and second gates as I expected. Instead I was beyond the second gate, in front of the palace itself. Apparently the stables and carriage house had openings directly into both courtyards, presumably to allow access for both honored visitors, like Jamila, and for the royals themselves, who rode all the way through the second gate to the doors of the palace.

Rising in front of me, its size overwhelming, was the palace of Sultan Kalmir.

*Zaid's home.* The thought was hard to comprehend.

The bright sun beat down, making my eyes ache from the brilliance of the gold and silver domes that rose above me. I had admired the palace from afar many times, but it was a different experience at close proximity. The smooth stone of the building and its towers was broken at regular intervals with windows, the intricate patterns of their latticed screens drawing my eye.

From the mountains I had glimpsed the greenery of the extensive palace gardens, but now I got my first proper look at their size and beauty. They extended around the base of the palace on both sides, and the heady fragrance of the colorful flowers lent the scene a sumptuous feel.

I took in the view, fighting not to gape like the newcomer I was. When my eyes latched on the gate back to the outer court, thoughts of the lavish beauty around me disappeared. I had hoped to find a small trickle of the public leaving the palace, their audience with the sultan completed, but no one walked anywhere near the gate except the doorkeepers. It must be too late in the day, the public audience already completed.

When a doorkeeper caught my gaze, I smiled, letting my eyes slide on after a brief second's pause. I could only keep moving and hope I looked natural—like someone whose legitimate business in the palace just happened to bring them through the courtyard. I had no choice but to keep moving until I could work out how to exit the palace without raising questions.

I passed the enormous main entrance to the building, with its vast double doors of polished mahogany, without stopping. Stepping onto one of the garden's carefully manicured paths, I continued on. But I couldn't keep walking forever—I had nearly reached the palace's inner wall.

A sound from behind gave me an excuse to glance back toward the gate. One of the doorkeepers was looking in my direction, despite the group dismounting just inside the courtyard. I recognized one of the newcomers as Malik, standing respectfully beside someone else's horse, and whisked myself back around, pulling open the closest door and stepping inside.

I closed the door behind me, only to open it again immediately for a girl in a green and gold kaftan that looked like a uniform. She was heading outside with her arms full of cut greenery, and she smiled an absent-minded thanks for my small service before disappearing around the curve of the wall toward a collection of low buildings that must house something to do with the gardeners.

I pulled the door closed again, refraining from looking toward the gate as I did so. I needed to stay out of sight until Malik had disappeared into whatever rooms people of his rank frequented. Thankfully the door I had found appeared to open into a part of the palace used by the servants, and I couldn't imagine Malik would find his way down here.

Unless he somehow knew the supposed thief his guards were chasing was here and was searching for me. I continued moving aimlessly, telling myself he couldn't possibly suspect me of having snuck into the royal palace. Even I hadn't intended to do so.

As I moved, my mind lingered on the scene beside the gate, which I had seen in the briefest flash. Malik hadn't been alone. From what I understood, only royalty dismounted in the inner courtyard. Malik must have already left his horse on the other side of the second gate, walking through beside his royal companion.

Prince Zain had returned to the palace with him.

I normally considered myself quick, grasping ideas and their many ramifications almost instantaneously. But I couldn't seem to wrap my mind around the revelation about Zaid. New aspects of it kept leaping out to strike at me, fresh confusions to cloud my mind. It could not be possible that my best friend was a royal prince, the heir to a kingdom, someone who rode all the way up to the palace itself.

Not that I was unfamiliar with royalty. But that had been in another life. In this life I was a qaleri—an orphan who camped in the ruins of Qalerim and spent her days exploring abandoned tunnels. I didn't consort with royals.

Somehow, without meaning to, I had moved deeper into the

palace. None of the servants I passed challenged me—this place must be large enough they didn't all know each other. Only when I opened a door that led out of the servants' corridors and into the main palace did I hesitate.

I hadn't been moving without purpose, after all—although it hadn't been a conscious one. I knew enough about castles and palaces to understand the layout of the servants' section and what it must mean for the rooms beyond. And I had headed straight for the area most likely to be occupied by the royals themselves. Without intending to do so, I was heading for Prince Zain. For Zaid.

I pulled myself up just before stepping out. Whatever my existing relationship with the prince—and I no longer quite knew what that was—I couldn't go wandering around the corridors and rooms reserved for the royal family. No one had questioned me while I strode the servants' halls, but they would most certainly do so out there.

Easing the door almost all the way closed, I examined the corridor beyond through the remaining gap. Polished fawn marble stretched before me—as if the sand of the desert had been taken and transformed into rich beauty.

Alcoves like those that decorated the rooms of Qalerim dotted the walls, but these ones contained elegant display items—carvings, ceramics, vases of bright flowers. They softened the hard stone, working with the rich velvet carpet to make the space inviting.

I reminded myself sternly that I had not been invited into it, and if I was discovered there, dire punishment would surely follow. Still I lingered, though, unable to bring myself to retreat back to a hidden corner and wait for my chance to escape. Zaid was here somewhere—with answers.

As if drawn by the intensity of my thoughts, a tall male figure strode around the closest corner, his brow deeply furrowed. I gasped audibly, unable to help myself, and his eyes shot to where I lurked behind the partially closed door.

I froze, my instincts at war as half of me felt the pull toward him, while the other half shouted to flee. A momentary thought that he might not be able to see me in the darkness behind the door was dispelled when he changed direction and strode over.

Ripping open the door, he stared down at me.

"Cassie! What are you doing here?" He sounded fierce, although he kept his voice low, shooting a glance up and down the corridor.

I nearly rolled my eyes at the amateur move. He couldn't have more clearly signaled he was doing something he didn't want anyone to see—and nothing made people look more closely than that. It was just fortunate for him we were alone.

I grabbed his arm, trying to tug him behind the door with me, but he stood firm. When I let go, he reversed our positions, seizing my arm and tugging me out into the corridor.

"I don't think I should be seen out here," I said uneasily.

He looked back at me, raising an eyebrow. "Oh, really? I can't imagine why you would think that when you were being chased through the city as a thief about five seconds ago."

When I only grimaced, he shook his head and let the matter drop.

He didn't lead us far, opening another door and thrusting me through ahead of him without checking who was inside. As soon as he had followed me, he shut us in.

# CHAPTER 19

"We'll be safe from interruptions in here." He paced away from me toward a window that was covered in a lattice screen with an intricate pattern.

When he thrust it open, leaning both hands on the windowsill, I frowned.

"I can hear your frown," he said without turning around. "It's a private garden. There's no one out there."

I gave a soft snort but relaxed, turning to take in my surroundings. We stood in a large, airy reception room, the long wall punctuated with a whole row of large windows. Glimpses of green through the lattice suggested they all looked out onto Zaid's private garden.

*Prince Zain*, I corrected my thoughts.

The other end of the room held a set of sofas arranged around a plush rug, but it was the only alleviation to the cool stone of the rest of the room. It produced an elegant, masculine feel that suited Zaid in some indefinable way.

"Is this your personal sitting room? *Prince Zain*."

Even from behind I could see his wince at my use of his title and true name. He turned slowly around to face me.

"Sitting room. Audience room." He shrugged. "You can call it what you like. But no one comes here without my invitation."

"I suppose I should feel honored." I couldn't keep the bite out of my voice.

"No, I didn't mean…" He seemed to deflate.

For a moment we just stood, looking at each other.

"Would you like to sit?" he asked eventually, gesturing toward the sofas.

"Not really." I walked over to join him at the window, gazing out at a lush oasis of vines, bushes, and small trees. "Is that a lemon tree?"

"What?" He looked from me out to the garden. "Oh. Yes, it is. There are several."

"I like lemon trees."

What was I talking about? Apparently all the shocks of the day had fried my brain.

Zaid stared down at me, a guilty, pained look in his eyes. He opened his mouth, and for a moment I thought he was going to apologize for the months of lies. But instead his words exploded at me.

"What were you doing back there? For that matter, what are you doing here now? You promised to stay away!"

I spun to face him, my hands flying to my hips. "What was I doing? I was looking for you! When I agreed to stay in Qalerim, I expected you to be gone a day or two—three at most. Not more than two weeks! I thought you'd accused Malik and been thrown in prison or been caught trying to find his secret room for yourself, or something."

His eyes flew to the door, as if he suspected Malik might have his ear to the keyhole. I lowered my voice.

"I went to Malik's house to find out if there was any talk in his household about an apprehended thief or…or spy, or something. I didn't expect to see Malik himself. I certainly didn't expect to see you!"

He ran a hand through his hair. "I've been away. I only got back yesterday. I invented an excuse to look through Malik's house at the first opportunity. I thought if I'd just been there, it might lend my story more weight with my father."

"I guess you forgot to tell me you were going away," I said with undisguised bitterness. "I suppose you were worried I might notice the dates of your absence lined up with the dates of the prince's delegation to Kuralan. Except I didn't know about that, either. I've just been tormenting myself for days, thinking I got my best friend killed!"

"Cassie." He reached out for my hand, but I whisked it away.

"Are we even friends? I don't know anything anymore. I guess I never did."

"Of course we're friends! Sometimes I feel like you and Kayla and the others are my only friends." He sighed. "I didn't want to go to Kuralan. I've been resisting doing so for months, so my parents ambushed me. When I last saw you up at Qalerim, I didn't know anything about the trip. But when I got back, they basically forced me straight out the door. I tried to argue, but…"

He broke off, turning to lean heavily on the windowsill, his eyes locked on the garden for a brief moment before he turned to look at me. "I know that's only a partial excuse, though. If I'd told you the truth, you would have known what happened to me. I should have told you, even if you don't trust me."

"I wonder why!" I threw my hands into the air and looked pointedly around the room. "Besides, when I found those vials in Malik's house, I went straight to you, didn't I? I trusted you enough to ask for your help!"

"After all these months!" he cried. "I'm glad you came to me for help, but I've been waiting months for you to tell me your story—and I still don't know it."

My eyes examined his face, my brows knitting. "Did you expect me to go first, then? Is that what you were waiting for?" I glanced around the room again. "Royal privilege?"

He winced. "No, of course not. It's not that I wanted you to be honest first. It was…"

"It was what?" I asked impatiently when he didn't finish. "I've spent my life seeking information about everything that was going on around me—until you. I thought you had the right to keep your secrets to yourself. But I never dreamed you were keeping a secret like this!" I shook my head. "Why would you be? The whole thing is nonsensical."

"I was afraid," he said softly.

I stared at him. In all the time I had known him, I'd never seen Zaid give any indication of fear.

"What do you mean? Afraid of me?" I laughed, unable to help myself. "I clearly wasn't a threat. I call myself an intelligencer, but I didn't even figure this out."

His eyes flew to mine. "An intelligencer? I've never heard you call yourself that. Aren't you a little young?"

I bit my lip. "I'm eighteen," I said stiffly. "You know that."

"But you weren't when you arrived," he said. "And you aren't one of ours. Are you Kuralani then? I suppose I've always known that was a possibility, but I thought maybe…"

I stared at him, shocked out of my indignation. "Thought maybe what?"

Did he know about the Four Kingdoms then? Was it a secret kept by the throne?

"I thought you might be one of the last members of the nomad clans. There were few enough of them left when I was a boy, but even those few have disappeared now. My father feared someone was targeting them, so I thought maybe…"

"So you really don't know? Even the royal family doesn't know?"

"Know what?" he frowned at me. "I knew it was unlikely you could be a nomad. Where are you from, Cassie?"

I shook my head. "Wherever I'm from, I can promise you I'm not *royalty*."

It hit me for the first time why I was so upset. It wasn't the deception, or even the weeks of anxiety, but the inevitable sense that I had lost him. The moment I discovered his identity, I lost my best friend.

The fight drained out of me.

Zaid sighed. "I might be a prince, but I'm still me, Cassie."

"Are you? Was any of it real?"

"Of course it was real." This time he did manage to grasp my hand. "All of it was real."

I gently slid my fingers out of his. "But how could it be real? We cooked rice and explored dusty tunnels. I told you about my fear of spiders."

He chuckled, and I shuddered, glaring at him.

"I don't think a spider would dare show itself in here." I gestured around the room. "No doubt an army of servants would instantly descend to remove it from the royal presence."

He sighed. "We're still people, Cassie. I'm still me."

"Zaid." I shook my head. "It's not even a good alias! It's way too close to Prince Zain. If I'd ever considered the idea that you might have a secret identity, I would have seen through it in an instant. But the thought never even crossed my mind. I guess it didn't occur to me that you might be hiding the fact you're secretly wealthy, powerful, and influential—on account of being next in line to run the kingdom!" I took a deep breath, having worked myself into a crescendo by the end of my rant.

"That's because it's not an alias," he said, regarding me warily, as if he thought I might be about to explode again. "It's just a nickname. When we met in Qalerim, it was obvious you didn't know who I was. We were exchanging names, so I told you mine. And since I was with friends, I used the version they use. It wasn't any more thought through than that. I acted on instinct, I suppose."

I took several more deep breaths, reminding myself to calm down and not allow my emotions to rule me.

"You wanted me to trust you. And you didn't think I'd trust your title." I said it as a fact, and he didn't contradict me. "But what about afterward? Why did you never tell me who you are?"

He sighed, the guilty expression coming back. "I liked you not knowing. I liked just being me around you. I've never known anyone else who didn't know my rank and position. Not everyone takes advantage of it, of course, I'm not saying that. Some people behave normally around me. But they still know. It can't help but color how we interact. But with you it was different. And your being there made the others different around me, too—more relaxed—because they couldn't treat me like royalty without giving away the secret. I..."

His eyes shifted away from mine, a look I couldn't read filling his face. For a moment it seemed like he was going to say more, but he didn't. When the pause grew too long, I leaned my hip against the windowsill.

"You didn't tell me because you liked not being a prince when you visited Qalerim." I could understand it, even if I didn't like the feeling of being a fool as I searched back over everything I ever said to him.

He grimaced. "It was selfish, I know. And I apologize. I never thought you'd find out like—" He stopped, anger descending over his face.

"What were you thinking back there? You told me you were always careful while spying on Malik. But you were just standing there in full view! And what possessed you to steal something? If I hadn't been as obstructive as I could get away with, they would have caught you."

"I didn't steal anything! It was just coincidence the maids had dropped their work right next to where I was standing. Malik made the assumption, and I wasn't about to correct him when I had no valid excuse for being there, hiding behind his bushes."

"You have to be more careful, Cassie! You've assured me

Malik is a dangerous man, and I know I'm not the only one with secrets. If he catches you, and I'm not there…"

He glowered at me, anger still radiating off him, but I didn't shrink away. He was only angry because he cared, and I couldn't resent that. Especially when he was right. I had let my curiosity goad me into being careless.

"You're right. I shouldn't have let myself be seen." I ran a hand over my eyes. "I'm not normally so rash. I guess it's just been a long few days." I glanced out at the garden. "And today just keeps getting longer."

"Yes, about that…did you follow me here?"

I stiffened. "Of course I didn't!"

"What are you doing here then? Don't tell me you're here to keep watch on Malik because talking of rash—"

"I actually didn't mean to come here at all."

He stared at me for a full second before bursting into unexpected laughter.

"I find you in the palace, near my personal rooms, having somehow bypassed the palace guards, and you tell me you didn't mean to end up here? And that you're an intelligencer, although you won't say for whom. I'm starting to think I should be worried."

Despite his talk of anxiety, a smile lingered around his mouth.

"It's my size," I said with a straight face. "No one sees me and thinks I'm a threat."

"If you're telling me my doorkeepers let you stroll through both gates and start wandering around the palace because you don't appear threatening, I'm going to have more than a few words with them."

"Maybe they thought I was coming for a public audience," I said provocatively.

He didn't look impressed. "The audience is finished for the day. And don't try to tell me you've been hiding in the palace since this morning because I saw you at Malik's earlier, remember. Besides, if you had come this morning for an audience, you would have been handed over from the doorkeepers to the ushers and shown directly to the throne room, not allowed to wander about the palace freely."

"Don't go blaming your doorkeepers, it's not their fault." I explained how I had attempted to get away from my pursuers and the unintended consequence when Jamila decided to visit the palace.

He laughed before suddenly sobering. "Ah yes. Which is why you saw me running back to my own rooms in such a hurry. I heard she was with my mother." He looked uncomfortable again, as if we'd reached a subject he didn't want to discuss.

Before I could force myself to ask the truth of the rumored betrothal, he continued talking.

"Only you would hide in a carriage you believed was on its way back to the place you were running from."

"I wasn't running from the place," I said matter-of-factly. "I was running from Malik's guards. And they were all searching through the park. I actually thought it was quite brilliant since the last place they would expect to find me was back at his house. I would have been able to slip away from there easily since I know his grounds so well."

"Maybe it was brilliant." A warmth came into his eyes that made me step away from the window, suddenly conscious of where I stood and who Zaid truly was. I couldn't joke with him like I used to do.

*But he wants you to,* a quiet voice said. *That's why he never told you the truth.* I mercilessly quashed it. What he wanted didn't matter any more than what I wanted. Growing too familiar with the handsome crown prince of Ardasira was only going to lead to pain.

*Too late,* the voice whispered, but I refused to listen to it. I took another step back.

"You've told me why you hid your true identity, but I still

don't understand what you were doing in Qalerim in the first place."

"I—" He seemed to bite off whatever words wanted to follow, leaving silence in their wake. After a moment, he shrugged. "I may not have told you everything, but I've never lied to you. It's important to me that you know that."

When I didn't reply, he stepped forward, gripping my shoulders and drawing my eyes irresistibly to his. "You do believe me?"

I thought about it for a moment before slowly nodding. "If you say so, I believe it." I bit my lip. "And I haven't lied to you either."

He nodded. "If I didn't believe that, I would have—" He once again cut himself off, leaving my mind to fill in the rest of the thought. It was easy to do. If he hadn't trusted me, he would have dragged me back to the palace and used his rank and position to force me to tell him who I was and where I came from.

"If I considered only what I want," he said, starting a new sentence, "I would tell you everything. But not all secrets are mine to tell. It was the qaleri that drew me to Qalerim. The rest of that truth is their story to share."

"The qaleri?" I frowned. So Zaid knew the truth of the mystery surrounding my friends. It wasn't much of a surprise.

"But what about you, Cassie?" His voice dropped low, intimate, and I was suddenly intensely conscious that his hands still gripped my arms, holding me close. "Is it your secrets you guard, or someone else's?"

I tried to look away from his eyes but couldn't tear myself free. I didn't answer, and the silence stretched between us, the air growing heavy despite the cool breeze blowing in from the garden.

"Well?" he asked at last, his voice a breath against my face. "Do you still not trust me?"

When I didn't answer, gripped by uncertainty and indecision, his hands dropped from my arms. He stepped abruptly back. His expression grew formal, and the breeze suddenly felt cold against my skin.

"Despite everything, I do trust you," I said in a rush. "But this is all very sudden. I need a chance to think. You say your story isn't yours alone—well mine involves others as well. And I'm not just talking to my friend Zaid anymore."

His face fell, and I wished I could wipe away the pain that leaped to his eyes. But I was afraid of the emotions coursing through me, close to raging out of control. It was myself I didn't trust.

"Exactly," he said and sighed. "This is exactly why I didn't tell you earlier."

I took a step toward him before stopping.

"You're right," I said. "And that's why I forgive you for any deception. I decided months ago that if I wanted to be friends with you while maintaining my privacy, then I had to respect yours too. And that hasn't changed just because the truth turned out to be so much bigger than I was imagining. But I've already been too rash today—more than once. I need a chance to think before I go blurting anything out."

I wished fleetingly for the decisiveness and clear-thinking of my younger years. But given my actions so far, I couldn't risk leaping with my heart.

A gurgle of almost hysterical laughter bubbled up. "If I'd known it was you in there, I promise I wouldn't have peeked through the window."

He looked like he wanted to bang his head against the wall. "That's not much consolation. Although it is a relief to know you weren't desperate enough to steal from him. I've been wondering why you would possibly resort to theft when you could have just asked me to bring clothes if one of the qaleri needed them so much."

"Well now I know just how many clothes you have, maybe I will next time," I said tartly.

"Cassie." He said my name like a groan, but I pushed on, having remembered the far more important issue that had been briefly obscured in my shock at discovering his identity.

"But I'm not worried about Malik's misunderstanding. Not anymore. He didn't catch me, which is the only thing that matters. But what about you? Did your visit achieve your purpose? I'm guessing his comprehensive tour didn't include his secret stockpile of deadly poison."

His lips twisted in dissatisfaction. "We didn't get very far, I'm afraid. Maybe if I hadn't been interrupted." He shot me another significant look.

I tried to hide my disappointment.

"We'll just have to think of something else. Although if your parents are considering a marriage alliance with Malik's daughter, your father must consider him above reproach." I tried to keep my voice neutral, although I didn't entirely succeed.

I waited hopefully for him to deny the talk of a betrothal, but instead the silence stretched out. My heart—which had been sternly told for months that it wasn't permitted to fall in love—cracked, just a little.

# CHAPTER 20

The frustration on Zaid's face changed to something deeper as he looked at me, but still he said nothing. Finally, when the pause grew too long, he spoke.

"His family have served mine for generations. His father was the Grand Vizier before him."

"Not all sons are like their fathers."

"In truth…"

"Well?" I prompted him. "We could do with more truth between us."

He smiled wryly before continuing. "In truth, it's not that my trust in him runs so deep. What I doubt is his drive, his capability."

I frowned. "From what I've seen, he's clever, devious, and ambitious. Very ambitious. I don't think drive is his problem."

"I believe you," Zaid said, "I do." But he said it with too much force, as if he were trying to convince himself rather than me. "I just don't see it in the person I know—in the person I've known my whole life. He has always completed his duties in a competent enough manner, but he lacks the creativity and energy I would prefer in my own Grand Vizier. He would never hold the role if it hadn't been his father's before him. He and my father grew up together, and Father didn't feel he could refuse him the position when his time came."

My brow creased. "That makes no sense. He must be an incredible actor."

"I just wish I could understand why." Zaid stirred restlessly, looking out at the plants. "I can't make any sense of it. Surely, if his aim was to fool us, he would have tried to impress us positively with his effort, loyalty, and excellence. Why would he spend years risking being dismissed for mild incompetence?"

"I only know what I've seen," I said. "I know nothing of his performance as Grand Vizier."

"Exactly." Zaid sounded frustrated, although I didn't think it was at me. "I know everything about his role as Grand Vizier and nothing of what you've observed. We each have a half of the picture, and when put together they don't seem to make a whole. How can I convince my father of any of this when he knows the same Malik I do?"

"He must have some deep purpose we have yet to discern. There's no other explanation." The thought made me uncomfortable. The last thing I wanted was to add to the list of things I didn't understand about Malik. I was supposed to be getting closer to answers about his invasion plans, not further away.

"He would have to be a very, very good actor." I could hear the discomfort in Zaid's words. He wanted to believe me, but he was struggling to do so against the evidence of his own experience.

"He's gathering an army," I blurted out.

"What?" Zaid straightened, staring at me with a new light in his eyes. "You didn't mention that before."

"I haven't seen it with my own eyes," I admitted, "not like the vials. I don't have proof. But he's paid off a captain of the guard who's gathering mercenaries from Kuralan and stashing them down south somewhere. I've heard them talking."

Zaid groaned. "I don't want to ask how you managed that, do

I?" He ran a hand down the side of his face. "Are you accusing him of planning a coup?"

"No, not a coup…"

Zaid relaxed slightly. "What else then?"

A knock on the door to the corridor made us both start. I turned a dismayed face to Zaid, but he was already moving. Whisking me off my feet, he scooped me up and dumped me out the open window. Before I had time to protest, I was sitting on the grass, out of sight in his private garden. Sighing, I straightened my jacket and waited, elbows on my knees.

Zaid wrenched open the door. "What is it? You know I'm not to be disturbed in he—"

"Your mother *insists* on your presence in her personal sitting room."

From the tone, it was clear Zaid's earlier flight had been in response to a direct summons. And clearly it must be an old and valued servant delivering the message now, given his willingness to cut off the crown prince.

Zaid groaned. "Very well. I'm coming."

Quick footsteps sounded, and the door closed. I waited a full minute before slowly rising and dusting myself off.

Was Zaid expecting me to wait here for him to return? Probably. I wasn't inclined to do so, however. While he had said this was his private room, where he wouldn't be disturbed, there were obviously limits to that. And I didn't want to have to explain my presence if a maid came in to clean—or a gardener, for that matter. This was clearly a well-manicured patch, for all its privacy. If I was found here, they wouldn't call the prince but one of the guard sergeants, and I didn't want to have to talk my way out of that. If Zaid wanted to talk further, he knew where to find me.

I had noticed a tall gate, hidden cleverly behind some falling vines, so I didn't bother to clamber back through the window. With the help of the vines, I quickly scaled the locked gate and dropped down to walk through a long alleyway, full of gardening equipment. I climbed another, similar gate before emerging into the larger gardens that ringed the palace.

Moving at a brisk pace, I aimed for one of the smaller side gates. On this side, there were only three strides separating the inner and outer wall, and I was soon back in the city again. Since I was exiting, not entering, the two guards posted to the gate let me through without comment, assuming I had been let in through the main gate on some legitimate errand.

Once in the city, I threaded quickly through the evening traffic, moving steadily for the western gate. No one accosted me, but after the unexpected turns of the day, I couldn't shake a feeling of unease.

I didn't breathe freely until I was out of the city and part way up the nearest mountain trail. As soon as a turn of the path put a spur of the mountain between me and the view of Qalerim, I stopped to take a deep breath. Had it all been a dream? Away from the bustle of the city, it felt surreal enough that it might have been.

I shook myself. I had never had any use for hiding from reality. I had berated my uncle for doing it in the past—I couldn't allow myself to fall into the same trap now.

Zaid, the person who had steadily wormed his way into my life until he felt like a solid and necessary part of it, was really the crown prince—meaning our paths would soon diverge. Malik was leading a life of such duplicity, not even those closest to him could see the truth of it. And we were no closer to finding a way to convince the sultan of Malik's crimes.

I began the uphill trudge back to my preferred entrance to Qalerim. I felt exhausted, mentally and emotionally wrung out despite only a short burst of physical exertion as I ran from the guards. And more drama lay in front of me. Zaid had claimed the rest of the secrets belonged to the other qaleri. I intended to ask them about those secrets as soon as I got back.

As I walked, my mood dipped even lower. It was hard to remember the confidence that had once filled me when I thought of meeting Aurora and fulfilling my dream of becoming an intelligencer. Despite stumbling on the find of a lifetime, I couldn't have failed more spectacularly. And yet I had no choice but to continue on. I couldn't report my failure to my spymaster and have her send someone else in my place. There was no one but me, and four kingdoms relying on me to pull myself together and do better.

I rounded another turn, my eyes on my feet, despite the glorious sunset painting the sky with oranges, yellows, and pinks.

"My dear girl!"

I started violently, my head whipping up to stare at the old man who hadn't been in my path a moment before. I stumbled several steps backward, taking care not to stray too near the edge of the path.

He wore a tattered robe, pulled up over his head, shadowing his face. Although he appeared to offer no physical threat, his presence still unnerved me in a strange way I couldn't put my finger on.

"My dear, dear girl," he repeated. "I've found you at last."

"Found me?" My hand strayed toward the hilt of the concealed dagger I wore.

"Of course, how foolish of me." He cracked a wide smile that was clearly meant to convey fond amusement, although the effect wasn't quite what he hoped. "You wouldn't know me. But I can't help but recognize your father in you. I am his uncle, newly returned from far off lands."

"What lands would those be?" I asked, my eyes narrowing.

He looked slightly irritated by my calling out his poetic language, but he responded promptly enough. "Kuralan, of course. Where else?" He chuckled as if my comment had been in jest.

"You're my father's long-lost uncle, returned from his adventuring in Kuralan?" I asked slowly.

The man cracked a broad smile. "Yes, exactly! And it warms my heart to see my kin again."

"I'm no kin of yours," I said abruptly. "And with your permission, I'll be on my way."

I couldn't imagine the purpose of this little scene, but I didn't have the patience for it on this of all days. If it had been another occasion, I might have approached the situation more subtly, prey to my curiosity. But my mind was fixed on my coming confrontation with Kayla, and I didn't want delays.

I strode forward, brushing past the old man on the narrow path. Before I could get fully clear, however, his hand shot out and grabbed my arm.

"Ah, but I don't give permission, Cassandra."

I tried to wrench myself free, but he held on with a strength that belied his age. I reached for the dagger, but a sharp prick in my back made me stop.

"I wouldn't do that if you want to live out this day."

I froze. The warbling crackle of age had dropped from his now-familiar voice. I looked around slowly, turning only my head. Most of the time I observed him from afar, trailing at a safe distance, so I had never seen him this close. But now that I could see beneath the shadow of his robe, there was no mistaking him.

Malik.

If I hadn't been so distracted...

"It didn't have to play out like this, you know," he said in conversational tones. "Young ladies ought to be more obliging."

"Like your daughter?" I snapped. "I've noticed she's the shy and retiring sort."

"Ah, Jamila." He chuckled. "Now there's a girl after my own heart."

"No compliment to either of you," I said through my teeth.

Now that he had dropped the act, he stood tall, no longer

stooping, and the desert robe he had wrapped around himself hung well above his ankles. I looked at it more closely, my heart sinking.

"Perhaps you're noticing the small holes," he said with malicious humor. "They come from a prickle bush, you know."

I met his eyes, firmly closing my mouth against the rising sick feeling in my stomach. Malik knew it had been me under his window earlier. He knew I had been spying on him.

He grinned, an unnerving expression. "I think you'll find you're better off doing what I ask. I don't mean you any harm, you know. I merely have a…business proposition for you."

"For me?"

"Don't underestimate yourself," he said, in a mock friendly way. "I have it on the excellent authority of Kayla that you know Qalerim better than anyone."

"Kayla?" I couldn't keep the alarm from my voice at the unexpected mention of my friend's name. Instantly my mind flashed to the secrets Zaid had mentioned. What did the qaleri have to do with Malik?

"Yes, Kayla. Our mutual friend. Did she never mention me?" He laughed, a nasty edge to his humor. "No, of course. She wouldn't have. Although she also didn't mention her new house mate to me until now, either." He sounded displeased.

"What have you done to her?" I asked through gritted teeth.

"Done? If you mean have I harmed her, certainly not." He leaned in close to whisper in my ear. "Yet."

I gulped. I had been debating making an escape attempt, despite the undesirability of starting a wrestling match on a thin mountain path. But his words made me pause. I didn't understand the threads connecting Malik and my friends, and if I managed to get away, he might go after them instead. He obviously knew where to find them—only Kayla could have told him which path I would take on my way home.

And he had said he wanted us to work together. If I played my cards right, this might be the chance I needed to finally find out all the details of his schemes.

With a force of will, I made my muscles relax and my suspicious look lessen.

"A business proposition, you say? What sort of business?"

He grinned, his grip loosening. "There's riches to be had, right enough. As much as you like."

I raised an eyebrow. "As much as I like? I fear you may have a failure of imagination there."

"As much as you can carry, then," he amended, with a tilt of his head. "You may stuff that satchel of yours full of far more valuable gems than those on the jacket you tried to take."

I didn't bother to correct him about my supposed attempt at thievery. Malik wasn't the sort of man who liked to be contradicted.

"And where are these jewels to come from? Not your treasury, I'm guessing."

"Certainly not. Despite what it must seem like to a penniless orphan, I am not made of gold."

"So what do you want from me, then? You want me to thieve for you?" I looked back toward Sirrala, but even as I did so, I remembered his earlier comment about how I knew Qalerim better than anyone.

My mouth dropped open as I realized his intention. "You mean the Treasure of Qalerim? You can't be serious. If Kayla said I know where to find it, she was exaggerating beyond all reason. I know nothing of the sort. And if I did," I couldn't help adding, "I wouldn't need your assistance to become wealthy."

"Ah, but you see *I* know where the treasure is to be found."

I raised an eyebrow. "I can't see why you need me, then. Go and retrieve the riches for yourself."

"I'm not interested in riches," he snapped before calming his voice with an effort and directing a piercing stare at me. "All I want is one small item, and you may have the rest."

198

"One small item?" I asked skeptically.

"A lamp, that is all."

His intent expression as he proclaimed the words warned me not to react to this revelation. I kept my face carefully unresponsive, as if I had never heard the old legends. But if he was truly after a lamp, then the qaleri weren't the only ones to believe in the tales.

"A lamp?" I shook my head. "How could you want nothing but a single lamp? Even one made of solid gold and studded with gems wouldn't be worth all this effort."

He looked satisfied with my reaction, brushing away my words.

"Never mind why I want it. Bring me that lamp, and you will be richer than you ever dreamed. And your friends will be unharmed."

"You haven't explained why you can't retrieve it for yourself." I frowned. "Why involve me at all?"

He let me go, finally, drawing out a small notebook. "I have discovered directions to the cave hiding the treasure. However, Kayla tells me she doesn't understand them. When I asked who knew the city best, I learned of your existence."

"If I help you, you have to swear you won't harm her," I said, disliking the tone of his voice when he referred to her having kept my presence in Qalerim a secret. "Or any of them."

"Of course," he said without hesitation. "I have no interest in harming them. As long as I have your cooperation, they may stay out of the matter entirely."

For a moment I weighed him with my eyes, but I could detect no insincerity, merely a slight impatience.

"Let's hear these directions, then," I said.

# CHAPTER 21

*H*e read aloud from his notebook. "Down the deepest pit, two rights and a left, then behind the grieving friends."

He looked up at me expectantly.

"That's all?" I stared at him. "No wonder Kayla couldn't help you. That's not directions!"

"I won't bore us both with the story of how and where I found the text that included that description, but I assure you it is most reliable," he said coldly. "And the book said those directions would allow anyone with knowledge of the mountain to find the cave. So I suggest you stop dissembling. Now that you have heard them, I won't permit you to go on your way, just so you can retrieve the treasure without my presence."

"I'm not *dissembling*," I snapped back. "You must be able to tell that there isn't nearly enough information in those directions. It's more like a riddle."

"The book said they would be sufficient for anyone with knowledge of the mountain. And I'm assured no one knows the mountain better than you. I'm told you've even mapped the tunnels."

I glared at him, angry at how much information he had

managed to prize from my friends. But anger wouldn't serve me now. I needed a clear mind. I drew in a long breath.

"It may be purposefully cryptic," I said in a strained voice. "Let me think for a moment."

Malik nodded once, his sharp eyes staying trained on me. I tried to put his presence out of my mind, focusing all my mental energy on deciphering the directions.

Whoever had written it had considered "the deepest pit" enough of a description to allow the reader to find the starting point of their path. Which meant it had to be something distinctive. My heart sank.

Even with a better description, Kayla wouldn't have been able to help him. Sometimes, in my explorations, I stumbled on corners of the mountain that I purposefully left out of my map book—places I kept quiet from the others.

After Elias's accident, I had expected them to slow down, at least a little—to be more cautious. But instead they had seemed spurred to new heights. And the more remote and hidden the section of the old city, the more interest it held for them.

But the city hadn't been maintained for generations, and some places were dangerous. To protect them, I had left those areas out of my maps, an easy enough thing to do given how much of the mountain still needed to be searched.

One such section could be described as a pit. I hadn't even attempted to descend the ladder that still poked up out of it, instead marking that area of my mental map with a large black cross. Given the number of missing rungs on the ladder, I suspected anyone who descended into that pit wouldn't be coming back up.

"You know where to go." Malik's satisfied words weren't a question.

"I know a possible place to start," I corrected him. "A dangerous place. If we go in there, we might never come out."

"I'm willing to take the chance."

I considered snapping back that I wasn't willing, but I knew I didn't really have a choice. It was better for him to think I was working with him willingly, rather than having him resort to threats and violence again.

"We have a long walk," I said instead. "And it's getting dark."

He pulled out an unlit torch from a bag which lay near his feet. "Don't worry about the dark. You just lead the way. And remember, soon you'll be richer than you ever dreamed."

I suppressed a sigh, starting up the track at a fast pace. I half expected him to lag behind until I reminded myself his feeble posture had been an act. He was significantly taller than me, his longer stride easily keeping up, even with my near trot.

Neither of us spoke as I led us unerringly through Qalerim. I made sure to skirt far around the part of the city that housed our apartments, not wanting to run into any of the others returning home as the light faded. If we ran into one of them by accident, Malik might insist on their joining us.

When the light from the various shafts dropped to near black, Malik lit his torch. I had never explored Qalerim in the dark—there was no need—so I had never experienced the way the dancing flames sent shadows skittering in all directions.

I reminded myself sternly that they weren't living creatures, circling us waiting to pounce, and continued on. Malik followed.

"You really do know this place well, don't you?" he said, his eyes fixed on me as if I were a curious specimen worthy of passing interest.

I shrugged.

"How old did you say you are?"

"I didn't," I replied coldly.

"Well?" Impatience twisted his face, and I decided it wasn't worth the fight.

"Eighteen."

"Pity." He brooded for a moment before brightening. "But soon that won't matter. You might be useful to me yet."

I glanced at him sideways. He spoke as if it would be an honor to serve him, but surely he couldn't think I would want anything to do with him once I possessed my promised riches. I gave an internal, sour laugh. Did he not realize he was giving away his intention to betray me? Or did he think I was too foolish to notice?

We went down several sets of stairs, moving lower and lower until we reached the deepest level. After winding through a number of tunnels, we arrived at a dead end, in front of which gaped a wide hole. I would have thought it a cave-in from the distant past, a hole to nowhere, if it wasn't for the top of a ladder poking out one side. Secured to the stone with metal bolts, it clearly wasn't the work of the qaleri.

Given its location, I had known they would find that ladder irresistible, so I had been especially careful never to mention its existence. So careful, in fact, I had nearly forgotten about it myself.

"Are you really sure you want to go down there?" I asked doubtfully. In the dark the hole looked even worse than I remembered.

Malik peered over the edge. Already the sleek, oiled appearance he had been hiding beneath my robe was marred by the dust of Qalerim, but he showed no indication he minded.

"I would have preferred a more stable entrance, but I will not be deterred. I've already stated that. Stop trying to delay us, and get on with it."

I didn't bother to protest his assumption that I would test the ladder by going down first. I was quite sure he had no intention of doing the job himself.

Drawing a steadying breath, I swung my satchel around so it lay over my back and crouched down by the ladder. Maneuvering to face backward, I lowered one foot until it hit the first rung. Carefully transferring my weight onto it, I tested it for several seconds before lowering my second leg.

"Hurry up!" Malik snapped.

"If you want to go faster, you can do it yourself," I said without looking up. "I can't speak for you, but I don't see much point in being rich if I'm also dead."

He went silent, not commenting on the heavy contempt dripping from my voice. Apparently he still retained some sense despite his desperate quest to possess the fabled enchanted lamp.

Five steps down, a rung was missing. I lowered my foot the extra distance to the next one down, but as soon as the ball of my foot placed weight on it, it snapped. Gasping, I grabbed at a rung in front of me as the unexpected movement caused my other foot to slip.

The fall wrenched my shoulders as I clung to the rung, my grip the only thing stopping me from plummeting to the rock below. My feet swung wildly, scrabbling against the wall and ladder until one of them found purchase on a new rung. I counted three frantic seconds before I let out my breath. This one had held.

I considered calling up to warn Malik there was a gap of two missing rungs but decided against it. He was the one forcing us to do this, and he could take the danger the same as me. I encountered two more missing rungs after that, but in both cases the next one down held. When my questing foot found solid ground, I paused, resting my head against the ladder and taking several shaky breaths. I'd made it.

I looked up at the distant light above me. We still had to make it back up again, so I wasn't safe yet.

"I'm at the bottom," I called, stepping away from the ladder.

"I'm throwing down the torch," Malik said, and a moment later, the light dropped toward me, nearly winking out from the whooshing air around it.

I darted forward and snatched it off the ground, relieved when it continued to burn. The last thing we needed was to be plunged into the pitch black. No doubt Malik would want us to continue by feel.

With the light in my hands, I turned to examine my surroundings. The air was even colder down here, and dank, as if the ingenious system of shafts that brought in fresh air and sunlight didn't reach this far.

I stood in a cave, although it was more like a wide tunnel that narrowed as it disappeared away from me. The walls looked rough, as if natural rather than hewn from the mountain by human hands. Despite myself, my pulse—which had just settled after my eventful descent—began to speed up.

Was it possible it was true? Did the Treasure of Qalerim really exist, hidden here many generations ago? And did that mean the enchanted lamp existed also? In my own lands, godmother gifts had been misused before, twisted from their original purpose as the brother in the story had done with the rings. And some such objects had lasted many generations before their power was depleted beyond use.

I glanced at the man descending toward me. If it was possible the lamp existed and possessed the powers claimed by the legend, I couldn't allow Malik to get his hands on it. But I couldn't act against him too soon, either. I still hoped to somehow use this opportunity to discover what plans he had put in motion. It was a fine balancing act, and I had no choice but to walk the edge as best I could.

As soon as he reached the bottom, Malik removed his knife from between his teeth, and snatched back the torch.

"Where next?" he asked.

I gestured into the darkness. "We walk, I suppose. It said two rights and a left. That seems fairly straightforward."

Malik gestured for me to go first, so I set off, relieved that he kept close behind with our one source of light. The tunnel soon branched, and I took the right fork without slowing. I nearly missed the second right because it wasn't a junction but a secondary tunnel that branched off from the right wall of the main one—just another looming black hole in the darkness that surrounded us.

"Are you sure about this?" Malik asked, a new edge of uneasiness in his voice.

"Of course not. Like I said from the beginning, the directions aren't exactly comprehensive." I halted, looking back at him. "But you want to go on, don't you?"

He growled, gesturing for me to continue, and I faced forward again, a slight smile pulling at my lips. There was something satisfying about seeing the sleek, controlled Malik coming apart in the dark depths of the mountain.

"You do know the way back out?" he asked a few steps further on.

I shrugged, not bothering to look back. "Just reverse the instructions. One left and two rights. Easy."

He didn't reply, and I could almost sense the waves of conflicting emotions rolling off him. From the way he talked, he had been searching for this lamp for years, and he finally had a chance of finding it. And yet no one with any sense could enjoy being down in this dank hole.

Our side tunnel ended at an intersection, and I took the left path, moving faster as I grew less and less willing to spend an extended period of time so deep in the mountain. I could feel the weight of it pressing above me, although the tunnel ceiling was considerably higher than my head.

The tunnel opened into an enormous cavern, our flickering light not making it to the furthest reaches.

"Where is it?" Malik spun around, his voice sounding both desperate and greedy at the same time.

"This isn't the cave with the treasure." I tried to hide my disgust. "There was another direction, remember?"

"That one made no sense. Behind the grieving friends? If

there were guards down here once, they've long since died and their bones turned to dust."

"I doubt it's that literal. Besides, it didn't sound like a warning about guards to me. It sounded like part of the list of directions."

Malik frowned. Although we couldn't see every corner of the cavern we stood in, it was clear it wasn't the mythical treasure cave he had expected, piled with gold and jewels in every direction. I could see in his eyes that he wanted to believe I was right.

"Well, then, what does it mean?" he asked.

I shrugged. "I said it sounded like part of the directions, not that I understood it. I suppose we should start by looking around."

I started for the closest wall, hoping that if I moved confidently, he would follow with our light. It worked, the circle of brightness moving with me as I reached the edge of the cave.

I could see no openings in either direction, other than the one we came through, but I started walking away from our entrance, keeping close to the cave wall. We would need to circle the whole cavern to see every part of it.

Before long we reached another tunnel entrance. I stopped to examine it in silence.

"This can't be it, surely. It's just a normal tunnel."

I shrugged. "Maybe. Maybe not. I don't know anything about this place or about the mind of the person who wrote those directions, for that matter."

But after a minute I kept moving. I wasn't willing to start down an unknown tunnel without some indication we were on the right track.

We passed another entrance and then another, but we barely stopped at either of them. I could hear Malik growing fidgety and impatient behind me, but I refused to hurry.

Larger and larger rocks dotted our path, and I had to weave around several of them. The wall was no longer smooth in this section, crevices opening and closing, reaching out rocky fingers for the center of the cavern.

"This is pointless," Malik said, and I glanced back to where he lagged several steps behind.

I stopped, sucking in a breath.

"What?" He hurried to my side, trying to follow my line of sight. "What do you see?"

"There." I pointed at a strange rock formation jutting out from the wall.

He frowned. "Don't waste my time. It's a rock. If you're trying to delay us, or—"

"The grieving friends." I cut him off. "I didn't see it from the other direction, but from this angle, it looks like two people. See, they're gripping each other's arms, and their heads are resting together."

Malik squinted in the direction of my finger. "I suppose it might look a little like that. But what does that have to do with…" His words trailed off, his tone turning thoughtful. "I might have read something about an ancient practice of grieving in such a way." He frowned at me. "But how did you know of it?"

I shrugged. I didn't feel the need to tell him that the desert traders of Lanover still continued the practice. Aron and Samar had called the traders traitors, suggesting they had broken away from these kingdoms. If the legends were true, perhaps when the original kingdom turned to desert, they had fled the other way, instead of chasing their king to the mountain. Or perhaps they were the nomads Zaid had spoken of—not dead but in a new home.

Malik didn't press me for an answer, instead hurrying toward the rock formation that almost resembled a statue. I kept close behind him, not wanting to be left behind in the dark.

Moisture filled the air in this section, dripping down from above in some places. I peered up at the roof of the cave above us, but it was too hard to make it out in the flickering shadows.

"I think this dripping water might have shaped the rock," I said. "Maybe it was a better likeness back when the directions were first written. It must have been a long time ago."

"Never mind that," Malik snapped. "Where's the cave? It said behind the grieving—" He cut himself off, leaping forward to peer at something I couldn't see. "There! Look!"

I circled around the rock to join him, peering down at an opening that wasn't so much a tunnel entrance as another pit. But this one was smaller, and a large boulder rose from the stone floor in front of it, hiding it from easy view. Without the clue, we would almost certainly have missed it.

My mouth went dry, my heart pulsing an irregular beat in my ears. It didn't seem possible, but had we really found the entrance to the missing treasure cave? I couldn't help a note of excitement, despite the terrifying idea of climbing into that hole. What wonders might we find in there?

CHAPTER 22

"*I*t's not very large," I said after a moment of silence in which we both stared at the opening.

Given the desperation he had shown so far, I expected Malik to dispute the underlying meaning behind my words. But he made no attempt to claim he could fit through the hole.

"Maybe this isn't it?" He sounded uncertain.

"Or maybe there was a larger opening that has disappeared in the intervening years." I shrugged.

Or maybe the younger brother was a particularly small man. Or a lot younger. The story hadn't said how old he was. I scrunched my nose at the distasteful thought that the blood-thirsty brother might have been a youth when he committed his crimes.

"Never mind that," Malik said. "Can we make it bigger?"

I stared at him. "Make it bigger? Did you bring an enchanted object that can cut through solid rock?"

He growled, waving a hand through the air as if to silence me. I gave him a disgusted look and walked over to the hole. When I sat down, swinging my legs over to dangle into the opening, he spoke.

"What are you doing?"

I raised an eyebrow at him. "Going in. That's what you were about to order me to do, wasn't it? You're clearly not going to fit, so it has to be me. Unless you want to give up on the whole thing?"

A large part of me hoped he would say yes and save me having to drop into a small, dark hole. But another part drove me forward, quite apart from Malik's threats. This was an adventure unlike any since Aron and Samar first brought me across the desert, and I wanted to know what I would find in this fabled cave.

Malik said nothing, so I continued, taking charge in the face of his consternation.

"It looked like the torchlight was reflecting off rock not too far down. I'll lower myself in, and hopefully reach ground before I have to let go. Once I'm down, you throw down the torch like you did last time."

I expected him to protest my taking the light and had a host of arguments ready. After all, I couldn't find him his precious lamp if I couldn't see. He said nothing, however, merely giving a reluctant grunt which I assumed signified his approval of my plan.

Taking a deep breath, I twisted around, rubbing against the rock edges of the hole as I did so. Once I faced Malik, I began to lower myself down. I had thought descending the ladder was nerve-wracking, but this was a whole different level. My legs swung free, my toes straining for purchase as I stretched them as far as they would go.

Soon three-quarters of my body was in the hole, my forearms and elbows resting on the ground at its lip, holding my weight. I could feel the narrowness of the entrance open up not too far down, but my feet hadn't found the bottom, so I had to go further. Moving even more slowly, I lowered myself again, seized by a sudden horrible certainty that my shoulders wouldn't fit, and I would be stuck here, half in the hole and half out until I starved to death. I certainly didn't trust Malik was going to make any effort to rescue me.

But my shoulders scraped through, the hole swallowing me completely, so that only my hands still gripped the edge. My steady pace faltered as I jerked to my full stretch, my straining arms struggling to keep their hold on the rock above me.

"I can feel the bottom!" I cried the words in triumph and relief, forgetting for a moment that I wasn't exploring with Zaid or Kayla.

Memory came rushing back, however, as I looked up at the glowing circle not far above my head, the black outline of Malik's head visible as he peered over the edge.

"Throw me down the torch," I called up, hoping he didn't mean to argue the matter at this point.

He still made no protest, however, and the torch appeared over the circle, held in his hand. I stepped back quickly as the flame dropped toward me, snatching it up as soon as it hit the ground. Looking up, I realized he was still surrounded by light.

"Seriously?" I muttered to myself. "You had another torch this whole time?" I didn't bother to voice my protest loudly enough for him to hear, however.

"I have a rope," he called down. "Bring me the lamp, and I'll lift you and your satchel of riches back out." His voice turned dark and threatening. "Fail, and I'll leave you to die alone in the dark."

"Thank you for telling me your plan," I muttered, rolling my eyes. Whether or not he actually had a rope, I didn't imagine he intended to use it.

"Don't touch any of the gold," he said, his voice urgent enough to make me pause. "The same book that led us here warned of a terrible enchantment on it."

I looked back up at him, frowning. If the legends about the ring and the lamp were true, it was possible the brother had managed to get his hands on other godmother objects as well. Maybe he had left traps among his treasure.

"You said I could take as much as I could carry," I said, trying to goad him into giving me more information.

"No, I promised you riches," he sneered. "Jewels, specifically. The jewels are safe, but the gold is forbidden. Except for the lamp. Stuff your satchel full of jewels, if you wish—legend says you won't find more valuable ones anywhere—and bring the lamp. Come straight back here, and I'll lift you out."

"That's your advice? Just don't touch the gold?"

"What other advice do you need? Hurry, girl!"

Grumbling quietly, I turned to face a narrow stone tunnel. At least I had a light.

I hurried forward, moving quickly because of my own excitement, not Malik's instruction. I hadn't decided what I intended to do if I actually found a lamp, my mind absorbed in the excitement of impending discovery.

When the tunnel continued to stretch on, doubt began to creep in. What if the tunnel led nowhere but a dead end? Malik would never believe me. The thought of being stuck here after my torch burned out lodged in my mind. The tunnel walls shrank toward me, and my breathing came heavier, as if I was running instead of walking. Any minute now, it would become too narrow for me to pass.

I moved deeper and deeper, and after a number of steps, I sternly scolded myself. The walls were still the same distance from me they had always been. I couldn't let the darkness and my fear distort my perceptions. I already had enough challenges working out how to fool Malik.

The end of the tunnel came abruptly, its approach impossible to see in the darkness. For a moment panic clawed at me again, but I suppressed it. Only when I stood at the end of the path did I see that the tunnel didn't finish but instead continued on with a sharp right turn.

I pivoted, took three steps forward, and gasped, rocking back on my heels.

It was real. The Treasure of Qalerim was real, and I had found it.

The tunnel opened into a small cavern, its walls rough, but the air crisp and dry, unlike the dank air in the cave where I had left Malik. A row of chests lined both the left and right walls, their lids thrown back and their contents gleaming in the light of my torch.

Gold. I had never seen so much gold—shining and glimmering as if it had been polished yesterday. I shivered. There was something unnatural about the bright yellow, unmarred by dust —as if it wasn't only human hands that didn't dare touch it. I had no trouble believing Malik's talk of enchantments.

I lingered anyway, though, walking slowly through the middle of the room. My eyes darted left and right as I tried to calculate what so many coins could buy. And not just coins. Heaped in among them were other golden items—goblets, chains, crowns. That much gold could do a lot of good for a lot of people.

That didn't mean I was foolhardy enough to touch it, however. When I reached the opening in the far side of the room, I paused, looking back at the chests. How wasteful to amass such wealth, and then just let it sit here where it could help no one. What greed had deposited it here?

A greed big enough to turn a kingdom into a desert, perhaps?

I turned away from the gold and stepped into the next tunnel. This one was short. Only a few steps led me out into a second, larger cave.

After Malik's talk of jewels, I was expecting more chests, these ones heaped with a range of colors. But I couldn't have anticipated the reality of this second cave.

For a brief moment, my confused mind thought I had stumbled out of the mountain altogether. Because while I had encountered goats enough in my explorations, and occasionally hardy shrubs growing where the shafts let in sunlight and the occa-sional rain, I had never encountered a small orchard of fruit trees.

But stone still surrounded me on all sides, and the darkness was still the impenetrable black of the mountain, rather than the moon-softened dark of night beneath the stars. I stood in a cave, slightly bigger than the one I had just left, so what stood ahead of me couldn't possibly be trees, despite their appearance.

I held up my torch and stepped closer to the first one. What I had taken for grained wood in the low, flickering light was actu-ally marble, in the same sandy color as the palace. Whoever had carved it into the shape of a tree had been a master artist, the details impossibly lifelike. And as I looked closer, I realized each tree was different, the effect contributing to the initial impres-sion of an orchard.

I should have realized immediately from the lack of leaves, however. Fruiting trees should have leaves. But the bright colors of the fruit itself had momentarily confused me. And what fruit these trees bore!

Every color of gemstone hung on the branches, carved—with as much skill as the trees themselves—into a myriad of different fruit. Rubies, emeralds, sapphires, amethysts, turquoises, even pearls, transformed into dates, apples, pears, grapes, figs, oranges, and more. I had never dreamed of such wondrous baubles and couldn't possibly guess at their worth.

Did Malik know these were here? When he told me I could fill my satchel with jewels, had these been the ones he meant?

A cold line of dread ran down my spine. If Malik knew this vast source of wealth stood here for the taking—its beauty alone enough to make its possessor famous—and yet wanted only the lamp, what power lay inside the lamp? I couldn't allow it to fall into his hands.

I hesitated for one more moment, reaching up a tentative hand to stroke one of the ruby apples. A part of me wanted to stay and enjoy the unbelievable beauty of this unique orchard. I couldn't linger, however. I had to find the lamp and a way out of this cave that didn't involve giving it to Malik.

Slowly I threaded my way through the tiny grove of trees, coming out in front of yet another tunnel entrance. Glancing once, regretfully, over my shoulder, I stepped out of the cave.

Almost immediately, I stumbled over a step, only just righting myself in time to prevent a fall. Looking up, I saw a pedestal that appeared to have been naturally formed by the cavern itself. Ascending the shallow steps, I carefully approached it.

Resting on the rock surface stood an ordinary looking brass lamp. I peered at it doubtfully. Its position suggested it was important, but could it truly be as powerful as the legends claimed?

I regarded it for a long moment before shrugging. If nothing else, it held power over my escape, and now that Malik knew of its location, I couldn't afford to leave it here.

Reaching out a trembling hand, I snatched it off the pedestal.

# CHAPTER 23

*I* waited for a moment for the ground to open and swallow me, or a great clanging cymbal to sound. Nothing happened.

Examining the lamp more closely, I looked for any sign it was something out of the ordinary. I found none. After a careful search, I shrugged and tucked it deep into my satchel.

Starting back down the stairs, my mind worked furiously. How could I convince Malik to get me out of here without handing over the lamp? He had no doubt been using my absence to consider every possible action I could take. Any stratagem I might use, he would have anticipated.

I walked back through the trees, lost in my thoughts. When I reached the last couple, I paused. Malik had said I might take whatever jewels I liked. And since he wanted me alive and whole until I delivered the lamp to him, it must mean he truly believed that unlike the gold, the jeweled fruit was safe to take.

I had no interest in vast wealth, but I couldn't resist their beauty, or the difference just one of them would make to the qaleri. They would never have to steal again.

I stopped and stripped the closest branches, stashing the gems in my satchel beside the lamp. I might not have the chance to ever return here.

As soon as I had filled my bag, I continued on, crossing back through the cave of gold without pausing. Nothing here drew me, and I felt no whisper of temptation. I wanted no part of whatever enchantment lay on this cave.

The return journey down the narrow passage felt far shorter than it had in the other direction. Part of me wanted to slow down, to take more time to think. But I didn't dare. I had no way to guess what Malik would do if he felt I had been gone too long, and I couldn't risk the possibility he would give up on me and leave.

I felt again the cloying grip of indecision and wished for the clarity of my younger years. It was hard not to feel that young Cassie would have known just what to do in this situation. But the way lay foggy before me, the best path unclear.

A flickering light appeared ahead of me, further than the reach of my torch. A hard knot of fear inside unwound. He hadn't left yet. My steps slowed, my thoughts whirling.

He must have heard me, however, because he called, his words echoing strangely from the rock.

"Did you find it? Tell me! Was the lamp there?"

I remained silent until I stood below the hole, looking up at him.

"How are you going to get me out? It's very small." I told myself the entrance couldn't have shrunk in my absence, but I hadn't remembered it being quite so tight. "It's going to be hard to pull me out."

"But did you find the lamp?" he cried, his words almost feverish.

"I did," I said slowly.

An almost manic light leaped to his eyes, and he fell back for a moment, disappearing from my sight. His rough laugh swelled, filling the cave and bouncing from the walls.

"At last! You have no idea how long I've been searching! At last!" His face reappeared, peering down at me. "Give it to me! Give it to me now!"

I shook my head, shifting to the balls of my feet and staring up at him.

"I'm not giving it to you until you get me out of here."

"Why, you—" He lunged down toward me, his reaching arms grabbing at the air.

I sidestepped easily, keeping just out of reach. As it was, he could have reached no more than my head, the small size of the opening keeping him from getting further than arm's length in.

"The lamp is right here." I tapped my satchel. "You can have it as soon as I'm out."

But the light had died from his eyes now, replaced with a scheming look that turned my stomach cold.

"What? Let you out so you can run off with my lamp? I'm not a fool. Throw it up immediately, or I'll leave you to die down there."

"But that means leaving your precious lamp."

He scoffed. "For now. But no one else knows of its location. I can come back later, when you are no longer an issue, with the tools to widen this hole."

I shifted uneasily. After all the heartless, unethical deals I had seen him broker, I didn't doubt he would do it for a second.

"Throw down two lengths of rope," I suggested. "I'll secure my feet before you pull me up. Then you'll know I can't run off."

"I don't have two lengths of rope," he said. "And I wouldn't trust you to tie the knot properly anyway."

"I'm not throwing up the lamp so *you* can run off and leave *me*," I snapped back, the darkness of the cave beyond our feeble torchlight making it hard to keep the air of authoritative calm I was striving for.

"The lamp is *mine*!" he shouted. The non-answer demonstrated I wasn't the only one affected by our prolonged time in the depths of the mountain.

When I didn't reply, he gave a low growl. Something dropped from above me, and I flinched back before I realized it was only a rope.

"I've secured it to a rock," he said. "Don't think I'm going to pull you up. I'm not having my hands full when you reach me. You can climb up yourself, and I'll be waiting between you and the exit with a sharp blade, so don't get any ideas."

I looked up at him and then at the rope that hung over the side of the hole. Could I pull myself up and then maneuver through that tight hole? Probably.

But once I got into the larger cavern, Malik had the decided advantage in terms of height, strength, and speed. If I climbed up that rope, how would I stop him getting the lamp? The familiar feelings of doubt and indecision swamped me. What would my younger self have done?

Malik had backed away from the edge at the end of his speech, but when I made no sound or response, he reappeared.

"What are you doing? Do you *want* to die down there? Get up here!"

Even in the dim light I could see the desire in his eyes. He might have the option of leaving me here to die and returning later, but he didn't want to walk away with the lamp so close.

I still said nothing.

With a shout of rage, he slammed the hilt of his dagger repeatedly against the stone at the edge of the hole, as if he thought he could chip it away until it was large enough for him to get through.

"What are you do—" My question cut off, changing to a wordless shout of surprise as a loud crack echoed through the cavern, reverberating and growing louder as several chunks of rock fell onto my head.

I didn't waste time looking for Malik. Ducking my head and

throwing my hands protectively over my neck, I dashed back down the tunnel, abandoning the torch which I had dropped in my surprise. A rumbling crash followed me, rock dust enveloping me and filling the air until it was hard to breathe.

The light winked out, snuffed by falling rock. I didn't stop, stumbling onward, always just in front of the collapsing stone.

The rumbling grew quieter, stopping just as my reaching hand found the end of the tunnel and propelled me sideways into the cavern of gold. I froze, not wanting to stumble into one of the chests by accident.

What had happened?

I drew in a deep breath, filling my panting lungs, only to cough violently at the dust that still hung in the air. When my coughing fit subsided, I wiped my streaming eyes and breathed more cautiously. The worst of the dust seemed to have settled, and I took stock of my body and surroundings.

Somehow I seemed to have avoided any serious injury, and I still had my satchel securely across my chest. And in one small positive twist, I wasn't in the pitch dark, either.

It took me several moments of confusion to realize the glow was emanating from the golden coins themselves. The light was faint enough I hadn't noticed it when I came through with my torch, but now that my eyes had adjusted to the darkness, it seemed bright—certainly bright enough to quieten some of the instinctive panic in my chest.

I crossed over to peer into the next cave. The faintest bit of light reached through the short connecting passage, but further beyond, the orchard lay in deep darkness. Reluctantly I pulled back into the cave of coins. If I had needed further evidence the gold was enchanted while the jewels were not, the magical glow provided it. But unfortunately, I needed the light and would have to stay in this room for now, however much it creeped me out.

I sat in the middle of the room, as far from the chests as I could get, and placed my satchel in front of me. With a corridor jammed full of broken stone between me and the entrance, underground survival had just become a far more pressing threat than Malik. I glanced in the direction of the jumbled stones that spilled into the cave.

Was he buried among them? Or had he escaped? If he was alive, I could imagine his rage would be great—despite having brought the situation on himself. Would he be able to find his way back through Qalerim and up the ladder without my direction?

I couldn't muster any sympathy for his plight. But since I intended to escape myself, neither could I dismiss all concern about his eventual fate. I pushed the questions to the back of my mind for now, however. Malik was no longer an immediate problem. I needed to focus on my own survival and escape. If I succeeded, I would have plenty of time to worry about Malik in the future.

I emptied out the jewel fruit, making a neat pile to one side. The lamp went on the other side. In the center, in front of me, I placed the other items from my satchel.

My water skin—sadly almost empty. An almost stale hunk of bread. Two dates. A short length of rope I had forgotten was in there. The pouch with the vial of nayera that accompanied me everywhere. That was it.

I had set out to spend the day in Sirrala, not Qalerim, so unfortunately I didn't have my tinder and flint or makeshift torch. Once I left this cave, I would be moving in the darkness. But as I gazed at my two dates, I knew hunger and thirst would eventually drive me to make the attempt.

The more I thought about it, however, the more certain I became that I couldn't afford to wait that long. If I huddled here in this small patch of light until desperation drove me away, I would be almost guaranteeing my failure. I had to explore now, while I still had strength and my wits.

I tore a chunk of the bread with my teeth, taking my anger

out on the food. It would be too stale to eat soon, so I might as well consume it now. My stomach gurgled at the offering, reminding me it had been far too long since I last ate or drank. I groaned. I would have preferred to start this ordeal in better shape.

When the bread was finished, and the last crumb picked from my lap and consumed, I slowly repacked my satchel. As I placed each jeweled piece of fruit in, I wished it were real. How ironic that if I was anywhere else, I could have purchased a lifetime's supply with just one of these imitations. But the size, brilliance, and craftsmanship of the ruby did me no good down here, while an actual apple might be the difference between life and death.

I shook my head as I placed the lamp on top and scrambled to my feet. I would just have to find a way out quickly, so it didn't come to that.

Shuffling slowly, I set off into the orchard cave. I moved along the wall this time, feeling for any openings with my outstretched hands, while every sense strained for some whisper of breeze that might suggest an opening higher up.

These caves seemed to have the ventilation I was used to in Qalerim, unlike the cavern that had held the entrance. Surely that meant these were connected to the main network in some other way. I tried not to think of the cave-in that had trapped me here. Another entrance could easily have suffered the same fate at some point in the past—whether by accident or human inter-vention.

Not that I understood what had caused the one that trapped me. Malik's blows shouldn't have been able to cause such damage. Unless it was a side effect of whatever enchantment guarded the coins? Perhaps in all this time it had been changing, growing less stable. I gulped at the thought. I needed to get out of here.

I reached the entrance to the stairs without finding anything and passed over it, continuing until I had fully circled the room.

Still nothing. Retracing my steps, I shuffled up the stairs, but they led nowhere except the dead end pedestal I had found previously.

My fingertips were rough and scratched now from running them over so much rock, and I was starting to imagine sounds in the darkness. I sat on the stairs to calm my breathing and recover my balance. I had been in tight corners before, places that others found intolerable, and I hadn't struggled like this. It was the darkness that was getting to me. I was never traveling without my torch again, no matter where I thought I was headed. As someone who lived in Qalerim, I should have known better.

Another count against me. I sighed. I had made too many mistakes. If only I hadn't been paralyzed by indecision, I could have climbed right out of the hole and found a way to deal with Malik afterward.

After several steadying moments, I made my slow way back to the cave of coins. The glow remained, and I was gladder to see it than I wanted to admit—even to myself.

But any small measure of relief quickly disappeared. I had found not even the tiniest hint of a way out. I sat down again, pulling open my satchel as if I thought I might suddenly find more helpful contents inside.

In the repacking, the lamp had found its way to the top, and I took it out in a spirit of pique. This object of legend, sought by so many, must once have come from the Palace of Light, delivered into the hands of a human by a godmother. Or at least the rings that created it had been. And yet, it did me no good now. It might command obedience, but I didn't need obedience—I needed a path out.

"I command you to show me an exit," I said in a stern tone to a shadow that looked a little like a person if I turned my head to one side.

"Cassie!?!" The startled shriek made me drop the lamp.

Twisting around, I half toppled over so that I ended up

sprawled awkwardly on the ground gazing up at Kayla, who stood behind me.

She ignored my strange position, staring at the chests full of glowing coins. "What's going on? How did I get here? *Where are we?*" Her pitch rose as her excitement mounted, a new note of awe entering her voice. "Did you find it? Is this it? The lost treasure?"

I finally managed to get my legs under me, scrambling to my feet and gripping her by both arms. "Forget how I got here! How did you get here? One second I was alone, and the next you were here."

Kayla finally stopped looking around us and focused on my face.

"It was the strangest thing. I heard your voice say something about finding you an exit, and then my body bent down, sort of like this." She pulled away from me and executed a jerky bow. "And then suddenly I was here."

She spun around, her eyes skimming over the blocked tunnel entrance before fixing on the one that led to the jewel orchard.

"What's through there?"

"The most amazing—" I cut myself off. "No, never mind that. You wouldn't be able to see it anyway because it's pitch black in there. Unless you brought a torch with you?" I asked, hopefully.

She shook her head, her eyes still wide and her expression distracted. "I didn't bring anything. I was standing in the living area, wondering where you were, actually, and then I was here. Like I told you."

Stooping down to pick up the lamp, I stared at it. "I was just playing around. I didn't expect anything to happen. The story didn't say anything about the lamp—"

Kayla shrieked, cutting off my sentence, and grasping at my arm as if her legs had gone weak.

"Is that…is that *the lamp*? *You* have the lamp?!"

"Um...yes?" I stared at her in some concern. "It was through that cavern and up some stairs. I just took it off the plinth."

"You just...took it off the plinth," she repeated weakly. "Don't you know what this means?"

"No," I said promptly. "I have no idea what it means. Don't get me wrong, I'm delighted to see you, but I'm also entirely confused." My mouth twisted wryly. "I don't like being confused, but it seems to be happening a lot lately."

"This changes *everything*."

I raised an eyebrow. "That seems a little dramatic." Kayla was prone to dramatics, but even for her the statement was a little extreme.

"No, you don't understand." She stopped and wrinkled her nose. "But, no, let's not go into all that here. Let's get home, and then I can explain it all in more comfort."

"I would love nothing more than to go home," I said with admirable restraint. "But if you haven't noticed, we're currently in a cave, deep in the mountain, and that—" I pointed at the blocked passage, "is our way out."

She frowned. "Are you sure? I think the way out is in there." She pointed toward the orchard cave.

I stared at her. "How would you know? You haven't been here before, have you?"

"No, of course not!" Her emphatic expression slowly changed to one of confusion. "I can't tell you why I'm so sure. I just know I'm utterly sure the exit we want is that way." Again she pointed toward the remaining opening.

I tucked the lamp into my satchel and secured it over my shoulder.

"By all means." I gestured ahead of us. "Show me the way."

## CHAPTER 24

Still frowning, Kayla moved away from the light. I expected her to slow and start feeling her way in the darkness, but she didn't break stride. I scrambled to keep up, instinctively slowing as my eyes failed me.

"Wait," I called, and the sounds of her movement stopped. I nearly collided with her, muttering a quick apology as I put a hand on her shoulder. "Now I won't get lost."

"Good idea."

She resumed the fast pace, and I stumbled along behind her, shutting down my instincts which screamed at me not to move so fast in the dark. As long as I focused on keeping the connection between us, I could keep up.

"Here." She sounded faintly surprised at her own declaration. "It's a tunnel entrance. We should go this way." She turned and walked into what had been a solid wall of rock the last time I was in this cave.

"A tunnel?" I faltered and had to lunge forward to grab her shoulder again before she got too far ahead of me. "I've been all the way around this cave. There isn't a tunnel here."

She shrugged. "Then what's this?"

I opened my mouth to reply but couldn't think of anything to

227

say. Instead I followed her in silence as we walked the steep uphill incline of the tunnel. By the time we came across the first set of stairs, the black around us had lifted, gradually becoming lighter until I was able to drop my hand from Kayla's shoulder and walk freely.

By the time we stepped out into a corridor I recognized, it was fully light.

"It's morning," I said, latching on to the least surprising aspect of the situation.

Kayla nodded. "I was about to make breakfast when…" She trailed off as if unsure how to describe what had just happened.

"That tunnel just appeared out of—" My mouth dropped open, my sentence dying as I glanced behind me at the place we had just exited. "It's gone!"

Kayla spun around, her mouth dropping open just as mine had when she saw the solid rock wall behind us. "Where did it go?"

"I was about to ask you that. You're the one who made it appear."

She shook her head vigorously. "No, I didn't. I don't know anything about it. All I know is that we wanted to get out of that cave, and I had the strongest sense about which direction we needed to go."

My hand tightened on the top of my satchel, my mouth going a little dry.

"I…" I faltered, looking around for any sign we weren't alone before going on. "Perhaps it would be a good idea to get back home before we continue this conversation."

"Exactly what I was saying!" she cried triumphantly. "Come on."

She took off running, and it was all I could do to keep up after my exhausting day and sleepless night. Despite keeping a sharp lookout, I could see no sign of either Malik or any of the other qaleri. And when we reached the central living area of our orderly apartment, both Selina and Elias had disappeared.

"I asked them to fetch water from the river," Kayla said when I commented on their absence. "So they'll be back at some point, I'm sure. But never mind them. What just happened?!"

I carefully withdrew the lamp and placed it on a low table surrounded by cushions.

"I think it was this."

"The lamp." Kayla breathed the words, her tone holding equal parts reverence and terror. "I can't believe you found it. All those hours and hours you spent making that map finally paid off."

"I didn't find it on my own," I said grimly, and her eyes flew to mine.

Once again, doubt and indecision pulled at me as I tried to decide how much I should say. And then the crash of falling stone filled my memory. My hesitation had nearly killed me. If I wanted to defeat Malik, save the Four Kingdoms, and prove myself as an intelligencer, I had to rediscover my confidence in myself. I had possessed it once, and I could possess it again. I hoped.

It was time to take a leap of faith and trust the friend who had sheltered me all these months. No more analyzing and doubting. It was time for action. I lowered myself onto a cushion, gesturing for Kayla to join me. Together we gazed at the lamp.

"Malik is after that lamp." I glanced up at her as she sat across from me. "The Grand Vizier," I clarified, when she didn't react at all to his name.

"I know who he is," she said quietly.

"He said you told him I know Qalerim better than anyone."

"You do," she said, sounding miserable. "I'm sorry, Cassie, I wouldn't have said anything if I could help it." She leaned forward suddenly. "So you understood those cryptic directions, then? They meant nothing to me, and he was so angry about it."

I nodded slowly, regarding her with concern. "Yes, I was able to work out what they meant. They led to a distant and dangerous corner of the mountain. And when we got to the entrance to the treasure caves, it was so small, he couldn't fit through. Selina could have, but I'm not sure you would have—and Elias certainly wouldn't."

Her mouth dropped open, and her tone turned slightly offended. "What's the point of an entrance only a child could use?" A grin briefly flashed across her face. "Sorry, Cassie."

I rolled my eyes, not offended at her reference to my small stature.

"It might have been part of the defenses of the cave? Or perhaps there used to be another entrance." I regarded the lamp. "Or maybe the owner of the lamp had another way in—one that didn't leave a trace for anyone else."

Kayla nodded. "After what just happened to us, I'd believe it."

"Whatever the reason, I had to be the one to go in. So I was the one to find the lamp, and I didn't want to give it to Malik. So he collapsed the cave on me."

"He what?" She gaped at me. "But you still had the lamp?"

My mouth twisted. "To be fair, I don't think he meant to collapse the cave. Whatever enchantments still lie over that place, they must be very old at this point. And apparently unstable. Or I suppose it's possible the stone had cracked at some point in the past and developed a weakness. Either way, I ended up trapped inside. When I commanded the lamp to find me a way out, I wasn't serious. I was just expressing my irritation at the uselessness of the treasure. I certainly didn't expect anything to happen. Doesn't the story say that the lamp binds people to obey it? There wasn't even anyone there."

"But I appeared." Kayla stared at me. "You commanded the servants of the lamp to assist you, and I appeared—along with an exit that didn't exist before. Malik always said...but I didn't know if it would really..."

She let out a sudden giggle. "It was kind of incredible, wasn't it? And now you have the lamp! You give the orders! This is amazing! I have to tell the others." She started to scramble to her feet, but I held out a hand to stop her.

"Hold on. Don't go anywhere just yet. What are you talking about? I don't understand."

"I can't...Or wait, maybe I can." Her eyes widened. "I suppose the old rules might not apply anymore. He always said the lamp was more powerful than the ring." She stared at me with a hopeful look on her face.

"Slow down," I said. "Start at the beginning. You mentioned servants of the lamp? I don't—"

"The people bound to the lamp," she said impatiently. "Like in the story. Those who swore an oath of loyalty to the owner of the lamp."

"But no one's sworn an oath of loyalty to me," I said. "And certainly not since I claimed the lamp. I haven't even seen anyone other than you."

Something tickled at the back of my mind—a familiar phrasing that pulled at my memory. Where had I heard something similar before? Without conscious intention, I slipped into the memory palace I had built around my uncle's castle, the one I used to store all the clues I had gathered about Malik—the one I had started long ago on our journey across the desert.

"Aron!" I exclaimed triumphantly, and Kayla started violently, her head whipping around to stare at the doorway as if she expected to see Malik's lieutenant standing there.

"He's not here," I explained hurriedly. "I just remembered that a long time ago, he said something about people being bound to the ring. When you talked about being bound to the lamp, it reminded me." My thoughts sped ahead. "In the story of the treasure, there was a lamp and a ring."

Pieces began to fall into place, although the tapestry they made still had holes, confusing the full picture.

"Kayla," I said slowly, "how do you know about Aron? And

231

why was Malik asking about me? What exactly has been going on here in Qalerim?"

She drew a deep breath, her face full of trepidation and hope.

"I'm bound to the ring," she said in a rush. "We all are. And now it appears Malik is right and that makes us servants of the lamp as well."

"Kayla!" Elias stood in the doorway staring at us, a large jug of water hanging limply from his hands. "How did you—"

"What? What is it? What's happened?" Selina asked, crowding in behind him.

Elias stepped into the apartment, making room for her to follow. "Kayla just told Cassie that we're bound to the ring."

He clapped a hand over his mouth as if he couldn't believe the words that had just come out of it. Both of them placed their jugs on the ground, and Elias closed the door behind them, moving slowly, his eyes on us, as if he wasn't even aware he was still completing the rote tasks.

Selina suddenly screeched and grabbed at his arm with both hands. "Is that the lamp!?" she asked.

"Yes." Kayla looked up at them both, her eyes shining. "That's the lamp, and *Cassie* found it. Wait until you hear what happened."

"From the beginning," I said, jumping in quickly before she could start telling them about her unexpected appearance in the cave. "I still don't really understand what's happening here."

So many times the qaleri had cut themselves off, not finishing sentences, or not even starting them at all. But finally it seemed they were ready to give me some answers, and I didn't want to miss anything.

"Malik found us all one by one and bound us to the ring," Selina said, plopping onto a cushion beside Kayla, her eyes glued to the lamp.

"Are you really orphans?" I asked. "How did he find you?"

"Yes, everything we've said about our backgrounds is true,"

Kayla confirmed as Elias stashed the jugs of water in the kitchen and joined us. "Malik found us living on the streets and promised us a better life." She looked around the apartment with a twist of her lip.

"It is a better life," Selina said, leaning against her. "I like living here with you. It's like having sisters. I always wanted sisters." She smiled at me. "And I like it a lot better in this apartment without all the mess of the others."

"Yes, it smells better, doesn't it?" Kayla added. "I like it here, too. Most of the time."

Warmth crept into my tired limbs. Despite all my fears about Malik's plans, I had enjoyed the companionship I had found among the qaleri as well. Selina wasn't the only one who had grown up longing for sisters. And now at last we were breaking down the remaining barriers that had separated us.

"But I miss living in Sirrala," Kayla added. "I miss the hustle and bustle of the city."

"And besides, this was never supposed to be forever," Elias said. "Malik always intended for us to find the cave and bring him to the lamp. And I don't think we would like the life he has planned for us after that …"

"But Cassie found it, not Malik," Kayla said. "And that changes everything."

"Does it?" he asked. "Are you sure?"

She nodded eagerly, but I jumped in again.

"You're going too fast. So Malik has the ring? The enchanted object from the legend?" All three of them nodded. "He found each of you and promised you a better life in exchange for your oath of loyalty. The oath bound you to the ring meaning you were forced to obey him. So he…sent you out here to Qalerim?" I thought of how they all spent their days. "To search for the lamp! He's had you here all these years searching for the lamp?"

Kayla sighed. "That's right. Obviously we didn't know that's what we would be doing when we turned ourselves into servants of the ring. But once he had us under his power, he forbade us to leave, except to make regular trips into Sirrala to fetch supplies from him. We were only permitted to take holidays on our birthdays or on procession days—and that was only after Sari joined us and made a compelling case that we would work better if we occasionally had some time off."

"And he forbade us from telling anyone about the ring, the lamp, our situation, him—any of it," Elias added.

"Wait, you mean you weren't stealing those supplies?" A faint flush rose up my cheeks as I realized my false assumption.

Kayla chuckled. "No, although it was obvious you thought so, and I couldn't tell you otherwise. I've been worried you were going to suggest you take a turn."

I grimaced. "I was tempted to steal from Malik a few times. I certainly wouldn't feel bad depriving him of any of his ill-gotten earnings."

"You wanted to steal from *Malik?*" Elias sounded impressed.

"She's not a servant of the ring, remember," Kayla said. "She's not bound to do him no harm like we are." She paused. "Were."

"Were? So we're not anymore?" Selina asked.

"I don't think so." Kayla leaned forward, excitement in every line of her body. "You know we've been working to piece together everything we know from the legends and our own experience, plus Malik's claims. And we know the lamp and the ring are bound to each other. Malik always said that those who are bound to the ring are also bound to the lamp. But the lamp is the more powerful of the two. The bearer of the ring commands loyalty, but the bearer of the lamp commands actual obedience—beyond the natural ability of the servant, even. That's what happened to us. Cassie demanded an exit, and I was able to lead her to one, even though it hadn't existed moments before. That's why Malik wants the lamp so badly. But he didn't find it. Cassie did."

"So now Cassie controls the lamp," Elias said. "We can make our own army of servants."

"Josef's bad influence is rubbing off on you," Kayla said with an eye roll. "Of course we're not going to do anything so self-centered."

"But you're saying we could?" I asked doubtfully, looking at the lamp that looked just as ordinary in the light of day as it had in the cave.

"No, Elias is forgetting," Selina said. "The lamp and the ring are connected, and they serve different purposes. It's the ring that binds new servants."

"So wouldn't that mean you're all still bound to Malik?" I asked. "Although you only have to give him loyalty, not actual obedience?"

"It's a fine line," Kayla said. "We couldn't work against his commands, but there was wiggle room. Like with the holidays. Once we all believed that we truly would be more effective with the occasional holiday, the binding let us take them. It wasn't disloyalty anymore."

So it was the other qaleri Sari had convinced, not Malik. That made more sense than Malik proving susceptible to the argument.

"So what happens if my commands as the bearer of the lamp go against loyalty to Malik as the bearer of the ring?"

"Given we're all telling you the secrets we haven't been able to speak for years, it looks like Malik was right that the lamp is stronger," Kayla said. "Its owner takes precedence. So while you can't bind new servants, you have control of the existing ones."

"I have no desire to bind anyone," I said, "so that's not a problem. I don't particularly want to issue you a lot of orders, either."

"But we can't not use the power of the lamp!" Kayla cried. "How else are we going to free ourselves from Malik forever?"

"Did you really create a new tunnel?" Selina asked.

Kayla nodded, bouncing in place from excitement as she

235

described her experience to the others—my disembodied voice, the jerky bow, her sudden appearance in the cave, and our impossible exit.

"So, you see," she said at the end, "the enchantment on the lamp will help us if the command is beyond our capacity."

"So we can do anything?" Selina asked, her mouth falling open.

"There must be limits," Kayla said. "We should work out what they are. Cassie, command us to do something."

"Why is Cassie giving out commands?" asked a new voice from the doorway.

We all jumped, spinning to look at the newcomer. Something leaped in Zaid's eyes as they met mine, mixing with the hint of guilt and relief already lurking there. With a flash, I remembered the revelation about his identity and my intention to confront Kayla about it. I hadn't dreamed anything would be able to drive the issue from my mind.

"Zaid."

I stood, but his eyes had moved from me to the lamp which still stood on the table, with us in a circle around it.

"What," he asked in a strangled voice, "is that?"

# CHAPTER 25

"Cassie found the lost Treasure of Qalerim," Selina said in a matter-of-fact voice. "That's the lamp made from the rings of the two older brothers."

"That's the lamp made from..." Zaid repeated her words in a dazed tone, his voice trailing away.

He took several steps toward me before stopping. "I came to make sure you'd made it back safely, and to continue our conversation." He frowned. "I came as quickly as I could get away."

"I've only just got back," I said. "I had an unexpected detour on the way."

"Ha! To the treasure cave!" Elias said. "I wish I'd had that kind of detour."

"No, you don't." Kayla gave him a loaded look. "If one of us had found the lamp, it would be in Malik's hands by now."

"Malik?" Zaid started. "You mean he's behind all this? So it really is true, then, that you're servants of the ring? I suspected it, but I could never get you to confirm, or tell me who had bound you. I certainly never guessed...so you've all been bound to Malik this whole time?"

He shook his head before turning to stare at me, and I could read in his face that he fully believed my story about Malik's perfidy for the first time. "But what does this have to do with the vials and the army?"

"Vials?" Kayla asked, as Elias exclaimed, "Army?"

"I imagine having a group of servants able to carry out any command—no matter how impossible—would be helpful with anything and everything," I said.

"We don't know we can carry out *any* command," Kayla said doubtfully. "We need to experiment."

"I just…" Zaid stopped, shaking his head. "I can't believe that all this time it was Malik. I never even suspected him. How could anyone suspect him when he's so…pallid?"

I shrugged, since I would never have described Malik that way. "But why didn't you tell me what you suspected about the other qaleri?" I asked.

He looked uncomfortable. "I didn't know anything for certain. I suspected they had been enslaved, and I couldn't just abandon them to that fate. But despite all my efforts, I couldn't discover anything else about their binding, let alone how to break it. But I did know that whatever was going on, you were safer not being involved."

"We knew he'd guessed," Kayla jumped in. "But we couldn't confirm it. Our forced loyalty to Malik wouldn't allow it."

"As a boy, I was obsessed with the legend of the lost treasure," Zaid said. "And unlike other boys, I grew into a youth who had free access to the royal library, able to read every book and scroll I could find that had any reference to the tale. Once I became old enough to escape the palace on my own, I started sneaking out to Qalerim to explore. That's how I met the qaleri. Although it was just Kayla and Josef in the early days."

"The supplies Malik gives us are pitiful," Kayla said. "Thank goodness Zaid took pity on us and has been bringing us extra food ever since. He knew we were searching for the treasure, and he'd done enough research to recognize the signs that gave us away as servants of the ring. But we couldn't tell him who had bound us."

"I never gave up hope of finding a way to free you all," he said. "I kept hoping I'd have the chance to follow you and see who you reported to. But you always waited to go for supplies when I had royal duties and couldn't get away. My father thinks it's all a fantasy, and that I'm still wrapped up in the dreams of my boyhood, hoping to find the lost treasure. He says I should enjoy myself while I still have the chance, so he indulges my desire to escape the palace, but he won't let me use any royal resources. Otherwise I would have assigned guards to watch you in my absence." He glanced at me. "It's that history that made me afraid he wouldn't believe me if I started making wild accusations about Malik."

Kayla grimaced. "Sorry about that. We recognized you were the prince immediately, of course, which meant we also knew when royal duties would prevent you from following us. Our binding wouldn't allow us to knowingly be followed."

She glanced up at me. "Now it probably wouldn't matter. If you ordered us not to be seen, we'd probably go invisible or something."

I sat back down on one of the cushions, gesturing for Zaid to join us. A lot of things that hadn't made sense to me before now did—including the qaleri themselves. Now that I understood the motley collection of youths had been forced together through no choice of their own, the whole dynamic of the group made far more sense. But my mind still raced with questions.

"Why did Malik limit himself to you?" I asked. "Why not enslave an army of adults?"

"Because the ring won't let him," Zaid said.

"What?" Kayla stared at him. "I've always wondered about that, but Malik only gives us bits and pieces of information. Why can't he?"

"It's something I found in my research. On its own, the ring has significantly limited powers. And one of those limits is that it can't bind anyone above the age of sixteen. Without the lamp, it only works on minds that are less formed."

"But that's…"

"Despicable?" Zaid cut me off. "Yes. It is. Only the lowest of criminals prey on children. I still can't quite believe Malik…"

"You only have to look into his eyes to see there is no limit to Malik's wickedness," Kayla said ominously.

I grimaced. "I might not have worded it quite so dramatically, but I agree. I don't find it at all hard to believe Malik is capable of evil."

Zaid looked uncomfortable, but he didn't argue.

"Can you free us, Cassie?" Selina asked hopefully.

Zaid shook his head. "The binding is controlled through the ring. The only way to release it is for the ring to be destroyed or for the person who bound you to die. As the owner of the lamp, Cassie can command you, but she can't release you."

"I'm sorry," I said. "I would if I could, of course."

For a moment we all fell silent, looking between each other and the lamp. Finally Elias spoke.

"So what now?"

"If what Zaid says is true," I said, "then Malik must have survived the cave-in. If he hadn't, you would all be released from the binding, and the lamp would have no effect on you."

"Cave-in?" Zaid looked at me sharply, and I once again summarized my adventures since leaving the palace.

When I described meeting Malik and his various threats, Zaid grew very quiet and very still. I kept waiting for an explosion, but it never came. When the tension grew too much, I stopped talking.

"I'm all right, Zaid. Really I am. And somehow, impossibly, it seems to have actually worked out for the best."

"Malik—a man I welcome into my home, who I sit and eat

with—was going to leave you to die in a hole in the ground. Believe me, it's not all right."

I bit my lip, trying to refrain from pointing out that I had been trying to tell him about Malik's true nature.

Kayla had no such restraint. "You and Josef can get together later and discuss all the terrible things you want to do to Malik. For now, can you please let Cassie finish her story, so I can find out what exactly she was doing at the palace?"

I laughed, and even Zaid relaxed, the tension somewhat defused.

Hurrying through the last of the tale, I turned to Kayla. "Yes, I was at the palace, and yes, I know who Zaid really is now. Don't think I've forgotten that you knew all along. And didn't tell me."

Kayla looked unapologetic. "He chose not to introduce himself with his title. I just went along with it. It wasn't my secret to tell."

"And you were worried he would stop bringing you sacks of flour if you spilled all his secrets," I grumbled quietly.

I couldn't find it in me to be truly angry with her, though. She had been friends with Zaid before me, and I admired her loyalty.

"So we finally all know the truth about each other," Selina said with satisfaction. "I never liked having secrets."

"Actually, I've got something more to share." I could sense the significance of the moment. If the barriers were coming down between us, then it was time for me to tell the full truth as well. It wouldn't change anything—my friends all had their own reasons for wanting to bring down Malik—but it mattered to me. I had said it was time to let go of uncertainty, and that meant following my gut. Zaid might be the crown prince, but I trusted him not to misuse the information about a world beyond the desert.

"More revelations?" Elias asked. "This has turned out to be a very unexpected day."

I chuckled. "That's for sure."

"So we're finally going to find out who you were fleeing

from?" Zaid asked. His voice was quiet, but his eyes were intense, focused on me in a way that told me he had been waiting for this information for a long time.

"You were running away?" Selina asked. "I thought you didn't have any family but an uncle somewhere. Were you running from him?"

I shook my head. "He always treated me like a daughter. The men I was running from captured me and dragged me here. They were taking me to Sirrala, but I escaped into Qalerim."

"They were a distinctive pair," Zaid said, "and I've been watching for them ever since."

Something dangerous in his voice told me Aron and Samar had been fortunate to be sent away from the city.

I purposely didn't meet his eyes, looking at Kayla instead. "You recognized the name of Aron."

She started almost as violently as she had the first time I said it.

"Aron captured you?" Elias's skin—already pale from lack of sun—turned even whiter.

"Aron and Samar. So you all know them?"

"We used to collect our supplies from them," Kayla said in a small voice. "I always had the impression they would rather slit all our throats and be done with it. Only the knowledge that Malik valued us kept them in check."

"Although Samar felt our value to Malik wouldn't be impaired by a few blows if he thought we'd looked at him the wrong way," Elias said. "But they haven't been there for a long time."

"Malik sent them to oversee his operations outside the city," Selina said. "I overheard him mention it once."

"Yes, they went a long way outside the city," I said, trying to think of the best way to introduce the kingdoms beyond the desert.

"And they found you there?" Zaid asked. "And decided to take you to Malik? But why?"

"I'm only fully understanding it now. I think my life was saved by how young I look. I was over sixteen when they captured me, but they must have thought I was younger. They were bringing me back so Malik could bind me to the ring. They thought I might have useful information for him." I shivered. "And if he'd bound me to the ring, I would have been compelled to share it with him."

Kayla gasped. "How strange. But it makes sense if you had no family. Malik never risks taking young people who might be missed."

"He hasn't wanted to attract attention to himself," Zaid said, the threat in his voice demonstrating why that was so.

"Oh, I'm sure I was missed," I said grimly. "Celine probably tore the kingdom apart looking for me. But she'll never find me here."

"But you're not bound like us," Selina said. "Why don't you just go home?"

I looked around at their confused faces. "Because I don't know how to get home. I don't come from Ardasira or Kuralan."

"What do you mean?" Kayla frowned. "There isn't anywhere else."

"Not since the last of the nomadic desert tribes died out, anyway," Zaid said. "Are you from the tribes after all?"

"No, but I did come from the desert. I came all the way from across the desert."

"Across the Great Desert?" Elias scoffed. "Everyone knows there's no way across the Great Desert."

"Yes," I said. "That's what everyone in the kingdoms on the other side of the desert thinks, too. But I can assure you there is a way. I came across it. Aron and Samar didn't take me because I had no family, they took me because they knew no one could follow us. No one would even guess where I had disappeared to."

"But that's..." Zaid didn't finish his thought.

"Impossible? Unbelievable? Yes, I know. That's why I never

said anything. But then yesterday I found out my best friend is a prince and, about two seconds later, I found a magic lamp that opened a tunnel through solid rock. Do kingdoms on the other side of the desert really sound that unbelievable?"

A slow grin worked its way up his face. "When you put it like that..." A moment later his brow creased, his mind obviously joining the dots at lightning speed. "You said Malik is gathering an army, but that he's not planning a coup. You're afraid he's going after your kingdom?"

"Not mine specifically. I'm from..." I stopped. Now wasn't the time to explain the intricacies of my origin. "Lanover is the nearest kingdom, and the most obvious target. But that's not where I first encountered Aron and Samar. I think they mean harm to all of the Four Kingdoms. They talked as if Malik intended to send them back across the desert at the head of an army. And from what I've overheard, he's just waiting for the weather to cool again."

"Malik is the Grand Vizier," Kayla said. "Does that mean the sultan approves an invasion? Why don't the people know anything about it?"

"No!" Zaid frowned. "Many lives would be lost in a war. And to what end? We cannot rule a kingdom across the Sea of Sand, even if we wished to do so. My father doesn't dream of conquest."

"Perhaps Malik wants to win a kingdom for himself," I said. "It makes sense from what I've seen of him. He must hate being forced to hide in your family's shadow."

Zaid frowned. "Whatever his reasoning, he won't be acting with my father's assistance."

"Even if he's gathered the soldiers, it's not a small matter to transport an invading army across the desert," I said. "Maybe he thinks he can convince your father. Maybe that's why he's been waiting?"

"Or maybe he needs the lamp."

At Kayla's words we all turned to look at it again.

"He might have thought we'd find it sooner," Elias suggested.

"He probably thinks that once he's family, he'll have an easier time convincing the sultan." Selina's words contained a note of accusation, her disapproving look directed at Zaid.

My heart gave a thump and then began to beat so wildly I had to fight back a flush. The unexpected events of the past day had driven more than Zaid's true identity from the forefront of my mind. He had said he came to finish our conversation. Was it his upcoming betrothal he wanted to talk about?

Out of the corner of my eye, I could see him trying to capture my gaze. I kept my eyes firmly turned away, however.

"It doesn't matter who I marry," he said after a moment. "My father will never agree to sanction an invasion. Of anyone."

"But how could you marry Malik's daughter of all people?" Selina cried.

I stood up.

"It's been a long time since I had a proper meal," I announced into the sudden silence. "I'm going to make some breakfast."

No one said a word as I marched out of the room toward the kitchen. I hadn't eaten, and I hadn't slept, and I had apparently just become the owner of a magic lamp. I couldn't sit there and talk about Zaid's betrothal like it was just another subject.

A piece of dry fruitcake from the day before rested on a stone bench that ran the full length of the room. I tore off a chunk with my teeth, closing my eyes and thinking of nothing but the food as I slowly chewed.

"I didn't know about my father's arrangement," a voice said behind me.

I stiffened, not turning around.

"He was hoping I would change my mind and agree to marry Princess Adara during my visit to Kuralan," Zaid continued. "I told him I wouldn't, but..." He sighed. "While I was away, he made an agreement with Malik that if I returned unbetrothed, I would marry Jamila. I never agreed."

"You're his only child," I said to the stone bench. "It's understandable he wants you to marry and secure your line. That's what princes have to do." I knew I sounded stiff, but I couldn't help it.

"Cassie." His voice was pleading.

When I still didn't turn, he placed a gentle hand on my arm and tugged me around.

"Aren't you going to ask why I've resisted all his efforts to choose me a bride?" he whispered.

I swallowed the lump of bread which had turned into a stone in my throat. When had he come so close? I could see every fleck of gold in his brown eyes, and they made my empty stomach contract painfully. Slowly I shook my head.

I was going to stop Malik, save the Four Kingdoms, and help free my friends. And then I was going to return home. It didn't matter to me who the prince of Ardasira did or didn't agree to marry.

"Cassie," he said again, leaning closer. His eyes dropped to my lips, and my lungs stopped working, the piece of bread falling from my suddenly nerveless fingers.

"It's a strange thing," Kayla said, barreling into the room only to pull herself up short with an audible gulp.

Zaid sighed, not turning to greet her, but I seized on her arrival with relief, pulling free and turning to look at her. My eyes struggled to focus on her expression, but I kept them turned determinedly away from Zaid.

"What's strange?" I asked and then forced out a chuckle. "Or perhaps I should be asking what isn't strange after the last day."

I swayed as I spoke, my fatigue overtaking me and driving out even the insistent voice of my stomach. Zaid caught me, steadying me with an arm around my shoulders.

"You need to go to bed," he said. "The next strange thing can wait until you've had some sleep."

"But I can't—"

"Yes," he insisted firmly. "You can."

"But maybe not here." A new note of uneasiness entered Kayla's voice. "Just in case Malik comes looking for you."

I winced. I should have thought of that for myself. My brain was reaching its limit. Zaid was right—I needed to sleep.

"I'll pick one of the other apartments at random, and I won't tell you which one," I said.

She nodded approvingly. "And take the lamp with you."

Selina came into the room, the lamp gingerly cradled in her hands. "Here it is. And your satchel, too." She unslung it from her shoulder and held it out to me.

Zaid took both items from her, stashing the lamp inside the bag. I watched him with a crease between my eyes.

"You're the crown prince," I said, my mind struggling to keep my thoughts straight. "You should take the lamp."

"I can't," he said, and I couldn't tell if there was a note of regret in his voice. "The lamp belongs to whoever retrieves it from the pedestal. It's like the ring. You would have to die for someone else to claim it."

"I suppose it doesn't matter where I leave it then." But I still accepted the satchel and slung it over my shoulder.

"Except it might be possible for Malik to take it," Kayla said.

I frowned at her. "But Zaid just said—"

"If there's one person who has researched the ring and the lamp more than Zaid, it's Malik. And he sent you into that cave to retrieve the lamp for him. He must believe you can give it to him."

I looked at Zaid. He was frowning at Kayla, but he didn't contradict her.

"Well?" I asked. "Is it possible he could take it?"

"I think it might be," he said slowly. "Malik owns the ring, and the two items are linked. It's like with the hierarchy of the lamp being stronger than the ring and overriding the commands of the ring's owner. The one who owns the ring has more claim to the lamp than the one who removed it from the plinth. But either way, no one can use the lamp to issue orders unless it's in their possession at the time. So I think it would be a good idea for you to keep it with you."

"A very good idea." Kayla looked as uneasy as I felt.

"We can worry about all that later. It's time to find you a bed." Zaid put a hand under my elbow and guided me toward the door. "You have several thousand to choose from. And I'll keep guard over you while you sleep."

I frowned at him as we exited the apartment. "But you're the prince. Don't you have responsibilities to be getting back to?"

He said nothing, a rebellious light in his eyes.

"Zaid—" I placed a hand on his arm as we walked side-by-side.

He drew in a slight breath, his arm tensing beneath my touch.

"Right now, you're the only thing that matters to me," he said.

"Because of the lamp," I said firmly, telling myself that made sense. "Since we can't let Malik get his hands on it. Here," I said quickly, turning into a side tunnel and choosing an apartment door at random before he could reply. "This one will do."

I led us inside and walked straight to a bed in one of the back rooms. Whoever had lived here had filled the shallow wooden frame with soft desert sand, and I sank into it with relief, not even staying awake long enough to hear if Zaid had shut the apartment door.

# PART III
# THE OASIS CITY

# CHAPTER 26

*W*hen I woke up, I was alone. I took my time getting up, stretching out my aching muscles. But I didn't linger too long, my empty stomach driving me out of the bedchamber.

In the main room, I found a simple meal laid out on an abandoned stone table. I inhaled the dates before picking up the bread and following a fresh breeze through a side entrance.

I emerged onto a small, natural terrace. Zaid sat there, gazing out at the view. When I dropped down to sit beside him, he smiled at me.

"You're still here," I said.

"Of course I am. I promised to watch over you while you slept."

"And watch over the lamp." I looked back over my shoulder. I'd forgotten to even check on it, distracted by the sight of the food.

"Don't worry, it's still there." He sounded amused.

Silence fell between us as I continued to eat, my eyes following the line of the mountain as it fell away, merging into the distant swell of desert dunes. At first I thought our terrace was perched on the edge of an inaccessible cliff, but as my eyes roamed over the landscape, I picked out the faintest signs of a path.

"Is that a goat track?" I pointed to it.

Zaid nodded. "I think so. You picked one of the few houses in Qalerim with an escape route." He gave me a quizzical look. "Did you do it on purpose?"

I shrugged. "If I did, it was instinctive. I wasn't thinking clearly by the time we got here."

"You're amazing," he said, the words soft. "You have the mind of one of my father's most cunning viziers, and yet you have no desire for power or to rule over others."

I finished chewing my final mouthful slowly, considering his words as I looked at the desert below us. When I'd finished, I licked the last of the sweet dates off my fingers before speaking.

"It's true that I have no particular desire to rule, and no thirst for pomp and display. But I don't think that means I have no desire for power. I think everyone does in some way. The power we seek just comes in different guises, depending on the person —and some people keep it under better control than others." My mouth twisted to one side. "I'm not sure I'm any great example, though."

"I think you don't give yourself enough credit. That lamp would be a temptation to most people."

I glanced back at where my satchel sat against the table. "Perhaps. I was certainly grateful for it in that cave." I shivered.

Zaid slipped an arm around me, rubbing his hand up and down my shoulder, as if he thought I was cold. I stilled beneath his touch. I knew I should say something, should push him away, but I couldn't bring myself to do it. Instead I considered his comment.

Was I tempted by the lamp?

Certainly not as a source of wealth. I had felt no pull to touch the enchanted coins, and even the jewels had only drawn me because of their beauty. In the hours since I escaped the cave, I had almost forgotten about the ones I had stashed in my bag. Wealth had its place—it could accomplish a great deal—but luxury had never interested me.

The thirst that drove me was the desire for recognition—not by admiring throngs, but by the people that mattered. My uncle. Aurora. I had spent a lifetime listening behind walls because of a fascination with knowledge and a certainty that I was at least equally as capable as the adults around me. And as I grew, I became more and more obsessed with proving myself. That was why I had thrown myself into the cart of two threatening strangers and ended up on the other side of the world.

But when my efforts went wrong, when the months passed without finding the key to Malik's plans or even a way back across the desert, I lost my confidence. And I had let my sense of failure undermine me. What I desired wasn't something the lamp could grant—that was what kept me safe from temptation. I wasn't superior to anyone else.

It wasn't the lamp that held the key to regaining my confidence and ability. It was me.

"I should have asked you for help sooner," I said, the truth of the words settling around me.

Telling Zaid hadn't changed the practical situation with Malik —at least not yet. But it had changed me. I had thought the failure was in me—a weakness that needed to be stamped out. But giving myself permission to trust my instincts had already lightened my load. And having Zaid behind me made me feel positively buoyant, despite the challenges ahead.

Zaid's hand stilled for a moment and then tightened around me.

"I wish you had. But then, I should have told you the truth about me sooner as well. If I had, you might have been open from the beginning."

I hadn't intended to talk about myself, but I was finished second-guessing my every action. Alone on the mountain, it felt like we were the only two people in the world. But I knew the moment was fleeting, and I wanted to make the most of it.

I told him my whole history—my childhood in Eldon, the delegation to the Four Kingdoms, my desire to win a place in Aurora's network, my capture by Aron and Samar, and our journey across the desert. But I didn't stop there. Zaid knew of my life in Qalerim, but he knew little of my second life—the one I lived as a shadow on the streets of Sirrala, lurking around Malik's house and following him as he walked the city at night.

"As my friend Zaid, I didn't want to involve you," I said at last. "But you're more than that. As Prince Zain, heir to the throne, will you help me save the Four Kingdoms and find a way home?"

He had listened quietly, making only occasional comments, but he stiffened at my request. For a painful moment, silence stretched between us. Then he sighed softly, his shoulders slumping.

"I will help you, Cassie. I will always help you. You only have to ask."

"What are we helping Cassie to do?" Kayla asked from behind us, and Zaid's hand fell away from my shoulders.

"To leave us," he said, the words almost succeeding at sounding light.

"What?" Kayla looked at me accusingly.

"I have to go home at some point," I said, "but I'm not going anywhere right now. But what are you doing here? How did you know where to find us?" I looked accusingly at Zaid. "I thought we were supposed to be keeping our location secret."

He shrugged unapologetically. "I needed to get you some breakfast. And I wanted to know if Malik had showed his face."

"We need to decide what we're doing next." Kayla dropped down to sit beside us. "Don't worry, I'm the only one who knows you're here, and I haven't seen any sign of Malik since he asked me to help him with the directions yesterday afternoon."

She looked out at the view. "This is nice. Why aren't we living in this apartment?"

"It only has two bedrooms," I said absently. "And besides, you know Elias would end up falling right off the edge of this terrace."

Kayla chuckled. "You're right. He would. It's a pity, though. It would be nice to have a view."

"When this is over and you're free, you can have a room in the highest tower of the palace," Zaid declared.

Kayla gave him a skeptical look. "The highest tower? Really?"

He grinned. "I'm actually not sure there are any bedchambers in the highest tower. It's mainly used for observation and astronomy. But I'll reserve you the highest available bedchamber."

I leaned back on my hands. "I'd prefer one that opens into a garden."

"Done," Zaid said quickly. "Stay in Ardasira, and I'll have the gardeners design you your own personal garden."

"Somehow I don't think Jamila is going to let us all move into the palace," Kayla said dryly. "Or are the tales Josef just brought back from the city about a betrothal celebration tomorrow untrue?"

Zaid winced while I tried to keep all emotion from my face.

"There's to be a celebration tomorrow," he acknowledged. "And Father and Malik are determined to announce the betrothal. I haven't agreed, however."

"So Malik supports the betrothal, then?" Kayla asked.

I shook my head. "You doubt it? His daughter would be sultana one day. For a man obsessed with power, how could he not?"

She shrugged. "I would have assumed the same, but that's the strange thing I mentioned before you went to sleep. When Malik appeared in Qalerim yesterday, he was ranting about the betrothal and Jamila being a fool. I couldn't understand it because he's made mention of his plans for Jamila to marry Zaid a number of times over the years."

"Wait, does he know Zaid comes out here?" I asked.

She shook her head. "We never told him since it had nothing to do with him or our search. Just like we never mentioned you until he asked a direct question that required me to name you."

"He was upset by the betrothal?" Zaid sounded as confused as Kayla.

She nodded. "He certainly seemed so. And he kept declaring he had to have the lamp immediately. He'd shown me the same directions in the past—or at least I remember the bit about the grieving friends—but I could make no sense of them. He kept insisting they were different this time, and they must mean something to me, but…" She shrugged. "Given I'm bound to him, he eventually had to accept I was telling the truth. That's when he said if I was that useless, there must be someone who knew the mountain better than me." She threw me an apologetic look. "Given all your exploration, plus your ability to remember paths —no matter how maze-like—you know Qalerim better than anyone these days."

"Don't worry." I gave her a sideways hug. "I'm not upset with you. It's not like you had a choice."

"But my father told me Malik was the one to suggest the betrothal." Zaid frowned. "While I was away, he came up with the idea of a backup plan in case I came back still unattached. Why would he be angry about it now?"

"Maybe he thought the whole process would be slow, but Jamila is driving it forward faster than he intended?" I slipped into my memory palace, walking the familiar corridors in my mind and examining the many clues I had gathered. "Maybe he wanted the lamp before he married Jamila off to you?"

"Do you think he means to use the servants of the lamp to force my father's hand somehow?" Zaid sounded worried. "From everything I've read, the servants of the lamp can perform magical feats of obedience greater than mere servants of the ring, but there are limits to their powers. And while having the lamp would allow him to bind adults, surely there's a limit to how many adults would be willing to swear loyalty to him."

His words about adults swearing loyalty brushed against something in my mind, but I couldn't grasp hold of it. Instead I kept getting distracted by the image of Jamila as a bride. I couldn't bear the thought of her marrying Zaid. She would make a terrible wife, and an even worse sultana. She thought of nothing but herself. Even filled with excitement about her own coming betrothal, she hadn't felt the least bit of fellow feeling for the bride in the park. She had been full of nothing but irritation at the minor disruption to her own plans.

How long ago that seemed, although it was barely more than a day. And now the city was preparing to celebrate again, on an even grander scale.

"Cassie said Malik's been gathering an army," Kayla was saying while my mind wandered. "His soldiers might be willing to swear loyalty. They're already willing to fight in exchange for gold—maybe they'll give their oath for the same reward."

Zaid swallowed, his face reflecting horror at the idea of a whole army of lamp bound. "Is there no limit then to how many he can bind? I thought I read somewhere there was a limit before the power stretched too thin, and he began to lose people?"

Their words mingled in my mind with the images of the wedding in the park, and horror washed over me as I realized the full scope of Malik's plans.

"He doesn't need to bind the whole army," I said, rejoining the conversation. "He just needs to bind its commander."

Both of them frowned at me.

"He can't bind people by force," Kayla said. "It doesn't work unless they make the oath."

"My father would never swear himself to Malik." Zaid spoke

with confidence. "He's the sultan. It's Malik who must swear loyalty to him."

"Except," I said, "in the marriage ceremony of his only child. I saw a marriage alliance happening only yesterday—doesn't the traditional ceremony include a promise of loyalty between the two families—usually exchanged by the two fathers?"

Horrified silence gripped the terrace as we all considered my words.

"That's why he was so angry and so desperate to find the lamp," Kayla whispered after a moment. "With Jamila pushing for the betrothal to happen immediately, he knew he didn't have long until the marriage ceremony. He couldn't afford to wait any longer."

"But he didn't succeed in getting the lamp." Zaid's voice sounded tight and grim. "And we're not going to let him."

"If the betrothal is supposed to be announced tomorrow, he'll be desperate, though," I said. "And desperate people do dangerous things."

"As long as he has the ring," Kayla added, "we can't be truly free, and the lamp is still a danger. We have to find a way to get the ring and destroy it."

"How in the kingdoms are we going to remove a ring from his finger? There's no way he would give it up willingly."

"Actually." Zaid straightened, his expression lightening. "There may be a way to trap him. Without the ring, he can't bind my father, and without the wedding ceremony, he won't be able to trick him into giving the oath. He needs both the ring and the ceremony for his plan to work. It's traditional for a betrothal to be marked by the exchange of gifts. At the celebration tomorrow, I'll tell him that I want the ring as my gift. I've read about its engravings and even seen a sketch in a book, so I'm confident I can describe it. I can pretend I've seen him wearing it and admired it. When he refuses, I can take offense and refuse to agree to the betrothal. My father will back me because he won't understand why Malik would value a ring over an alliance with our family. It will be a great insult."

"What if your father's desperate enough for an heir to overlook the insult?" I asked. "He might consider your demand unreasonable."

"Then we give him another option to consider." The grin spreading over Kayla's face filled me with apprehension. "We dangle a more appealing alliance. He'll be thanking Malik for providing him with an excuse to back out of their arrangement."

"What sort of alliance?" I asked suspiciously. "Zaid has already refused to marry the Kuralani princess."

"But you've just told me she's not the only princess, after all," Kayla said. "You've just told me there are four new kingdoms to make alliances with."

"The Four Kingdoms?" I snorted. "I could barely convince you they existed. What hope do we have of convincing the sultan?"

I considered each of them, anyway—running through the royal families in my mind. "Besides, none of them even have any eligible princesses. They're all already married or too young."

"But my father doesn't know that." Zaid was grinning as well. "And if Malik knows it, he can't admit to the knowledge without giving away his double dealing."

"Exactly." Kayla nodded enthusiastically. "So we present him with a princess—someone who can answer any question he might have about these new lands."

"Oh, no. Just wait. You can't think I'm going to…" My words trailed off as I looked between the two of them—both regarding me with almost identical expressions of barely contained glee. "You think this is funny, don't you?" I accused.

"Of course not." Kayla tried and failed to keep a straight face. "This is a serious and dangerous situation."

"My father doesn't have to be completely convinced," Zaid said. "We just have to sow enough doubt that he'll side with me and repudiate the betrothal before it's announced. Since I haven't agreed yet, the final commitment hasn't been made. We can still withdraw with honor."

"You should use the name of one of the actual princesses," Kayla said. "If Malik recognizes it, it might throw him off stride. He might think the Four Kingdoms really have found their way across the desert. The princess could have been widowed in the time since he got his information or something."

"Absolutely not. If I have to masquerade as a princess, I'm at least using my own name." I considered for a moment. "Lanover has a Prince Cassian. I'll introduce myself as Princess Cass of Lanover. That should be enough to make Malik pause. He might think he has the details wrong."

"I suppose that will work." She sounded a bit disappointed, but I had already moved on to the next difficulty.

"I can hardly turn up completely alone at the doors of the palace and claim to be a princess. No one would believe that."

"No, of course not," Kayla said. "But don't forget you now command a whole team of servants." She bowed elaborately from her seated position. "Elias and Josef would look quite impressive as matching guards. They're not quite old enough, but their height will disguise that. And I could be your serving maid. You can claim you left the rest of your delegation in the city so as not to inconvenience the sultan."

I considered the idea. As reluctant as I was to involve the qaleri, I couldn't exclude them. They had been entangled with Malik for longer than I had.

"Actually, Selina can be my serving maid. I have another purpose for you," I said. "I need a team to watch Malik. If we're going to bring him down, we need to find evidence to present to the sultan."

"An intelligencer!" Her eyes glowed. "How romantic."

"Don't get too excited. The reality is small bursts of fear couched in long periods of boredom. There's a lot of waiting around."

"With the power of the lamp at our disposal, we'll be the best intelligencers ever."

I frowned. "I'm not going to use the lamp. I don't need to control you—we're working as a team."

"Don't be silly. Of course you'll use the lamp." She dismissed my words with a wave of her hand.

I opened my mouth to protest, but Zaid spoke first.

"Actually, Cassie, I think she's right. It would be one thing if we only had the ring, but they'll be far more capable with the power of the lamp to aid them. None of the qaleri are trained as intelligencers, so they'll be safer with the magic of the lamp behind them."

I met his eyes for a moment and knew we were thinking the same thing. It was more than just their capability or safety—although both were valid points. I would be safer that way too. With the lamp to bind them, they couldn't betray me through either choice or accident.

"Very well," I said with a sigh. "I guess it's time to find out how this lamp works."

# CHAPTER 27

*Z*aid was the first to rise, reluctance in every line of his body.

"If this plan is going to work, I need to convince my father I'm at least considering the possibility of cooperating. Which means I need to get back home before he sends half the guard out looking for me. It will be dark soon enough."

I glanced at the sun, hanging low in the afternoon sky. I had slept the day away.

"You go," I said. "And we'll see you at the celebrations tomorrow."

"You're sure you don't need—"

"Go!" Kayla said. "We'll be fine." She smiled in a satisfied way. "After all, we have the lamp to help us."

"Yes," I said uneasily. "The lamp."

Zaid looked like he wanted to say something else, but he merely wished us farewell, moving toward the door.

"Wait!" I cried, and he spun around so fast he must have been looking for an excuse to linger.

"As soon as he sees me at the celebration, Malik will recognize me. He'll know I survived the cave-in, and he'll guess I have the lamp. He might try to seize it from me right there."

Kayla looked from me to Zaid before holding out a flat hand toward him expectantly.

"It's a good point. Hand it over."

He glared at her, but I read acceptance behind his resistance.

I looked suspiciously between them. "Hand over what? Zaid, what's she talking about?"

Kayla raised an eyebrow. "How do you think Ardasira's one and only prince manages to stroll between Sirrala and Qalerim at will, as if he was an ordinary person? He has an enchanted object of his own."

"What?" I almost shouted at Zaid. "Is that true?"

He sighed and pulled a leather cord from his pocket. A small, shiny black stone hung from it. I stared at it with knitted brows.

"I've never seen that before. Do you usually wear it?"

"He only puts it on after he leaves Qalerim," Kayla said. "It renders the wearer not invisible, but…inconspicuous, I suppose. To anyone who doesn't know them, they look like themselves. But for anyone who does know them, they appear like a random passerby—the eye just sort of slides over them. Their own mother could walk past them in the street and not recognize them."

I gasped. "That's how you disappeared that day!"

"You tried to follow me?" Zaid looked more amused than surprised at the possibility. "Of course you did."

"Only once," I said. "It was after that I decided that if I had my secrets, I had to let you have yours. But you can't imagine how it undermined my confidence to lose you so easily."

"If you wear this, Malik will see nothing amiss," he promised. "You don't have to wear it around your neck. Tie it around an arm or a leg, or something. As long as the leather strap is encircling some part of your body."

"And what about you?" I asked. "Will you recognize me?"

He nodded. "I've seen the charm and held it. It won't work on me now. Like this one." He pointed at Kayla. "She used to harass me constantly until I finally showed her how I managed to get out of the city so often without being stopped."

I accepted the object from him. "Will you be able to get back into Sirrala without it?"

He glanced around the room which still had the musty smell of long disuse. "Somehow I don't think it will matter too much if I'm recognized this time. I suspect I won't be coming back here."

My breath caught. He was right, of course. One way or another, our life here in the ancient city was coming to an end.

"And I, for one, couldn't be more glad," Kayla said promptly. "Now go and make sure our future is in a palace, not in service to Malik."

He rolled his eyes but farewelled us again before jogging away.

I stared down at the object he had bequeathed me, amazed at the easy way he had handed over what must be a treasured possession.

"Yes, he trusts you. Yes, it's all very moving. Now we need to hurry up ourselves," Kayla said, prodding me in the side.

I gave her a reluctant smile, forcing my brain to switch tracks. "I want watchers on Malik as soon as possible. I'll need two three-person shifts so we can cover the whole night. I'll send—"

"I'm sure you know what you're doing," Kayla interrupted. "You don't need to convince me. Let's find the others and make it happen."

I collected my satchel, checking that the lamp and the jewels were still tucked inside, and followed Kayla out the door. We hurried onto the main corridor, picking up our pace as the light increased, flowing in from the enormous entrance. By the time we reached our familiar doorway, we were almost running.

Kayla had barely touched the handle when it flung away from us, pulled open by someone inside.

"There you are!" Elias cried. "We were starting to think you were never coming back."

Kayla rolled her eyes. "We had to come up with a plan to defeat Malik, and that takes a little time."

"You came up with something?" Selina's hopeful eyes peered around Elias. "What's the plan?"

"Cassie is going to use the lamp to give us all tasks. With its help, we'll be experts at everything. But we don't want to waste any time, so come on. We need the others."

Kayla abandoned our doorway for the next one along. Selina and Elias crowded close behind her, exclaiming in eager voices, while I trailed at the back. I seemed to be the only one less than enthusiastic about using the power of the lamp on my friends.

The other three burst into the apartment that had once been their home, calling excitedly for the others. I followed behind, wrinkling my nose at the musty, unpleasant smell and the mess strewn everywhere. The others kept their kitchen clean—no one fancied getting food poisoning—but the motivation finished there. As far as I could tell, the mess didn't even bother any of the others. It seemed obvious now that this group had been brought together by force rather than choice—the only wonder was that they hadn't split into two apartments a long time ago.

"What's going on?" Sari called to Kayla. "Josef saw Malik going into your apartment yesterday. He never comes to Qalerim."

Tension simmered just below the surface of the room, every qaleri present and on edge. I had been surprised to see them all together when I walked through the door, but I realized now they were anxious about what new havoc Malik planned to wreak on their lives.

"Are you ready to tell me what's happening, *Cousin?*" Josef asked Elias, the dissatisfaction in his voice suggesting he had asked before without success.

"Cassie found the lamp!" Elias announced with a self-impor-tant grin.

Kayla elbowed him as chaos broke out among the others.

"What?" He rubbed his side and glared at her. "We were coming to tell them, weren't we?"

I hid a grin. No doubt Kayla had been intending to make the announcement herself.

"Is it true?" Patrin called to her from the back of the clump of qaleri, every single one of whom had leaped to their feet.

"Yes, it's true," Kayla said. "Everyone settle down. We're not free of Malik yet, but we have a plan, and everyone needs to play a part."

She quickly outlined our strategy, keeping the story focused on Malik and the part the qaleri needed to play. When she finished, she gestured to me.

I stepped forward. "I'm going to issue some commands, and because you're bound to the lamp through the ring, you'll be forced to obey me. But I'm only doing it because this plan is to help all of us—if we succeed, I intend to destroy the lamp and the ring. And if any of you don't want to be part of this, you can speak up now."

"I've been waiting years to find a way to be free of Malik. If you think you can destroy him, I'll willingly obey your orders for a day," Josef said. "Especially if it gives me magic powers in the process." He grinned as the others murmured their agreement.

I took the time to meet each of their eyes separately before I nodded acknowledgment.

"Very well, then. I need two teams of three to watch Malik's home and Malik himself. The first team will go straight away, while the other team sleeps, ready to relieve them later."

"I'll lead a team." Josef stepped forward, Patrin close behind him.

"Actually, I need you to act as one of my guards, along with Elias," I said. "Patrin can lead a team, and Kayla will lead the other." The others would follow the two of them willingly enough.

"Go on, then." Kayla nodded encouragingly. "Give the commands."

I wasn't sure if I needed to be touching the lamp while I did it, or if having it in my bag was enough, but I figured it couldn't hurt. Pulling the lamp out, I held it in both hands.

"I command you, qaleri, not to tell anyone about me or about the lamp—by word, by deed, or by inaction. And not to let yourselves be seen by Malik or anyone else not in this room, except Zaid."

"How are we supposed to do that?" Sari interrupted to ask.

"You all lived on the streets before you came here," I replied. "You know how to avoid drawing attention to yourselves. Just do that, and trust in the lamp to help with the rest."

"I think we're going to be invisible," Kayla said gleefully, and some of the younger qaleri muttered excitedly to each other.

I ignored them, eager to get this part out of the way as quickly as possible. "I command you to watch Malik and his home, and to report to me immediately if there is any unusual activity, or if you discover anything of interest."

All of them bowed, bending in half at the hips as if pushed from behind by a large hand. Several of them gave cries of surprise, but Kayla just met my eye when she straightened, nodding significantly toward Selina.

"Oh yes, Josef, Elias, and Selina," I added. "You're not to go spying. I command you to play the roles of guards and serving maid of Princess Cass of Lanover."

The three of them made a second, awkward bow. Josef and I hadn't always seen eye to eye—on room cleanliness for one—but he straightened back up with a grin on his face.

"This is going to be fun." He cracked his knuckles. "I can't wait to see Malik's face when he finds out we've fooled him."

Several of the others laughed before Patrin broke off to assemble his team of three and head out of Qalerim.

"How will we know how to find you?" he asked me as they

scattered to gather whatever supplies they deemed necessary. "In case we have something to report."

"I'm hoping the lamp will help with that," I said.

"It will." Kayla spoke with confidence. "Just follow your instincts—however little they make sense. If you feel a strong sense that the answer to your problem is in a certain direction, that's the lamp directing you to its solution."

Patrin looked bemused, but he accepted her explanation, and it was soon just Elias, Josef, Selina, Kayla, and me left in the room.

"What next?" Selina asked.

"Next is the fun part." Kayla rubbed her hands together gleefully. "Cassie needs an outfit."

Josef and Elias gave matching groans, and Selina looked less than impressed.

"Our part doesn't start until the morning," I said. "Why don't you all try to rest. Who knows what tomorrow will be like?"

Reluctantly, the others scattered, an air of anticlimax hanging about them. Kayla remained undaunted, however, tugging me back toward our apartment.

As soon as we were alone, I voiced my doubts. "I know you should be sleeping like the other members of your team, but what *am* I going to wear? I hadn't even thought of that yet." I tapped my satchel. "I could buy something, except I'd rather not part with any of the fruit. It will attract too much attention, and I have other plans for them."

"The fruit?" Kayla stared at me as if I'd lost my mind.

"From the cave. Didn't you see? Oh, of course, it was too dark when you arrived. Here, look." I pulled my satchel open and tipped it toward her. "There were carved trees full of these."

Kayla's jaw dropped open as she pulled out an emerald apple and examined it. "You've just been carrying those around in your bag? You have a fortune in there!"

"Yes, but it's a distinctive one. Coin would be more useful for this purpose."

"What are you planning to do with it?" she asked. "You said you had a different plan? Are you going to take it back home with you?"

"I'm going to present them to the sultan," I said. "As a gift from the fictional Princess Cass. I'm hoping it will make him more inclined to believe I really am a foreign princess—and one from a wealthy kingdom worth allying himself with."

She nodded vigorously. "He'll have to believe you're a princess if you casually give away a pile of these!"

"But he won't think that if I turn up dressed in rags." I looked down at my jacket which was dirty and torn after my adventures in the cave.

"You're forgetting the lamp." She reluctantly placed the apple back in my bag. "Try commanding me to give you a royal celebration gown fit for a Lanoverian princess."

"Do you think one will just appear?" I asked.

She bounced up and down on her toes. "Maybe? Let's try!"

Curious despite myself, I retrieved the lamp and repeated the command. Nothing happened. I peered around the room.

"I don't see a gown anywhere."

"No." Kayla looked disappointed but also intrigued. "And I didn't bow. I guess that's how you know the command is beyond the capacities of the lamp."

"Maybe it can't produce items from nothing? Let me try wording it differently." I thought for a moment. "I command you to make me a gown fit for a Lanoverian princess."

"Oh!" She jerked downward again, a movement that was fast making me uncomfortable. "I'm feeling a strong inclination to work on that dress you gave me to patch last week." She hurried over to a neat pile of mending in the far corner of the room and retrieved the gown I had been wearing when I first arrived in Qalerim.

My uncle had ordered it made especially for my trip in one of the styles popular in the Four Kingdoms, so I had never worn it into Sirrala, not wanting anything to draw attention to me. But I had worn it through the tunnels of Qalerim often enough that the material had started to give way.

"I don't think there's any way that gown can be made to look fit for a royal celebration," I said doubtfully.

Kayla just shook her head. "Give me a chance. Or rather, give the lamp a chance."

She sank onto a cushion, pulling her sewing kit near and selecting needle and thread. Within moments, she was making neat stitches in the gown.

"Describe what you have in mind," she said as she worked. "You'll want something in a Lanoverian style."

"A ballgown, of course," I said, watching her flying fingers. "In softest silk, with a long flowing skirt."

"What color?" she asked.

I laughed. "Since we're dreaming here, how about a dusky pink? With a train, of course, and half sleeves. And embroidery on the bodice. Oh, and a sheer cloak of the same color, to go over the top. And rose gold jewelry to wear at my throat and..."

My voice stuttered, dying away as something strange began to happen beneath Kayla's fingers. A dusky pink spread out from her flying needle, staining the fabric which seemed to be growing, falling voluminously over her lap in silken folds. Within a minute, the entire gown had transformed.

"It looks like it needs something to work with, as a starting place," Kayla said, the same astonishment in her voice that I was feeling.

"Or maybe it needs you to do something?" I suggested. "After all, it's supposed to be an enchantment based around obedience."

Kayla shrugged and grinned. "I don't care why it works, as long as it works. You'd better order me to make outfits for Selina and the two boys as well."

I did so, watching with fascination as she turned other items from the mending pile into two elaborate guards' outfits and a uniform for Selina that would make her look more like a lady-in-waiting than a servant.

"Maybe they'll actually believe I'm foreign royalty," I said, starting to think for the first time that this plan might work.

"Of course they're going to," Kayla said, her voice suddenly fierce. "They have to."

# CHAPTER 28

*J* tried to hold on to that confidence the next afternoon
as I stepped out of a side entrance to Qalerim, my soft
train gathered in one hand. I had scampered down the goat track
in front of me countless times but never in a gown like this.

"I can't arrive at the palace covered in dust," I said doubtfully.
"I don't know why I didn't think of it earlier."

"You're supposed to be a princess. You shouldn't be walking at
all." Josef, having fully entered into his role in our little drama,
frowned at me thoughtfully. "We should have something to carry
you. That would be proper."

"Carry me?" I laughed. "All the way down the mountain? Just
the three of you?"

"Don't forget the lamp," Josef said. "If it works like you say it
does, it should make you light as a feather—or make us immea-
surably strong, or something."

"Oh, of course! The lamp. That's the answer for the chair as
well."

I slipped my hand into the silk purse Kayla had made for me.
It brushed against a small collection of shiny gold coins, and I
shook my head. The lamp certainly didn't hold back when it
came to royalty. At Kayla's suggestion, I had commanded her to

create me a purse fit for a princess, and apparently such an article wasn't complete without coins hidden inside.

But it was the lamp I wanted now. My hand fastened around it.

"I command you to make me a chair fit for a princess." I glanced around. "Out of that wood over there. And then carry me in it to the royal palace."

All three of them fell into jerky bows, then hurried to obey, grinning at each other. They had all heard the story of their outfits from Kayla, and they were eager to try it for themselves.

As they lashed together the branches from beneath a twisted tree, the wood transformed, growing strong and beautiful. When they trotted back to me, Elias and Josef each held the handles of one end of an elaborate, enclosed carrying chair.

They placed it on the ground, and Elias gave an exaggerated bow. "Your chair, my princess."

I snorted but climbed inside, gaping at the jewels that now lined the frame. Josef was also eyeing them.

"Do you think they're permanent?" he asked. "Or will the whole thing disappear once you no longer have need of it?"

"I have no idea, and I don't much care." I arranged my skirts so they weren't at risk of trailing into the dirt. "All I care about is defeating Malik."

"Speak for yourself," Josef muttered, but he picked up his end of the chair without complaint.

"Well, am I light as a feather?"

"Maybe not quite a feather," Elias said, "but light enough that we can make it all the way to the palace without exhausting ourselves."

They started down the mountain, picking their way without much care.

"Please don't tip me out," I said nervously. "That will ruin the dress for sure."

"We won't," Josef said confidently. "You ordered us to carry you to the palace. I've never been so certain of my steps on this trail before, or felt so sure-footed. We'll get you there, never fear."

I shook my head. "I'm starting to understand why Malik spent so long searching for the treasure cave."

"What was it like?" Josef asked, and I spent the rest of the way down the mountain describing its wonders to them.

We weren't the only ones entering the city for the celebrations, but the richness of my chair and our garments drew whispered exclamations from the other travelers waiting at the gate. And the guards who let us through all gave bows of respect.

Word seemed to ripple ahead of us because our path toward the palace cleared, people stopping what they were doing to watch us go by. Here in the city, the preparations already looked complete, and a celebratory atmosphere pervaded the air. The shops of the merchants had been transformed with fine carpets, cushions, and green boughs, and everywhere illuminations hung, ready for night to fall.

"A princess!"

"She must be!"

The whispers ran ahead of us, and I drank them in, letting my role settle over me. An intelligencer might be called on to act the part of a princess as easily as a street orphan, I reminded myself. It was all just part of the illusion.

The road led us past the houses of the nobles, their connected gardens lining our path with green on both sides. People emerged from some of them, joining us on foot, on horseback, by carriage, or in carried chairs of their own. I noted none of the conveyances were as rich or beautiful as ours, though.

The palace rose before us, its gold and silver towers reflecting the sun. All too soon we reached the first gate. Most of the crowd around us dismounted, ready to walk the rest of the way, but a select few continued on to dismount at the second gate. I caught the self-important, pompous look on the face of one such noble, and wrinkled my nose. But we had discussed what should happen here, and I reminded myself it was a necessary part of the act.

Josef and Elias attempted to carry me through the gate, only to be stopped by a doorkeeper who gave polite instructions for me to dismount.

"Our mistress is royalty," Josef announced in a loud voice from his position at the front of my chair. "She will dismount at the palace door, as befits her station."

The doorkeeper fell back, startled, before exchanging looks with his brethren. The other guests in our vicinity looked over, whispers breaking out and spreading in all directions.

The head doorkeeper of the outer gate approached, his manner respectful.

"Ardasira has no princess." His eyes darted around, taking in my gown, the expensive outfits of my servants, and the chair itself. They almost started from his head when he saw the size of the jewels embedded in the wood.

"I am not from Ardasira," I said, glad for the extra height provided by the chair since I was normally too short to look down my nose at anyone. "I bring greetings from my own people to Their Majesties, Sultan Kalmir and Sultana Nadira. Do you intend to bar my passage?"

He hesitated, his eyes darting once more to the gems on my chair, before he stepped back and gave a deep bow.

"No, of course not, Your Highness. Please forgive my mistake."

One of the other doorkeepers murmured something, but the one speaking to us shot her a silencing look. When his gaze slid toward the doorkeepers at the second gate, I realized he had decided to pass on the problem of my identity to his superiors at the inner gate.

Josef and Elias moved forward again, carrying me through the outer courtyard toward the second gate, Selina walking close beside. One of the doorkeepers ran ahead of us, whispering to those waiting, although the rumor of our arrival had already preceded us.

The head doorkeeper of the inner gate stepped forward to meet us with a deep bow, apparently not wanting to risk giving offense despite the uncertainty around my status.

"I apologize, Your Highness. We weren't expecting you."

"I have traveled a vast distance to see your sultan," I said. "And I am told there is a great celebration underway. I did not wish to miss the opportunity of presenting my gift to your ruler."

As I spoke, I shifted the large bowl in my lap, peeling back the simple white linen that covered it. The head doorkeeper leaned forward to peer inside.

For a long moment he stood frozen, eyes wide. Then he visibly pulled himself together, drawing back and stuttering for a moment before bowing deeply again.

"I am certain our sultan will receive you most graciously, Your Highness." His eyes passed over my two guards and one serving maid. "You desire entrance only for the four of you?"

"It is a party, is it not?" I kept my voice light. "I left my guards in the city as I would not insult your sultan by implying any lack of trust. But I must have someone to carry my chair, and a girl to help with my gown."

"Naturally." He bowed again, and I could almost see the calculations going on behind his eyes.

The four of us could be no great threat to the sultan in his own home. And the risk that I might not be royalty must be weighed against that bowl of jewels. How could anyone but a princess bring such a gift? If he turned me away now, I might take insult and leave, thus denying the sultan possession of those wondrous jewels. Who knew what punishment might come his way in that case?

"We are honored by your presence." He held out a welcoming arm, gesturing for us to pass on, and I caught a flash of Josef's triumphant smile as my chair started forward again.

We had passed the first hurdle.

The chair stopped at the foot of the shallow steps that ran up to the vast double doors. I took a fortifying breath and handed the bowl to Selina as I dismounted, checking as I did that I could still feel the cord of Zaid's enchanted object secured out of sight around my ankle. It pressed reassuringly against my skin.

Selina gave the bowl back, falling into step one pace behind me while ushers directed Elias and Josef where to carry my now empty chair.

When I reached the top of the stairs, I paused, waiting for them, and they hurried across the courtyard to flank Selina.

A lush red velvet carpet ran from the entrance to the door of the throne room, which had been thrown wide for the occasion. I walked the path it provided slowly, my attendants at my back, all my attention on not tripping over my long skirt.

The few people in front of us made way, stepping to either side as whispers engulfed us, fanning out from our passage. By now half the city must have heard that an unknown foreign princess had arrived.

I reached the door of the great throne room, and an usher hurried forward to take my name. He passed it on to a herald who stared at me in confusion.

I ignored him, waiting with an imperious air and stiff spine. My confidence must have convinced him because he shrugged and signaled to the trumpeter. A short fanfare—the type reserved for royalty—made the room fall silent. Into the quiet, he announced my arrival in a loud voice.

"Her Royal Highness, Princess Cass of the kingdom of Lanover."

With all eyes on me, I stepped into the room.

# CHAPTER 29

*D*irectly ahead of me, Sultan Kalmir sat, his throne on a raised dais. At my entrance, he stood, and I could see the confused question on his lips, although the distance was too great for me to hear his words.

Two familiar figures stepped to his side in response, and my heart contracted at the sight of Zaid in the formal robes of a prince. He had always looked commanding in the dusty, abandoned splendor of the mountain, but now he was dressed for the part.

Reluctantly my eyes slid away from Zaid, catching on the man who stood on the sultan's other side. My hands fisted in my skirts. Malik.

Having sought approval from his father, Zaid leaped down from the dais, hurrying through the crowd to stop in front of me. When he smiled down at me, I wanted to scold him for the intimacy of the expression. He couldn't give me the special smile I had received so often in Qalerim. We were supposed to be strangers.

"Greetings, Princess Cass." He gave a shallow bow. "Your arrival is most unexpected." His eyes laughed, making it hard not to respond in kind.

"Greetings," I said. "I have come bearing a gift for Sultan Kalmir."

His eyes flew to the bowl in my hands, his face finally registering the appropriate air of surprise. He had left before we discussed my plan for the jewels.

"He is most anxious to meet you." He offered me his arm.

I handed the bowl to Josef and placed my fingers lightly on his elbow, allowing him to guide me down the long room.

"Please excuse my people," Zaid said in a loud voice. "They are merely stunned at your beauty and elegance."

I couldn't suppress a disbelieving chuckle that bordered on a snort, but his words had the desired effect. The frozen room began to move and talk again, although those closest to us still openly watched our passage.

The music resumed, the sound of stringed instruments and woodwinds blending together to provide a melodious background to the hundreds of hushed conversations.

"There's no going back now," I murmured in an under voice. "Word of the existence of the Four Kingdoms will be all over Sirrala by nightfall—whether or not it's believed."

"It will be believed," he said, with confidence in his quiet voice. "No one looking at you right now is asking themselves if you're truly a princess."

I flushed at the warm admiration in his eyes, unintentionally ensuring we presented the perfect picture as we arrived together at the foot of the dais. Looking up at the sultan and seeing the way his eyes lingered on his son, I doubted he would need prompting from Zaid to see the potential for an alliance.

Malik had disappeared during our procession down the room, and Zaid's mother had taken his place beside the sultan. The sultana wore an elegant robe of dark green silk brocade that glittered with gold thread. A draped shawl half covered the elaborate arrangement of her dark hair, the golden embroidery which edged it matching thin gold chains threaded through her tresses. The overall effect of both opulence and refined elegance made me grateful to be wearing a gown produced by the lamp.

I glanced sideways at Zaid. He had inherited his commanding air from both parents.

Zaid gave them the same shallow bow he had afforded me.

"Father, Mother, may I present Princess Cass of Lanover."

"I am not familiar with the kingdom of Lanover," Sultan Kalmir said, in neutral tones. "Nor of any kingdom beyond Ardasira and our neighbor, Kuralan. From what region do you come, and how have you reached us?"

I bowed deeply, gesturing for Josef to step forward with the bowl.

"I have come from across the Great Desert, Your Majesty, where my kingdom is one among many. I wish to offer you this gift as a token of my goodwill and of my wishes that our lands might find mutual prosperity through an alliance of friendship."

Josef dropped to one knee and held the bowl up while I pulled off the covering. All three members of the royal family gasped as the many lights in the throne room caused the fruit inside to glitter and shine.

The sultana descended the two steps of the dais to lift a small cluster of amethyst grapes from the bowl. She examined them from every angle before placing them gently back and glancing up at her husband.

"I have never seen such a treasure. Each one is unique and valuable beyond price."

"But not," I said, "as valuable as friendship between our two peoples."

"Very prettily said." She smiled for the first time, the expression lighting her face and softening the assessing gleam in her eyes.

I instantly desired her approval—not just for the sake of our mission but on a personal level. It was easy to see why Zaid's father had chosen her. No doubt he was only one of many who had gone to great lengths to earn her smile.

"I mean it with all my heart, Your Majesty," I said softly. "I would give you twenty such bowls in exchange for peace and prosperity between us."

"Be careful," she said softly, "or my husband might indeed name such a price."

My eyes flew to hers, a smile leaping to my face at the amused gleam in the depths of her gaze.

"Would any price be too high to pay?" I asked and caught the soft glance she threw at her son.

"No, none."

I cleared my throat. Somehow we had strayed directly into deep waters, and I couldn't let myself forget I didn't really have an alliance to offer—although I would willingly talk to the Lanoverian king and queen on the Ardasirans' behalf if I ever made it back across the desert.

The sultan gestured, and a servant leaped forward, taking possession of the bowl. At another sign, a second servant appeared with a small wooden table which he placed beside the throne. The first servant positioned the bowl upon it so it stood at the sultan's elbow, and then they both bowed and withdrew.

"No one bearing such a gift could be unwelcome, Princess Cass," the sultan said. "And I hope to have leisure in the future to examine the beauty of each jewel more closely. But greater still is my interest in the claims you make about lands beyond the desert. I had thought the rumors of such mere legend."

"As my people long thought about your kingdom," I said. "I welcome such a discussion—at a more suitable occasion."

Sultan Kalmir glanced around the room. "Indeed. Tonight you shall be a guest in my palace, and we shall meet in the morning."

I bowed again. "I thank you, Your Majesty. Perhaps my servants might be shown to our rooms now?"

Approval leaped into his eyes at this suggestion, as if he had suspected I meant to disappear at the first opportunity. Royal servants were once again beckoned forth and soon led the three qaleri away. Selina glanced backward over her shoulder as she went, and I gave her a reassuring smile. Hopefully they could keep safely out of sight for the rest of the evening. As reliable as the lamp had so far been, I saw no need to test its abilities.

"May I escort you to the refreshment table, Princess?" Zaid asked.

I agreed, and we moved away from his parents.

"Where did you get those?" he asked in a whisper. "When you said you had a gift, I couldn't think what it might be. I certainly didn't imagine such a wonder."

"From the cave, of course," I replied in even quieter tones. "I brought them out in my satchel, and it's a good thing I did. I'm not sure I would have gained entry here tonight without them— or received such a favorable reception from your father. My impossible claims seem more believable when I bear such a gift as if it is no great thing."

"It was well done." The approving light in his eyes reminded me of his words on the terrace, and I had to fight to keep down another flush.

When he handed me a laden plate, our fingers brushed, and my heart lurched in response. Seeing him here as his true self was affecting me more than I wanted to admit. Or maybe my heightened responses were a consequence of our conversation on the terrace.

He turned from me for a moment to respond to someone on his other side, and I took the chance to study his profile. How familiar it was, despite the new setting. My heart thumped again, and a sense of certainty that felt almost like peace settled over me.

My head had refused to fall in love with someone so full of secrets, but my heart hadn't listened. And my repeated denials didn't make it any less true. I had been in love with Zaid for months.

For a moment I wondered if I was so mercenary that it had taken the revelation of his rank for me to acknowledge my feelings. But I rejected the thought almost immediately. And it wasn't even the removal of the barrier caused by our secrets that had made me willing to admit my love, although that had played a part.

The change had come from inside me. From early in my life, I had tried to distance myself from the role my uncle wanted me to play—convinced that to be an intelligencer, I needed to prove that it was my head in control, not my heart. And the rash mistakes I made as soon as I left home seemed to confirm that idea. If I wanted to save people and make a difference, then I would do it by listening only to my head. But that approach hadn't worked. As more time passed, my ongoing failure bred uncertainty, and my decisions became slower and poorer.

I had denied the role my instincts played. And in doing so, I had reduced myself, limiting my true potential. My mistakes had come from youth and inexperience, not because emotions were weakness. In a world populated by people, there would always be a role for the heart in understanding what was going on around me.

It was true that I had seen too much and gained too many new experiences to ever return to the certainty that came only with extreme youth. But that was inevitable. And I could use that experience to make wiser, better decisions—decisions that used both my head and my heart, working in unity. I needed to trust my instincts—the very instincts that had saved me when Malik nearly discovered me in the room of vials. I needed to let my heart play its part, responding to things my head couldn't even see.

After the treasure cave, when I finally accepted that my heart was as much a part of me as my head, I had begun the process that had led me here. I had opened the way to hear what my heart had been shouting at me all along.

Of course I was in love with Zaid.

My eyes caught on someone standing half way across the room, her furious gaze locked on me. I gulped. How much of my emotion had been visible on my face?

Too much from Jamila's expression. She spun around, marching away in the direction of the throne. I leaned toward Zaid, and he responded instantly to my small movement, closing the conversation with the person on his other side to turn back to me. I bit my lip. How closely had he been attuned to me that whole time? Had he read me like Jamila seemed to have done?

But I couldn't allow myself to get caught up in my own feelings. We hadn't come here tonight for ourselves, but for something much more important.

"Look at the dais," I said quietly, not turning myself. "I don't think Jamila is happy."

His gaze locked over my shoulder, and he sucked in a breath. "She and Malik are talking to my father now. This might be my opportunity to bring up the ring."

"Go!" I hissed. "Hurry, before it's too late."

He strode away, and this time I did turn to watch him go. We shouldn't have strayed so far from his parents. It would have been too easy to miss our chance.

I drifted toward the dais, moving as naturally as I could through the crowd so as to hide my true destination. At first no one spoke to me since there was no one with me to make introductions. But just as I reached my goal, an older nobleman grew emboldened enough to approach.

Positioning myself so my back was to the throne, I seized the excuse to linger in the area, exchanging bows with the man. Unsurprisingly, his first question was about my origin. The news that I came from across the Great Desert was met with a self-satisfied response as he launched into an extended tale about his long-ago boyhood, claiming to have been friends with one of the last remaining desert nomad families.

At first I was interested to hear his account since he talked of the family knowing a secret way across the desert. But as the story dragged on—becoming more and more about himself—I realized the only member of the family he had actually spoken with was another young child. Disappointment filled me as I realized he was speaking of nothing more than the exaggerated tales exchanged between young children. After that, I continued to nod and murmur at appropriate intervals, but my attention wandered to the hushed conversation happening on the dais.

"We cannot trust her, Your Majesty," said Malik's familiar voice. "This talk of a kingdom across the desert is nonsense."

"Perhaps," the sultan acknowledged. "But tell me, Malik. Could you produce such items as these? Do you know of a local craftsman with such skill, or local mines that produce such jewels?"

I almost smiled at the frustration Malik must be feeling. Did he know what treasures the cave contained other than the lamp? Was he tormenting himself wondering who I really was and how I had gotten my hands on the cave's riches? I hoped so.

"There has always been the occasional rumor," Zaid said. "I see no reason to dismiss her claim out of hand. If there are more kingdoms across the sand, it could be a lucrative opportunity."

I could hear the double meaning in his words, although he wouldn't openly mention a marriage alliance in the presence of Malik and his daughter.

"This was supposed to be an occasion for celebration, not business," Jamila said in her sweetest voice. "When will you announce our happy news so that all of Sirrala can celebrate with us?"

"Nothing is finally settled," Zaid said quickly. "Although I have been giving the matter serious consideration."

I changed my angle slightly so some of the group came into

view in the side of my vision. I was just in time to see Jamila elbow someone—presumably her father—although Zaid's back blocked my view of Malik.

"And what has been your conclusion, Your Highness?" Malik asked hurriedly.

Zaid gave a quick upward jerk of his shoulders. "I am willing to agree—if you are willing to give me a ring I have long admired as my betrothal gift. It is a family heirloom of yours, I believe, and will remind me of the long history that lies between our families. It is a very old ring and, as you know, I have always had an interest in antiquities."

"What ring would that be, Your Highness?" Malik asked, wariness tinging his voice.

"It is made of gold, encircled with interlocking diamonds, and on the inside, the shape of clasped hands. I have always marveled at how such an intricate symbol could be made in such a tiny size."

Zaid's mother sighed softly, and I wondered if she dreaded the prospect of Jamila as a daughter-in-law.

"My...my father's ring, Your Highness?" Malik stammered. "I don't know how you could have seen me—" He cut himself off as if he had suddenly remembered that he shouldn't reveal he never openly wore the ring.

His voice held neither confidence nor the menace I was used to hearing in it, and he seemed to be stalling for time, as if he didn't know how to respond. I frowned slightly, confused, and the nobleman in front of me faltered. I quickly pasted a smile back on my face, and he resumed the thread of his conversation.

"Certainly that ring," Zaid said lightly.

"It is a family heirloom," Malik replied, still seeming flustered, and I caught a soft growl from the sultan.

Zaid had been right. His father didn't approve of his Grand Vizier hesitating over such a trifle. Apparently Jamila didn't either because she jumped in.

"And that is exactly why it is the perfect gift for my husband. My father has no son of his own to hand it down to, and he could not ask for a more worthy recipient than you, Prince Zain." Her conversational tone changed, her volume rising so that those on this side of the room could hear her words. "At our wedding, he will place it on your finger himself to welcome you as the son he never had."

A wave of applause rippled through the audience who had come expecting to hear a betrothal announcement. The sultan hesitated for a moment before accepting the situation, possibly thinking himself fortunate to win his son's acceptance of a betrothal with so little trouble.

He raised his own voice.

"Let drinks be poured for all that we may drink the good health of my son and future daughter-in-law."

More applause sounded, and servants began to circulate bearing jugs of chilled juices.

Forgetting the man in front of me, I turned to gaze in horror at Zaid's back. Our plan had failed in the worst possible way. The sultan was a man of honor and would now consider himself committed to the marriage. But Malik had no honor. As soon as the oaths of loyalty had been made, he would have no qualms with refusing to hand over the ring. And at that point, there would be nothing the sultan could do about it.

We had intended to make the betrothal itself conditional on his handing over the ring, but now he had gained the time between now and the wedding to find and seize the lamp.

Zaid stood frozen, facing away from me, so I couldn't see his expression. But it didn't matter. I needed to get out of here and join the qaleri surveilling Malik's house. They had the lamp's help, but none of them were trained in spycraft. But if I joined them, perhaps, together, we could find the sort of hard evidence the sultan would need to break his word to Malik.

As I resolved to flee the room immediately, Zaid finally

moved. Urged by his father, he took a single step toward Jamila, clearing my view of Malik. The Vizier was watching his daughter with a slightly dazed expression and didn't even notice me.

But it wouldn't have mattered if he had. Even if I had somehow lost the protection afforded by Zaid's enchanted object, I doubted Malik would have recognized me. Because I had never spoken to the man standing on the dais in my life.

He might sound like Malik, but he was not the man I had followed so many nights, the one who had taken me to the treasure cave. From afar they looked identical, but I had always had a knack for remembering faces. Up close, although the differences were subtle, there was no question. That was not Malik.

$\mathcal{I}$ fell back a step, my mind whirling, unable to explain what I was seeing. The royal family clearly thought they were interacting with Malik. No one in the whole room saw anything wrong but me.

His voice was the same—how was that possible? Although now that I thought about it, I had noticed a difference. Not so much in the timbre itself, but in his manner. All my conversations with Zaid about Malik flashed through my head. He had struggled to believe me because he claimed the Malik I described couldn't possibly be the one he knew. Somehow, impossibly, it seemed he was right.

"Are you unwell, Your Highness?" The concerned voice of the nobleman I had been ignoring broke through my shock. "You don't look well."

"I am well enough," I said. "But I have traveled far. I will retire now. But I don't wish to disturb your sultan at such a joyous moment. Perhaps you could let him know I have withdrawn to my room at a later point in the evening?"

"Certainly, if you wish it." The man gave me an odd look, but I didn't heed it, already fleeing for the side door my friends had disappeared through. I had to find them as quickly as I could.

I almost stumbled over my skirts in my initial haste, brushing against several people in the process and nearly knocking a tray of drinks out of a server's hands. Forcing myself to slow down, I smiled at those who tried to speak to me but stopped for no one. It didn't matter now if they thought the princess from Lanover rude. Everything had fallen apart.

The mystery of Malik hadn't changed the situation. I still needed to get to his house and use my knowledge to help the qaleri find the evidence we needed. And in the process, perhaps I might find answers about him as well.

I slipped through the door, finding myself in a large room instead of the corridor I had expected. I paused, looking around as I tried to orient myself. Rich, luxurious carpet softened my footfalls, and large, plush stools lined the walls. A number of tables held jugs of water and wash cloths of various sizes.

At my entrance, a girl a couple of years younger than me leaped to her feet from one of the stools. When she saw it was me, she relaxed, resuming her seat. From her clothes, she appeared to be a serving maid of some sort, although she didn't wear the green and gold of the palace servants.

I walked slowly into the middle of the room. The girl watched me with large, curious eyes. She had ebony hair and a slender figure that suggested a coiled energy at odds with her small frame. Although I'd never met her before, I was struck by an instant sense of fellow feeling—a certainty that if given the chance, this girl and I could be friends.

"You're the foreign princess everyone is talking about," she said, still regarding me with interest.

"I'm Cass."

"I'm Zaria. Your maid came through earlier, but she said your instructions were for her to go to your rooms. If you need something, I can assist you. My mistress probably won't need my help for hours."

I realized I was in a refreshing room of some sort, and this girl must be personal maid to one of the other guests.

"Thank you, but I don't need anything." But even as I said it, I realized that wasn't quite true. "Unless you could direct me to the rooms where they sent my servants?"

"Sorry," Zaria smiled apologetically. "I'm not familiar with the palace. My mistress and I are Kuralani, and it's my first time in Ardasira. I must say, I didn't expect it to be quite so exciting."

From her expression, she meant the words seriously, although sitting alone in an empty room for hours didn't strike me as especially exciting.

"Are you really from across the desert?" she asked.

"Yes." I nearly asked if all Kuralani were so informal but restrained myself. I didn't have time to waste.

Who knew what the real Malik was doing right now?

Looking around the room, I tried to decide what to do next. I needed to find one of the palace servants so they could direct me to Selina.

"There are usually others in here," Zaria said, as if I had spoken aloud. "If you wait, I'm sure someone will come along. Although I can't promise they'll know which rooms you've been assigned. But they could probably take you to someone who does."

For the first time it occurred to me that I wasn't really here as part of a foreign delegation, and I didn't have a trunk of clothes waiting in my room. I didn't even have needle and thread so Selina could use the lamp's power to sew me something more appropriate for wandering the city at night.

My eyes fell on Zaria again. My head told me I knew nothing about this girl, but every instinct shouted that I could trust her. And I had decided it was time to go back to listening to my instincts, especially about people.

"Actually," I said, "there is a way you could help me." I eyed her up and down. "I think we're about the same size. Would you be willing to swap clothes with me?"

"Swap clothes?" Her already large eyes grew enormous. "But...you're wearing..." She gestured at my dress, apparently unable to find words to sufficiently describe my outfit.

"Yes, exactly," I said. "It's too distinctive."

She raised an eyebrow. "Effecting an escape, are you? Already?" She grinned at her own joke.

I hesitated for only the briefest moment before hurrying on. "Actually, my kingdom is in danger. And the people of Ardasira and Kuralan as well." Given most of the mercenaries making up Malik's army were Kuralani, it didn't seem like much of an exaggeration.

She straightened, her face going instantly alert.

"I can't explain, I'm just asking you to trust me. I know you have no reason to do so, but all I need from you is your clothes."

"You don't want me to try to pose as you or something, do you?" she asked with knitted brows.

I shook my head. "Goodness, no. I just need to get out of here without being recognized."

"I'm not sure a change of clothes will be enough for that," she said with a disbelieving look.

I shrugged, not willing to tell her about the enchanted object secured to my ankle. If I could get rid of the distinctive clothes, I wouldn't have to worry about anyone recognizing me.

"If all you need is a change of clothes, my mistress brought one." She gestured at one of the wardrobes in the corner. "Her husband, Kasim, is only a merchant, so they don't get a lot of royal invitations. But since they were invited all the way from Karema by the Grand Vizier himself, they received an invite for this one. She's determined to make the most of the opportunity and didn't want to risk having to go home early if something was spilled on her first outfit."

I paused at the mention of Malik.

"Your mistress's husband was invited all the way from Kuralan by the Grand Vizier? What does he sell?"

"A bit of this and a bit of that," she said cheerfully. "But he's best known for dealing in antiquities—especially ancient texts." She grinned. "There's not a huge market for them, though, so he sells other wares as well."

I hesitated for a moment. Ancient texts?

"And did the Grand Vizier buy anything from him?" I asked.

Zaria wrinkled her nose. "Only a single book, which was too bad of him and well below my mistress's expectations given the lengthy correspondence between Kasim and him over the last year. It only made her doubly determined to make the most of the celebrations tonight. She's hoping they can secure some valuable connections within the Ardasiran nobility."

Had this Kasim been the source of the directions Malik had found? Perhaps he had hoped that by consulting the original text, rather than a copy, he would find some new insight. How typical that he had manipulated the merchant into delivering it in person, at great expense and inconvenience, given the size of the sale.

But I couldn't stay here asking Zaria more questions. The others were already at Malik's house, and we couldn't waste the opportunity afforded by his presence at the party. I was losing valuable time. Perhaps I could track Zaria down later, though. For now, I needed to focus on getting an appropriate change of clothes.

"I need something simple and plain," I said. "Something that won't draw attention in the city."

"In the city? No, you won't want her clothes, then. They're not exactly unobtrusive." She wrinkled her nose again as if she disapproved of her mistress's fashion sense.

"Your outfit would be perfect." I gave her a pleading look. "Please?"

After another moment's hesitation, she capitulated. Having

made the decision, she wasted no time in beginning to strip off her clothes. Within seconds she was handing me an ankle-length outer robe in the Kuralani style, a long sheer chemise, and a pair of trousers.

"Will you need my shoes, too?" she asked doubtfully. "I have very small feet."

I grinned. "So do I, actually. But I think I can keep my own shoes."

I had already shed my cloak, but I needed her help with the fastenings of the dress. When I stepped out of it, I saw her eyes flick to the odd lump of the stone tied to my ankle. She didn't comment, however.

Within moments I was dressed in her clothes and helping her to fasten my gown. When I had finished, I stepped back and admired the effect. It was a beautiful dress, and she wore it at least as well as I had.

"Now everyone will think you're a foreign princess." I smiled. "And you are foreign, at least, so they won't be completely wrong."

"Ha! I won't be leaving the room dressed like this, I assure you. As it is, my mistress will probably have a heart attack when she gets back and sees me. She'll accuse me of stealing it and check all the wardrobes for your dead body." She chuckled, a musical sound that reminded me of bubbling streams.

"I hope you're able to get back to your accommodation without trouble." I hesitated. "At least the dress should be worth some money."

"*Some* money?" she raised an eyebrow. "The material alone is worth more than I make in a year. Not that I would ever sell it, or let anyone cut it up. I'll keep it just so I can take it out sometimes and admire myself in the mirror." She laughed again, as if delighted at her own foolishness.

I snatched up my silk purse, now out of place with my new

outfit. I wasn't going to leave it behind, though. I would just have to hope no one thought I had stolen it.

"Good luck," Zaria said when I reached the outer door of the room. "With saving your kingdom and everyone else."

I paused for only a moment to look back at the unexpected girl. A brief pang went through me that we hadn't met in other circumstances. I would have liked her for a friend, and I was sure Kayla would as well.

"I hope we meet again, Zaria."

"As do I, Princess Cass."

I closed the door softly behind me, looking up and down the long corridor beyond. To my right, I caught a glimpse of red. I hurried toward the long carpet that had led from the entrance to the throne room.

A few people still walked it, heading into the celebration, but I saw three people going in the other direction. Good. I wouldn't completely stand out, then.

Unlike on the way in, neither the ushers nor the doorkeepers paid me the least attention. On my way through the outer courtyard, I glanced toward the neat rows of vehicles lined up against the far wall. I could see no sign of my chair until my eyes caught on a haphazard pile of sticks.

"That answers that question," I muttered to myself. Josef would be disappointed.

Guilt pricked me as I realized Zaria's new dress would likely transform back to its original state now that I was no longer wearing it. But she had talked as if the dress might cause her trouble, so perhaps it was for the best. She would certainly avoid a lot of awkward questions this way. I would ask Zaid to send her a gift of coin so she could buy a beautiful dress of her own choosing in its place.

Once outside the palace, I began to run. My disappearance, coupled with the destruction of my chair, might lead to trouble for Josef, Elias, and Selina. When I reached Malik's house and the others, I would use the lamp to bring the qaleri from the palace to join us. It would be a far easier way to bring us all together than trying to send them a message.

I was slightly winded by the time I reached the right house, my confused jumble of thoughts having driven my feet faster than my usual pace. Few vehicles were on the road at this point in the day. Evening had arrived, and the streets were instead full of celebrating people.

I weaved my way through them, everyone too full of good cheer to pay me any heed, even when I bumped against them. The gardens had all been hung with illuminations, like the shops, but they hadn't been lit yet. In this twilight period, when the bite of the sun had gone but the light still lingered, people clustered around the shops and squares. Later the crowds would move to the gardens to enjoy the effect of the lights among the beauty of the plants.

"Kayla," I hissed when I reached the nearest wall of Malik's house. "Where are you?"

She appeared from nowhere almost directly in front of me, and I had to bite back a scream. My hand flew to my heart as I took several gulping breaths.

"Sorry," Kayla said contritely. "I can't control it."

"I know. It was just a surprise."

"What are you doing here?" She looked me up and down in concern. "Where's your dress?"

"Never mind that. I need to know if you've found anything of interest."

She frowned. "Uh oh. What went wrong?"

"Everything. Jamila found a way around our stratagem. The betrothal is now official, but Malik's only promised to give the ring *after* the wedding."

"But he'll never give it up!"

"Exactly," I said grimly. "The whole thing is a disaster."

"Wait." Kayla glanced over her shoulder at the silent house.

"You said Malik promised to give up the ring? You saw him? He was at the palace?"

"He was when I left. He and Jamila were accepting congratulations on her betrothal."

She frowned. "You turned up just as I was trying to decide what to do. Malik left in a carriage with Jamila some hours ago. Sari and I followed them as far as the palace, and she stayed near the carriage to tail them back home again while I returned here immediately. But Malik just arrived home—alone and on foot, and not in his official robes. And there's been no sign of Sari. I was starting to worry about her."

"Malik's here?" I shook my head, trying to make sense of it. "Did you get a good look at him?"

She nodded. "He walked right past me. It was definitely him."

"So our Malik is here now, while Zaid's Malik is up at the palace—or was when I left. He wouldn't leave just as his daughter's betrothal was announced, and I'm sure he wouldn't have beaten me here even if he had. He's not the type to run."

"What do you mean, our Malik and Zaid's Malik?" Kayla stared at me with concern, as if she thought I was losing my wits. "I don't understand."

"Neither do I. But it appears there are two Maliks. There's the one we know—the dangerous one who bound you and who commands Aron and Samar. And then there's the one Zaid knows—the Grand Vizier who visits the palace and whom Zaid kept claiming was too weak and ineffectual to mastermind anything. Have you ever seen the Grand Vizier up close when he was with Zaid or operating in an official capacity?"

Kayla gaped at me, clearly in shock. "No, I haven't. I don't exactly get invites to the palace."

"And, of course, Zaid has never seen Malik when he's with either of us. They look close enough alike that anyone would be fooled at a distance, and most people could probably be fooled in close proximity, too—at least for a short time."

"So you're saying Malik has a twin brother?"

I shrugged. "Given how alike they look, it's the only thing that makes sense. But it also makes no sense. Malik's father was the Grand Vizier before him. Their family has always been close with the royal family. How could they not know he has a twin?"

She shook her head, looking dazed. "What now, then?"

"We need to find indisputable evidence of Malik's illegal scheming so Zaid can break his betrothal. Malik will be desperate to get his hands on the lamp, so we might not have long. I'm hoping that with my experience and your lamp abilities, we'll be able to do much more than either of us could on our own."

"Indisputable evidence...like two Maliks?" Kayla raised an eyebrow at me.

I stared at her. "Of course! The other Malik is still up at the palace, but you said our Malik is here. If we apprehended him and dragged him up there to present to the sultan, he would have to launch a full investigation. That's brilliant, Kayla."

She grinned, not bothering to pretend modesty. "Ordinarily I would doubt our ability to capture him and carry him up there, but with the powers of the lamp, it shouldn't be any problem at all."

"I'm going to call the others," I said. "Even with the lamp, I'll feel better if we're working together. And I'm sure they won't want to miss this."

Reaching into my bag, I groped around for the lamp. I still wasn't sure if I needed to be touching it, but this wasn't the time for experimentation.

My searching fingers found nothing.

"Kayla! It's not there!" I dropped to my knees and tipped the bag upside down, turning it inside out and even shaking it in my desperation.

"What isn't there?" Kayla asked, but I could see in her expression that she knew.

"The lamp. We agreed I needed to keep it with me at all times, so I carried it to the palace in this bag. It was right here. But it's gone." I tried to think clearly. "Maybe it fell out on the way here?"

Kayla gasped suddenly, the sound too delayed to be a response to the lost lamp. I looked up just in time to see her bend in half before she disappeared.

# CHAPTER 31

"Kayla!" I cried her name, but it was too late. She was gone.

Tears filled my eyes. I could no longer pretend I had dropped the lamp in my hurry through the streets. From what the others had said, only one other person could use the lamp to control my friend.

Malik had the lamp.

I slowly put my remaining few possessions back in my bag, moisture still obscuring my vision. My friend was gone, not only lost to me but enslaved to Malik. Zaid was locked into a betrothal with Malik's daughter. And I no longer had any hope of capturing Malik and dragging him to the palace.

Time had just become even more urgent, since Malik would surely now push for the wedding to happen as soon as possible, but the only one left to search for evidence was me. How soon would he be able to start recruiting his army of lamp bound?

"Cassie! Are you all right?" Someone dropped to one knee beside me, concerned hands touching my shoulders.

I sniffed, wiping an arm across my eyes.

"No, I'm not all right," I said, turning into Zaid and resting my head against his shoulders. "I've failed."

"I think you mean I've failed," he said grimly. "What happened back there was my fault."

I shook my head against his shirt. "That's not what I'm talking about. Malik has the lamp."

Zaid sucked in a breath, drawing back to meet my eyes. "He took it from you? Did he hurt you?"

I shook my head, and he looked relieved, although the expression quickly changed to one of confusion.

"But how? When? He was still at the palace, accepting congratulations with Jamila, when I snuck away."

"I don't know how he did it. I never even saw him. And I brushed against enough people in my race here—both at the palace and in the city—that it could have been anywhere. But when I said Malik has the lamp, I didn't mean the man at the palace with Jamila. I meant the other one. There are two Maliks."

I held up a hand to forestall his protest. "Don't tell me that makes no sense—I'm well aware of that. All I know for sure is that the man you were talking to at the palace isn't the Malik the qaleri and I know. He sounds like him, and they look almost identical, but there are slight differences. Once I saw him up close, there was no mistaking it."

Zaid rocked back on his heels. "Two Maliks?" He shook his head. "It seems impossible—and yet it explains why the man you've been describing sounded nothing like the one I grew up knowing. But then who's the second one?"

I stood up, and he rose with me. "I don't know. But I intend to find out." I pointed at the house. "The answers must be in there. I followed him from this house countless times, watching as he went about his underhanded business. That was the Malik I know. And you had a tour here, presumably with the Malik you know. So they must both live here."

Zaid shook his head again. "It's hard to fathom...the size of the deception! You described him living a double life, but neither of us could have guessed the extent of it. I suppose his two existences must have been separate enough that no one person saw him up close in both. The disreputable merchants the other Malik dealt with don't get invitations to the palace."

"Even if none of the servants know, Jamila must. Surely she would recognize her own father."

"And I intend to hold her to account." Zaid sounded furious, and I guessed he was thinking of her trick at the palace.

"I'm going in there right now, and I'm going to find some evidence—something you can take to your father and use to convince him. Our story just keeps getting more unbelievable, so we'll need something he can't possibly argue against." I swallowed. "If I'm not back at the palace by morning, you'll have to try telling him the truth anyway."

"You can't think I'm going to leave you to go in there alone!"

"Of course you will. They'll already be looking for you up at the palace, I'm sure. You can't disappear from your own betrothal party."

"I won't be marrying Jamila, no matter what I have to do to get out of it," Zaid said grimly. "As far as I'm concerned, there is no betrothal."

"Still. It's too dangerous." I tried not to feel glad at his words, but I couldn't help the lift in my heart.

Zaid put a hand on each shoulder and looked me straight in the eyes. "Listen to me. There is no chance whatsoever that I'm going to allow you to go into that house without me. If you had the lamp and the qaleri to help you, maybe. But you're not going in alone."

"Zaid, no one else knows what's going on here. You have to tell your father. And that's not even mentioning the fact that you're the crown prince, and the kingdom's only heir. You're important, Zaid. You have to stop putting yourself at risk."

He didn't move, and I could see the stubborn determination on his face. But as he watched me, his expression softened.

"You never did ask me why I've been refusing my father's

attempts to marry me off," he said quietly. "It's because of you, Cassie. I saw you launch yourself off that camel and scrabble your way up a cliff by sheer determination alone. I was too far away to help, but I went looking for you afterward, and I found you in the river cavern. You were exhausted but not in the least daunted. And you looked at me and saw only Zaid." He smiled, his eyes alight. "Ever since that moment, I haven't been able to stomach the idea of any of the brides my father has suggested."

"Zaid…" My voice sounded weak to my own ears, but I didn't know how to respond.

We weren't Zaid of Sirrala and Cassie of Qalerim. He was a crown prince, and I was an intelligencer for a foreign kingdom at best, and a homeless street orphan at worst. My act tonight had been just that—an act.

But I loved him. I had acknowledged that tonight, and the awareness of it burned through every inch of me. Just standing so close to him, I felt more alive than I had felt in years. I didn't know if I could resist him if he talked to me like this.

"I can see you trying to resist me," he said, in a husky voice. "But I'm finished waiting for you to realize you love me back."

He swept his arms all the way around me, pressing me against his chest. I looked up at him, my emotions spilling out of my eyes, and he gave a sound that was half satisfied sigh, half groan before pressing his lips to mine.

For one glorious moment, I could think of nothing but Zaid. I was his and he was mine, and nothing else mattered. Then reality came crashing back.

I pulled away, panting, fresh tears in my eyes.

"Someone who claims Malik's identity is in that house right now, plotting to use your people to destroy mine. I can't kiss you and talk of love as if all our plans aren't in ruins at our feet."

"Love?" Zaid raised an eyebrow, one side of his mouth tugging upward. "So you admit you love me?"

"Leave and go back to the palace, and I'll admit anything you like."

He shook his head, the stubborn look back. "I'll just have to help you find that evidence, arrest Malik, and explain your true identity to my father. Then you'll have no excuses left."

"Are you serious?" My hands gripped his sleeves, my eyes trying to read every line of his face. "Do you really believe there's a chance your father would ever accept me?"

Zaid leaned in close, his breath brushing against the hair beside my ear. "I hear it on good authority you're the only one who knows the location of the richest treasure this kingdom has ever seen. Not even a king could reject such a dowry."

Hope filled me, ballooning inside and filling every crevice. I had once desperately wanted a place in Aurora's network, but that wish paled now beside my desire to spend the rest of my life at Zaid's side.

"In that case," I said, "we need to move quickly. Now that Malik has the lamp, he'll be able to empty the rest of the cave easily."

Zaid took my hand, and I let him, enjoying the feel of his warmth and strength. I had to trot to keep up with his long strides, but I didn't tell him to slow down. When we reached the edge of the house, he paused, however, stepping back and gesturing me forward.

"You're the one who knows what you're doing. I'll follow your lead."

"Thankfully for us, most of the servants should be out enjoying the festivities. As long as we avoid the servants' hall, I don't think we should need any great skill not to run into anyone."

"Shouldn't there be guards, at least?" he asked.

"Malik employs guards for when he goes out during the day, but they don't stand watch over the house. Instead he relies on locks." I pulled out a set of lock picks and grinned. "Which is foolish of him."

Within minutes we were both standing in a dark, silent hallway, and I had locked the door behind us.

"As easy as that?" Zaid whispered.

I rolled my eyes. "It took me three years to learn to pick locks that well. And we couldn't have done it at this time of night if the whole city wasn't out celebrating."

I gestured for him to follow me down the hall, thinking as we walked. I had searched this whole house and found no indication of a second Malik living here in secret. But he must eat and sleep like every other person.

The one thing I had found, however, was a secret room. A secret room with a second door. Did Malik's fireplace conceal a whole hidden wing?

"We're going to start with the room where I found the vials," I whispered to Zaid. "It's hidden behind the wall, and it had another door. I'm hoping it might lead to wherever Malik is hiding himself."

"False Malik," Zaid whispered back, and I shrugged.

It didn't matter to me who was the real Malik, as long as they were both held to account for their crimes.

Twice I had to freeze, holding out a hand to signal Zaid to do the same. To his credit, he responded instantly both times, not babbling questions, or shifting his weight at the wrong moment. On both occasions, the servant moving through the house passed by without noticing us, and we were soon on our way again.

The lanterns in the garden had now been lit, and enough light came in through the screens to provide some illumination. The semi-darkness felt comforting and familiar, and I found my way with ease.

After a brief pause for me to pick the lock of Malik's study, we both stood inside.

"Now what?" Zaid asked in a slightly louder whisper. "Should we check the room for evidence?"

I shook my head. "I've looked through all the papers he keeps here. They concern his above-board business dealings only. No, we're in here because of this."

I crossed over to the mantel and pressed the small rose that released the hidden door. Without a sound, the back of the enormous fireplace slid aside. I gave a dramatic flourish, enjoying the expression of astonishment on Zaid's face, despite the tension of the moment.

"I might not have found it," I confessed, "if I hadn't noticed that the fireplace looked like it had never been used. Malik doesn't seem like the hardy, enduring sort, so it was a detail that didn't fit."

"Are you ready for this?" Zaid asked.

I took a deep breath. "No. But we have to do it anyway."

I stepped forward through the fireplace. Zaid followed, ducking his head to make it under the mantel.

"As you can see," I said, "this is where he stores all the vi—" I cut myself off mid-word.

The walls were lined with bare shelves, and the room was otherwise empty. Not a single vial or jug remained.

# CHAPTER 32

"*W*here—" This time it was Zaid who cut me off with a warning hand on my arm.

I went instantly silent, straining my ears for whatever he might have heard.

The faint sound of voices filtered into the room from somewhere beyond. Both of our gazes focused on the door in the far wall. Moving together, we crept closer.

When I pressed my ear against the wood, the voices grew louder, but not loud enough to discern the words. I looked up at Zaid.

He shrugged, needing no words to say what we both knew was true. With time working against us, there was only one way to find out what was on the other side of that door.

When he reached for the handle, I shook my head and pushed his hand away. I had a childhood full of practice at this.

He stepped back, gesturing for me to take his place. Inch by inch, I turned the round knob of the handle, keeping my movements both slow and smooth. Sudden movement attracted the eye.

The rhythm of the muffled conversation didn't change, so when the handle finally finished turning, I pulled the door gently open by the smallest possible margin. Still there were no cries of alarm or sudden silences.

Opening it wide enough to press my eye to the gap, I peered through. On the other side was a long, narrow room. Clearly someone lived here, although without any source of natural light, it would be dark and depressing even during the day. Everywhere I could see the signs of regular life, from the table, surrounded by four solid chairs, to the pitcher of water on a stand at the far end.

Other doors opened off the room, but only one stood ajar, giving me a view of a large four poster, strewn with clothes and other possessions.

I frowned. It almost looked like someone had been packing.

The low sound of voices came from a dozen people clumped together to one side of the room, crowding the space. With a sinking heart, I realized that I knew every one of them.

It wasn't only Kayla Malik had summoned. He had gathered every one of the qaleri and now stood at their head, Aron and Samar flanking him.

The large bag at his feet seemed to confirm the impression that he had just finished packing, but from the cases and crates weighing down every one of his companions, he had packed a lot more than his clothes. I turned back to look at the empty shelves around us, a terrible idea forming.

Malik had the ring, the lamp, and the betrothal. He had just gained everything he needed for his plan to succeed. And he hadn't wasted a moment in packing up to leave.

He knew I was still alive—by now he must know I knew Zaid. So he was ensuring that if the sultan did come looking, he would find nothing here to indict his Grand Vizier.

A gleam of gold from the object in Malik's hand caught my eye. He was holding the lamp as he cast what looked like a final glance around before placing a hand on Aron's arm.

Abandoning subtlety, I thrust the door all the way open.

"Zaid!" I screamed in warning, and he leaped into the room beside me.

Malik's face twisted, and his words came faster as we raced across the distance separating us. A flurry of bodies jerked forward in the hateful bow, and I launched myself the final distance, my fingers reaching for the closest arm.

It reached back.

My hand clamped around the one extended toward me, just as everything went black and a whooshing sensation made my stomach heave. For one dizzying second, my feet had no purchase, and then the ground reformed beneath them.

I let go of Kayla's hand and staggered, trying to find my balance in the darkness.

"Lanterns!" Malik's voice barked, and the rustle of movement sounded all around me.

Someone gripped my upper arm, and I flinched, trying to pull away. But the familiar voice whispering in my ear was Zaid's.

"Where are we?"

I started to say I had no idea but stopped myself before I could utter the words. They were false.

Instinctively I did know where we were. The taste and feel of the air filled in what my sight could not. Rather than speaking, I pulled Zaid away from the crush of milling bodies.

Now that my eyes had adjusted, I thought I could see the faintest of glows just beyond the sound of Malik's voice. I led the way in the other direction, feeling our path through the stone trees with outstretched hands.

Zaid stumbled behind me, colliding with a tree. A moment later he gave a soft gasp. His questing hands must have found the fruit, their shape allowing him to guess where we were.

But while the trees offered us some meager protection, there was nowhere in the treasure cave for us to hide and no exit for us to slip out of. I should have realized this was the perfect place for Malik to stash the nayera. Now that he had the lamp, no one could access it without him issuing the command to send them here. And yet with an army of soldiers to turn into servants of the lamp, he would have no problem retrieving it whenever he pleased.

A sickening thought hit me. Could he order his forces straight across the desert? We had just seen proof that they could take supplies with them—and even other people. Unless there was a geographic limit to how far he could order his servants to go, even the desert itself was no longer a barrier to him.

Light blossomed behind us, exposing the stone trunks and bouncing off the fruit in a rainbow of brilliant light.

"There!" Malik cried. "I saw her. Grab them both."

Back in the hidden room, I had acted fast, giving my instinct full rein, afraid Malik would disappear and our chance of finding proof along with him. But now I needed my mind to play its part and think us out of this impossible situation.

The ringing sound of drawn steel at my side informed me Zaid had brought his sword. But one weapon wouldn't be enough against a dozen people, especially with the power of the lamp behind them. And we couldn't hurt any of the qaleri, anyway.

But what if it was just Aron and Samar? Could Zaid hold them off if it was only the two of them? The qaleri would turn against Malik in an instant if I could get hold of the lamp.

Which meant everything relied on me.

As soon as he revealed his sword, Aron and Samar both focused on Zaid. I could see them rushing toward him, glimpses of their movement appearing and disappearing between the stone branches, the colors of the fruit flashing off their skin and clothing in strange ways. The clang of steel indicated battle had been joined, and it took all my strength to turn away and leave Zaid to face them alone.

The remaining qaleri hadn't yet reached me only because they moved slowly, their attention caught by the wonders around them. Most of them hadn't seen the fruit I brought back, and even Kayla and Josef stared in awe at the effect of the jewels hanging on the trees.

"Faster!" Malik shouted, his voice dripping with frustration, but I had already used their distraction to slip around them, circling out of the trees and down the far side of the cave. It was darker over here, and the cries and clangs of Zaid's furious fight with Aron and Samar obscured my absence for a moment.

Malik shouted something else, but I didn't catch it this time. His voice echoed strangely off the walls, and as I made it closer to the tunnel, I could see why. Despite his numerical and magical advantage, he was slowly backing away from the skirmish. As Josef spotted me—shouting my name and sending the rest of the qaleri rushing toward me—Malik stepped all the way backward into the cave of gold.

In the semi-darkness, trying to move quickly, my friends tripped and stumbled over the many crates of nayera that had been abandoned across the open stretch of ground between me and them. The obstacles wouldn't delay them for long, but they gave me a few precious seconds. This was my one chance to catch Malik alone.

But as I stepped into the tunnel, a short, sharp cry echoed through the cave, bouncing off the walls. Unable to help myself, I looked back toward Zaid.

Aron and Samar had forced him most of the way through the orchard, his back now exposed to the qaleri who were leaping over the crates. His movements, once lightning quick, had slowed, and blood ran down his arms from multiple cuts.

Aron's blade flashed forward, flipping Zaid's weapon from his hands and sending it flying into the trees. Zaid instantly dropped to the ground, moving just quick enough to avoid Samar's heavy swing. When he leaped back to his feet, he held two lengths of wood as if they were haryat batons, a determined look on his face.

But even proper batons wouldn't hold long against two swords. And these versions were just thin planks ripped from a crate.

I didn't hesitate. I wouldn't let Zaid die—not even to stop Malik. Reversing direction, I ran toward the battle, my hands plunging into the silk purse that still hung at my side. Apparently the enchantment that had created the bag would last until it was no longer of use to me, and seeing all those crates had reminded me of one of the items I carried inside it. I did have a weapon after all.

I tried to dart through the middle of the qaleri, but Patrin caught me by the left arm, hauling me backward. I screamed, pulling against him, but Elias caught me from behind, wrapping his arms around my waist.

Zaid stepped back, blocking Aron's blade with one of his makeshift batons. The blade cut deep into the wood and caught there.

My right hand pulled free of my purse, the vial I had been carrying with me for months gripped in my fingers. I just needed to get a little closer…

I strained against my captors, trying to move toward Zaid, but Elias lifted me off my feet. Someone else tried to grab at my free right arm, but I swung it back.

"Get out of the way!" I screamed at Zaid, releasing the vial.

As it sailed through the air toward him, he didn't hesitate. Dropping both sticks, he threw himself backward. As I watched, helpless, he tripped over a crate and fell, hard.

The vial smashed against Samar's shoulder, fracturing into several jagged pieces.

"What…?" Aron—stooping to pick up his sword from where it had fallen, still caught in Zaid's baton—followed the missile's trajectory and met my eyes.

For half a second, everyone remained frozen, waiting to see

what would happen. A faint whiff of familiar smell floated toward me, and I held my breath.

Samar staggered. Knocking against Aron, he drove him to the ground, collapsing beside him. Neither of them got up. Neither did Zaid.

# CHAPTER 33

"*Z*aid!" I renewed my struggles.

Had he also been knocked out by the nayera? Or had he hit his head when he fell?

"Elias!" I pleaded. "It's Zaid! I just want to check he's alive."

"Marik commanded us to bring you to him. I'm sorry, Cassie." He sounded tormented. "I don't have a choice."

I stopped fighting, slumping in resignation. I had no hope against ten opponents and no desire to accidentally hurt any of them. My struggles could serve no purpose now.

As soon as I calmed, Patrin let go, and Elias placed me gently back on my feet. But they resumed a loose grip on either arm almost immediately.

Kayla and Selina crowded close behind, their faces miserable and their eyes saying the apologies their lips did not. The rest of the qaleri followed, moving as a group toward Malik and the glowing gold in the other room.

"You called him Marik, not Malik," I said to Elias, hoping to get an answer before we reached the tunnel.

"I accused him of not being Malik, and he admitted it openly," Kayla's glum voice said in my ear. "He said there's no need for secrets from us now since there's nothing we can do to stop him."

"Malik and Marik?" I shook my head. "So they are twins?"

"Only by blood," Marik said as Elias pushed me ahead of him into the cave so Marik and I stood alone between the rows of chests. "I'm ashamed to lay claim to such a weak-willed piece of—"

"He's your brother!" I cut off his diatribe, shocked at his anger, despite everything. "You've been living in his house and using his name for months—if not years!"

"You mean my family's house," he said. "The house that could have been mine—*should* have been mine—if capability and intelligence meant more than five minutes of seniority. My brother cares about nothing but petty comforts and keeping up appearances. Manipulating him has been child's play."

"Why did he let you impersonate him all this time?" I asked, although I suspected I knew the answer. Malik clearly had a weak will, unable to stand firm before a far stronger one. No doubt he had come up with all sorts of excuses for why he didn't expose Marik.

"How could he refuse to take in his own twin—abandoned all this time because of a simple accident of birth?" Marik spread his arms wide, his gloating expression sickening. "And by the time he began to understand a little of my activities, it was easy enough to make him see how he, too, would suffer the consequences if he made any attempt to expose me."

"You're the younger twin," I said, several things becoming clear.

"Well, I'm certainly not the Grand Vizier." His snide tone didn't quite mask his true bitterness about the matter.

"You'd have made a better one," I said, the words popping out before my brain could catch up.

They were true, though. Clearly Malik had allowed himself to be manipulated by his stronger, more dominant brother—taking the easier road of little resistance. And Malik's weakness had done as much harm to the kingdom as purposeful sabotage would have achieved.

A dark, twisted root of bitterness colored Marik's words—the result of being born the second son and excluded, for some reason, from the chance to follow in his father's footsteps as royal advisor. A Grand Vizier needed the sort of cunning mind Marik clearly possessed. Without the bitterness, there was every chance he would have turned that cunning toward the service of his sultan and the honor of his family line.

My praise, limited though it was, caught Marik by surprise. For a moment he stared at me, as if he suspected me of mocking him somehow.

I shrugged. "Your brother clearly didn't inherit the brains of the family."

"No," Marik snapped. "He just inherited everything else—the name, the family, the house, the position. And what was I left with? Nothing."

He gestured around at the piles of gold. "But not for long. Soon I'll have everything."

He held up the lamp. "You're smart, Cassandra. I could use a servant like you. Swear loyalty on my ring, and you won't be harmed."

I glared at him, about to repudiate the suggestion, but a groan from the orchard cave made me pause. Zaid. He was alive.

My legs trembled, my fear rushing back. What did Marik intend to do with Zaid now that he knew the truth about him? He couldn't believe Zaid would agree to marry Jamila now.

A grin spread over Marik's face. "Ah yes, the touching romance."

I bit my tongue. Had Marik been at the betrothal party? Hidden behind some disguise? Had he seen Zaid and me interacting there?

Marik took a step toward me. "Despite your insolence, I actually rather like you, Cassandra. You remind me a little of my younger self. Swear loyalty to me, and you can have your prince."

"What?" I gaped at him.

"I had intended him to marry my niece, but Jamila has become rather trying of late. She helped keep her father in line in exchange for the promise of a throne, but then she got greedy and decided she didn't want to wait any longer. She could have ruined everything." His voice turned dangerous. "And now I find I'm disinclined to give her a kingdom after all. She will learn that, in our family, shared blood is no protection against being cast off."

His eyes refocused on me.

"You can have her place. All you have to do is swear your loyalty and convince your prince to swear his. I will claim you as my daughter and take your father's place in the wedding ceremony without any need of pretending to be my brother. You can marry your prince and become a princess. What is an oath of loyalty next to that?"

"You don't intend to dethrone Sultan Kalmir?" It was hard to believe.

Marik looked bored. "I have no interest in dealing with insurrection in Ardasira while I am occupied across the desert with a far more valuable conquest. Kalmir and his heirs can sit in their golden palace and play ruler as much as they like—bound by loyalty to me, of course."

I stared at him, my mind whirring. He thought I was a tool—valuable for the moment, not least because he hoped I would convince Zaid to swear his loyalty. But his treatment of Jamila demonstrated what happened to his tools once they ceased to be of use to him.

Despite the fleeting temptation of a life with Zaid, I could never agree to bind myself to a person like Marik. There had to be another way out. I just needed a little longer to think of it.

He seemed willing to talk, clearly seeing me as no threat. I needed to encourage that and hope an opportunity presented itself.

"If you really are Malik's twin, why doesn't anyone know of your existence?" I asked. "I thought Malik and the sultan grew up together."

"You're full of questions," he said, his cold eyes dissecting me.

I kept my spine straight, and my gaze firm. He seemed to appreciate boldness, as long as I didn't go too far.

"You want me to swear loyalty to you in exchange for becoming a princess. But how do I know you'll keep your word? I'll be helpless once I make the oath. You need to convince me I can trust you."

He threw back his head and laughed.

"You want to know if you can trust my word? Very well. You can't. But I think you already know that."

I shivered, taking a step back despite myself. The anger and bitterness had festered in him so long that he no longer cared whom he hurt or what he tore down in his quest to take what he believed had been stolen from him.

"But there's one thing you can trust," he continued. "I will never rest until I have more than my brother could ever imagine. And anyone who stands in my way will be annihilated. You can join me, or you and your prince can die."

"What did Malik do to you?" I asked.

"He existed," Marik said through his teeth. "The firstborn son our father desired. According to my nurse, our father was so delighted to receive the news that his wife had borne him a son that he sent a messenger straight to the palace with the joyful tidings of Malik's birth. But the doctor had missed that our mother carried twins. Within minutes, the contractions started again, and another son was born. But the second time it didn't go so smoothly. She didn't survive."

He said the words without feeling, as if he had no connection to the story he was telling and no grief for the mother he never knew.

"Your father blamed you for her death." It was a tragic ending, but a predictable one.

"He ordered my nurse to take me and to be gone from his house. He declared he only had one son, and he never wanted to hear the other spoken of again."

"What did she do?" I asked, compassion stirring despite myself.

"She left, of course," he said in a flat voice. "She took me to Kuralan, to my mother's family. And there they raised me, deprived of everything that should be my birthright."

He glanced at the closest chest, his eyes lingering on a crown that perched on top of the pile of coins. "I inherited only one thing from my mother's father. A ring. A family heirloom. And using only that ring, I have carved for myself an inheritance greater than Ardasira itself."

I considered pointing out the inaccuracies of that statement— starting with the fact that he had used his brother's name, wealth, and home to carry out his plans, not the ring alone—but I held my tongue.

Marik didn't know me at all. He thought he could maneuver me into serving him, and I needed him to keep believing it. Because the moment he stopped, Zaid and I were both dead.

"I'm guessing your grandfather didn't know the true properties of the ring," I said.

Marik made a disgusted noise in his throat. "Of course he did not. None of them did, or they would never have given it to me." It sounded as if he resented more than just the Ardasiran branch of his family.

Again his eyes strayed to the crown, and I could see a yearning behind their coldness. How many years had he worked with single minded determination toward the goal of conquest? He had set out to make himself into an emperor, and everything he had sought to achieve was at last within his grasp. Every piece was falling into place.

But still he had to wait. He needed to orchestrate a wedding ceremony, bind an army, and lead an invasion. No one would be able to stop him, but it would all take time. And then more time would be needed before he could fully subdue the Four Kingdoms and ascend a throne.

Right now, he felt triumphant, and I could read in his eyes the desire to enjoy the fruits of that triumph. He wanted to pick up the crown and feel the weight of it in his hands. He wanted to know it was his. The only thing stopping him was the warning about the enchantment on the gold.

A desperate plan unfolded in my mind. It had as much chance of failure as success, but I had to try something.

"I suppose you mean to take all this with you." I indicated the many chests. "You won't have any issue funding your conquest now."

He frowned. "No one can touch it, it's enchanted. I warned you of that the first time you came here."

"Did you?" I shrugged. "I wasn't paying attention. Not that it mattered. Whatever enchantment was once here is long gone."

Marik's eyes remained on me for a moment before they betrayed him by sliding sideways to the chest. In the light of the lantern, it was impossible to discern the faint, unnatural light the gold gave off in the pitch dark.

"How do you know?" he asked, suspicion coloring his voice.

He glanced across at the silent qaleri as if he suspected us of conspiring against him. They clustered in the tunnel, awaiting their next order, and it was true that resentment filled their eyes, although they knew nothing of my intentions.

"I took some of it," I said. "And nothing happened."

His attention snapped back to me. "You touched the gold? Took some?"

I nodded, as if it were no big deal. "I wasn't sure how easy it would be to sell the jewels, so after I piled them into my satchel, I filled all the space around them with coins."

"I don't believe you." His eyes fell on the qaleri again. "You'll no doubt be more truthful when I command one of your friends to pick up a coin. Selina perhaps?"

I kept my face impassive despite the fear churning inside. Everything depended on what happened next.

"No need," I said. "I'll pick one up myself."

His eyes widened as I stepped toward the chest with the crown. Bending over, I let my purse swing forward so it hung in front of me.

Concealed from Marik by my body, one hand slipped into the purse and retrieved one of the coins created by the lamp—a shiny, golden coin that had never been held in a human hand, its sheen matching that of those filling the chests. Straightening, I held it out to him as if I had just retrieved it from the chest.

"See. No enchantment."

Marik didn't immediately move, an uncharacteristic hesitance holding him captive. But after a long pause, he reached over and removed the coin from my palm. Holding it up, he examined the shine on the gold.

For a second, he just stood there, and I thought all my careful acting was for nothing. But then he stooped toward the chest, snatching up the crown.

Instantly a rumbling sounded. Startled, he looked up at the roof of the cave in time to see a chunk of rock break loose. Jumping sideways, he narrowly avoided being struck.

Twisting toward me, he snarled. "You!"

More chunks of stone rained down as he surged toward me. But I was already in motion. The other qaleri drew back, moving out of the range of falling stone, but I lunged toward Marik.

We collided with enough force to send him staggering backward, directly into the path of a fist-sized chunk of rock.

It smashed into his shoulder, making him flinch and list sideways, but I clung on. Snatching at the lamp, I tried to haul it out of his grip.

A bellow from behind the qaleri nearly startled me into letting go. Glancing back in their direction, I saw a hulking figure striding through their midst. Samar had woken and was rushing into the cavern to defend his master.

Marik's attention was divided now, torn between the falling stone and Samar's arrival, and his stance was still out of balance from the blow. Taking advantage of his distraction, I hooked both hands around the lamp's handle and pulled with all my strength.

At any other time, he would have succeeded in maintaining his hold on it. But the blow from the stone had made him loosen his grip, and I ripped it free. Dancing backward, I spat out my words as fast as I could.

"Negate everything Marik ordered and, instead, arrest him. Don't let him escape."

I opened my mouth to issue another stream of commands—this time based around fighting and subduing Samar. But in front of my astonished eyes, Samar jerked downward, just as my friends did.

Samar was bound to the lamp?

I stared at him in shock, wondering how I'd missed seeing him make the gesture back in the hidden room, but he didn't notice. Reacting to my command with greater enthusiasm than the others, he strode toward Marik, murderous intent on his face.

"Traitor!" Marik cried, leaping backward out of Samar's reach, although there was nowhere for him to go.

Samar continued to pursue him just as the loudest crack yet announced the fall of a new section of ceiling. A piece of rock as large as my head came loose. Once again, Marik dodged, but Samar was too intent on his prey to see it coming. It struck him on the top of his head, and he swayed for less than a second before once again crumpling to the ground.

# CHAPTER 34

The qaleri surged out of the tunnel, driven by my command to apprehend Marik. He tried to run, but with the entrance blocked, there was nowhere to go. Josef and Patrin led the charge, each seizing one of his arms. They showed none of the gentleness my friends had earlier shown me as they hauled him back through the tunnel.

A creak sounded, and I looked up at the ceiling in alarm. The rocks had all been concentrated above Marik, as if the enchantment recognized who had touched the gold and was aiming to bury him in an avalanche of stone. Fear that my friends would suffer the same fate as Samar gripped me, but this time the ceiling held.

I took a breath and then another. Nothing else happened.

"Is that all?" Sari also stared upward. "That wasn't much of an enchantment."

"It was enough to kill Samar," Kayla said in a quiet voice.

"He's dead?" I hurried over to join her where she knelt beside his still form. "Are you sure?"

She nodded. With trembling fingers, she closed his eyes. I placed a hand on her shoulder and squeezed. It must have taken courage for her to check on him. The last time he had fallen in these caves, he had found his way back to his feet.

"I think the enchantment used to be much more powerful," I said to Sari. "But it seems to have weakened and warped over the centuries." I pointed toward the blocked entrance. "And I suspect it used up the bulk of its remaining strength two nights ago. What we just saw was more like a dying gasp."

"Thank goodness." Selina shuddered, staring at the boulders that now filled the old tunnel. "Or we might have all died."

I bit my lip. "I'm sorry for putting you at risk. I was hoping the tunnel would be safe."

"Don't apologize," Kayla said firmly, coming to her feet. "Any one of us would have agreed to that gamble to be free from Marik."

A familiar voice reached me from the other cave, and I took off running. Bursting through the tunnel, I jumped over several crates and threw myself into Zaid's arms.

He broke off his conversation with Patrin to crush me against him.

"I heard the falling stone," he said. "That's what brought me properly back to consciousness. I was worried…"

"Not as worried as me! I didn't even know if you were alive until we heard you groaning earlier."

He shook his head. "Patrin just filled me in on what happened. Well played."

Now that it was all over, and Zaid's arms were wrapped firmly around me, I began to tremble.

"It could have turned out differently. It nearly did."

He shook his head. "You held your nerve and took the only option open to you. No one could ask more than that. And it worked."

I looked up into his smile, warmth spreading through me. But a flash of red and a feeling of damp beneath my hands made me pull back.

"Your arms," I cried. Blood seeped out of three long cuts.

"They look worse than they are," he said, dismissively. "They're shallow."

"But you've been bleeding that whole time! We need to get them bandaged." I looked around, trying to think what we could use. "Kayla? Do you have something we could use to bind Zaid's cuts?"

She popped up beside me, a grin on her face. "Would you like me to do it?"

I couldn't remember her ever mentioning any particular experience in wound care, but she seemed enthusiastic.

"Yes, please."

Her grin broadened as she bobbed down like a puppet.

"That will make it much easier," she said as she straightened. "I'll have him bound up as expertly as any doctor in no time."

Zaid eyed the lamp I had forgotten was still clutched in my hand. "That's certainly a very useful object," he said thoughtfully.

"Don't get any ideas," I said. "We're destroying it immediately. In fact…"

I turned, looking for Josef and Patrin. They stood to one side, still holding tight to Marik. I hurried over, my face set.

"Josef, retrieve the ring for me."

Josef complied with good cheer, wresting the ring from Marik's finger without thought for his comfort. Their prisoner uttered a guttural growl, but neither boy paid him any attention.

"You're a fool," Marik spat at me. "I offered you everything, and you've thrown it all away. Do you think the sultan will let his son marry a nameless orphan? And don't think you can hide behind the lamp. When he realizes you made a fool of him, parading around as a foreign princess, he'll cast you out. And when he does, I'll come for you myself."

"Just because you don't know my family doesn't mean I don't have any," I said. "I may not be a princess, but I am foreign. And if the sultan is interested in an alliance, I'll do everything I can to help secure him one."

"Cassie will never be cast out of the palace or Ardasira," Zaid said firmly, slipping an arm around my waist.

Marik ignored him, staring at me. "*You're* from across the desert? *You're* the one Aron let escape?"

He began to thrash violently against Patrin. Josef, who was bringing me the ring, tossed it in my direction, leaping back to help his friend. The tiny piece of jewelry hit the ground, tinkling against the rock, and I stooped to pick it up.

I examined it for a moment, noting the interlocking diamonds Zaid had described. Marik feared I meant to claim it, but I had no interest in being a slave master.

I did, however, have a very great interest in getting us all out of this cave.

"Elias and Selina," I called. "Could you extinguish all the lights for a moment?"

"All of them?" Elias sounded nervous.

"Just for a moment."

Selina shrugged and blew on the nearest lantern. It shouldn't have done anything, but the flame immediately winked out. The smallest pang flittered through me. Life certainly was easy with the lamp. But every time I saw one of the qaleri forced into a bow, I remembered it wasn't worth it.

Within moments we all stood in the pitch dark.

"Now what?" Josef asked.

"Is anyone standing near the tunnel? Can you see any light from the gold? Even the faintest glow?"

"I'm by the tunnel," Sari called. "Give me a moment." I heard footsteps against stone and then she spoke again. "It's just as dark in here as out there."

"Good." I nodded although no one could see me. "Elias and Selina, light the lanterns again, please."

Within seconds, the first flare of illumination pierced the darkness. Soon a rosy glow surrounded us.

"What does it mean?" Zaid asked.

"It confirms my theory that the last of the protective enchantment on the gold is gone." I looked around at all the crates and cases still scattered haphazardly.

"Everyone except Josef and Patrin, empty these crates of nayera, and fill them with gold and jewels instead. We're leaving here as soon as possible, and no one is ever coming back. Just be careful not to smash any of the vials!"

"You're just going to leave the nayera here?" Zaid sounded unsure.

"Why not?" I gestured around. "I can't think of a more secure place. We can take back a small case of it, if you think it would be useful for the royal apothecary. But I thought you said even he's only allowed to have it in small quantities."

Zaid looked around at the thick stone walls. "I suppose that makes sense."

The qaleri finished removing the nayera in an impossibly short time, filling the cases with the jewel fruit and carting in the chests of gold. Once it was all gathered together in an impressive pile, I looked back at the now barren forest. The trunks themselves were beautiful works of art. With the help of the lamp, the qaleri could carry enormously heavy loads. Working together, they should be able to transport them.

"Everyone except Josef and Patrin, start ferrying loads directly into the royal treasury." I glanced at Zaid. "I assume it will be locked?"

He nodded.

"Good. That means you won't be disturbed. Keep going until all the trees, the jewels, and the gold have been safely deposited."

"I can help, too," Josef offered, a disquieting gleam in his eyes.

I gave him a stern look. "You will stay here. And everyone

else, don't keep any of it for yourselves, and don't touch anything else in the treasury. This wealth is for all of Ardasira."

Zaid gave me a swift squeeze.

"I will personally make sure my father uses it for the benefit of everyone." He smiled. "And I'm sure that will include a reward for each of you, for the part you've played in finding and retrieving it."

A small cheer went up, and the qaleri resumed work with fresh enthusiasm. I smiled up at Zaid, the expression growing when he bent down toward me. But as soon as he pressed his lips to mine, eliciting a quiet gagging noise from Josef, a loud groan made us spring apart.

"Aron!" I swung around to stare at the tall man as he slowly sat up, one hand held to his head.

"I forgot he was there in all the chaos," I said to Zaid. "He must have breathed more of the gas than you or Samar."

As soon as Aron's eyes locked on me, he surged to his feet. Afraid of his intentions, I spoke quickly, hoping I understood the source of his antagonism.

"You are freed from any commands Marik placed on you."

His eyes widened, traveling from me to Marik and back to the lamp I held in my hands.

"I'm...free?" He spoke the word as if it was unfamiliar.

Marik let out a long stream of curses, and I guessed he had been placing the last of his hope on his one remaining lieutenant.

Aron's eyes stayed on the lamp. "I am not free. I just answer to a different master."

I shook my head. "Only for now. We need its power to get us out of this cave. But then you'll be truly free."

He didn't look like he believed me, and I couldn't blame him.

"How is it possible you and Samar were bound to the ring?" Zaid asked. "You're long past sixteen."

The ghost of amusement crossed his face. "But we were all

sixteen once. And younger even, though it's hard to remember now." He rubbed again at the lump on his head.

"You mean you've been bound to Marik all that time? He must have been almost a child himself when you swore your oath."

"The foolishness of youth," Aron said. "If I'd had a mother to tell me bedtime stories, I would have known the tale of the Treasure, and I would not have fallen for the same stratagem that felled the older brothers in that history. But my father was more interested in the labor of his hands than in stories."

He looked at Marik with burning anger in his eyes.

On our long ago trip through the desert, I had never thought I might end up feeling compassion for Aron, but it stirred in me now. He had paid a heavy price for choosing the wrong childhood friend.

Zaid, however, looked less moved. "While I concede your life has been bound to Marik, you spent most of those years as a servant to the ring. Only in the last few hours have you been a servant of the lamp, bound to obey as more puppet than person. I've watched the qaleri for years now. They were still free to make their own choices, within the bounds of the tasks they were given. You share some responsibility for the crimes you've committed."

He met Aron's eyes steadily, his own expression implacable. There was no doubt that he spoke as crown prince.

After a long moment of silence, Aron gave a single nod in acknowledgment of Zaid's words.

"I suggest a trade," he said.

"A trade?" Zaid raised an eyebrow.

"I will show you the way across the Sea of Sand, and in exchange, you will hand me over to my own people, to be tried and judged by them for my crimes, according to our ancient treaties."

Home. He was offering a way home. Hope rose in me.

"Your own people?" Zaid frowned. "What people would that be?"

"I am of the desert nomads." Aron glanced at me. "Those you know as the desert traders. Once we were one people, although our paths diverged many generations ago."

"So it's true!" I cried.

"Is that where they all went?" Zaid asked. "My father always hoped they had found new lands and not perished among the dunes."

"Many of them had chosen to make the crossing before I was born," Aron said. "And those who remained went after." He turned a burning look on Marik. "After I told my friend about the kingdoms on the other side of the desert, he made it his mission to track down any remaining nomads. He desired to be the only one with knowledge of the crossing."

"And yet you're willing to stand trial among those same people?" Zaid asked.

Aron met his gaze. "The girl spoke of freedom. Without absolution, I can never be free."

"Very well." Zaid didn't hesitate. "If you show us the way across the Sea of Sand, we will safely deliver you to these desert traders to dispense justice as they see fit."

Kayla appeared at my elbow, making me start.

"We've transferred everything into the treasury now."

I looked around the now empty cave in surprise. I had been too absorbed in Aron's words to notice their progress. Kayla, on the other hand, seemed all too aware of what occupied us. Her concerned gaze kept flicking to Aron.

"I will not harm you," he said, noticing her reaction. "While you sought the lamp you were my enemy. Its discovery served to take what freedom I still possessed. But I care nothing for you now."

"I didn't seek it by choice," Kayla said, her eyes narrowing. But then her voice softened. "We none of us had a choice."

Before Aron could reply, an enraged shout sounded behind us. I whirled to face Marik, instinctively stepping between him and Kayla.

Apparently Patrin and Josef had also been distracted by Kayla's arrival because Marik had somehow wrenched himself free of their hold. But he made no attempt to retrieve the lamp, or to attack either Zaid or me. Instead he just stared at me with hate-filled eyes.

"I was the one who was supposed to have everything," he snarled. "You may have the lamp, but it cannot carry you across the desert—it's too far. You're never going home." His eyes flashed to Aron, remaining there for a full second before he exploded into movement.

Zaid and Josef both raced forward from different directions to restrain him, but he surprised them both. Instead of running toward Aron, he darted to one side, aiming for the wall instead. Aron pursued him, moving faster than either of the others. The same anger reflected on his face as had driven Samar in his last moments.

"Wait!" I cried, seeing Marik's goal and realizing his intentions.

But I was too late.

# CHAPTER 35

$S$eizing four of the vials from the top of a neat pile, Marik turned around and propelled himself straight into Aron, turning the man's own momentum against him.

The glass of the vials shattered against Aron's chest, and a small cloud of gas enveloped them. Both men fell.

"No!" I cried, trying to race toward them, but Zaid held me back.

"Give the gas a moment to disperse." He sounded a little sick.

"So much gas…" I shivered. "What happens if you get exposed to that much?" Even as I asked the question, I didn't want to hear my fears confirmed.

"Such a dosage is likely fatal," he said softly.

"But Aron…And home…" A tear ran down my cheek.

Zaid removed his restraining hands, leading the way to the fallen men. Marik lay slightly nearer, and he bent over him first. After a few seconds he looked up at me and shook his head. But when he moved to Aron, he paused, frowning and leaning closer.

"He lives!" he said. "His breathing is slow and shallow, and I can't be sure he'll wake—but for now he's alive."

"He's larger than Marik," I said. "He would need more gas for a deadly dose."

Kayla came over to join us. "We should get him to the royal doctors. I can carry him."

When I looked at her blankly, she nodded at the lamp with an impatient expression. "Just give the order."

"Oh!" I glanced down at Marik's body and then up at Zaid.

"Leave him," he said. "Let him lie here with the poison he amassed. It's a fitting resting place. As for the rest of us, we should go to the throne room. The guests will be gone by now, but my parents are likely awake and frantic about my disappearance—either frantic or furious, at any rate."

I drew a deep breath and nodded, taking a final look around the empty cave. No part of me wanted to see it ever again.

Stooping, I untied Zaid's stone from around my leg, handing it back to him. The time for hiding and for deception had passed. I would face those at the palace as myself.

Clutching the lamp, I ordered all of its servants to gather in the throne room, bringing Zaid, Aron, and me with them. Kayla picked up Aron's prone body, slinging him over her shoulder, although his feet nearly trailed on the ground. Patrin, meanwhile, placed one hand on Zaid's shoulder and one on mine.

The same whooshing sensation overturned my stomach, but this time the darkness lasted only seconds. When we appeared, blinking, in the throne room, candles still burned everywhere as servants busied themselves removing the detritus of the festivities.

Every one of them stopped to stare at us, and the sultan turned from where he had been having a conversation with Malik and the captain of the guard. Unlike the servants, he hadn't seen the method of our arrival, his face expressing only frustration as he spied Zaid.

"Son!" He hurried over. "Where have you been? To leave like that—" He paused and looked at all the servants standing motionless around the room. "Leave us, please. Clean up may resume in the morning."

At first the servants didn't move, all of them still gaping at us. But the captain of the guard cleared his throat, and they poured out the doors, still sending incredulous glances over their shoulders as they left.

Once we were the only ones remaining, the sultan fixed a confused look on the qaleri and me. "Who are these people? And why have you brought them here? Your departure shamed your mother and me."

"No." Zaid met his father's anger with steady calm. "It is Malik and his daughter who shames us. There will be no betrothal."

"How dare you!" Malik cried, but his voice sounded feeble, and he was staring at Aron, lying flat on the floor.

"We need a doctor for this man," Kayla said, interrupting the unfolding drama. "He's inhaled too much nayera."

The sultan frowned at Aron, but after the briefest pause he gestured for his captain of the guard to fetch a doctor. The man raced away at full speed, no doubt wanting to return to his ruler's side as quickly as possible given the strangeness of the circumstances.

"Of course you will marry Jamila, Son," the sultan said. "Your betrothal has been announced to the whole city."

"Malik and his daughter are traitors," Zaid replied. "They have aided a man who sought to bring death and destruction to many. This is the girl I'm going to marry."

He took my hand and gently pulled me forward. I stepped up beside him, a strange calm coming over me instead of the nerves I had expected. Zaid loved me, and that was enough. Everything else we could overcome together.

Sultana Nadira joined her husband. Our eyes met, and a smile spread across her face.

"Princess Cass, you're still here. We feared you had fled our kingdom."

I took a deep breath. "I'm afraid I'm not a princess, Your Majesty."

Her smile dropped, and her eyes flicked down to Zaid and my clasped hands.

"The deception was a necessary one, which you'll understand when you hear the whole story," Zaid said firmly. "And while Cassie might not be royalty, her uncle is a noble from a land across the desert. Not that her origin makes a difference to my choice. I intend to make her my wife no matter what you say."

The sultan's brows knitted, a storm gathering as he took a breath to speak.

Zaid held up a hand to forestall him. "Before you say anything, you might wish to visit the treasury. Cassie has already had her dowry delivered directly there. The bowl of jewels sitting on that table is just the smallest fraction of their riches."

The sultan stopped. For a long moment he examined his son.

"Little of what you say makes sense to me. But I trust understanding will come in time. If you say my Grand Vizier has transgressed, then a full investigation will be conducted."

He turned to his captain who had just reappeared at his side after directing a team of doctors to carry Aron from the room. "Arrest Malik."

Lifting up his heavy robes, Malik tried to run. He didn't get far.

The guard led him away, and the sultan turned back to us, his expression slightly dazed.

"Thank you for trusting me, Father," Zaid said quietly. "I think we will soon discover that while Malik wasn't the architect of this treason, he was actively involved in keeping any word of it from reaching us."

This time when Sultan Kalmir looked at his son, there was a softness in his gaze.

"I trust your judgment," he said. "And it would take a fool not to see that something extraordinary is going on here. Who are all these children?"

Josef bristled at being called a child but didn't dare protest the word's of the sultan.

"You always thought my head was in the clouds, Father, but I was right," Zaid said. "The Treasure of Qalerim is real—along with the ring and its lamp. And these are the servants of the lamp."

"But not any more." I turned, looking for my friend. When I caught Kayla's eyes, I beckoned her forward.

"Destroy this ring." I held it out to her.

Her eyes grew wide as she slowly took it from me. For a moment we looked at each other, and then she gave a solemn nod, her body bending in its last unnatural bow.

I had no idea how such an item could be destroyed, but the lamp would know. It seemed a fitting final order for it.

"The ring?" The sultan seemed to finally catch on, speaking in urgent tones. "Wait!"

But he was too late. Kayla took the closest lantern from Selina and thrust the ring inside its flame. It shouldn't have been hot enough for the purpose, but the fire immediately leaped up, forcing her to drop the lantern and step back.

The flame turned blue, its heat rising as the gold ring inside melted. As soon as it disappeared—the liquid metal dripping down the insides of the lantern—the enormous blue flame winked out.

We all stood in silence, staring at.

"What have you done?" the sultan asked hoarsely.

"What needed to be done, Your Majesty," I said.

Rulers carried great burdens on their shoulders, and I could understand why they might think the benefits of the ring and the lamp outweighed the dangers. But that was why they needed good advisors.

"Cassie hasn't acted alone," Zaid said. "She and I are in agreement. The ring had to be destroyed."

"You are right, Son," his mother said. She gave her husband a look. "And your father will see that when he has had a moment to reflect."

She eyed the lamp still clutched in my hand. "And what of that?"

"Without the ring it's useless," I said. "Just a lamp. The ring was required to bind anyone to it." I glanced at Kayla. "Fetch me some breakfast."

"No!"

She grinned, throwing her arms around Selina and giving a happy giggle. "Absolutely not. No breakfast for you."

The sultana gave her an odd look, but a broad grin spread over my face.

"Just a lamp," I repeated, placing it on the ground at my feet.

"I think," the sultan said, "that I need to sit down. And then I think the two of you have a story to tell. A proper one, with all the details." He gave me a piercing look. "But the lands across the desert are real?"

I nodded. "And if Aron ever wakes up, he can take us there."

When the sultan would have spoken again, his wife laid a restraining hand on his shoulder, silencing him.

"I think what my husband means to say is that we're very happy for you both." Her warm eyes rested on her son's face as he gazed down at me. "We will welcome you into our family at the earliest opportunity. And we'll be even happier when you provide us with some grandchildren."

"Mother!" Zaid cried, outraged, but she just laughed.

"I also think some breakfast would be in order," she said to the group at large. "It must be nearly dawn."

Approving murmurs passed around the group, and Elias grinned at me.

"I like this place."

A servant appeared on cue, summonsed by some invisible means, and the qaleri were led away. Kayla flashed an excited grin at me over her shoulder, and I wondered if she was thinking of her promised room in the tallest tower. Seeing her smile, my own mind wandered to the garden I'd requested.

"We did it," Zaid said quietly while everyone was distracted. He slipped his arms around my waist, pulling me close.

"We did, didn't we." I smiled up at him in sleepy contentment, my body suddenly reminding me that most of the night had passed.

"Do you think you can bear to live here?" he asked, glancing around the elaborate room. But beneath the humor in his voice, I could hear a trace of real anxiety.

I cupped his face in my hands, reveling in the feel of his skin beneath my fingers.

"All I've ever wanted was a place to belong and for someone to see me for who I truly am. And that person is you. My home is with you, Zaid, and I will happily live wherever we can be together."

His arms tightened around me, and my sleepiness disappeared. As he dipped his head and pressed his lips against mine, fire burned through me. For once, my head went completely quiet, and my heart took over. I could almost hear its satisfied sigh. It was about time.

*Z*aid clasped my hand, the point of our connection hidden by the folds of my elegant gown. Had it really been two years since we had joined hands and made our wedding vows? It seemed hard to believe so much time had passed, and yet, at the same time, it was hard to remember my life before Zaid.

The caravan master in front of us regarded us with a steady gaze. He was retiring from the party already since his group were to leave the capital at an early hour in the morning to return to the desert.

"Farewell, Prince Zaid and Princess Cassandra. I will pass on your offer to the other caravans. We will need to discuss the matter, of course. Some will not approve of rejecting the old ways and again teaching our youngsters the location of the oases that lead across the desert. There are dangers for a caravan in such a long journey. But I am certain there are others who will welcome the opportunity—now that we know Ardasira has become such a prosperous kingdom, and that the recent danger posed by Marik is passed."

He paused. "As for the man you have handed to our keeping. There are desert nomads within Caravan Adira who remember this man and the way he stood by and let his companion complete his deadly work. Seeing him in custody has brought them a measure of closure—as has understanding that he was in some way bound by an enchantment. We will ensure justice is done despite the complexity of the situation."

"I do not doubt it," Zaid said. "We thank you again for your hospitality. We appreciated the company on the last leg of our desert journey, as well as the chance to learn from you about what we might expect here in Lanare."

At the mention of the Lanoverian capital, the caravan master's mood brightened, a smile lighting his face.

"It is true that others would not have been so accommodating as to leave their caravan and accompany you all the way to the capital. But then other masters do not have a daughter who gave up the caravan life for a title and a life in a palace."

He sounded a little wistful, but I had seen the joyous reunion between him and his daughter and grandchildren. Princess Tillara's ties to her people clearly remained strong, despite having left Caravan Adira to marry Lanover's Prince Cassian.

"I would give up all kinds of lives for the chance to marry a handsome prince and live in a palace," Kayla said with a dreamy sigh as soon as the caravan master had bowed and retreated.

Selina rolled her eyes. "You do live in a palace, Kayla. You may remember you insisted on taking the larger room."

"I'm older," she said promptly, "I need more space."

Selina rolled her eyes again.

"You are not allowed to marry a foreign prince," I said firmly. "Either of you. There are plenty of young men in Sirrala for you to choose from. Since all my old friends live across a giant desert, I need my new friends to stay on the right side of it."

Lanover's crown princess, Evangeline, approached, leading Kayla and Selina to the refreshment table, while an elegant woman joined Zaid and me.

"And which side would be the right side?" the newcomer's musical voice asked in an amused lilt.

"The Ardasiran side, of course," I said promptly.

As always when I saw Princess Celeste of Northhelm after even a momentary absence, I was struck again by her beauty. So far a week had passed, and I had not grown more accustomed to it. Her golden skin, dark hair, and perfect features had a timeless quality that made it difficult to pick her age, although I knew from Celine that her older sister must be around thirty. Her young age made her accomplishments even more impressive.

As hard as it was to believe that such a face could ever go unnoticed, Celine had assured me that the perfect princess could search a house and wield a knife with as much ease as any intelligencer. Not that the great spymaster Aurora needed to search houses herself. She had a whole network for that.

To my astonishment, when she spoke again it was to offer that network to us—or more accurately, to extend it into Ardasira. She spoke as if her offer was of no great significance, but I could feel its weight. Celine had told me her sister ran her spy network for the good of all the kingdoms since her marriage to Northhelm's crown prince, and an offer to include us in that cooperation was more than I had looked for on our first visit.

Zaid stepped in while I was still searching for the right words. His elegantly stated thanks kept his refusal from sounding churlish, and my heart swelled with pride for him. It had meant a lot that his father was willing to trust him with this trip, and so far he had ably earned his father's good opinion.

"Of course," Celeste said immediately, making no attempt to change his mind. "Our peoples are barely known to one another. I am precipitate." Someone approached to speak to Zaid, and she focused her sparkling eyes on me, her next words delivered in a whisper.

"I hope in time, however, that our lands will grow tighter

bonds of friendship. And perhaps when that day comes, our networks can merge."

When I turned startled eyes on her, she winked. "Celine writes very long letters. I knew your name long before you disappeared from your delegation, and it's not hard to guess what role you've taken up in your new home."

Emboldened, I smiled back. "I learned from the best that it's possible to be both crown princess and spymaster."

She acknowledged my words with a tilt of her head. "It has its difficulties, certainly, but it is rewarding in its own way. I wish you all success, Princess Cassie."

"But keep my intelligencers out of your kingdoms?" I asked, with a teasing grin.

"Naturally." She smiled back. "I will collect up any that forget which is the right side of the desert and send them back to you."

"So kind and thoughtful," I murmured, and her smile grew into a grin.

I had been both flattered and awed when we arrived at the palace in Lanare to be greeted not only by the resident royals, but by Princess Celeste and her husband as well. Given the vast distance between Lanare and her own northern residence, two kingdoms away, I could only marvel at the speed of her movements. She must have heard of our arrival impossibly quickly after we made contact with Caravan Adira.

Of course, she claimed the purpose of the visit was to allow her eight-year-old daughter to visit her grandparents, but it didn't take much chatter from the servants to discover the visit had been unplanned and her arrival only a day before ours. Not that I blamed her. How could a spymaster resist getting firsthand information on an entire new set of kingdoms?

"I leave in the morning," she said quietly.

"So soon?" I asked. "I had understood you meant to visit for several weeks."

"My family will stay here, but I must travel with the traders to meet their caravan on the edge of the desert."

"Aron," I said, instantly understanding.

She nodded. "Caravan Adira has granted me permission to interview the prisoner." Steel shone from her eyes. "When next Ardasira sends a delegation across the sand, I will have rooted out every last member of this conspiracy against our people."

I didn't doubt her for a second. Even I had felt a moment of fear when I saw her face after Zaid shared what we knew of the plot hatched against the Four Kingdoms by Malik.

Aron and Samar had traveled throughout these lands, recruiting malcontents as agents for Marik. Each one had been given gold and a pouch with two vials of nayera so they could test Marik's claims about his marvelous potion for themselves. They were instructed to lie in wait until contacted again, at which point the bulk of their payment would be received in exchange for tipping a jug of liquid into their nearest large water source.

Of course none of the recruits had been informed that in its liquid form, nayera was fatal—an oversight that would likely make them easier for Aurora to work with. Their loyalty to Marik was unlikely to last beyond that piece of information.

"It's just a pity it's been so long," she said, frustration leaking into her voice. "I know it couldn't be helped, but it will make chasing all the trails harder."

"It was certainly a long wait on my end," I said. "But the doctors did everything they could to wake Aron earlier. If he hadn't been in a coma for eighteen months, we would have been here much sooner. I had given up hope before he just returned to consciousness one day. And once he woke, we came as soon as a delegation could be arranged."

"Of course," she sounded sympathetic. "I'm sure you're eager to see your family. Although I hear you won't travel as far as Eldon this trip."

I sighed. "It's a long way. But now that contact has been established, we hope to have regular caravans crossing the desert. Next time we'll give plenty of warning before our arrival, and I hope my uncle might travel here to meet me."

"I'm sure he will do so. And likely Celine as well." She chuckled. "My youngest sister has never liked being away from where the action is happening."

I laughed, and Aurora announced it was time for her to head for her bed ahead of the traders' early start. We said our farewells, and I watched her go with bemusement. My old dreams of joining her network now seemed hazy and distant. But Aurora herself, at least, had lived up to every one of my imaginings. It seemed impossibly surreal that I was standing here, conversing with her as an equal.

An arm slipped around my waist, and Zaid bent down to press a quick kiss against my lips.

"I missed you," he said, his eyes warm as they smiled down into mine.

"You were gone for five minutes."

He shrugged. "I can miss you in less time than that."

"I wish my uncle was here," I said. "I'm sure he's been worried about me, although I'm told the godmothers reassured everyone about my safety. At least the letter I wrote him has now been posted." I shook my head. "I can't believe I have a godmother, even if she did keep out of sight."

"I can believe it. You deserve one."

I shook my head, but he looked stubborn, so I let it drop. Gazing out over the party, put on in our honor, my mind wandered to home.

"I wonder what the other qaleri would make of Lanover?"

"They aren't qaleri anymore." Zaid smiled as he always did when he corrected me on the point.

"They always will be to me." I laid my head on his shoulder.

"I think the others are happy in the apprenticeships they

chose," he said. "Even Elias wouldn't have come if he hadn't received special dispensation to travel as a trainee guard."

I caught sight of the tall young man out of the corner of my eye and smiled at him. He nodded gravely back. He took his duties very seriously—a phase that brought him great mockery from his cousin but that his captain assured me would pass soon enough.

"I keep thinking about Josef," I said. "I think he could easily have ended up like Aron—if he had been a servant of the ring for longer, or if he had only had Samar for company. And yet now he's so productive and happy working with the goldsmith you found to take him on."

"It's a sobering reminder," Zaid agreed. "But not the right one for a party. Come dance with me. I'll even listen again while you tell me how much you admire Princess Celeste and explain some agonizing detail of spy craft that she demonstrated to you."

"She didn't demonstrate anything to me," I protested laughingly. "But I learn so much just from watching her. Yesterday, she—"

"See!" He spun me around and pulled me close. "You do want to talk about spy craft. I knew it. I'm an excellent husband."

"You certainly are." I wrapped both arms around his neck, holding the position longer than the dance required. "The very best."

He leaned down to drop a kiss on my nose. "Only because I have the very best of wives."

"I do listen to you talk about irrigation a lot," I agreed.

His eyes instantly brightened, as they did whenever his favorite topic came up. "Just think how amazing it would be if we could irrigate the desert. Even just shrinking its size would make a difference for the journey across. We could—"

"Not at a party," I said firmly. "I may be the best of wives, but I'm not that good."

"Very well," the twinkle in his eyes gave him away even before he continued. "We can save the conversation for the meeting I've organized on the topic for tomorrow morning."

"You can have the conversation, then," I said firmly. "I'm going to write to Celine so the letter can go with the next ship heading back to Eldon. She was the one to invite me on the delegation to the Four Kingdoms, all that time ago. And I think it's about time she heard the results."

# NOTE FROM THE AUTHOR

Explore Kuralan and get to know Zaria as she discovers the second fabled treasure cave of the younger brother in The Golden Princess: A Retelling of Ali Baba and the Forty Thieves, coming in 2022.

Or if you missed discovering the western part of the Great Desert and meeting Caravan Adira and the desert traders, read The Princess Search: A Retelling of The Ugly Duckling.

Or read about how Cassie helped save her home kingdom of Eldon in A Crown of Snow and Ice: A Retelling of the Snow Queen.

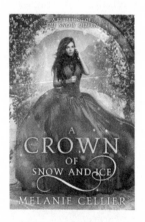

To be kept informed of my new releases, please sign up to my mailing list at www.melaniecellier.com. At my website, you'll also find an array of free extra content.

Thank you for taking the time to read my book. I hope you enjoyed it. If you did, please spread the word! You could start by leaving a review on <u>Amazon</u> (or <u>Goodreads</u> or <u>Facebook</u> or any other social media site). Your review would be very much appreciated and would make a big difference!

# ACKNOWLEDGMENTS

The original tale of Aladdin with its many jinni is a story flowing with all the gold, jewels and luxury you could possibly imagine—one that indulges our imagination beyond the realm of any possible reality. Unfortunately I'm too practical minded a person to fully embrace that vision. (Am I the only one who couldn't stop wondering when the influx of jinni gold was going to reach the point that gold became devalued, crashing the whole economy of this completely imaginary kingdom? Yes? Good! Because honestly, talk about being a killjoy.) My story, consequently, doesn't strive for the heights of the original—but I have attempted to touch on something of the lush feel that is so central to Aladdin. And I look forward to venturing back across the Great Desert to Kuralan in my next fairy tale on the hunt for another hidden cave full of gold and treasure.

Writing The Desert Princess took more out of me than I expected—not least because it occupied me during a time of great global turmoil. Now more than ever, many of us need the opportunity to occasionally step into an oasis of peace and to sit there for a while before we venture back out into the chaos of normal life. I hope, if nothing else, this book has given you some moments of peace away from whatever worries you carry.

Of course, the burdens of the current era bear down on everyone else, just as they do on me, and yet my team have once again gone above and beyond to support me through the writing of this book. To my editors and beta readers—Priya, Katie, Rachel, Greg, Ber, Mary, Deborah, and my dad—I am so thankful for each and every one of you. I could not be more fortunate in having such a fantastic support network for both writing and life. And the same goes for my author friends. You are always on the other side of a keyboard (or video screen) and it's never mattered less that most of you are on the other side of the world. (Except for you, Marina! Having 0ne writing buddy and sprint mate in (nearly) the same timezone is both good fun and extremely helpful for my productivity.)

And thank you, Karri, for another beautiful cover. Somehow these fairy tale covers still manage to amaze me, even after so many, and this one incorporates some of my favorite colors and shades.

I don't have a magic lamp to fulfill my every wish, but my family did an incredible job of supporting me through the exhausting journey that writing this book turned out to be. I couldn't imagine a better reward than to continue to live life with you all. I thank God for you constantly, and for the beautiful, wondrous, exhausting gift of creativity which ensures our lives will never reach the blissfully ordered state I sometimes dare to dream about.

# ABOUT THE AUTHOR

 Melanie Cellier grew up on a staple diet of books, books and more books. And although she got older, she never stopped loving children's and young adult novels.

She always wanted to write one herself, but it took three careers and three different continents before she actually managed it.

She now feels incredibly fortunate to spend her time writing from her home in Adelaide, Australia where she keeps an eye out for koalas in her backyard. Her staple diet hasn't changed much, although she's added choc mint Rooibos tea and Chicken Crimpies to the list.

She writes young adult fantasy including books in her *Spoken Mage* world, and her three *Four Kingdoms and Beyond* series which are made up of linked stand-alone stories that retell classic fairy tales.

Made in United States
North Haven, CT
27 November 2021

11580499R00225